ISLAND INTERN

Published by

Stoney Creek Publishing Group

StoneyCreekPublishing.com

ISBN: 978-1-965766-12-5
ISBN (ebook): 978-1-965766-09-5
Library of Congress Control Number: 2024926286

Cover design by Kimberly James
Printed in the United States

Island Intern

Paul Remmers

For my wife, Clara

Part 1

"The pleasure of a physician is little, the gratitude of patients is rare, and even rarer is material reward, but these things will never deter the student who feels the call within him."

—Theodor Billroth, M.D., Surgeon, Vienna, Austria, 1894

CHAPTER 1

I didn't hear the words I said.

"I swear by Apollo Physician and Asclepius and Hygieia and Panaceia and all the gods and goddesses, making them my witnesses, that I will fulfill according to my ability and judgment this oath and this covenant:"

My mind was not on the words but on my future. It seemed hard to imagine that I completed medical school as I stood with my right hand raised and recited the Hippocratic Oath, along with Dr. Randall and the rest of the graduating class. I memorized the words a few days ago and that was easy, but how would my new life as a doctor be? That was hard to imagine. Everyone said that it would be forever different, forever better than my father's life. Would I make decisions that would help people or hurt people? And now I had to make decisions on my own, without the faculty.

"I will not use the knife, not even on sufferers from stone, but will withdraw in favor of such men as are engaged in this work."

As I looked around the room, I knew that we all felt that way, me and all forty-two of my soon-to-be ex-classmates. "Sufferers from stone"?

"Whatever houses I may visit, I will come for the benefit of the sick, remaining free of all intentional injustice, of all mischief and in particular of sexual relations with both female and male persons, be they free or slaves."

My internship was just a few weeks away. A few of us were staying here in Galveston at the Medical Department of the University of Texas to be house interns at the John Sealy Hospital for a year of "supplemental training," as the faculty called it. They said it would make me a real physician by the sweat of my brow.

"I may see or hear in the course of the treatment or even outside of the treatment in regard to the life of men, which on no account one must spread abroad, I will keep to myself, holding such things shameful to be spoken about."

I was a doctor because my father had insisted that I become one. For as long as I could remember, he said that ranching was too hard a life and that a doctor would be more respected in the world, even though there was no one in my family who had ever been a doctor. And I loved our ranch.

"I fulfill this oath and do not violate it, may it be granted to me to enjoy life and art, being honored with fame among all men for all time to come; if I transgress it and swear falsely, may the opposite of all this be my lot."

As I lowered my hand and sat back down and the ceremony continued, I wondered whether my father was right. I was never opposed to it, but it was my life now, and his decision would take my life in a different direction from his. Yes, I was excited to be a doctor, especially because of the year, this year. I knew that I was living in a modern time. A modern era for medicine was beginning, as the faculty told us over and over. The old remedies and potions of the past were being replaced by science, undeniable science. I became a doctor just as medicine was entering an era of great discovery. It was modern medicine at the beginning of a modern century, the twentieth. The year was 1900.

Dr. Randall now called my name to receive my diploma: "Douglas Heinrich Schuler."

After the ceremony and the congratulations from my family and fellow students, I was happy. I didn't care that none of the faculty came over to shake my hand or to meet my family, except Dr. Randall. My family seemed happier than me. With a big grin from a weathered face, my father said my graduation was a dream come true. After he shook my hand, he put his arm around me and squeezed me hard. I don't remember him ever doing that.

My family had never been to Galveston. I knew it would not be easy for my family to visit me during my four years here. I was the oldest of six children, and our cattle ranch was all I knew. My father worked hard on our massive ranch all his life. We would ride for hours together with our hired vaqueros herding cattle to the far end of the ranch, then coming back to the house at the end of the day. He said ranching was a lonely life and liked the idea of me coming here for medical school. They had heard that it was the best in the Southwest. And our family doctor said it was where I should go. I was twenty-two when I came to Galveston.

We all walked downtown from the Medical Department building to the Tremont Hotel where my family was staying. Once in their room all eight of us sat together, my four younger sisters on the bed and my brother on the floor. They were all staring at me. Did I look a little different now to them? Four years was a long time, we all thought. My mother would come over to my chair and hug me over and over. My only brother, Henry, would hug me his way, from behind me, choking me. He had gotten stronger.

"This is from Doc Wallace and his wife," my father said as he handed me a box wrapped in brown paper. I unwrapped the box and saw that it was a doctor's bag, black with two small handles and a brass clasp with the initials D.H.S embossed in gold letters above it.

"This isn't leather, is it?"

"No, I think it's alligator," my father said.

"I can't carry around such a nice bag. The professors will think that I think I'm already a physician."

"But aren't you?" my mother added.

"Yeah, I am, but not really. I mean everyone will call me one, but I'm really still in training. But I have to tell you something first. I'm not coming home now. It's been a hard decision but I'm going to be a house intern for a year here before I come home. Then I'll know I know what I'm doing."

"You're not coming with us?" my mother stood up again with her hands on her hips.

"No, I wrote to you about this. I really should do this if I'm going to be a doctor worthy of the title."

"Your letter didn't say anything about staying. You mean it's not necessary to do that year?" my mother asked.

"No, it's not, but I feel I just have to."

"Then you've decided?" my father interrupted us both.

"Yes."

"All right," my father said as he put his arm around my mother's shoulders.

He continued, "Well, I don't know how to advise you further on this. But I think if you feel you have to, then you have to. But there is another person who will be sad that you're not coming home. You know whom I am talking about."

He meant Anna. This was the conversation I dreaded. It hurt them after all they did for me. I did long to go home. I missed so many things about our large home in the middle of our ranch surrounded by sprawling oak trees, not like the homes built on top of each other here in Galveston. I missed sitting at the kitchen table, feeling the breeze blow in on a hot summer day. The quiet at night, except for the cicadas. It was loud here day and night.

My sisters each gave me a gift they had made. Some things to wear, mainly. I guess my clothes had gotten pretty worn. My brother gave me a knife with my initials engraved on the handle and a longhorn steer branded on the leather sheath.

"You could wear it on your belt," he said.

"No, I couldn't, how would it look wearing a knife in front of a patient?"

"Pretty good, I bet. It's sharp. I pared one of the horse's hooves with it the other day. You could easily remove a toe with it, I bet. Have you ever cut on anybody?" he asked, smiling.

"No, not yet, but we use scalpels. They are smaller but sharper than this knife. I've gotten pretty good at sharpening them."

"Then you're not a real doctor yet," Henry said. "What have you done, anything?"

"I helped one of my professors sew up a guy after an alligator bit him across his stomach. He was fishing in the bay when it surprised him. We took one of my sharp scalpels and removed his spleen, then I sewed him up. It took me forever to close such a large laceration. But he was drunk, so it made it easier to work on him. And he survived."

"Have you delivered a baby yet?" my youngest sister Rachel asked.

"The first one I delivered I managed to drop, it was so slippery. And the mother still wanted to name the baby after me when she saw that it was a boy. I told her my name was Albert, after Professor Clopton. But me and some other students were reprimanded when they heard how we've been using their names for the male babies born at the hospital. But most babies are born at home."

"Thank you very much, now, I am nauseated," my mother interrupted, then stood. "No more stories. I want to change the subject. This is a lot for me to think about now that you changed our plans."

I went to hug my mother. "Forgive me for staying."

"We bought you something while we were in San Antonio."

She handed me a package wrapped in light pink paper. When I opened it, I saw the dark black double rubber tubing stethoscope. It had a bright metal bell and a black diaphragm opposite the bell at one end. On the other end below the metal earpieces was a small metal clasp holding the tubing together engraved with my initials. I was one of the few in my class that still didn't have a stethoscope. I didn't have the money and couldn't bring myself to write for the money to buy one. The faculty kept them for life, I was told. I opened the metal arms to the earpieces and put it around my neck and felt the pinch. Everyone was watching me.

"I think that part goes in your ears," my brother chimed in. Everyone laughed and I took it off my neck and stuffed it into my coat pocket and then grabbed him by the neck.

The next few days together were especially nice. My brother and sisters had never seen the Gulf of Mexico, so they spent hours rolling around in the surf. My mother was trying to make the most of the short time with me, to make sure I had what I needed. I didn't need much, I told her. I lived in a one-room carriage house in an alley near the medical school. It had a small cot and a table and chair, and a kerosene lamp to study by. I didn't feel the need for curtains in the small windows. But my mother said she was going to make some and that I had better hang them.

It was late May and the weather was beautiful. There weren't many mosquitoes in the air and so far there were no reported cases of yellow fever for the year. There were a few seamen who had arrived on a steamer from the Caribbean and were quarantined downtown with high fevers suspected to have it, or malaria or dengue.

My father reminded me that he wanted to visit the German Society here in Galveston before they left. So we all took the electric trolley from 25th Street then south toward the beach to Avenue O. We got off and walked several blocks west. At 27th Street we saw several signs on homes and small buildings in German. My father approached the steps and entered the small building of the Garten Verein, or Garden Club. There was no one inside. The bulletins on the wall were written in German. My father read a few of these, then crossed the large lobby and headed out the back door. We followed behind him. It was the middle of the afternoon and there were several older men gathered on a bench talking and laughing loudly in a beautiful garden area. They put down their beers on a small table when they saw us. My father produced a letter from his coat pocket and, speaking German, asked to see to August Schlueter. One man stood quickly and said that it was he. He shook my father's hand, said "das Willkommen" and accepted the letter. I saw my father's eyes big and wide with amazement because they still had beer to drink this late in spring. They poured their beer from a large brown bottle nested in a tub of ice!

"My name is Henrich Schuler and I have a letter of introduction for my son, Douglas Schuler. We are from Santa Clara and are members of the German Society of New Berlin, near Seguin, in Guadalupe County."

"Your son is living here?" Mr. Schlueter asked as he quickly read the letter. Then added, "Why is he living here?"

"Yes, he has been living here for several years attending the Medical College. But he has not made association with the German Society here as we have requested him to do. He has graduated and will be working as a house intern for a year before returning home. His mother and I wish that he could be made a member."

"Yes, of course. I assume he speaks German as well as you?"

My father and mother were born here in Texas and their German was good, better than mine. But Mr. Schlueter was older than my father and was from Germany, and he made the point that he spoke German better than we did. Mr. Schlueter looked at me and asked me in German several brief questions about where I was living and how did I enjoy my time here in Galveston, and if I had family in Germany. I had been told that our family came from Stuttgart. I spoke in German in response to his questions and he initially acted as if he didn't understand me well. But then he smiled and walked over to me and put his arm around me. My father was pleased when he handed us each a stein of cold beer.

"We will take good care of him here in our society. All Germans are welcome no matter where they immigrated from in Germany. I think we have some Swiss and Austrian members as well, who say they are German," he said with a smile and a wink. "And we will help your son improve his German."

My parents were embarrassed by my response, but they knew that I did the best I could. I had forgotten much of the language even though it was still spoken often in our home and we had German language classes every Saturday at our local German Society Hall in New Berlin. We spoke a mixture of Texan, German, and a little Spanish.

"Let me show you and your family around our club, Henrich."

We walked through the grounds and were amazed at what they had created here. As we strolled through landscaped paths we saw grass tennis courts and lawn bowling lanes, and several women playing croquet on a large grassy lawn surrounded by low hedges. At the far end of the property was a large fountain made of stone with large goldfish swimming around.

"Henrich, this is our most recent addition to the club, what do you think?"

"This is magnificent!" my father exclaimed, holding the empty stein.

He had never seen anything so grand. My mother stood holding my sisters back from the water. I held my brother back. The German Society Club in New Berlin was small and, besides, the clubhouse was not much to brag about. I explained to my father what a tennis court was and the game that was played there. Several of the mansions here in Galveston had them, too. Once I peeked over their brick walls after hearing young girls laughing while playing the game.

We walked away from the fountain and back toward the clubhouse and saw the large dance pavilion at the southern end of the property. It was a large beautiful green and white painted building in the shape of an octagon, with a tall spire and large windows on all sides. We were speechless. My sisters could not be contained and ran toward it.

"This is our dancing pavilion. Every Saturday evening in the spring and summer, we have a gathering of all members and dance late into the evening with a polka trio."

My mother spoke up this time in her broken German. "It is so large, so beautiful! Do you need such a large building?"

Back home, our club members would dance outside on the grass by candlelight on Saturday nights to Hans Wurzbach singing and playing the accordion. There were never more than fifty members there and most of the Germans in the county attended. Beer was made and served only in the winter. We didn't have ice.

"We have over five hundred members," Mr. Schlueter said. "The building is electrified and bright with lights at night. It was built more than ten years ago. I own a lumber yard and donated the wood to build it. My lumber yard has provided the wood for many of the homes built here, too. You should all stay and join us in the fun this Saturday night. We welcome all Germans here in Galveston, and in Texas, too."

We peered through the large windows into the pavilion. We could see the electric lights hanging from the ceiling in large brass fixtures. There was a stage on one side, and a long bar on the opposite side. All of their club members could fit into the building and would dance round and round. But my family was leaving the next day.

"I want to thank you for your kindness, Mr. Schlueter, and the tour of your beautiful club, but we are leaving tomorrow," my father said.

Mr. Schlueter shook my father's hand and said that he understood. And he told me that he would like to see me soon on a Saturday evening. I smiled back and said that I would come. My parents had wanted me to join the club when I moved here but it didn't interest me. But it did now!

Before they left, my father gave me money to have a new suit made. The one I wore during the graduation was dirty and stained. And there was enough money to buy a new pair of shoes to go with it, he said. We were all quiet as I stood with them next to their departing train the next morning. The goodbyes were short. I knew it would be a year before I returned home for good. My mother hugged me hard and pinched my waist and reminded me that I looked too thin and needed to eat more.

They boarded the train and then all looked back at me and waved as the train slowly pulled away, except for my father. It would leave the island by the railway bridge to the mainland and to Houston, and then to connect to another bound for San Antonio. They would get off at Seguin.

CHAPTER 2

It was getting dark as I walked home from the corner store where I bought a ham sandwich wrapped tight in white paper. I entered the alley and walked in the deep sand along the back fence line to my place. I pulled a ripe peach from a branch hanging over the short wooden fence and then turned into an opening in the fence and walked up the narrow wooden stairs and opened the screen door and sat down at the small table in my back house. I sat in the only chair at the table. After I ate, I lit the kerosene lamp and sat quietly for a moment then rewrapped the small part of the sandwich leftover. It was quiet tonight. Sometimes, I heard the horses on the ground floor beneath me neighing or moving in their stalls.

I had to do it, I had to write her back. The letters to Anna had gotten harder to write. But writing this letter was especially tough as I had to break the news to her that I wasn't coming home, not yet. My father reminded me about Anna, the one I promised to marry. Maybe she already knew by now. It had been nearly three weeks since my family left and even though I told them not to tell her, I knew that she knew I should have been the one to break the news to her. In my last letter, I didn't tell her that I wasn't coming home after I graduated, but I didn't say that I would see her soon either. I had trouble keeping up with her letters during these four years.

She and I planned to be married right after I returned home. We weren't officially engaged. She was upset when I told her last year that the curriculum had been changed, from three years to four like most of the medical schools back East. And now, with my internship, she would have to wait another year after already waiting another year.

I didn't know what else to say in the letter. I told her in every letter that the years would go by fast, and how much I missed her. I had a small photo of her on the table in front of me. It was when she was sixteen. I loved her long auburn hair and her hazel eyes. I tried hard to imagine those colors in my mind now. Maybe she looked different now. My mother said that she didn't. She didn't include a new photograph with her graduation gift—a thin flat white box with a black necktie wrapped in white tissue. I put down my pencil and looked out of the small kitchen window. Every night was the same in the summer; it was hot and I was sweating. The sea breeze felt stronger as the sun went down, though.

I went outside to feel the breeze. After a few minutes, I went down the stairs and walked to the cistern in back of the main house. I put some water in a metal bucket and then went to the privy before going to sleep. I went back upstairs and inside. I sat on the edge of my bed and rinsed the sweat off my face and then blew out the lamp. I lay down on my short bed with my feet over the end of it and listened to the horses beneath me and to the noises in the alley. There were always people coming and going in the alley, some whistling a tune, some coughing, or some laughing with another person, but lately, the young children of the Petteway family were still running around after dark.

Moses and Angelina Petteway and their three small children lived directly across the alley, no more than ten feet from my stairs. Moses was a longshoreman and Angelina cleaned for the rich family in the front house. The children played together so well, so full of energy, so daring, so happy. They would play until dark and sometimes afterward despite the insistence of their mother that they come inside. In the summer it was dark until late and even then they were usually not ready to stop playing. Every sound would echo up and down the alley. After they finally went inside, it was quiet and I could hear the horses breathing and snorting—there were two of them. And later in the evening, the voices I didn't know, adults who didn't live here but hid in the alley for the night.

Next to my place in a small two-room back house was Grandma Sam's little house. She lived alone and was a widow. Her inside wood stove was always smoking, and she was always working in and around her little place. I always tried to guess what she was cooking. She would feed me sometimes when she said I look pitifully skinny. I hoped she would invite me over after a long day at the hospital or the Medical Department building. I had never had food like hers until I moved to Galveston, I guess because she was Black. I learned to eat pigs feet and greens with hot water cornbread. We would sit together in her small kitchen and eat it at her small round wooden table that wobbled. I never knew if it was the table or the slanted floor. She didn't want me stealing any of her plates, she said. She called me "child," even though I knew that she knew my name. She said that she felt the need to worry about others, so she was going to worry about me too.

She worked so hard doing laundry for others in a metal bucket over a fire in her small yard. That was how she earned a little money. I never saw anybody help her. Several years ago, after walking home after an exam, I saw my clothes hanging from her line, blowing in the wind—my underwear too. When she saw me climbing my steps, she stopped working to yell at me about how filthy I had become and that I was stinking up the alley, worse than the horses. I smelled like those dead bodies they keep at the school. Since that time, I realized that she would walk into my place during the day to gather my clothes. The water in her bucket was always scalding and the lye smell was strong, but I appreciated all that she did for me. I offered to pay her, but she refused. I would leave a dollar under the dinner plate after she fed me.

She and her husband lived in that little house for many years and raised their two boys there. After they were grown, they moved out of Galveston, one to Chicago and the other to New Orleans. Both were dockworkers like their father, who died a decade ago. She was born in Nacogdoches in '44 and was raised on a farm outside the city. She and her whole family were slaves. She got married after the war, then they came to Galveston for work. She told me that she had never learned to read because she never went to school. When she got a letter from one of her sons, she would bring it to my place for me to read it to her. They were long, beautiful letters that expressed their love for her and their desire to send her money. She would always cry a little, and then smile a little, and then snatch the letter back from me. She never wanted to know what I thought about the letter. That brief smile revealed that she only has few teeth left. The joints on her hands and wrists and knees were large and round from her arthritis. By the dark splotches on her face—facial hyperpigmentation—she probably had diabetes.

On the other side of me in a one-room house was a new family, Italians who have recently immigrated. They had two small children who spoke a little English. They were accepted by the other kids in the alley, and they all played stickball together and none wore shoes. They stopped the game only to clear the way for the horses and carriages that came through. The parents tried hard to keep their children from playing in the trash bins or the gigantic potholes, especially after it rained.

There were always a few drunk men who either lived here or were chased off the small porches in the morning by the owners. It was hard to tell who was living there, or just passing through, but we didn't worry too much about it. In the alley everybody talked to each other, talked about the current situation of the alley and what could make it better, like the people in the big front houses did.

The square city blocks were divided east to west by an alley. The alley ran behind the big houses on the block. These little "back houses" were crowded together in between and on top stables and servants' quarters. So many people lived in the alley, maybe more than in the big houses on the block. They were the cheapest residences in town to rent and people would come and go, mostly unnoticed. People hid out here from their spouses, or the bosses, or the law. When the law was looking for someone, the authorities would forget to check the alleys. And there were thriving businesses in some alleys, mostly small, unmarked gambling joints or bars. The houses of prostitution were not in the alleys, they were in large houses downtown.

All these little alley houses were painted white with green shutters. The salty sea breeze was tough on the paint and made it peel. There was never a fresh coat of pain for an alley house. The alley was a street turned outside in. We didn't have much to do with the people who lived on the street, and they didn't have much to do with us. On the street, it was a real neighborhood with clean sidewalks in front of shiny black wrought iron fences protecting real houses in perfect order. It was not far from us, just around the corner.

I rented from the Hendersons, the family in the front house. They had a beautiful home, tall and elegant, with bright white paint with tall dark blue shutters. The sea breeze didn't peel their paint. The front porch was broad and deep with large, decorated columns all gracefully tied together by well-placed carved wooden accents. Mr. Henderson was a banker, and he and Mrs. Henderson had three daughters. The oldest, Angel was nearly eighteen, and the twins Cassandra and Clara were about seven. I never spent any time with the family in the front house. I wasn't sure if Mr. Henderson didn't like doctors or he was afraid of the influence that I might have on Angel. I paid eight dollars a month to rent the small house over their stables and during my four years here he never increased the rent. Each month I placed the money in an envelope and pushed it through the mail chute near the large front door. With the May rent I included an invitation to my graduation, but they didn't attend.

I had never seen the twins outside in the backyard without shoes, nor were they allowed to cross the small picket fence that separated the carriage house from the main yard behind the home. The twins would smile and wave to me outside the large dining room window in the back of the house when I would get water from the cistern in the main yard. I repaired the mosquito netting over the cistern several times a year while the twin girls watched. Their eyes became wide when they saw me high on the ladder. Maybe they thought I might jump in to cool off. Everybody drank the rainwater from the cistern. From my small porch at night, I looked into the brightly lit house. I would sometimes see Angel sitting in the parlor alone reading or pressing flowers into a book or brushing her hair. She had long beautiful blonde hair falling over her shoulders that shimmered in the light from the chandelier above her. She never noticed me in the dark. Electricity hadn't made it to the dwellings in the alleys.

Where I lived wasn't far from the hospital, about ten blocks. In front of the old hospital was the new John Sealy Hospital on 9th Street and Strand, directly east from the business district downtown. It was next to the Medical Department building finished the following year. Both were magnificent, modern buildings, built side by side, with tall spires, long balconies, and magnificent stone entryways. Wide grand stairways led up to the second floors main double doors, which were tall and heavy and carved. Under the stairways were arched side entries to which a carriage could pass through gaining access to the first floor.

I particularly admired the Medical Department building. It was built with imported red brick, and more than four stories high. The tops of each window were covered with intricate terra cotta designs. Each end of the building was circular and capped with a tall spire surrounded with skylights. We heard that it was designed after a medical building in Europe. I knew that our school was new and lacking the longstanding traditions of the schools from the East Coast, but this building gave it a sense of permanence and prestige. It shone bright red in the morning sun.

Next to it was the hospital, John Sealy Hospital. It glowed white in the sun from its limestone walls. It was just as tall and just as magnificent. Each end of the building was squared off and on its roof was a single central broad spire. Underneath the spire was the surgical amphitheater, the only structure on the fourth floor. It had wrought iron balconies on each side of the front of the building, adjacent to the grand central stairs that also entered from the south side of the building. The archway beneath the stairs was where the ambulance carriage entered and unloaded on the first floor.

The State of Texas mandated the construction of these modern buildings in Galveston, the largest and most prosperous city in Texas. I had heard that many in the community didn't see the need for the school and didn't think it would last. The Texas Medical College had closed its doors here two decades ago but was in several small buildings that were insignificant. Businessmen in town like Mr. Henderson probably had little patience for the idea of training students to be doctors and nurses for the rest of Texas. Many of our faculty were from schools back East and Europe, and didn't relate well to the local wealthy businessmen and their families. They were probably not included in Galveston society parties nor cared to be. Many men had gotten very rich here in Galveston, and they had their mansions on Broadway to prove it. A great deal of money had been made in the past few decades here exporting cotton brought by rail from East Texas and the Midwest. And in exchange, the wealthy imported the finest things from Europe to fill these mansions.

The heat from the day finally relented and the alley kids were bathed and put to bed and the horses were asleep, too. My letter to Anna was unfinished, again.

CHAPTER 3

My legs were beginning to ache standing here at the end of the bed of my new patient, Mr. Cyrus Malloy, on the east ward. It seemed like forever while Dr. James Thompson, Professor of Surgery, was critiquing my presentation of the presenting illness. I spent at least three hours in the middle of the night talking to Mr. Malloy and examining him, and I knew exactly what was wrong with him. I did all the talking with Dr. Thompson now during our morning rounds. There were the two other house interns standing beside me remaining completely quiet, Carl Heath and Homer (whom we called Tex) Hornsby.

Mr. Malloy was lying quietly in bed listening to Dr. Thompson and the rest of us, with the bed sheet pulled up to his chin. Dr. Thompson had awakened him so that he could hear my presentation and my diagnosis and my plan for his recovery. Dr. Thompson was tall, over six feet, and broad shouldered and with a booming voice. He wore what we all did, a black suit, with a high-collared starched white shirt and a black tie. But his suit was always clean and pressed. He had a broad waxed mustache on top of a heavy beard and grey, well-oiled hair combed over his head. He had spectacles ready in his outer coat pocket.

Dr. Thompson began after my presentation, "Mr. Malloy, do you agree with your doctor about the events that led to your admission here?"

"Yessir, completely," Mr. Malloy said, then added, "But I didn't drink as much as he said I did."

"Yes, I'm sure you didn't," Dr. Thompson said. To us, he continued, "Dr. Schuler, you can double the amount of wine he quoted you last night. You didn't comment on his skin, besides the upper body spiders that you mentioned."

He reached down and yanked the bed sheet covering Mr. Malloy away, leaving him naked. Mr. Malloy quickly covered his genitals with his hands but didn't protest. The sun was shining into the room through the east window directly on the patient. He was obviously thin with his extremity muscles wasted but his abdomen protuberant, and he was jaundiced in the sunlight.

"Yes, he is icteric, Dr. Thompson. I'm sorry but I didn't notice it last night." I could see clearly this morning that his skin appeared a light-yellow color, especially his upper chest to his face.

"Only sunlight will reveal the true color of his skin." To the patient, Dr. Thompson said, "Sir, put your hands by your side, please."

To Carl he said, "Dr. Heath, reach down and examine the man's testicles".

Carl walked from the foot of the bed to the right side of the bed and felt both of his testicles, one at a time. Mr. Malloy closed his eyes for the exam.

"Well, Dr. Heath, anything unusual about this man's anatomy to you?"

"Yes, Dr. Thompson, he is missing his right testicle and has a very small left testicle."

Dr. Thompson now asked the patient, "What happened to your right one?"

"A horse kicked me when I was a boy and ..."

Raising his hand to stop the patient, Dr. Thompson said, "And his only testicle is atrophied because he drinks without responsibility, and if you look closely at his chest, you see that he has developed gynecomastia. Do you know, Mr. Malloy, that you have the breasts of a small woman?"

This was all new information for the patient as he couldn't decide whether to cover his genitalia or his breasts. He was going back and forth when Dr. Thompson said to me, "Dr. Schuler, I want you to show me how you percuss the chest."

I walked around to the head of the bed and had the patient sit up and then swing his legs over the side of the bed. The patient then asked if he could have his bed sheet back and Dr. Thompson said no. I took the stethoscope out of my suit pocket, put the metal arms around my neck, and then placed my left hand on the right lateral side of the patient's upper back and with my right middle finger, I thumped the last knuckle on my left third finger. I heard resonance through the lungs.

"Stop, put your stethoscope back in your pocket, and begin again," Dr. Thompson interrupted. I did, but then continued percussing his chest, now both sides and noting the difference in the sounds from each side. At the left lung, at the lower lobe I was hearing a clear resonant sound. And on the right side of his chest, I clearly heard a dull sound.

Dr. Thompson came to the right side of the bed and leaned over and said, "Do that again." I knew he had heard it, as well as did Carl and Tex. We were all leaning in on the patient.

He added, "First of all, you didn't learn chest percussion properly and it is only by chance that I could tell the difference."

I straightened up, took a deep breath, and glanced quickly at my friends. They had stepped back to the foot of the bed. Dr. Thompson asked them if they heard the difference in the percussive sounds and in unison, they both said, "No".

Dr. Thompson smiled at them and to me asked, "What do make of the dullness in his right chest? Your colleagues are not able to help you now, Dr. Schuler."

I spoke up. "He has a large pleural effusion in his right chest."

The patient interrupted. "Can I lay back down now?" He looked directly at Dr. Thompson rather than me. I was his doctor, but the patients always could tell who was in charge at morning rounds.

"Dr. Schuler, now take your new stethoscope and listen for breath sounds." I did and placed the earpieces in my ears and the bell on his right chest. Dr. Thompson continued, "Do you hear clear breath sounds on the right, in the area that was dull to percussion?"

To the patient, he added, "Be quiet and take some deep breaths in and out of your mouth."

I did not hear breath sounds on the right side of his chest as I did on the left. I spoke up. "I still feel that he has a right chest pleural effusion, Dr. Thompson."

Dr. Thompson responded, "And how would you determine the etiology of the obvious fluid in the right chest?"

"I would place a large needle between his posterior ribs and draw off the fluid and examine it by sunlight to know if it is a transudate."

Dr. Thompson responded loudly, so loudly that all the other patients in the ward heard him, "Not on your life would I allow you to do that to this man, wasting a good sharp needle on an alley cat like him. I know it's a transudate and like everything you see about him, it is all due to his incapacitated liver from his weakness for alcohol, day after day drinking away his dignity."

This man was obviously a drunk and had a very sick liver that made him bright yellow, but he was better this morning, thanks to me. He seemed like a happy man, ready to leave the hospital and knock down a few more before lunch. He was trembling now. Dr. Thompson continued, "Mr. Malloy, get dressed, please, and go home or to whatever curbside you call home as your life in this world will be brief." He then turned and walked off the ward, leaving us all with little to say, and even the chatty Mr. Malloy was speechless, and he began to tremble a little. All the other patients were watching us.

I folded the stethoscope and put it back in my suit pocket and told the patient, "Mr. Malloy, please get dressed and go home."

I looked at Carl and Tex and they just smiled back at me. I didn't want the patient to go into delirium tremens, which would truly make matters worse for me. He just needed another drink of whiskey and that would steady him. I knew he had cirrhosis of the liver and didn't have long for this world. The fluid collection in his chest was large and I wanted to draw off most of that fluid from his chest before he left. That would help his breathing. I wanted to know what was in the fluid; that was my original plan. I told my friends that I was going to draw off the fluid anyway, since I could, I was a doctor now. But both Carl and Tex told me not to. Word might get back to Dr. Thompson from the nurses. We walked away from Mr. Malloy as he was grabbing his clothes from under the bed.

I thought we might receive a little more respect from Dr. Thompson now that I graduated. He acknowledged that I was a medical doctor, just as he was. But the way he said "Dr. Schuler" was done sarcastically. I took a deep breath and looked across the ward at the other patients I admitted during the night. Tex and Carl came up to me, smiling.

Carl put his arm around my shoulder and said, "Well, Dr. Schuler, I have a spare needle and syringe if you want it. Mr. Malloy would have been good practice."

Tex added, "Wow, Doug, that was painful just to watch. I had to look away several times."

"It was like you two weren't even in the room with me. I know I percussed Malloy's chest the right way. You heard it right?"

"Yeah, you're the best at it. We heard it," Carl said.

We all walked slowly back to the nurses' table after smelling fresh coffee and eyeballing the other patients to make sure they were all still breathing. Their beds were in two long rows, and we walked between them down the middle at the foot of their beds. In an adjoining storage room was a small stove with a steel coffeepot blowing steam. We all sat in chairs at a small table in the corner. The aroma was soothing. I opened the cupboard to look for some cups. Two nurses, one young and one old walked into the room. The young one was very pretty, with dark eyes and wavy hair underneath her tiny nurses cap. She smiled at me and gently took the cup from my hand and poured it full of hot coffee. How beautiful they looked together.

The old nurse said to her, "Take Dr. Thompson his coffee, he's on the west wing."

The young nurse placed the cup on a saucer and a saucer on a decorative metal tray and walked out. The older nurse was taller and heavier but dressed the same, a heavily starched white apron over a long blue dress.

She just glared at us and said, "None of you belong in here."

This was the head nurse, Nurse Sanders, and she glared at us motionless until we left. When we were students and loitering in the ward, she would demand that we leave. We were interns now and we deserved to stay.

She stopped me and said, "That urine specimen in the jar doesn't belong here, either. Take it with you."

With a cold smile she added, "Having a good first week, Schuler?" I picked up the jar of Mr. Malloy's urine and left.

On my way out, I said, "You know I'm a doctor now."

"I know you are," she said, and then looking at the table in the corner she added, "And don't forget your little doctor bag, too."

I grabbed by bag and put it under my arm and went to the window and held the jar of urine up to the sunlight. It was the color of tea, from a high bilirubin in the blood that turned his skin yellow and his urine brown. The sunlight revealed it clearly. I left the jar on the nurses' table in the middle of the ward for them to dispose. It wasn't my job anymore.

I was proud of my little doctor bag that our family doctor gave me because Dr. Wallace gave us all his time and his care. He took care of my Oma as she was dying in our house, in a room behind the kitchen, when I was nine years old. She and my grandfather on my father's side were immigrants from Germany. They arrived as newlyweds to the "promised land of Texas" when they bought their one-way tickets. They were given free land to farm and ranch in Guadalupe County. Along with other German immigrants, they farmed and ranched that hard, dry land and called it New Berlin. It was near Seguin, near Cibolo Creek. My Opa died when I was three and my Oma came to live with us right away. I always remember lying in bed next to her on top of her quilt on her dark spool bed, and her stroking my hair as she told me stories about Germany, in German. I could just imagine how beautiful it was, with its lush forests and towering mountains. She never learned to speak English.

On my mother's side, my grandparents also had immigrated from Germany and lived with other immigrants in Kendall County. They called it Bergheim. They had left the protection of established New Braunfels in Comal County to move west, just outside the city to open a small general store along a winding road that left the city. An Austrian born man joined them in the area and began to build up the small community. It was risky living where they did, my mother would tell me. But they and the other Germans had no trouble with the Comanches. They all followed the peace treaty that had been signed between them. They would trade with them along with the white settlers at my grandfather's store. I remember the moccasins that he gave me when I was younger, and the beaded necklaces that he gave to my sisters.

The other white settlers, mainly Irish or English, went farther west and had regular skirmishes with the Comanches. They refused to sign a peace treaty with them. Nobody knows who killed my grandparents at their store one evening in 1882. They were shot and then robbed. Many in the community felt that young Comanche Indians did it, but my father and mother didn't believe it. They were sure that some white men killed them and then rode off with the looted goods, going west toward the Nueces River, where a lot of criminals hid. But no one ever found out who killed them. My uncle now runs the store.

As my Oma was dying that night, I sneaked to her room when Dr. Wallace was there and watched him by candlelight sitting by her side as she was sleeping. He himself was dozing off in that squeaky rocker while holding her hand. He would have me translate his observations to her. He wasn't German but it didn't matter, I knew my Oma trusted him. My father said there were no German doctors here. I told him that she knew she was dying and that she wasn't afraid, and that she wasn't looking for a miracle. He would wake if her breathing changed and then look over and see me standing by the bed, and smile. The gentleness in his smile is what I remember most. His big smile would appear slowly out of a white bearded face that was round, and a head covered with white hair. He had all of his teeth, but my Oma only had a few left. I looked closely at her still face, too. She hardly looked like she was breathing but then with a deep sigh she would startle me. Dr. Wallace remained calm.

"Go get me a pillow for my back, boy," he would say as he stroked her hand and the rocker went silent.

He was not the angel of death. I liked it when he came to see her. He was always confident and calm. He walked slowly into the house, letting the screen door slam after he entered the front door. He greeted the men with a handshake, even me and my brother. He would speak to my father a little, then make his way back to my grandmother's room carrying his little black bag, making the floor creak with his heavy pointed boots. After a few moments, my Oma would then yell for me to come translate. He had the same type of doctor bag that he gave me.

A year after her death, I remember him back at our house, this time standing over me with his washed hands in the air and his shirt sleeves rolled up, ready to take out my tonsils on the kitchen table. He smiled and winked at me through his round spectacles as my father tightly held my feet together at the end of the table. I looked up into his eyes and winked back.

I was tired after being up the whole night admitting new patients and caring for all the patients on both wards. It was what we did as interns on a call night, which came every third night. When I met Mr. Malloy at about two in the morning, he was sound asleep, but he woke after a dose a tonic of Lupulin and Capsicum and a few rakes across his chest with my knuckles. Then, unfortunately, he talked my ear off, even singing while I was trying to close a large laceration in his forehead. It took me forever to sew it together. He was brought here by the police carriage after they closed a bar downtown on Church Street. As he sobered in the morning, he told me before rounds that he worked every night as a carriage driver, was married, and had two teenage children to feed. And that he had to work again tonight. He said he needed the money. He didn't know much of it was used to buy alcohol.

I admitted several other people last night, including an older man nearly comatose with diabetes and severe dehydration. His mouth was so dry, his tongue was practically sealed to his palate. His breath reeked of sugar. He was only taking small sips of water despite the nurse's demands. The family was resigned to the hopelessness of the situation. A milkman from a dairy on the east end of the island was admitted with a large, swollen, painful right leg and foot. It was either gout or cellulitis, an infection from a microorganism from his cows.

One patient who worried me more than Mr. Malloy was a seaman brought to us from a steamship that sailed into the harbor late yesterday. The ship's physician told of this man's protracted fevers and periodic confusion. The physician spoke directly with Dr. Randall, who in turn shared it with me. Dr. Randall came to the hospital last night about 11 p.m., leaving a dinner party early, it seemed, by the way he was dressed. He didn't stay long but after looking at the patient from a distance, he gave me instructions to not let the sailor die.

The patient was Ignacio Mendez from Manzanillo, Cuba. He was forty-eight years old and a veteran Atlantic seaman, currently first mate on the steam paddle wheeler Carlotta. The ship was loaded with bales of jute from India. He was well in Veracruz, the last port of call, until four days go when he began with high fever. He continued to work until yesterday, but he became confused and agitated, hallucinating and calling for his dead mother. The Carlotta's physician brought him over himself in the ship's long boat. The ship was anchored in the ship channel following routine quarantine laws for all ships.

When his carriage reached the hospital, he was on a stretcher, disoriented, pale, and palpably feverish. Dr. Randall came to the bedside early this morning while I was listening to the patient's chest. Mr. Mendez was no longer disoriented but moaning in pain, and rarely moving his extremities. He had been given a cool water sponge bath and was lying nearly motionless in a loose, white gown. Dr. Randall looked concerned.

"What's your impression, Douglas?"

"He's tachycardic, but without a murmur, and he's not able to move his extremities. He doesn't respond to pain. I think his fever is breaking now; he's more alert this morning."

Dr. Randall pulled out his stethoscope and listened carefully to his heart, then his chest, counting his respirations, and then listened to his abdomen. He coiled his stethoscope in his hands and replaced it in his coat pocket. He palpated his abdomen gently then deeply and the patient did not grimace from pain. He next examined his legs and saw that they were not swollen. He reached up and pulled down on a lower eyelid and saw that the conjunctiva was pale. He lifted his head slightly off the pillow and Mr. Mendez winced and moaned. Dr. Randall did it again with the same result. Why was he lifting his head, checking for meningitis? The patient didn't open his eyes or respond when Dr. Randall called his name. I asked him in Spanish last night and he briefly opened his eyes for me.

"I don't like the way this man looks," Dr. Randall said after several minutes thinking, staring at the patient.

"I don't either."

The patient seemed less responsive now. Dr. Randall reached over and lightly slapped his face, both sides, with very little response.

"I just don't like what's happening here," he said, still staring at the patient.

"I don't either, Dr. Randall," I said as I stared at the patient, too.

"No, I suppose you don't." He glanced up at me and then back at the patient. "Douglas, tell me your impression."

"I think he has malaria."

"Why do you think he has malaria?"

"Well, he's been traveling in endemic areas for the past month—India, the Caribbean. The ship's physician recorded very high fevers with rigors for the past few days. He's febrile now."

"The ship's physician never mentioned rigors to me."

"Well, I got that from the patient last night when he was mentally clear for a short while after a cool sponge bath."

"How did he describe them?"

"He said that with the fevers he had hard shaking chills like he had never had before."

"Okay, that sounds like rigors to me too. Yes, I think he could have malaria. Have you ever seen a case of malaria?" Dr. Randall said.

"No, I don't think so."

"You won't forget him now, if that's what he has. He's going to keep us busy till we can get some quinine into him. Now that it's light, examine his blood smear, see if his red cells are infected. "

"I gave him a dose last night after you left."

"Good," Dr. Randall said as he was walking away.

I always followed instructions from Dr. Edward Randall even if I didn't completely understand them. When he said "don't let the man die" I knew what he meant. Keep him alive through the night until morning rounds, was what he meant. I had always watched the way he carried himself, especially at the bedside, the way he thought carefully at the bedside before he spoke, before he gave his opinion. He told us over and over, "Share with the patient the truth, but keep your opinions to yourself." As students we were scolded often for the telling the patient what we thought was wrong with them before we knew. And our initial diagnosis based on our first impressions was often wrong. He would say also that it was acceptable to the patient to tell them that you didn't know what was wrong with them. Being correct about a first diagnosis was acceptable to the patient as long as it was the truth.

Dr. Randall was Professor of Materia Medica and Therapeutics, was probably in his forties, thin and tall, and with very understanding eyes—at least, when he spoke to the patients. He was always composed and dignified, and unlike the other faculty, almost always calm. Just having him here at the bedside gave me greater confidence in my own ability as a physician. And I learned to share with patients their diagnosis only after I had the correct one, which was the one that he agreed with.

I was amazed at the broad scope of his understanding of diseases, especially infectious ones, like malaria, but his main interest was of the diseases of the heart. In his lab at the Medical Department building, he had put together a string galvanometer to read the electrical conduction of the heart. As students, Carl, Tex, and I took our turn hooked up to it. Wire leads attached to metal plates were placed on our arms and one leg by rubber straps with electrical gel against our skin forming a triangle of wires across our body with our heart in the middle. Dr. Randall called it Einthoven's triangle after the famous doctor in the Netherlands with his electrocardiogram machine. We lay motionless while the little needle measured small electrical blips with each heartbeat. He called his set up an electrometer. He compared our tracings to the tracings of patients who had previous heart attacks. There was a very small difference in the electrical conduction pattern that only he could see, but we all agreed that there was.

Dr. Randall had even rigged up a stationary unicycle with the help of a local blacksmith so that we could sit and pedal and raise our heart rate. We peddled for hours while sitting on that wooden triangular seat. Carl was the best at it. He never tired. He wasn't as tall as Tex or me, but he was broad shouldered and strong in the legs. And he got his heart rate higher than ours. He was an expert on a real bicycle, he told us. I had never seen a bicycle before coming to Galveston. Carl had his own since he was a child. He was from the big city, from Dallas, and he learned to ride an adult bicycle as a kid. He dared me to ride one once while we were downtown. He laughed and said that I was afraid to try, but I wasn't.

After studying a full day one of us would assist Dr. Randall in his lab, usually on a Friday night. We had to lie perfectly still on the wooden table or pedal for what seemed like hours, but we didn't mind. That wooden seat hurt me more than a saddle ever did. He appreciated our help and would give us a little money for our time. As students then we rarely carried spare change in our pockets. The other faculty we assisted in their lab never paid us. He especially appreciated Carl and his heart rate and paid him more. And we knew he was in charge of the intern selection for the hospital.

After morning rounds with the faculty, I was back on the east ward and wanted to get the blood sample from Mr. Mendez. I went to his bedside and found him still unconscious. I touched his face with the back of my hand and his skin felt cool now. He didn't make a sound when I lifted his head slightly off the pillow, no grimace either. I put the tourniquet around his arm and slapped the arm beneath it to find a vein. With the needle and syringe I withdrew enough blood to fill it, then removed it. With my free hand, I placed pressure on his arm for hemostasis for a few seconds.

I left the ward with the syringe in my pocket and went down the hall to the storage room and found the microscope. I took it off the counter and placed it on the large table near the window. The window was facing east to capture the light in the mirror on the microscope. I took several drops of blood from the syringe and placed it on the glass slide and then smeared the blood with the glass cover slip. I made several more slides, varying the thickness of the smears. I stained them with a dropper of Giemsa solution from a glass vial. I searched the smears for the red blood cells that now were purple, focusing on their appearance. There were no abnormal blood cells or malaria organisms. Why didn't I see them? I looked at each slide closely again and didn't see any signs of the malaria parasite. Nothing unusual, except elevated numbers of white blood cells. I marked the slides with a wax pencil and wrapped them in a cotton cloth and placed them in my outside suit coat pocket.

I walked slowly back to the east ward and back to Mr. Mendez. I sat down on the end of his bed. He was lying very still and breathing regularly. I reached up and felt his radial pulse, still fast and thready. Could he have hepatitis, or maybe yellow fever? There were no obvious signs, no wounds, no rash, no localizing symptoms. I sat a little while longer with him and listened to his heart again, then left to see Dr. Randall.

His office was a floor below. He was in the corner by the window holding a fluid filled test tube to the light. I knocked on the open door and he motioned me to come in. I took a seat in the chair in front of his large desk.

"How's our patient, still with fever?"

"101 this morning at ten."

He went to his desk and sat. "His mental status?"

"Still couldn't rouse him."

"Did you examine his blood smear?"

"Yes, sir, and I didn't see anything abnormal, just a few elevated white blood cells."

"You know, we get several cases of malaria a year here, mainly local people during the summer months. Let me see those slides and have a look myself."

I handed the slides to him, and he went to the shelf by the window to his microscope. He spent several minutes looking at each slide while I admired his office, especially his wall of medical books and the human skull on his desk as a paper weight.

"Well," he began, "I don't find any evidence of malaria."

I sat up straight again, "Yes, sir." I was right on this one.

"He may not be showing the infected red cell or other malarial forms yet. It's still early in the course of the disease. You're going to have to keep checking the blood smears until you find it. Go out and keep a close eye on him." He handed the slides back to me.

"Yes, of course, I will."

As I left the office, I suddenly felt very fatigued. I hadn't slept in over twenty-four hours but my day was not over. I went back to the west ward and found Carl sitting at the bedside of a patient, writing in the chart, a little old lady tucked under the sheets snoring. He was talking with the student nurse who was standing at the foot of the bed and holding a shiny metal bedpan.

"Carl, what are you doing?"

"Making rounds with Edith."

"Let me talk to you about a patient I admitted yesterday. He's a sailor with three days of fever and ..."

"I know about him, the patient of Randall's with malaria on the east side."

"His blood smears were negative. If he dies on me, I'll never hear the end of it."

"Relax, Dougie," he said, still looking at Edith. "I know what's wrong with him."

"No, you don't."

"He suffered the untimely bite by a member of the arachnid family."

"What are you talking about, Carl?" My mind was exhausted.

"You know, a spider bite!" Mr. Mendez had a large spider tattoo in the middle of his back.

"Very funny." Why does he do this to me? "Hey, lend me fifty cents."

He did and I walked away. When Mr. Mendez was brought to the hospital, I asked Carl to help me roll him over onto the stretcher. We admired the tattoo, a black widow, I think, that covered his whole back.

Carl stood up and put his hand on my shoulder and said, "Don't worry about this guy, he'll get better. These sailors are tougher that you and I. Right now this malaria bug is having it out with his circulating syphilis, and the syphilis wins every time. Then he'll be good as new."

It was almost noon, and I was hungry. I had been hungry since last night but there was nothing to eat. I went out the front door of the hospital and down the steps and walked next door to the Medical Department building looking for something to eat. I found a lady with a small wooden cart in the basement and bought a dried beef sandwich and a piece of pound cake with one of the two quarters in my pocket. I was going to find some typical histopath slides for malaria and compare them to Mr. Mendez' slides. I had to make sure. I wasn't sure of myself about everything like Carl was. Someday, it would come back to him.

It was almost five o'clock and I was back at the hospital. I didn't see any evidence of malaria on the slides I had made. My last set was at four o'clock and again they were negative. Mr. Mendez had a normal temperature now but again was difficult to rouse.

The old man with diabetes died at 2:58 p.m. and just in time, as I wanted to go home. We had the body sent to the morgue and I spoke with his daughter. His wish was to die in the hospital, she said, rather than at home. He was fortunate. While examining another patient, Nurse Sanders brought me a note and then said as she always does, " I hope you're washing your hands between each patient, Dr. Schuler." I didn't have the time or the desire to do that. The note was from Dr. Randall who wanted to see me in his office immediately.

I went downstairs to his office and knocked. The door was open but he wasn't there. I went in and sat down on the small chair in front of his desk. I began to look around. There were so many books, all beautifully aligned from floor to ceiling, texts of surgery, pharmacology, and many others, all in deep shades of burgundy, navy, green, and black. Would he mind if I browsed through a few? I didn't dare. Dr. Randall had studied abroad before coming to Galveston. We all had heard how he met Pasteur and Lister and studied under Carl Braun and Billroth in Vienna. He never spoke of these old days and these legends of science and medicine. Instead, he spoke of the exciting times that we lived in now, at the beginning of a new century. He was recently fascinated with the development of roentgen rays, or as we called them X-rays. How it would open up the secrets of the human body, by simply taking a photograph. He wanted a machine for the hospital. He said it might change the way we approach the patient, maybe even make the physical exam obsolete. And, after I had just learned it.

He was a man of vision, but I never got to hear it in our conversations when I was a student. I overheard many of the conversations he had with the other faculty physicians while we all stood together over a patient. The students stood in the back and our opinions were not welcomed. Now that I was an intern, I wanted to hear of his travels, his conversations with the great ones in our field. I imagined he and I talking about the future of medicine together, modern medicine as he called it. Was I a colleague now, free to share my ideas? No.

He walked into the room quickly and I stood up immediately. I had fallen asleep in the chair. I knew how he expected that we stand in his presence. Would he reprimand me now? He went right around me as if he didn't notice me and sat down at his desk.

"Sit down," he said. "What about the smears for this afternoon?"

I wiped the drool from my mouth, "No, I didn't see anything abnormal."

"I spoke with the ship's physician today. They're sailing again tonight. They've loaded cargo and the captain is pressuring the ship's physician to sail. We've got to come up with a diagnosis. This physician has planned a series of bleedings and purgings for Mr. Mendez. When will they let go of that antiquated practice? You've started the quinine already? How many doses has he had?"

"Three."

"Let's rethink what could be wrong before they decide to take him back to the ship and sail away with a dying man on board."

Could something else be the source of his fever? My mind was tired, and I was at a loss for coming up with something new. I knew I looked bad, unkempt, unshaven, and now sweaty. I sat forward in the chair and looked at Dr. Randall, who looked perfect—clean shaven, hair neat, a dark pressed suit. I wondered what he thought of my appearance, especially after a night on call.

"Let me see the blood smears, Doug," he said leaning back in his chair. I reached in my pants pocket and gave him the slides. The cloth was sticky with blood now. He took the slides from me and pulled the microscope close to him. He carefully lifted the cloth off the slides. He took his time examining all the slides as I began to doze off again.

I was dreaming when he finally spoke up. "Well, I don't see any malarial forms, either. I've examined him today also and besides his systolic cardiac murmur, I don't find anything to help us."

I had heard the murmur also and didn't know what to make of it. I really felt we had to think more of a venereal disease, like Carl said.

"1 was impressed with the increased number of white corpuscles, especially," I said.

"Yes, I noticed that, but did you notice the inclusions within the white cells?"

"No", I said. I was too tired to lie.

"Possibly bacteria. Let's go take another look at Mr. Mendez, together."

We both stood and went upstairs to the east ward. Mr. Mendez was still difficult to awaken, and again hot to touch. Dr. Randall pulled back the sheet covering him and there was a bright red rash over his chest.

"Well, Doug. What about this?" he said without looking at me. This was new. I walked to the other side of the bed and touched the rash. It was even hotter than the rest of his body. I watched Dr. Randall reach down and check the patient's eyes. His pupils were dilated but reactive to the light. The whites of his eyes were still white, but his conjunctiva was pale with a few hemorrhages. The more I saw the more I was confused. It was now dusk and the light very dim now on the ward. We both heard footsteps now and saw an older man walking over to us slowly. The footsteps echoed loudly throughout the ward and most of the patients were now watching him. It was the ship's physician. An older man with a long white beard, under a tanned and wrinkled face, wearing a weathered white shirt and striped pants. He spoke with a thick Scottish accent.

"I've come to collect Mendez, Dr. Randall. We sail at dawn."

"Dr. MacCubbin, must you? We have not diagnosed nor treated this man yet, and he's most likely worse now."

"I realize that, but my orders from the captain are clear. We've loaded her up a day early, so we're sailing right away. Mendez must return to the ship."

"Can't he be left with us until the ship returns to port? You told me that it makes quarterly visits here? What good is he to the ship in this shape?"

"I'm taking him now, Dr Randall. He'll be under my close care. For a sailor, being sick on land feels like death. He needs the pitch and roll of the ship to purge him of his sicknesses. Have an orderly carry him to your ambulance, if you will".

Dr. Randall stared down at the patient, then looked up at me on the other side of the bed and said, "Go get an orderly and escort them to the dock." I took off my suit coat.

Mr. Mendez was carried off the ward and down the front steps of the hospital and gently placed in the back of the hospital ambulance, a long black covered carriage with the writing "John Sealy Hospital Ambulance" on the side door. A light gray horse drew it. Dr. MacCubbin and I got into the carriage and sat next to the patient and across from each other. He sat there staring at me, then looked away and lit a cigarette. We rode slowly down Strand Street toward downtown. I was watching the patient's breathing.

At the hospital, we often had sick sailors, but they never stayed long. We worked as fast as we could, but the ship's captain ruled their fate on sea as well as on land. We never knew what happened to these men after their short but interesting stay here. At least, we never had the drunk sailors brought to the hospital. The bars were full of them downtown on most nights. And they were left to sleep it off in the street. Dr. MacCubbin was probably still recovering from his drunken state. He smelled like the rest of the sailors after a day in port.

"My boy, you must not fret over such a man as Mendez. He is a seaman, born and baptized in the sea, coddled on hard tack and rum. He is different from you and me. Have a smoke and try to relax,"

I was ignoring him as he rambled on about life at sea. He was as a quack. He had no regard for this man, Mendez. Did anybody? I never knew if he had a family in some port waiting for him. I cared more for him, yet he only spoke to me while in a half-conscious state of mind. Dr. MacCubbin had no more passion for Mendez nor for other humanity than an undertaker or a butcher. The orderly took the ambulance slowly to 22nd Street and turned north to Pier 21. The ship had been towed from the dock and was anchored in the bay. The doctor had a longboat tied at the dock, with a young sailor waiting. We carried Mr. Mendez, still limp and febrile, carefully down the wooden steps covered in green algae to the boat and placed him gently in the center. He never made a sound.

The doctor climbed into the boat and said, "Untie us and shove us off, young man."

I stepped quickly into the boat and said, "I need to escort him to the ship. Dr. Randall insists that I go."

"Very well, then, get in and shove us off,"' he replied. I untied the bowline and pushed hard on the dock.

The young sailor rowed slowly, and we made headway as the water in the bay was calm. It was by now a clear night as we headed into the last of the sunset over the harbor. The winds were mild, out of the southeast. The farther we rowed from shore the darker the sky seemed. I checked the radial pulse of Mr. Mendez. He had a weak one and he was still breathing. The doctor just looked at me and shook his head. I hadn't helped this man under my care. I received almost no information from him, just hearsay from this old physician in the boat with me. We pulled alongside the ship, and I threw the line to a sailor on deck.

"Dr. MacCubbin, may I inspect his quarters?"

"Yes, boy, but it won't help you."

"I will be quick, and I won't take anything."

"Go ahead but stay clear of the captain."

Several of the sailors carried Mr. Mendez on board and to sickbay with the doctor behind them carrying his clothes. Another led me into the hold of the ship to the forecastle and motioned me to the small quarters of the patient. I had lifted a lit lamp hanging by the quarterdeck. His hammock was hung against the wall and in the corner was his sea chest. I opened it and began to look through his things. The air was stale and hot, and it was quiet. I was the only one here. The chest was full of things from a life at sea—half-done scrimshaw carving, some silver Spanish currency, some documents, and a needle and spool of black thread. There were some old letters tucked in the lid of the chest. I wanted to open them and read about the people in his life to gain some clue of his world. I dug deeper into the chest and found several small glass bottles with small corks, both half full of a white powder. I held the bottle up to the light and noticed a slight yellowish discoloration of the powder. I put one of them in my pocket and closed the chest. I looked around the cramped quarters that was his world. I walked up the steps to the deck and around the cargo to the handrail. It was quiet. The ship was loaded with bales of cotton, fore and aft. I looked across the bay to the city as I walked across the deck. The lights from the gas lamps downtown were beautiful, flickering as people walked by them. I could make out the top hats of the men with their canes and the women in their long wide skirts. The fresh air felt good. A sailor tapped me on the shoulder and motioned me over to the gangway to enter the longboat.

I walked past one of the ship's immense paddle wheels sitting motionless and down the steps and stepped into the longboat. I shoved off at the bow as the sailor began to row slowly back to the city. I sat in the stern, and I leaned back onto the boat and stared at the city lights, now rolling. So was the voice of the sailor. He was very talkative about his life at sea, and his own personal fears of ever ending up in a hospital like Mendez and how happy he was to be sailing with a capable doc, like Doc MacCubbin. If he ever had to take a man's leg off, he could take it quick. That was important to every seaman, he said.

I felt the sailor kicking me in the leg. "Get up mate, I need to back to the ship straight away," he said.

He was drunk and laughing about how foolish I looked slumped in the stern. I think he had spit on me, too. My face and neck felt wet. I sat up as quickly as I could. How long had I been asleep here?

"l tried to wake you when we reached the dock, but I couldn't, and I got tired of trying. You know with the ladies all waiting for me. Don't think ill of me, but there was gin to drink and no time to waste.'"

"I'll be al right," I added back, wiping my face with my rolled-up shirtsleeve. 1 climbed out of the boat and walked up the slippery steps to the top of the bulkhead. The sailor was singing as he began to row back to the ship.

Once I had my bearings, I walked past the bales of cotton stacked high on the dock and toward the Strand. What time was it? There were very few people walking on the streets now. But there was still music coming from several taverns on the Strand and on Market Street. I walked eastward toward home. I ached all over as I walked. I kept walking block after block, and then turned the last corner into my alley and my feet sunk in the sand as I walked toward my place. The alley was quiet and dark. I climbed the steps to my place and opened the door and walked in and sat down on the edge of the cot. I kicked off my shoes on the floor and took off my clothes and threw them into the corner and lay back on the cot. I was hungry, but more tired than hungry. I tried to recall it all, all the patients I cared for as a real doctor. I was a doctor. Did I make a mistake?

CHAPTER 4

So far it had been a better day today. I ran into a few of my friends at work and we discussed some of the latest hospital gossip. One of the medical students working with us was convinced of his diagnosis about a man under our care with abdominal pain. He was so sure it was gout. True, the man was robust in his body habits, but we told the student that he had a spasm of the common bile duct most likely due to an impacted gallstone. I could palpate his swollen and distended gallbladder when I pushed hard under his right rib margin. He would need his gallbladder removed but fortunately Dr. Thompson was not here for the rest of the summer. Like many of the faculty, he traveled in Europe for a month and was not scheduled back until mid-September. We felt more relaxed with him gone.

I was not due on call for another night and wanted to escape the hospital. I walked down the front steps of the hospital after telling Tex about my patients for the night. He had night duty on a Friday night. I stared at the student nurses' boarding house across the street. It seemed quiet over there for a summer evening, no one on the front steps that I recognized. But I really didn't know anyone there like Carl did. He made sure that he got to know every incoming nursing student class. He dated a few but it never lasted. He wanted me to join him tonight downtown for a party at a private club.

Last Saturday night I invited him to a party at the German Club.

I had received an engraved invitation at the hospital to attend the annual Bach festival at the dance pavilion. He saw the invitation and wanted to join me and said that he knew a few words of German, like *fraulein,* or *bier.* We went and I introduced him around as just Carl. They were gracious and didn't ask his last name. I had been there a few times before since my parents came, mainly to sit outside and play cards and drink a bottle of last year's beer. I had told them about Anna, and they reminded me of the importance of keeping my promise to her.

The dance pavilion was spectacular that evening, with food and music, and to my amazement, beer on ice. It was in large wooden kegs in metal troughs packed tight with ice. The large chandeliers set high in the ceiling with large glass domes that shone brightly. The band at one end of the stage played polka music. Carl and I danced with several of the young frauleins round and round the octagonal building and then we all sat quietly and listened while the orchestra played Bach. We drank beer out of large, imported glass steins. It was so cold it gave me a headache.

Carl suggested that I should get to know one or two or three of the young girls there, and there were several in their late teens or early twenties whom I admired. They were very friendly to us, as were their parents, but it all reminded me of our club back home and of Anna. I told him about Anna, but he always said that I needed a girlfriend here in Galveston, too. He was a natural with the ladies and even their parents. After several steins they didn't mind that he didn't speak German. He could carry a conversation for hours, no matter where he was or who he was with, and the language didn't seem to matter. All the patrons spoke German early on, but it gave way to English as the evening progressed. How did he do it? We left late in the evening and Carl promised several girls that we would return the next weekend. They looked at him more than they looked at me that night. They always did, but I made better marks in school than he did.

I told Carl I didn't want to go to the private party. He said there would be some real women there. But I was hungry, so I walked alone toward my place. But I didn't have any food, there, so I went down Strand Avenue for several blocks and tried to smell someone cooking outside. I kept walking farther down past 13th Street; a few blocks farther was the Mexican barrio. I turned the corner heading south on 15th Street to Mechanic Street and in a small house was a family that sold food on the weekends. I walked around the side of the house and looked over the fence. There on the ground was a slaughtered pig's head with a mass of swarming flies and blood in a sticky pool on the ground. They were making something out of pork today. I rang the metal bell outside and a short but muscular man with thick hands opened the door and motioned me inside with a smile. Mr. Lozano was in his forties and had thick hair and a wide mustache. I sat at a small table in the front room of this small house by myself. I leaned over to peek into the kitchen, hoping to see his daughter.

She was there and as I was nearly on the floor leaning on the back legs of the chair she turned around while working at the kitchen table and gave me a quick look. It was a blank look, but it was a look. She turned back around and as I was rocking back again, I could see her bare ankles and calves, smooth and well-shaped, below her dress. Her father went into the kitchen, and I heard him speak to his family in Spanish: "The gringo is hungry again." He looked out of the kitchen at me, and I smiled back. His daughter walked out of the kitchen carrying a fork and asked, "What do you want?"

"It doesn't matter, whatever you want to bring me," I said to her in Spanish.

She didn't smile and said in English "Why? You know my little sister brings you the food. I'm busy now."

She was wearing a simple tan dress with a small V-neck collar.

An apron was tied over her dress. She was wearing simple sandals. Her neck was thin, and her hair was dark and wavy and long. It was not all together, but it hung down behind her head with a few locks in front which she now pushed back. She had dark, cool eyes that made me warm all over. I knew she was younger than me, but not by much.

She went back into the kitchen. Maybe she would she bring me the food? After a few minutes, she came out with a wooden plate of steaming enchiladas, rice, tamales, and corn tortillas. She put the plate down in front of me.

"Please sit with me," I said in Spanish.

She spoke to me in English, but I spoke to her in Spanish. Maybe she would warm to me if I spoke Spanish? But she wasn't smiling, in fact, she seemed irritated that I could speak it. I learned to speak Spanish working with my father and the vaqueros on our ranch. I worked with them for long days at a time and they didn't speak English. After a long day, at the very end of our ranch, miles from the house, I would sleep outside with them under a cluster of oak trees at the creek. They would cook by campfire, and they would feed me, mostly beans and rice and corn tortillas. They would tell me stories about their life always on the move, wherever there was work. They were superstitious and wouldn't sleep near the creek because of La Llorona. They said that you could hear her ghost wailing for her children that she had drowned after her lover abandoned her. And if you got too close to the creek, she could pull you in and drown you. After the fire went out, lying on my blanket with my head on my saddle, I would listen for her crying, her wailing. I only heard coyotes. They called the creek Arroyo de La Llorona. We came to call it Woman Hollering Creek.

"You look so pretty tonight, Rosita," I said in Spanish.

"No, it's Rosa. How can you say that I look pretty? And how do you know Spanish? We need to speak English, okay?"

"Please, please sit with me. My name is Doug," I said in English.

"You've told me your name before."

She looked back in the kitchen and her father was sitting at the table with his back to the doorway, so she sat down across the table from me. It was hot in the front room, and we were both sweating. I looked down at myself, I had forgotten how awful I looked. My wrinkled white shirt, with the sleeves rolled up. There was no blood today on my shirt, thankfully. My black pants were stained with some white powder, from the hospital. My shoes were dusty, and my hair was not combed. I straightened it with my fingers.

I smiled at her and began to eat. She got up and went into the kitchen and came back out with a glass of water for me.

"Gracias, Rosa"

"You're welcome"

"So, you're not married?" I asked with a stupid smile.

"What do you think?" she said with a frown.

"Neither am I"

"1 know, I can tell."

The food was delicious. I hoped I was not eating too fast, but she wasn't watching me. She seemed anxious but she stayed while I ate. She had gotten up once to get her baby brother, who was crying in the room behind the kitchen. He was quiet now in her arms and she seemed less anxious.

"Why do you come here so much?" she said. We were the only ones at the table this evening as no one else had come for a meal. She was looking directly at me with those beautiful dark eyes.

"Well, you see I work all the time at the hospital and live by myself, and I get hungry, and your food is my favorite," I said as slowly and sincerely as I could.

"Liar!" she scoffed in Spanish.

"Now wait, I'm not lying, it's all true. I'm a doctor and I need to eat to better treat my patients." She was rocking the baby in the chair and not looking at me anymore.

So I kept eating but slowed down a little.

She looked back at me. "I don't believe you. All you doctors at that hospital do is kill people. Everybody says that people get sick and go there for help and they don't get any better and then come home and just die."

She carried her brother back to his bed; he was asleep now. She came back in after a few minutes and sat back down. She had taken off her apron now and brought a book to read. I tried to see the title of the book.

"What are you reading?" I asked. She kept reading without looking up at me. I wanted her to look at me, but I was at a loss for words. I finished my meal and was expected to leave now. I put a quarter on the table and stood up.

"Will you walk out with me?" I asked.

"Why?" she snapped back.

"Will you sit with me on the steps for a while... please," I said. "We could feel the breeze off the gulf."

She had a pained look on her face now as she looked back into the kitchen.

"Okay, but not for too long."

She stood up and walked out through the screen door ahead of me, on to the front porch and sat down on the top step. I was right behind her and sat down close to her. She moved away a little. My feet were shuffling in the sand at the bottom of the steps. She kept her feet on the bottom step. Was she used to this, other men coming over here to eat the food and then trying to speak with her? She looked annoyed.

It was cooling down and the night was clear, and the moon was out and shining down on her. She was beautiful, even though she had masa in her hair. After a few moments she seemed more relaxed and looked at me and smiled a little. She was enjoying the cool breeze. I kept my distance.

"Were you born here, Rosa?"

"Yes, in this house." She said, looking at me, "You're not from here, are you?"

"No, I'm from Santa Clara, near Seguin. My family lives on a ranch there. I was born there."

"In the barn?"

"No… in the house."

She was smiling now and laughed. I laughed, too. We sat there quietly and listened to the breeze through the trees. A carriage went by slowly, then, another in the other direction.

"You've been coming here for several years now. Why?" she asked.

"To see you."

"Is that right? You eat like an animal, so fast and loud. I've never seen someone so hungry. My father lets us serve you more food than we normally do. I tell him we should charge you double but he won't."

She looked at me as she spoke now. I was entranced by her eyes, especially now reflecting the moonlight.

She continued, "You come here and see me cooking, wearing an apron, with masa in my hair. I don't believe you. It's not fair, I always look terrible when you show up."

"I come after work, hungry and tired, without my hair combed."

"Come see me on a Saturday night, you know, make a date, and so I know you're coming and can look better than this. Then I might believe you." I thought she always looked beautiful.

"This Saturday night then, can I come to see you?"

"What time?"

"Seven, I'll look better than this too, I promise."

"Then go ask my father."

I stood up to go inside but hesitated at the door. Her father was looking at me through the screen door. She had her father's penetrating eyes.

I took a few steps back and said, "Can I come to see your daughter this Saturday?"

He stared at me and spoke to her in Spanish, "Rosa, do you want him to come?"

She hesitated, not looking directly at him or me, and said, "Yes."

"Come inside, Rosa" he said.

Our eyes met as I walked past her down the steps to the street. I smiled as I passed her, but she didn't look at me. But she said yes, yes to her father, and yes to me.

I walked home, turning corner after corner, running my hand over the tops of the small iron fences on the streets. Some of the houses were still lit up with their electric lights but I preferred the moonlight. I was close to home now and when I reached the alley, I walked slowly down it, shuffling my shoes in the sand as the horses do.

CHAPTER 5

We were called into Dr. Randall's office, Carl, Tex, and I early this morning. Would we be reprimanded?

Instead, he said, "I want you three to do me a favor."

"Anything for you, Dr. Randall," Carl snapped back with a quick smile.

"Yes, uh, well," he continued without smiling, "Dr. Clopton phoned me this morning and is coming to the hospital and wants to make rounds with the new house interns. He'll meet you on the west ward at nine. You pick the patient; it shouldn't take more than an hour."

He said this sitting at his desk without looking up from his medicus. What could we say? We walked slowly out of his office looking at each other. We would never tell him no, but now this was a giant favor from our favorite professor. A favor of this magnitude deserved some payback, but I learned it wouldn't materialize for an intern. Everyday courtesy didn't apply to us.

Dr. Albert Clopton was a legend at the hospital. Yes, he was a member of the original faculty, as Professor of Physiology and Hygiene. And he came to fame during the War Between the States, as a dyed-in-the-wool Confederate and secessionist, coming from Jefferson, Texas, as a member of the Second Infantry Company and Wood's Brigade. My grandparents supported the Union during the war as most German Texans did. He reminded us all the time of his military achievements; he weaved that into our student lectures.

As a first-year student, I remember his long-winded orations, more like sermons, on physiology. I wanted to walk out of his lectures but that was not tolerated; neither was sleeping through them. We all thought he should retire, but I would come to know that physicians never completely retired.

"Carl, what do you think?" I looked in desperation.

"I've got the perfect patient for him. He'll never know what hit him. "

"Then you present the case," Tex said.

Carl was always the best presenter of patients, very smooth and very careful not to present too many details that could reveal mistakes. This valuable skill served him well as a student. But he was overconfident, and someone was going to realize that he didn't know as much as he let on. He was smooth with the student nurses, too. Tex, Carl, and I were all alumni members of the Jolly Bone Jugglers, our fraternity as medical students. This brotherhood was created and dedicated to the conquering of social barriers. Carl, as a senior student, had become the Grand Mogul, and Tex and I were Bone Warriors in charge of vital activities such as providing names and descriptions of incoming nursing students. At our meetings, we would all wear our robes over our suits, half-black, half-white, divided down the middle, with skull and crossbones on the left chest and with the letters "JBJ" between the bones. We felt we were popular as students, but now as interns we had moved on, and there was no time.

It was nearly nine and we walked slowly to the west ward for another cup of coffee, but Dr. Clopton was at the nurses' table in the middle of the ward talking loudly to Nurse Sanders. He was short but had an air of importance that she correctly recognized. He had a long face with a prominent nose and well combed white hair and a bushy moustache. All the moustaches that the older doctors had were so long, nearly covering their bottom lips. That was the old way. All of us were clean-shaven, much to the dislike of Dr. Clopton and the faculty. He wore a black suit with a high collar and a black tie. He leaned on a polished black cane with a brass knob. In the other hand, he had a small, worn black doctor's bag with some of the tubing of his stethoscope sticking out the top. Carl walked over to him with the two of us right behind him.

"Dr. Clopton," he said extending his right hand, "it is the thrill of a lifetime to finally meet you."

He glanced back at Carl for a split second but kept speaking to the nurse. Was he deaf? We all looked at each other and didn't know what to say next. She gave us her usual glare for interrupting her conversation.

She concluded, "It has been the joy of a lifetime to spend these few minutes speaking together and I only wish I had more time from my duties to speak with you further." She glared at me.

Dr. Clopton nodded to her and then turned to look at us. He wasn't smiling anymore but staring at us all from head to toe.

"I'm Dr. Clopton. Who are the three of you?" We all introduced ourselves, and then he shook our hands. His grip was stronger than ours, we thought as we looked at each other. He didn't recognize us as we were students here for the past four years.

"Well, lead the way, before I change my mind," he said.

Carl led us over to the bedside of Mrs. Sophia Salter. She was a middle-aged woman whom he admitted last week with persistent fevers. I was not that familiar with her case. By looking at her, she obviously had a high fever; she was flushed and tremulous, and hot to touch. She looked at us with only partial interest, but Dr. Clopton caught her attention, and she looked up at him and forced a smile. He put down his bag on the mattress near the foot of the bed and gave me his cane to hold. He walked to her right side of the bed and introduced himself. He bent at the waist and stared over her with dark, penetrating eyes and touched the back of his hand to her cheek. She closed her eyes being reassured by his presence. He checked her right radial pulse, and then examined her hand, then her fingernails. "Give me my stethoscope," he told me without looking at me. He placed the bell of the stethoscope very gently on her left chest and listened for a few seconds, through her gown, just to the left of her sternum in the intercostal space. All along Mrs. Salter seemed very much at ease. We were taught to completely disrobe the patient when performing a physical exam and to listen to the heart in all five auscultatory locations on the chest. He didn't so much as have her sit up to listen to her lungs, and he gave her no chest percussions from behind her. But she seemed so comfortable in his presence.

He stood up straight and looked at Carl and said, "Tell me about this woman's illness."

Carl began with many of the details of her presenting illness as we had been drilled to do. But immediately Dr. Clopton looked uninterested, especially as Carl began to go through each organ system and body part of the physical exam. Dr. Clopton looked at each one of us slowly, no longer uninterested but now irritated with a deep scowl beneath his moustache.

"Stop," he said, "I said, stop with this ridiculous regurgitation of inane details. What you have done is molest this poor woman. She came to you in dire straits, and you proceeded without any therapy but with gregarious observations and scientific hypotheses of no consequence. I will not stand for another ounce of this quackery you speak."

I looked away from his stare. Why does he do this to us?

Even louder, he continued, "What kind of practitioner is being trained at this university, a school that I fought for and razed from the ground with my bare hands?"

Now pointing at Carl, he said, "You sir, are destined to be the instigator of much suffering and morbidity among the common man and I cannot let you go on doing such a thing. I will speak with Dr. Randall about you and you and you. The two of you are just as guilty in your silence. You throw mud in the face of the great men of Texas medicine."

He grabbed the cane from my hand and walked off the ward talking to himself and shaking his cane in the air. He grabbed his top hat from Nurse Sanders and left the ward.

I looked at Carl and Tex, then back at Carl. The patients that were conscious sat up to hear better. Nurse Sanders stood with her hands on her hips. I gave it back.

Carl looked at us and said, "I thought it went pretty well."

Nothing bothers him, nothing. We all smiled at each other, but then we had to hide our true feelings as the patients were watching. Mrs. Salter was staring at us with a frown and shaking her head. Nurse Sanders walked over to us and stood very straight with her arms folded and her face red.

"What did you three do to Dr. Clopton? Dr. Randall is going to hear about this."

"Let's go," I said.

We walked away from her. She made everything worse for us. We kept walking and didn't stop at the nurses' table. We left the floor to go to the basement, to the morgue; it would be quiet there.

"Don't worry about it," Carl said. "He's from another time, a left-over relic. Science is the true source of modern medicine, and it has left him far behind."

Tex added, "That's right, we all know it, he knows it. Did you see the extent of his examination? And he didn't offer any opinion about a diagnosis."

"But why was the patient so taken with him?" I asked.

"He's old and has the old style," Tex answered. "He talks about touching and healing with magic potions. I thought he was going to pull out a bottle of DL William's Pink Pills for Pale People. He was waiting for the infamous black vomit, I'm sure of it. He swears every fever is yellow fever. There hasn't been a case of yellow fever here in twenty years."

"I could use some pink pills right now for my cephalalgia," I said.

"Doug, just say headache," Tex said.

"I thought he was going to recommend a good bleeding for her," Carl laughed and we joined him.

"Let's find some coffee somewhere, maybe at the student nurses' home. Caffeine helps a headache," I said.

"My favorite place," Carl retorted.

We walked down the front steps of the hospital and across the street to the student nursing home. It was an older wood frame house with a small porch. We climbed the small set of stairs and slowly opened the door. We walked inside, past the stairs and peeked into the parlor. The housemother wasn't there. The nurses' quarters were upstairs, at the top of the stairwell. We weren't supposed to be here or go up there. We walked to the back of the house to the kitchen, swung open the door and smelled the coffee. The coffee pot was full and hot. We each poured the thick black coffee into small white porcelain cups without the saucers and drank with our eyes on the swinging kitchen door. After one cup, we didn't run into anyone like we had hoped, no student nurses returning from the hospital after their morning rounds. Not even the housemother was around. We would be reported if she saw us. So, we just left and returned to the hospital after another cup.

We all had our regular duties for the afternoon—checking on all the patients, documenting their progress next to their vital signs in their chart, talking with family members gathered at the bedside, handling any discharges for the afternoon, examining new admissions. The most difficult duty was telling a family member that their loved one had died. This duty was left to us by the faculty most of the time.

The families always wanted to know why they died, but that wasn't always so easy to say. Many times we didn't know, and we shared our opinions with them, but it was usually not easy to convince them. We would then escort them downstairs to the morgue to see the body. We tried to clean up the bodies a little beforehand, wipe away any blood or body fluids. They would spend some time with their dead loved one and then leave but return to collect the body. Most of the time, families would shake my hand and say, "Thank you, doctor."

But the absolutely most difficult thing that I had to do that I never got used to was to tell a family member after the death of their child. That was heart wrenching for everyone, even us. I will never forget one young girl who was brought to the hospital one night, my second night on call as a doctor. She was unconscious and with a high fever. She came by the ambulance with her mother. As the orderlies carried her up the stairs to the ward on a stretcher, with one look I could tell she was near death. Her mother left the ward and returned home. She was only seven years old.

By her exam, her neck was rigid and she not moving any of her extremities. Her pulse was barely palpable. I phoned Dr. Randall at his home late that night after she began to vomit. I suspected that she had meningitis as she began to develop a spotty rash over her arms and upper body. Dr. Randall told me that he agreed with me, but it was unlikely that she would improve. I was at a loss as how to help her. Several of the nursing students stayed by her side during the night, bringing down her temperature with cool water rinses. I was able to control her vomiting by getting her to swallow some antimony sulphide. Her rapid pulse was controlled with a dose of Digitalis. But she didn't drink any liquids.

By sunrise she had died. I went to the bedside after I was notified by Nurse Willow. The two student nurses were there hugging each other and crying, and I wanted to cry with them. I was already thinking about what I could have done differently. The student nurses stopped hugging each when Nurse Willow returned to the bedside. She bent over the metal footboard resting on her elbows, speechless. She was wiping away tears with a lace white handkerchief. I passed them and carefully examined the young girl. She had no carotid pulse, and she wasn't breathing, and her body was cool, so I pronounced her dead. We were all dying on the inside, but this was our duty. We saw firsthand the very worst of life and the reality of death, and we weren't spared any of it. We were deeply wounded by her death, even though we didn't know her, and she had never spoken a word to us. She was a healthy kid less than twenty-four hours ago.

Her mother and father would return that morning. What would I say to them? We left the body in her bed and surrounded it with portable curtains on metal folding stands. When they came, they were escorted by Nurse Willow to the bedside around the curtains. Her mother let out a scream as she slid the curtain away and saw her daughter. I went to the bedside. The father was holding up her sobbing mother. I spoke to him about her lethal diagnosis, spinal meningitis. I knew they had never heard of it by their eyes. And I said there was nothing we could have done to save her.

After they had taken it all in, after my endless talking, it was quiet on the ward. Their confused, tortured faces relaxed a little and they thanked me for doing the best that I could. The tears only then rolled down my cheeks. I will never forget her and all the details of her short stay with us, or her tiny body lying still in the large bed. I never saw her eyes open. I had only opened them when I examined her and pronounced her dead.

Our afternoon was fortunately uneventful; no looming disasters, no special requests. By six in the evening, I had told Carl about all the patients under my care before I left. He was on call tonight. I found Tex about the same time, and we left together. It was a Friday.

"Hey Doug, I am starving. Let's find some food," Tex said.

"Definitely, I can barely think I am so hungry," I agreed.

We walked a few blocks east toward downtown on the Strand and a few blocks south to a corner store run by an Italian family that Tex knew. We walked in as they were about to close and stood in line for a homemade sandwich. The whole place smelled of fresh baked bread and raw fish. The father was barking out orders to the rest of the family in Italian. We left with our sandwiches wrapped in white paper and ate them as we walked back to Strand and caught the horse trolley that took us downtown. At 25th and Strand we took the electric trolley across town heading south across Broadway. After a few more blocks we got off and then caught another mule trolley going west ten blocks or so. Tex had the idea of buying a bag of oysters at O'Neill Oyster Farm. It was just west of the city where the houses were small and scattered. We wandered around a little after getting off the trolley. Then we saw the sign for the farm several blocks away. We went into the small tan wooden building with a large green sign above the porch that said O'Neill Oyster Farm and bought a large burlap bag of freshly caught oysters. I could see the oyster boat docked behind the building in a small swampy inlet from the bay. On the property were large piles of opened oyster shells all around the building.

"How did you know about this place?" I asked Tex.

"I took care of old man O'Neill, and he said I could come by any time for a bag of free oysters."

He spoke with him as the old man stood behind the counter, then shook hands with him and then we met the whole family as they wandered in. Afterward he lifted the heavy bag over his shoulder, and we left. Tex was tall and lanky, but I knew he was strong by his crushing handshake. He would laugh as he shook everybody's hand and watched them recoil with pain, the men, at least. He had a big laugh and a big West Texas accent but he was shy around women, unlike Carl. He had light wavy blond hair that needed to be cut. All of the faculty complained about the interns needing regular haircuts, which we didn't often get. We didn't have the time or the money. As medical students we cut our own hair regularly.

We found our way back to 25th Street and the electric trolley. We got off at Broadway and took another electric trolley all the way down, eastward toward the beach and toward his apartment at the Lucas Terrace Apartments. It was a large three-story red brick building at the east end of Broadway as it ran into the beach. We received some puzzled and offended looks on the trolley as fellow passengers could smell the oysters.

It was dusk now as we left the trolley and walked to Tex's apartment building. I had been there before when we were students. He had enough money from his family to afford to live there. He had a great view of the Gulf over the several blocks of small homes from the window of his third-floor apartment.

"Take the bag down to the beach, I'll meet you there," Tex said as he handed me the bag of oysters. He leaped up the front steps of the stone columned entry. I walked around the side of the building and down several blocks of small homes to the beach. There were dunes at the end of the street, and I found a trail between them. I dumped the bag of oysters in the sand. It was a nice breezy evening and starting to cool down. I walked around the edge of the dunes and gathered some driftwood to make a fire. I took it back to where I left the oysters. Tex came through the same trail holding a bottle of wine.

"Tex, you eat oysters and drink wine? How is that for a West Texas boy?" I asked.

He laughed and said, "I know, I can't believe it, either. I got hooked on these things last year when I was invited to an oyster roast in the park downtown. There was a band playing and we drank wine."

"I thought you were strictly a beef man, maybe pork, but oysters? I only had them once and raw and couldn't stomach it."

"No, you got to roast them. Let's get a fire going and I'll show you how to shuck these."

"And where did you get the wine?"

"I bought it downtown from a wine merchant. It's a German white wine, goes good with the oysters, and with crabs. Dean Payne had me over to his house for dinner last year before we graduated, and he taught me about wine."

After he opened the bottle he added, "Us West Texas boys know how to live."

I piled the wood away from the dune on the firmer sand near the water. Tex had some matches, and we easily got the fire going. The dry driftwood burned quickly and was easy to light. He went behind the dunes and pulled out a wood plank and two small sawhorses. He brought them next to the fire and set them up.

"I keep my oyster shucking setup hidden in the dune," he said, grinning.

"I see. Now show me how it's done."

He pulled the pocketknife out of his pocket and reached into the bag and chipped away an oyster from the others. He pried open the oyster easily and threw down the top shell. He loosened the oyster in the bottom shell. He poured just a dash of wine in the oyster and placed it on the hot coals. It was dark now, but I could see what he was doing from the light of the fire. I tried to pry one open with my pocketknife and it took me several tries. He poured a little wine on mine, too.

It was dark and there was only a sliver of a moon above the water. We stuck our knife in the boiling oysters and took them out of the shell and then ate them. Now these were good! We kneeled in the sand by the fire, and we finished the bottle and opened another. We took turns drinking from it. The fine people of Galveston would never drink wine out of the bottle.

After eating at least a dozen or so oysters each, we sat back and relaxed a bit. Some girls were walking by with their parents, following the water's edge. One of them waved and said hello to Tex. He invited them over for some oysters and they slowed down to look at us. But their parents kept stride and nodded back to them to keep up.

"Do you know them?" I asked.

"They're a family that lives in the apartments. The girls are friendly, probably in their late teens, but the father won't say a word to me. He thinks I shouldn't be allowed to live there with the other families. But I don't care. I won't be here much longer after our year is up."

"Are you going to move back home?"

"I think so. My family expects me to. Even the mayor told me that I should come back, that they need a doctor in town. Every little town probably needs a doctor, right?"

"What is the name of your hometown??"

"Sweetwater, outside of Abilene; it's in the middle of nowhere. My family farms and ranches there. They didn't want me to leave, even for school. But our family has been friends with the longtime mayor who convinced me and my mother to become a doctor. He told my father about the hospital training I could get here. How it would help the community to have a real trained doctor. My father wasn't happy with my decision to be a doctor. He doesn't trust them. The mayor knew that my father wouldn't agree to it, so he first convinced my mother. I remember my father not seeing me off at the train station in Abilene with the rest of my family. He's not one to write a letter, either. But when I first came here, I fell in love with Galveston, all the people, all the pretty girls, the beach, the finer things in life. But now, I guess, I'm tired of it and I think I'm ready to head back home. People haven't really accepted me here."

"I feel the same way. People here look down on me, too. But I have a girl here now. She was born here, and her family is here. So. maybe I will stay after all."

"I have a girl waiting for me back home. We write letters a lot. But I haven't been home in so long." He pulled out her picture from his back pocket. I could see it well by the firelight.

He added, "I hope she hasn't forgotten about me."

"She's really pretty," I said as he pulled back the picture to look at it again.

I added, "I have a girl back home too, but I don't know how she feels about me now, after four years."

"Or how you feel about her?" Tex said.

"Well, I guess, I don't know now. I haven't seen her in so long, too. But my girl here is not like the other girls in Galveston, she's not from a rich family."

I didn't carry a picture of my girl back home, Anna, like I used to when I first moved here. She had sent me several more, but I didn't carry them. either.

"What's her name, your girl here?"

"Rosa. She has dark brown hair and dark eyes and..."

"Is she one of those Italian girls that live here? I think they are beautiful, with their olive skin. I know the daughter of the owner of the corner store where we got the sandwiches. She smiles at me a little when I walk in, but I have never had the nerve to talk to her."

"No, Rosa is not Italian."

"Well, Doug, I guess you and I will have some decisions to make pretty soon."

"If we can make it through the year, through the internship."

I could always talk with Tex. We have known each other since we started as students, Carl too. As interns, we were unsure about what the faculty thought about us. So far, we agreed that we have been treated differently than when we were students, worse. We didn't expect that, but we have each other. Over these past few months, we had slowly gained confidence in our ability as doctors, and now we often spoke up to disagree with the faculty. As a student we never dared to do that.

PART 2

"Heaven defend me from a busy doctor."

— Welsh proverb

CHAPTER 6

I was sound asleep when I felt one of my shirts hit my face. I pulled it down to my chest and saw Grandma Sam staring down at me. I was wearing little but just enough. She was standing over me, mad and sweaty and tight-lipped, with her hair in a red scarf. She had her arthritic hands on her hips. She wore a hard-pressed, white dress.

"This place is a mess. The rats are gonna takeover here then come over to my house and I'm gonna kill you if that happens. We have enough rats around here and you be the king of them all," she said as she began picking up clothes from all four corners of the room.

"Get up. I got no time for you. It's Saturday and if you want breakfast you better get it now or I'll give it to the dogs," she added as she opened and then slammed the screen door closed. She walked down the steps as she always does, with heavy feet. She was always mad about something.

I grabbed some clothes off the floor and got dressed. I couldn't find my shoes. I went down the steps, out the little wooden gate and tiptoed a few feet over to her house. I walked in without knocking and sat down at the small square wooden table. I smelled the bacon right away. She brought me a plate of two fried eggs, bacon, and a biscuit.

"Don't you have any coffee?"

"Yes, I do, and you are gonna want sugar in that coffee, aren't ya?

But I ain't got any because you don't never bring me no sugar from that hospital like you used to. Of course, I am gonna use most of it up. But you still expect some here for you when you eat the food I paid for. Boy, bring me my sugar." She held that large cooking spoon up like she was going to hit me with it, her other hand back on her hip.

"I will, I promise," I said looking down at the food.

She was calming down now. "You look bad, you know, dirty, your hair is too long. When did you last take a bath? I do for everybody around here and you don't bring me no sugar!"

"It doesn't matter, but I gotta look good tonight, I have a date."

"With who, with some no good...."

"No, no, with a real nice girl, I know you'd like her. Do you have any butter?" She just looked angrily at me. I smiled back and she turned away. I knew she didn't have any butter, or milk. She might have some, at times, if she was given some from some of the ladies that she did laundry for.

She put a letter on the table, next to my plate and said, "Read this to me."

It was a letter from her son in New Orleans. I opened the envelope and in it was a letter, with a picture, and a five-dollar bill. The picture was of her son and his wife holding their daughter standing in front of a small house.

"How many grandbabies do you have, Grandma Sam?"

"Here, give it to me," she said as she took the picture and the money out of my hand. I opened the letter. The paper was soft and the ink a little smeared probably from the humidity. I started reading aloud.

Dear Mama,

How are you? We are doing fine. Here is a picture of me and Millie and your new grandbaby, Phoebe. She has your ears and your mouth, Ma. I am so proud. We are standing outside our new house. I hope you have everything you need. Please come live with us here in New Orleans. The docks are always full of ships and that means work, plenty of it. I will write you again very soon. I hope that white boy is still next door so he can read this letter to you. I love you, Mama.

Your son,

Willie

Grandma Sam put the picture on the small windowsill next to several other yellowed pictures of her family and put the letter and the money in her dress pocket. She stood and looked at the picture for a short while and said, "Another grandbaby, the first for Willie and Millie. I think I have five now. He's my baby and I'm proud of him. But I ain't gonna move over there and live with him and his wife. I don't like this Millie. She is a New Orleans girl and I hope I never have to meet her."

"Grandma Sam, do you want to write him back? I can do that for you."

She shook her head "no."

"You better go now, I got more work than you know, especially since you gonna want clean clothes for tonight when you go out with your new girl."

I stood and touched her forearm and said, "But you're my girl, Grandma Sam."

She let me hold her arm a little longer this time. She pulled away and went out the back door to her washing pot. I left her place through the front door and went up the stairs to my room. I had to get dressed quickly for work.

I walked into the hospital up to the third floor and then straight to the east ward. Things looked the same; hopefully no patient of mine died last night. Carl was coming off call and gave me the details on all the patients during the night and a few he admitted. One was a child from the orphanage with high fever and vomiting and diarrhea. There was an old lady with right-sided paralysis and aphasia due to a cerebral attack, most likely. And an old man with a heart attack. Carl already had ordered several hypodermics of morphine for him. The others were stable, so I went to check on the boy first.

I walked down the aisle between the rows of beds, foot boards facing footboards, and found the young boy in the last bed lying on his side with his legs pulled up close under his chest. He wore a clean starched gown tied in the back that was too big for him. He was facing away from the other patients, looking out the window into the bay. I picked up the metal file hanging at the end of the bed. Our eyes met, and I smiled but he looked away quickly. His name was Archibald McDowell. He was ten years old and his temp has been 102 since last night. I walked over to his side of the bed and sat next to him.

"Archie, I'm Dr. Schuler, I'm going to be your doctor."

I was still smiling but he was scared and obviously didn't feel well. He didn't look at me right away. He had been crying.

"Where is that other doctor, from last night?"

"He went home to sleep. I'm the chief now. How long have you been feeling bad?"

"Since yesterday. I started throwing up and couldn't stop. I feel like I gonna throw up right now."

"Hold on, hold on ... talk to me first."

"I can't help it."

I stood up quickly and waved at the nurse down on the other end of the ward to come down. She came quickly and I gave her the emesis basin. She sat next to the boy while he vomited into the basin. He continued to gag and heave for several more minutes, then lay back down on his side in a ball after it passed. She took the basin away. I continued looking through his chart while he vomited. The nurse showed me that the emesis was small in amount and only blood tinged. I sat back down next to him. He was still lying on his side and crying, but with no tears.

"Archie, roll on your back for me."'

He did and I stood up and went over to right side of the bed. He was pale and his eyes were sunken. His skin was hot and dry. I pulled down his lower eyelid and his conjunctiva was dry and pale, and when he opened his mouth his mucus membranes were dry and sticky. There were no palpable lymph nodes. With my stethoscope I heard that his lungs were clear, and his heart was beating fast and regularly with no murmurs. When I put my stethoscope on his abdomen, it was quiet and very tender throughout. He was guarding his abdomen to keep me from palpating it, but I did anyway. I had to push down hard and when I let go quickly, he winced in pain. He was very dehydrated.

"Have any of the other kids at the orphanage been vomiting, too?"

"Yea, I think so."

I held his hand and said, "You're gonna be okay, we're gonna get you better."

"What's wrong with me?"

"Well, I don't know yet, but I want you to do this one thing for me first. I'm gonna bring you this water to drink and every few minutes I want you to take a few sips of it. You might still vomit again but don't be afraid, just keep sipping that water. It won't taste real good but act like it's root beer, Okay?"

"Okay, I will."

"You promise?"

"I will, l promise."

Archie was scared. There was nobody to take care of him here, to sit by his side, to hold him, to kiss his forehead. The nuns at the orphanage had too many kids to care for as it was. They were known for their discipline, not for their affection. What he really needed was a mother to take care of him.

The sick kids always made us nervous. Older people had their whole lives behind them. They were going to die anyway. But for the kids, the hospital is the last place they wanted to be, even the lonely kids from the orphanage. Children thought that the hospital was the place where you go to die. I bet the other kids thought Archie was as good as dead when he left for the hospital. I was running my fingers through his light brown hair as we spoke. I stood up next to the bed and before I could speak, he had rolled back over toward the window, back into a ball.

I couldn't give him anything for pain now until the diagnosis had declared itself. It would be soon. I went from bed to bed now on my rounds, reviewing each bedside file, then briefly talking and examining each patient. All the rest were old people, some on their last legs, especially a local fisherman, Mr. Vincenzo Negrini. He literally would be on his last leg after we amputated the other one later today. Carl had told me that the gangrene was wet and progressing toward the knee and no matter how well or how often the nurses wrapped and unwrapped that leg, it continued to smell. The nurses were sending their students to do this awful job rather than themselves. I knew that smell and it was one that was hard to take. The terrible odor permeated the whole ward, even the whole floor. The nurse in charge pressed me again about the urgency for the amputation. I promised that we would not wait until Monday to do the amputation. The other patients were starting to complain.

But as I made my rounds, I would look back at Archie to see if he drank any of the solution. We put table salt with sugar in potable water in a large glass with a paper straw on a small table next to him. Even the potable water here in Galveston was a little salty, but you got used to it. He only reached for the water once that I saw, but he hadn't vomited anymore. He seemed like a tough boy; he was an orphan, so he had to be.

There were many patients under my care this morning, but my mind was on tonight, my date with Rosa. What would I say to her? What does she think of me? I had seen her for several years, but never had time for her, even just to be friendly. My habit was to go to her house, eat, then leave, all in about ten minutes. Her little sister would bring the food to me. She was eight years old and was always glad to see me. I would hear Rosa arguing with her parents in the kitchen, but she would never come out. Sometimes our eyes would meet in passing but never for very long. Back then, I had other things and other women on my mind. But now, it was different.

I met with Dr. Randall later in the morning and reviewed with him the patients under my care. We sat in his office nearly every morning like this, even on Saturdays. I was on my own on Sundays. Dr. Randall seemed particularly interested in the boy and had more questions than I had answers. I never made up answers for Dr. Randall, he could see through my reasoning.

"Were any of the other children at the orphanage vomiting?" Dr. Randall asked, sitting back now in his desk chair.

"Yes, I believe so."

"Has there been an epidemic of fever at the orphanage?"

"Carl said that the ambulance driver reported that Archibald was the sickest one, he didn't mention any others with fever."

"Several orphans die every year because of various contagions, it is a perfect breeding ground. You had better ask Carl again about any sick kids there. What's your plan for the boy?"

"1 have him on clear liquids for now, but he's not taking much so far. I'm going back soon to examine him again."

"Keep a close eye on him, but hopefully with some hydration, he'll be fine. Watch his input and output closely. And by the way, somebody on the wards needs an amputation. I've smelled it all morning. Don't wait until Monday to do it."

I had forgotten to tell him about Mr. Negrini. I knew I would have a full day even today. I had to see Dr. West today about the amputation in the operating theater on the fourth floor. I had told the patient that it had to be done today. He didn't look at me but just cussed me in Italian. I went to the Medical Building next door to find Dr. West. His office was locked, so I phoned him at home about the amputation. He said that he was unaware of this patient, and that the decision to amputate was up to him and not to be decided by a house intern. He would come in to see the patient this afternoon.

Dr. Hamilton A. West had been a longtime resident of Galveston and for many years the house surgeon at the old Galveston City Hospital. He was well known in town and hopefully not caught up in too many local social functions to perform the amputation this afternoon.

He came in at 1 p.m. and we went to the ward to see the patient. The fisherman lay there with his left leg wrapped and elevated. I could tell by the look on Dr. West's face that the smell from the leg was overwhelming. He unwrapped the leg and didn't look away. From the knee down, it was dark purple, ulcerating, and draining. I glanced over at Archie, who was lying very still on his side with his knees up close. He hadn't taken in much of the solution. I examined again him before I met with Dr. West and he was in more pain, especially in the right lower quadrant of the abdomen now. Dr. West told Mr. Negrini about the need for immediate amputation, or he would die. The patient grumbled something that we took for a "yes."

I transported Mr. Negrini with the orderly to the operating theater on the fourth floor. There was an elevator that connected the wards on the third floor to the operating theater above. The patient was talking loudly now, delirious. I held him down by his arms as the orderly operated the elevator. His breathing was still regular and his color good. One of the nursing students who was Italian said that he stepped on a stingray barb on the deck of his boat several days ago. Would he be able to fish again in his boat, working his nets as he did before? A tough man like Mr. Negrini wouldn't let this minor setback stop him. Maybe there was a carpenter in the family who could make him a new leg. We'll never see him again after he heals.

The fisherman's leg was truly gone. He didn't flinch when I pinched his calf hard with a hemostat, but we gave him the ether anyway. I administered the anesthetic for a few minutes and then stood across Dr. West. He was short in height but strong in frame, about fifty, with well-groomed salt and pepper hair, and a thick mustache and sideburns. He wore a white high-collar shirt with a black tie that was tied perfectly, but his sleeves were rolled up. He had dark eyes that never focused on me, even when he spoke. Most of the faculty had the custom of not looking directly at us when they spoke.

The nurse had given us thick white cotton smocks to wear to cover our clothes. Dr West rolled his eyes when the nurse insisted that we wear them. He told me that he never felt comfortable wearing these while operating but it kept the carbolic disinfectant spray off our clothes. Our nurses were staunch advocates of asepsis but would always seem to over spray the carbolic solution to clean the surgical field. Just the smell of it burned my nose. Dr. Thompson had taken to wearing a cloth facial mask to keep from smelling it. He became irritated when we didn't understand him as he yelled out orders to us.

Dr. West began to saw the leg off just below the knee. The leg was large and heavy, and I was tiring under its weight. I got one of the nurses to find a medical student to help me hold it. The student was eager because he had never seen an amputation before. It was late August, and of course, very hot and sticky. As he sawed, my mind began to wonder. The whole scene captivated the student and Dr.

West began to quiz him about the basic anatomy of the leg. Sweat was dripping down my face, just like it would in the summer sun at home as my brother and I would herd cattle with the ranch hands. All day on my horse riding in the August sun. It was a slow pace, a solitude that soothed me. My brother and I would break away from the hands and head for the river, the San Marcos River. It took forever to get our boots off and then we would dive into the cool, clear water. The breeze was cool on our wet heads. Back with the herd, I would rope the new calf, and the vaqueros would place the cherry red-hot brand on its hip. The smell of burning flesh with the wind was a scent burned into my memory.

But medicine was my life now and the smell of a gangrenous leg in the stagnant air of the amphitheater was overwhelming my dreaming and imprinting itself in my mind instead. How to keep these smells out of my brain? This leg wasn't the first and it wouldn't be the last either, but I wanted to focus on Rosa and how nice it was going to be to finally speak to her alone. To really show her the type of person I was.

All three of us were now sweating heavily and breathing hard. Dr. West kept snapping at us to hold the leg still as he sawed through the tibia. Removing that leg was like removing a tree limb. All the smells at the hospital were worse, much worse than anything the ranch would produce. Since being a student, I had seen many shocking things: blood, dying flesh, pus, broken limbs. The sight of these things no longer bothered me, but it was their smell that I couldn't forget.

The stump wasn't bleeding much, which concerned Dr. West. But the more he trimmed the stump closer to the knee the more it bled. We covered the wound now with the posterior skin flap and he told me to suture the wound. Our hands were covered with a thick coating of dried blood. Dr. West had removed his smock and was washing his hands in a basin while giving me orders. He dried his hands.

"Dr. West, there is a young boy under my care, an orphan boy, who I believe has acute appendicitis and will probably need to be operated on as soon as possible."

"I told you, Dr. Schuler, I'll decide when the operation in necessary. I'm very busy today and I wasn't planning more than this one case this afternoon.

"I'm very worried about him. He has nobody here with him and he's not taking in fluids, not much at all. I'm not sure where to go next with him. I hate to give him any morphine for now. I can hardly palpate his abdomen. He's guarding terribly".

"All right, I'll take a look at him."

I began suturing the large wound with the thick catgut sutures, but it was taking longer than I thought. I didn't want Dr. West to leave. I told the medical student to finish the job. The patient was breathing slow and regular. His pulse was strong and his skin cool and dry. His pupils were equal. Throughout the entire procedure he never said a word. The ether would wear off soon, so I told the medical student to hurry, and not to worry about how neat the wound would end up. The amputated leg was wrapped in a white sheet and carried off by an orderly to be incinerated. My job now was to keep the patient alive. The amputation went well. The student finished the sutures, and we carried the patient back to his bed. He was still asleep. I hurried over to Archie's bed and Dr. West was standing over him. He had examined him and then told him that he would need immediate surgery to remove his appendix. Archie was very upset now and crying.

Dr. West slowly added, "Now son, this will go well, and you will feel better afterward. Not to worry."

Archie looked at me and said, "What should I do, am I going to die? The pain won't go away. I'm so sorry but I couldn't drink that water."

I walked over to the other side and held his hand. Poor boy, he had nobody now but me?

"I'll be in the surgery theater. Get him ready for surgery, Douglas. And bring him up right away," Dr. West said.

Archie stared at me and held my hand tight. "I'm afraid."

"Trust me Archie, okay? But you have to have surgery. There's a piece of your stomach on the inside, that has to come out. We have to do it now. Then you'll be good as new. "

"Okay, but do you promise?

"Yes, Archie, I promise."

"Doctor, take care of me good, please."

I sat down next to him and gave him a hug. He buried his rolled-up body into my chest. I had to get him ready. I stood up and walked over to the stretcher that was by the fisherman's bed and brought it next to Archie's. I waved to the medical student to come over and help me. We gently placed him on the stretcher, which was excruciating. We rolled him slowly down from the ward. Archie was terrified but quiet. He yelled out when we bumped the stretcher against the last bed on the ward. We headed toward the elevator.

Dr. West was waiting for us in the theater, with his smock, the same one he wore for the first operation and his hands on his hips. We gently placed Archie on the table. He was wide-eyed after one look at that bloody smock, but he didn't say anything. He kept his eyes on me. I smiled back at him. I sat near the head of the table and told him about the ether. I covered his face with the gauze and placed a few drops of ether on it. He had terror in his eyes, but he was a brave kid. He calmed down when I told him to take slow, deep breaths. I waved at the nurse and grabbed my smock and pointed to Dr. West's to bring us clean ones. Dr. West reached out and pinched the skin of his abdomen with a hemostat and he didn't move. He was breathing regularly, and his skin was hot and dry. Dr. West opened the right lower quadrant of the abdomen with a short diagonal incision. He slowly went through each layer of the abdominal musculature, until he reached the abdominal cavity. I stood up and went to the other side of the table. I held the spreaders for a better look.

"Take a look at this, Douglas."

He showed me a purplish fingerlike projection from the colon. It was inflamed but intact.

"It hasn't ruptured yet?"

"No, I don't believe so. The peritoneum seems clean. I'm going to remove it and make this young man live to be an old man like me." I had never seen Dr. West smile.

He sewed the opening to the appendix closed at the colon and then slowly sliced it away. Dr. West was very dexterous. His hands had some signs of arthritis, but he was very skillful with the scalpel. I always enjoyed watching quick hands in the operating room, especially Dr. Thompson's. He was legendary here at the hospital. It was worth the verbal mistreatment you received to operate with him. On those occasions, I would look up and see the theater full of eager students. It was a Saturday and the theater was empty. I was glad, for Archie's sake.

The surgery went well. Archie had been still throughout. After Dr. West resected the appendix, I made sure that the abdomen and skin were neatly and cleanly sutured. This scar would be a constant reminder of the hospital, but maybe of me, too. The student and I rolled Archie back to his room. I sat with him for a while. It was late afternoon and Archie was still asleep. I combed his hair with my fingers and felt the skin on his chest with my palm. He was still warm, just a low-grade fever. Archie was going to get better. A patient's pain wasn't as real as it was to me now. It wasn't simply because I was the one in charge, or the one to blame. I had to get used to that now as a doctor. As a student, I was more aloof, less committed. I knew the day would come for me to assume the responsibility that I had been trained to accept. But that was what terrified me most about being a physician, especially when caring for a poor helpless young guy like Archie.

I checked on Archie several times before I left. He was awake and in less pain. He even smiled for me once as I shook his hand. I had gotten a student nurse on the floor to take special care of him for the night. They warmed to each other right away. He promised her he would drink our hydrating solution and she promised no more bad tasting medicine. And it was okay to hold him if she wanted to. I relaxed a little and concentrated on being with Rosa tonight.

CHAPTER 7

I left the hospital by late afternoon and walked home as quickly as I could. I drew some water from the cistern and bathed and put on a clean, pressed suit. As I looked in the mirror, I needed a haircut. After shining my shoes, I left my place and walked down to the Strand and found a barbershop. I got a shave, too.

Her father received me at the front door, but not with a smile. He waved me inside and pulled out a chair from the table for me to sit as he walked from the front room. Rosa came to join me in the front room, and I saw her as I had never seen her before. Her long dark hair was pulled back and tied loosely with a red ribbon. She wore a long white ruffled dress with a high soft collar. She was beautiful and she smelled so good. I was sweating now. She pulled up a small chair next to me and smiled.

I tried not to say it, but I couldn't stop myself. "You are beautiful."

She smiled, didn't say anything back but looked around the room at her father now sitting in a chair against the wall reading the newspaper, *The Galveston Daily News*. Her father asked without raising his eyes from the paper, "What are your plans for the evening, Douglas?"

"Well, I thought we would go downtown to get a bite to eat and then head down to the water and stroll along the beach."

Mr. Lozano yelled to his wife in the kitchen, *"El gringo quiere que vayamos todos a comer y despues caminar por la playa. Estas lista?"*

I looked quickly at Rosa, and she looked back with a half-smile.

I knew what he had said. The whole family was going with us. I had been out lots of times with groups of students to all sorts of cafes and taverns at all hours of the night, but not with their families. They all filed into the room, her younger sister Isabel carrying her baby brother, Carlitos. Her mother took off her apron and walked into the room from the kitchen. I introduced myself, in Spanish. She smiled back. She didn't speak English.

Rosa, looking a little worried, said, "I think we are all ready, Doug."

We left the house and walked westward toward downtown. I waved down a carriage at 15th and Market.

"Well, I knew today would be a special one, now that I run across my doc on the street," It was Cyrus Malloy, the driver of the carriage.

The family was already climbing into the carriage when I realized who it was.

"Hello, Mr. Malloy, feeling better these days?" I said trying not to look at him. I hoped they couldn't smell the gin on his breath. It was a breezy night and this was an open carriage.

"I am, and I took your advice. As soon as you saw fit to release me, I told the misses to open that special bottle of gin, the one that we had been saving for our thirtieth and to take my medicine straight away. It took no time and I was a new man. See how steady," he said, holding his hand out over us.

"Que dice," Rosa's mother asked her husband what he said.

"That the doctor feels that his liquor is a good medicine for him," her father said. Mrs. Lozano stared back at me. Mr. Lozano understood English well.

The evening hadn't started well but was getting worse. Her father probably thinks I'm a gin doctor. I was no longer optimistic about spending any time with Rosa alone. And Mr. Malloy talked nonstop until we reached 22nd Street. Here at the corner of Postoffice street was a drinking fountain for the horses. We stayed for a while as the horse couldn't get enough water. We all looked over at the Opera House here on Postoffice Street with its elegant carved stone entrance in the shape of a half-moon. And the dark red brick facade with its posters of upcoming acts pasted in a row of window cases. People were loudly milling around outside and then slowly walking in. Well-dressed men in their expensive suits and top hats. Women in their long European dresses and big feathery hats. I looked back across the carriage at Rosa, and she seemed annoyed, as did her father. I hoped not with me? As I was struggling to find the words to make a conversation, the horse had had enough water, and the carriage lunged forward and we headed down Postoffice Street. Once we stopped at 24th Street, I helped everyone out as quickly as I could and tried to pay Mr. Malloy but he refused, saying that he might need a doctor like me in the future. We left him while he was still talking to me.

Mr. Lozano suggested a small corner café on 24th and Church Street. We walked a block to reach it. We went inside and were ushered to a corner table next to the other Mexican families. Mr. Lozano ordered for his family, including Rosa, speaking English, while I ordered the same as Rosa. Mr. Lozano spoke directly to me almost the entire time. He was in a much better mood now. He asked a lot of questions about where I was from and my plans for the future. I told him I wasn't sure where I was going to end up, though, I had thought about going back home and practicing there.

After eating we walked another block to 25th Street, where we caught the electric trolley heading south across Broadway and down to the beach. I sat by myself directly behind Rosa. We were all looking out the window at the tightly rowed houses, mostly two-storied, with broad porches and tall shutters, all painted in different colors. Twenty-fifth Street was a broad street with a central parkway lined with oleander bushes as tall as the trolley, blooming in bright pink, white, and red flowers. Many people were out walking or were sitting on their porches. It was now dusk and quite crowded on the trolley. After reaching the beach we stepped out of the trolley and walked the short distance to the beach. The surf was calm and the breeze pleasant. The moon was rising over the water. It was a hazy yellow moon, reflecting softly over the water, and as we strolled together, we seemed to walk just before it. Rosa and I together took a deep breath and smiled at each other as we took it all in. I walked closer to her now.

"Did you order such a beautiful moon for tonight?" she asked.

"Of course, I did." That was all I could think to say.

I wanted her to get to know me now. But not as my friends knew me from school, but as a man, stable, dependable, and reliable.

"We don't come here often, but it's something special for me every time I do. I'm glad you decided to bring me—I mean, us." she said as she walked close to me. We were beginning to drift away from her family now. She stopped and leaned on me with one hand on my arm and with the other she unlaced her shoes. She headed for the water's edge with her shoes in one hand. Several pelicans appeared gliding in formation breaking the moonlight off the water and then disappearing again, one by one.

As I came close to her, she smiled and gently said, "Can you feel the water through your shoes?"

Yes, I was standing in ankle deep water. I quickly pulled off my socks and shoes and rolled up my pants and ran to catch up to her.

"I'm sorry about the carriage ride with that patient of mine. I hope you and your family don't think badly of me. He drinks a lot of alcohol, but not me."

She laughed, "1 know you don't. My mother is naturally nervous about you, but after we left the carriage, she calmed down. I think my father likes you. I know my sister does. Do you like what you do, Doug?"

"Yes, so far I do. I'm trying to learn as much as I can before I go back home."

"So, you're going back to Seguin soon?" she asked after pausing a few seconds. Why did I say that? She won't bother with me any further if I have plans to leave. I have grown to like it here in Galveston but have always seen it as a temporary place. Rosa doesn't seem so temporary, though.

"Well, I'm not sure what I'll do after next summer when my internship is over. '

"Would you stay here?"

"Yes, I would, I mean, I could."

"I've lived here all my life, and it's home to me. All my family is here. My father and mother came here from Mexico after they were married. My grandparents followed them later. I could never leave. I know what it means to be near your family."

"How old are you, Rosa?" I was staring at her smooth ankles in the foamy surf as they swayed from beneath her skirt.

"Twenty-three."

"I should tell you my age too, twenty-six." My heart was beating faster.

"I wasn't going to ask you. It doesn't matter to me a man's age just as long as he is good to me, and that he loves me."

No one had spoken so seriously so soon to me. I didn't know what to think or say now. I just kept walking slowly in the shallow surf. What would I say now?

"Do you write to your family often?" she asked, walking closer with me again.

"Well, I'm always so busy at the hospital. I mean to write but, no, not very often."

"I'm sure your mother writes you regularly. Then she waits and waits for your letter," she said with a smile, holding my forearm. "Or do you write your girl back home instead?"

She had a way of keeping me speechless. But I had to answer her.

"There is a friend I have back home, one that I've known for a long time, I mean we sort of grew up together. Anyway, she has written me a few times and I did answer a few times but just short letters, to let her know about school, work."

"She is probably dying to hear from you too, just like you mother, huh?

"No, not really. I don't have a girlfriend; I mean, I'm not promised to anyone. Are you, Rosa?"

"No, I'm not. I wouldn't keep anyone guessing as to my feelings. It's not fair, even if you're not sure, I couldn't mislead anyone. It's best to be completely honest in matters such as these, don't you think, Doug?"

"Of course, I do. I agree completely."

"Good."

I had to change the subject. "What I love about Galveston is living so close to the ocean. I used to dream of what the ocean would be like. I could only imagine the waves and endless horizon. I feel relaxed when I'm out here with the waves."

"What do you want in life, Doug?" she asked.

"Right now, I don't know. I mean, I shouldn't say that I know what I want. I wish I could tell you more. I do want to be with someone who I can love and take care of." Where did that come from?

She was looking up at me with those beautiful dark eyes. They were like black pearls in the moonlight.

She said back, "I like what you've said, Doug. I had no idea that you thought that deeply about things, that you truly cared about people's feelings. I mean, I know you take very good care of your patients, but I didn't think that you cared much about a woman's feelings."

It was a wonderful night, but it was getting late. There were still many families out walking tonight. Down the beach, we could see the bright red light from the lanterns at the Pagodas Bath house on piers above the surf. Rosa and I had talked most of the evening and I still wanted more time with her. Her family was in tow most of the evening, but we hardly noticed them. Her father would occasionally send her sister to walk with us and between us. We were truly enjoying each other. She was happy, laughing with me. We all turned around and walked back to 25th Street and instead of taking the trolley we walked slowly down the oleander-lined parkway, between the trolley lines. She looked beautiful in the shadows of the oleanders, between the dangling blossoms swaying around her in the breeze. Their light, clear fragrance was filling my lungs and my head. The sharp shadows of the leaves played across her like little daggers.

We crossed Broadway and the large monument in the middle of the street. We walked together all the way to Market Street and from the corner I hailed a carriage for the slow ride home. Her father had several questions for me now, but her mother never spoke. When we reached their home, she went inside with the young children while I waited with Rosa and her father on the front porch. He looked back at me with a quick half smile and said goodnight, and he and Rosa went inside and shut the door. She gave me a quick smile and a wave before she went in. I said *"buenas noches"* as the door shut, then stood there on the porch for a few moments, staring at the door. I turned and went slowly down the few steps to the well-worn grass below and over the brick curb to the street. I was the only one out now, walking down the middle of the red brick street. The sea breeze was cool and my heart swelling in my chest. I could still smell her and the oleander flowers. She was wonderful. It was all wonderful. I could take care of her.

I awoke the next morning still thinking about Rosa. How did she feel about me? I wanted to lie back and dwell on the evening, but I knew I had to get dressed and get to the hospital soon. As I sat on the edge of the cot the scent of bacon and eggs from somewhere in the alley made me hungry. I had a few pieces of dried bread wrapped in a linen cloth, but they were now too hard to eat. I looked outside in the alley and saw one of the Petteway boys playing stickball. Angelina soon yelled to him to come in and eat. I quickly dressed in my undershirt and trousers and went down the steps to the alley. I walked across the alley through the sand in bare feet and climbed the step to the short, crooked porch and knocked on the Petteways' door. Moses opened the solid door and smiled at me.

"Let me guess, you're hungry," he said.

I quickly smiled back, "I sure am, can you tell?"

"Doug, what happened to you, you sure look bad. Angelina, do we got some food for the young doc?"

I heard Angelina give a slow "yes", and then she asked Moses, "Did he bring any sugar?"

As I heard her question, I ran back to my house and grabbed the small burlap bag stamped "John Sealy Hospital" and trotted back through the sand holding the bag of sugar in my right hand and holding up my trousers in my left. I walked inside and the whole family was sitting at the large table in the small room with plates of food in front of them and with no available seat for me. I saw a small wooden plate on the potbelly stove with bacon and eggs. I grabbed the plate and went to the table to find an extra fork. No one spoke to me as we all ate. As I stood behind Moses, I smiled at Jessie, his youngest daughter and she smiled back with a mouth full of food. The quiet in the room lasted as we all finished breakfast. It was broken with the sound of a wooden chair screeching as Jessie stood up and went to the bedroom. She brought out a checkerboard and a flat black box. She sat down next to her grandpa at the corner of the table and opened the worn red-and-black board and began to set up the checkers. She had a light blue ribbon in her hair amongst the braids and was wearing a long, clean, white dress. She and I were barefooted. The room was a dull white with grease stains on the wall next to the stove.

Her grandpa hadn't looked up from his plate yet, but said to her, "You just don't give up, do you?"

She suddenly stood up again and with one hand on her hip she pointed at him and said loudly, "I am going to beat you this time."

"We will see, we will see," he said, still eating his eggs.

She sat back down and pulled the chair close sitting perfectly straight. She made her first move slowly, and then her grandpa made his after he cleaned his plate. Angelina sat back and smiled her bright white smile at me. We were all wiping the sweat off our faces and necks on this hot August morning.

"Doug, Doug, Doug, you can eat, you can sure eat," Angelina said.

We were all drinking our sweetened coffee except grandpa.

"Angelina, how do you do those eggs so good?" I asked.

"I knew you liked them fried and I had a feeling you would show up this morning without an invitation. But it feels good to help the hungry like you. If you go to jail for stealing that sugar, I'll send Moses over with a cake made from it."

"Like I said before, Angelina, I didn't steal it, they give us rations."

Moses leaned his large body on the back legs of his chair and laughed, "Sure, Doug, you know I won't tell. We love your sugar. I'm going to bring home some bananas from the steamer we're unloading today. I'll hang a bunch under the porch, and you come grab some. You see, we're gonna give you rations, too."

The Petteways have been good to me these past four years. They gave me "rations," things off the boat, and never let me pay. Of course, I never had money either, until last month. As a house intern, I am paid a little.

I shaved with my dull razor, combed my hair and adjusted my tie and left my house to go back to the hospital. I walked down the alley and turned the corner to the street and doubled back and walked down the sidewalk in front of the Hendersons' home. The black rod iron fence was dripping in dew, as were my eyelashes. It all smelled fresh. I walked down the cleanly swept sidewalk made of square black-and-red paving stones, like a checkerboard on diagonal. Did Jesse beat her grandpa for the first time?

The sidewalks of the homes were different from each other, but all were perfectly laid. There were iron fences with alternating pickets low and high with matching gates. And blooming jasmine vines in beds behind the fences obediently grew between the pickets and set the mood with their perfume. Palms that were planted near the porches grew taller than expected and reached the second-floor balconies extending their wide fronds on thin branches bending back down to the first floor. I walked this street many times. The colors from the gardens were always changing by the season, by the day. The tall, well-painted houses were close together and close to the street. They were standing tall in the morning sun and seemed even taller with their long windows and open shudders.

What was waiting for me at the hospital? Whenever I entered the wards for the morning, there were always surprises—new patients, unexpected readmissions, higher fevers, unexpected deaths, and unexpected survivors. I climbed the front steps of the hospital, opened the heavy doors, and then climbed the stairs in the central hallway. I had been thinking about Archie off and on since descending these stairs yesterday. My anxiety about him was building as I worked my way to the ward. He had to be better today.

I looked across the ward to find him. He was sitting up, on the edge of the bed looking out the window. He was better. I looked at his bedside chart at the nursing table in center of the room. The nurse said that he ate a little this morning and hadn't vomited since the surgery. And there was no fever during the night. He turned around and then stood slowly as he heard my footsteps over the yellow pine floor.

"Hey, sit back down," I said. He did slowly with some pain. I took his little ten-year-old hand in mine and he gave me back a big smile. I sat down on a chair across from him. I looked behind me to see Mr. Negrini several beds over, asleep, snoring loudly. Archie and I laughed as we looked at him.

"How are you doing, Archie?" He was wearing an adult hospital gown that hung down over his feet.

"I feel better. What did you do to me?"

"You don't remember?"

"This hurts me, you know," he said as he lifted the gown and pointed to the sutured wound.

"A monkey with an oyster shell climbed in the window last night and did this to you. I had to sew it up. He didn't take out much, just a few bananas that you ate last week." He laughed a little because it hurt. I continued, "Pretty, isn't it? You can show all your friends. Lie back for me now."

I poked the incision for any fluctuance, any swelling. The incision was red, but it was clean and well opposed. He withdrew a little from me so I would stop prodding.

"What did you and that old doctor do to me, tell me the truth?"

"Well, we took out a little piece of your intestine, called your appendix. It's about as big as your little finger, you know. You won't miss it. Have you ever heard of an appendix?" I grabbed his hand and showed him his fifth finger.

"No. So I won't need it?"

"No, I had mine out when I was about your age too and I haven't missed it."

"So, what do I do now? Can I leave?"

"Just lie here now for one more day and eat all the food they bring you and do what that nurse over there tells you to do. Can you do all that?"

"Yea."

"I'm going to check on my other patients now and I'll be back to see you later. Before I do, I have to ask that nurse if you've been following orders." I smiled and let go of his hand and stood to leave.

"Wait, Dr. Schuler, can I ask you a question?

"Sure. "

"What happened to that man's leg?"

"Well. We had to cut it off. It was dying off, and...."

"Where did you put it?"

"We threw it away. You know, he is a fisherman, so we threw it back to the fish, out there. He's going to get a new one, a wooden one. Hey, will you do what I told you? And don't sneak out of here."

He was smiling again, "I will, I mean, I won't sneak out of here."

"You promise?"

"I promise."

I went back to the nursing desk and reviewed some of the charts of the other patients under my care. So far nothing emergent, no crises during the night. Several went home early this morning. I was still looking after Mrs. Landes, Dr. Randall's special patient, admitted several days ago for severe arthritis. I went to her bedside last. I pulled the curtain barrier away from her bedside and found her asleep. The student nurse, especially assigned to her, sat quietly with her chart in her lap. She motioned to me to keep quiet, with a slowly placed finger to her lips. I didn't want to wake her, but I knew Dr. Randall would ask me about her progress when he arrived. I also knew that she would only be receptive to Dr. Randall. She was breathing normally and didn't seem to be in pain from her arthritis. I lightly felt her right radial artery and her pulse was not too fast.

I turned back and went to the nursing station looking for a cup of coffee. I had a better chance of finding one without Nurse Sanders on duty this Sunday. The black metal coffee pot on the small desk was heavy and hot to touch. I found a small white mug and poured a cup of black coffee. I sat on the corner of the desk and drank my coffee. What should I do for Mrs. Landes? I had heard that she was one of the more important people in town, and that she and Mr. Landes were instrumental in locating the medical branch of the University of Texas in Galveston. She had never actually been a patient here until now. I finished the coffee and went to Dr. Randall's office. It was mid-Sunday morning and the door to his office was shut. I knocked and opened it slowly.

"Good morning, Dr. Randall."

"Doug," he said looking up from a thick book he was reading. "Sit down, let's talk about your patients."

He closed the book and sat back in his chair and looked the same as he always did, black suit with tall white collar and tightly tied necktie. As we spoke, he had the habit of looking at his gold pocket watch. He would dexterously unlatch the gold cover and close it just as quickly, after a quick glance down. It was ten o' clock.

After I spoke of everyone under my care and of their progress, he asked, "And Mrs. Landes? You forgot her."

"Well, she rested well during the night and was without fever or complaints."

"Any complaints by her now? You know, I admitted her after a house call the other day. Her arthritis was worse, and she summoned me to her home to address her pain. She has tried various poultices and tonics but gets more relief from just soaking her hands in hot water each morning. She insisted that I admit her immediately to run tests and to once and for all properly deal with her pain." He said this with a smirk.

"She looked comfortable. I was afraid to wake her. Her student nurse said that she had a quiet night."

"I don't blame you for not waking her. I was just glad the other patients didn't keep her up."

He sat forward and reached into a drawer and pulled out a glass jar full of bright white coarse powder and with a broad white label with black bold lettering.

"What do you think, Doug?" he asked as he passed it to me.

"I have never seen this before," I said as I rolled the bottle to the label side. "Aspirin?"

"Yes, it's acetyl salicylic acid, a new product from the Bayer Company in Germany, ideal for arthritis pain. I had this shipped to me several months ago, but I haven't had the nerve to try it on any patients yet. We have to be very careful with newer treatments. We don't want to use them prematurely. But I was thinking about a trial treatment period for Mrs. Landes."

"Yes, I have heard of it, maybe we should give it a try?"

"I'm really not sure about it. Doug, don't forget our first obligation in patient care is to do no harm. You haven't forgot that part of the Hippocratic Oath already?" he said with a slight smile.

"No sir, of course not, but what else can we do with her?"

"I don't know, maybe I'll think of something as we're talking to her."

We rose together and went out to the east ward to see Mrs. Landes. She was now awake and talking quietly with the student. Mr. Landes was sitting next to her in a small cane bottom chair, dressed formally with shoes shined and stiff shirt collar. He and the nurse stood as we walked to her bed.

"Good morning, Mr. and Mrs. Landes," Dr. Randall began. We all shook hands except Mrs. Landes who keep her arthritic hands folded across her chest, resting on her soft, floral nightgown. She was not wearing the usual stiff, white hospital gown that was required. She wasn't smiling.

"Well, Dr. Randall, what is your plan for my recovery?" she asked after the round of greetings.

Mr. Landes spoke up. "Yes, Dr. Randall, we were hoping to have made some progress at this point, but she still suffers terribly. We don't feel that Mrs. Landes should return home until she has made some improvement. The servants miss her, and our home is chaos without her, but I do feel that the time has come for an answer."

I looked at the student nurse. Our eyebrows rose in unison.

But Dr. Randall answered confidently, "Mr. Landes, because of the severity of your wife's arthritis, I feel we need to throw out all customary treatments and begin a trial of a completely new therapy, actually one that has grown very popular in Europe."

Mrs. Landes now looked directly at Dr. Randall and began to smile. She was a pale elderly woman, but now I saw a little color return to her face, probably at the thought of trying something no one else in Galveston had ever been offered.

"It's called Aspirin, a new product developed by the chemists at the Bayer Company in Germany. But, Mrs. Landes, I must add that it is experimental. There is a risk in taking the medication. We are not sure of the potential side effects."

"Young man, I have lived with this curse for many years, and I am ready for the cure. I do want this new therapy, and, in fact, I do not want to leave until I have tried it."

Dr. Randall pulled out the same bottle from his coat pocket and then gave it to Mrs. Landes to examine. She held it tightly with her arthritic fingers as she stared at the bright white powder reflecting the sunlight. She was nodding in approval while reading the instructions on a small label written in German on the other side.

"Well, we can give a trial dose today," Dr. Randall added after breathing deeply.

Mrs. Landes had now reached a hand for Mr. Landes to hold and the two were nearly giddy. We walked away, back to the nurse's station after taking our leave. Dr. Randall had an unusual look on his face now. He was staring at the bottle with a deeply concerned look, a look of optimism mixed with a healthy dose of dread.

He instructed me to mix five grains of the Aspirin powder in water and bring it to her. He was going back to his office. I mixed the powder as he said and brought the glass to her. She briefly examined it, and then drank it all. I began to feel the same dread that Dr. Randall felt. Mrs. Landes handed the glass back to me and then asked for another glass of water, this time with ice. From the moment I introduced myself as her doctor she treated me as her servant, ordering me around before I could interrupt her.

I walked back to the nurse's station with the glass. Where would I find ice?

CHAPTER 8

It was late August. I never found ice for Mrs. Landes. Ice was hard to come by this time of year and I longed for it every summer. Often, I would see the Galveston Polar Ice Company carriages delivering ice in our neighborhood, only to the rich. Large smoking blocks of ice hanging delicately from iron tongs like one large, delicious drop of water. Once it was stored in an ice chest in the kitchen, it was picked apart to smaller and smaller pieces by servants and placed carefully in tall glasses of tea with sprigs of peppermint to cool down the throats of wealthy Galvestonians on a scorching summer afternoon. Life was effortless for the rich but so much work for everyone else.

Patients were admitted to me daily, usually very sick with much of the same things—tuberculosis, pneumonia, gout, strokes. Who got better or didn't was hard to predict. The older ones had a harder time of it, and, of course, the younger ones fared better. Tuberculosis was particularly devastating to all. Whole families were at times infected, even young children. Dr. Randall and I went to one home close to the hospital where TB had taken hold. Small children were coughing as loudly as the adults, producing bloody phlegm, too. They were trained to carry a white handkerchief and to cover their face when they coughed. These handkerchiefs were all tinged with blood. We covered our faces, too. There wasn't much that could be done. Quarantining the family head was devastating. They became social outcasts and then, one by one, slowly consumed by the disease. They were so thin before they died.

I reported to Dr. Randall in his office at mid-morning. I sat before his desk and waited, then stood when he walked into the room. He began talking as he walked around me to the front of the desk. I reached into my pants pocket and pulled out the small bottle that I had taken from Mr. Mendez's sea chest a few weeks ago. After Dr. Randall reviewed my last patient, I showed him the bottle. The white powder in the small, corked bottle was now light yellow but still dry and loose. He tilted the bottle then opened it and hesitantly smelled the cork.

"I know you've opened it, already. It's yellowed from exposure to the air. Why did you go to ship?"

"I was worried about Mr. Mendez, especially after talking to the ship's doctor. I wanted to find something more about him."

"Did you see anything else in the chest?"

"Nothing else really."

"Well, Doug, I don't know what to make of it, I doubt if we will ever see or hear from him again. Show this to Dr. Smith next door. He'll know what it is."

As I was leaving, he said, "By the way, Doug, I'll be leaving the island soon and will be gone for a few weeks. I believe you and Tex and Carl can care for things without me. Also, this Friday you are to attend a dinner in my behalf at the Landes home. Mrs. Landes wants to announce to the community the miracle therapy for her arthritis."

"Yes sir, I will."

"Of course, I tried to remind her of the experimental nature of the Aspirin therapy, and that if her pain returned after stopping the medicine, I would be more convinced that it was helping her. But she won't stop it. She has demanded that I acquire more from the Bayer Company in Germany as soon as possible. When it arrives, you will then need to convert it to pill form."

"I will."

"She wanted you, my 'assistant,' as she called you, to be there as well."

I had plans to drop by Rosa's for a meal and to spend the evening with her family if they would have me.

"Yes, Dr. Randall, I am free Friday."

Dr. Alan Smith, our Toxicology professor, wasn't seen much on the wards by anyone but he was famous for his unusual talents. Down in the bottom floor of the Medical Department building, Dr. Smith kept to himself but was often visited by students with questions about poisons or different concoctions taken by their family members. He would expound about the uses of arsenic and strychnine and create scenarios of death and dying for the entertainment of the students, any method of death the students could imagine. In his lab he was hard to see, barely noticeable moving among the beakers and flasks that he handled at eye level. I found him during the lunch hour sitting at a large table in the middle of the lab handling a sandwich in one hand and several serum samples in another, positioned above a test tube tray, and bending over an opened volume of something.

"Dr. Smith, do you have a minute?"

He only briefly glanced up at me through his small spectacles, and then looked back at his text and said, "No, not really".

I waited a few minutes and then he stopped what he was doing now and straightened up to face me.

"So, you're a doctor now, Douglas?"

"Yes, I am."

I remembered he was at the graduation, but he didn't see me or anybody graduate. He was sitting in the back of the faculty section reading a large volume of something, probably bored by it all. But none of the graduates minded; at least he was there.

I held out the small bottle and walked toward him. "I need your help, I found this among the personal belongings of a patient of mine, a seaman. He was febrile, comatose, and we never came to know what was wrong with him. I was hoping if you weren't too busy you might be able to analyze this for me, and of course, Dr. Randall."

He was interested now. He looked at me long enough to put down the sandwich and to accept the small bottle from my hand. He walked over to the window to examine it in the sunlight. He removed the cork and smelled the light-yellow powder without hesitation. He tilted the small bottle over on the tip of his index finger and tasted a few of the crystals.

"Hmmm, Schuler, it's bitter and at the same time numbing to my tongue. Could be opium, or codeine, or cocaine? I've not tasted anything like it before. I'll analyze this material for you. I believe I can identify it."

I would not have tasted the powder but I'm glad he did. I knew that I would never see Mr. Mendez again, but I wanted to know what was in that little bottle. I had to close the book on his case. I held out my hand to shake Dr. Smith's, but he had gone back to his lab bench. He placed the bottle in his coat pocket. Should I stay a while, like I used to as a student? He didn't like a student looking over his shoulder. And he, in turn, thought nothing of injecting lingering students with unknown substances, all for the sake of advancing science.

Tex was the victim of one of Dr. Smith's little experiments. He was injected with the serum of a febrile boy suspected of having yellow fever. Tex was sick for a week, with alternating chills and sweats, even a temp of 105 degrees. But he recovered in time for final exams. Dr. Smith would track him down at the hospital demanding more blood smears to complete his studies. Tex, being tall and thin, of course, has great veins in his arms. Once while working on the ward, Tex climbed on an empty stretcher and grabbed a sheet from a nursing student and threw it over himself when he heard

Dr. Smith coming. Dr. Smith passed by thinking the body on the stretcher was a corpse. We said we hadn't seen him, then we pushed the stretcher down the hall and placed it in the elevator.

Archie was getting better. He was eating and walking around the ward and frustrating the nurses with questions. He was scheduled to go back to the orphanage when the ambulance returned. I told the nurses I would take him back to the orphanage myself. I went to his bed and told him to put on his clothes that were under the bed. He didn't have shoes, but I saw how calloused his feet were when he was admitted. I checked his incision one last time. It wasn't tender to touch, he said. We left the front door of the hospital, and we went down the stairs and he didn't have pain in his abdomen as he walked. We walked most of the way through town, but at 25th Street one block off Strand we found a horse stable and rented a horse. I put him on the horse, and we walked the horse down to the beach. There was no saddle, so he held tightly to the mane. At the water's edge, he moved to the back of the horse, and I got on in front of him. We rode the horse in the sand westward to the orphanage. We walked the horse at first, then ran it as he held on tight to my waist. We talked about life in the orphanage, the only life he had known.

We saw the orphanage from a distance, standing alone behind the dunes and the low salt cedar trees. It was a two-story structure with long balconies facing the Gulf. Archie said all the boys lived upstairs together in a large room. He didn't remember how many boys there were now, but there were a lot. There were no other buildings or homes in sight. Isolation meant that epidemics such as yellow fever were less likely to infect the kids sleeping close to one another.

We went through the double doors of the front entrance. I spoke to a few nuns there about his appendectomy and his recovery. I couldn't restrict his activity because that would be impossible after spending four days in the hospital. All the other kids ran over to him and were lifting his shirt to see his scar, but he had orders from me to not let anybody touch it.

Archie was anxious to see his best friend, Frankie Madera. Archie told me about him one night in the hospital. They had treasure buried in the dunes in front of the orphanage. Archie was not allowed to tell anyone what was buried there. He didn't tell me even after I told him that I saved his life. Frankie was smaller than Archie, but he quickly had Archie's arm twisted behind his back and screaming uncle. I stayed for a while there and met all of Archie's other friends at the orphanage. They were so happy to see him. They thought that they would never see him again. Other kids never returned to the orphanage after leaving for the hospital, they said. He had returned a conqueror! He had cheated death!

I was only allowed to be gone from the hospital for a short time. I gave Frankie and Archie a ride on the horse in the dunes before I left. Frankie was loud, with thick brown hair and a deviated nasal septum from a previous broken nose. He was a little fighter, no doubt, as they all had to be. I said goodbye to them, and he gave me his best handshake. The nurses had given him too many hugs as he left the hospital, he said. I rode slowly back down the beach after running the horse for a few blocks. I practically lived on a horse back home. I was free. Since being in Galveston, living on an island, I was a prisoner. Carl said we should take a boating trip to feel free, and girls liked it, too. I walked back to the hospital from the stables after I bought an ice cream cone at an ice cream shop. It was dripping down my hand faster than I could eat it. I held some crushed ice in my other hand and rubbed it on the back of my neck as it melted.

This week had been a busy one for the interns. Too many sick patients for which I could do very little, but who talked to me incessantly, one after another. Sometimes they were too sick to talk but if they weren't sick enough, they would ask so many questions. One patient would hear the question of another patient and ask it again, and then I was stuck on the ward explaining and reassuring them. But reassurance was harder to pull off. Dr. Randall was good at it. And he was right when he said that reassurance only goes so far. Patients heard what they want to hear most of the time, good or bad.

Dr. Smith was convinced that the powder in that little bottle of Mr. Mendez's was cocaine hydrochloride. Dr. Randall felt he was probably heating the powder, then injecting it as a liquid. He most likely suffered a fatal brain hemorrhage and was dead.

I had been too busy to take Rosa out again, but she expected me on Friday. I couldn't tell her that I had to be at a dinner party at the Landes home. I was a regular nuisance at her home over these past few weeks, only dropping by late in the evening. I was allowed to sit with her in the front room and speak with her in private. Her younger sister frequently sat with us and dominated our conversation, even singing and dancing for us. Those evenings were so pleasant and reminiscent of my home life, of my younger sisters. Her parents rarely spoke to me and her mother would leave the room when I entered the house. Her father occasionally asked me about what I did. He didn't seem too impressed with my desire to help people as a doctor, but he didn't allow me to pay for any meals there anymore.

I walked up to the home of Mr. and Mrs. Landes on the corner of 16th St. and Postoffice. It was a large, red brick home with tall windows, each window covered with green painted shudders and topped with a mosaic half-moon-shaped tile insert. The house was crowned with towers and a parapet, like a castle. It had large black wrought iron balconies and pale yellow and blue ornamental tiles on the porches. Stone steps led up to the entry porch. Guests arrived by carriage at the west entrance as they swept around the back of the house in front of the servants' quarters.

This late summer evening was hot but breezy. I climbed the

steps and entered the home through the large heavily carved double doors. I wouldn't know anybody there besides the Landes.

But I was wrong; Mr. and Mrs. Henderson were there. They looked my way and noticed my wrinkled suit but not me. Angel was there, too, and she didn't notice me either. I went to stand near her. Her soft blue eyes matched her well-sewn dress that matched the ribbon in her hair. She wore a diamond pendant on a gold necklace. Before I spoke, she left my side of the room and joined her parents.

Mr. Henry A. Landes came to my side and slapped me on the back and dragged me to his study to meet his friends and have a smoke before dinner. It was a large room with a high ceiling and dark wood paneled walls with brass lighting fixtures every few feet. Several men sat in large leather chairs that were placed inside a large Persian rug. He introduced me to his friends as Dr. Randall's "boy," but at least he had remembered my name. I never had to give him Dr. Randall's excuse for not being there. As the men all began to talk below the smoky cloud, I looked back into the main room to see Angel looking away from me and laughing at the jokes of another man. Rosa never treated me that way.

Later all the guests sat down to dinner at the large carved dinner table placed perfectly under a large electricity-fed chandelier. There were at least thirty of us. I couldn't stop staring at the chandelier, all that crystal reflecting all that light! I overheard one woman seated near me say that Mrs. Landes had it imported from Paris. She wasn't as impressed as I was. The table was perfectly set with bright white plates of different sizes with gold edges and a long-stemmed wine glass. Why were there two forks? The food was served by well-dressed servants and came to us course after course. Mrs. Landes, seated at one end of the table, was talkative and gesturing freely during the dinner without any sign of her rheumatism. Mr. Landes, seated at the other end, rose and toasted his wife's complete recovery and the innovations of modern medicine of which John

Sealy Hospital now afforded them easy access. That the University of Texas was more than just a school for the young men of Texas graduating to become tomorrow's doctors, it was a portal to the great European schools of medicine. I agreed whole-heartedly with everything he said, except that we did have one woman who graduated with us. Her name was Charlotte Schaffer. She left for Chicago after we graduated, I think. She was the smartest in the class, but didn't get the award for it.

I handed Mr. Landes another bottle of aspirin pills after dinner. We all went to the parlor where Mrs. Landes played the grand piano, with her now revived and pliable hands. All present cheered her performance of several classical pieces. At the end, she stood next to the piano and bowed. She held her hands behind her and rubbed them together as we clapped. I backed out of the room and slipped out into the yard through the servant's entrance, and then to the alley.

It was late when I made my way to Rosa's house, just a few blocks away, but in a totally different neighborhood. I climbed the few wooden steps to her small porch. It was dark inside. Was anyone awake? I looked in a window and saw a candle lit in the back of the house and someone reading by it at a table. I had to see her, so I knocked. No one came. I knocked again, harder, and after a few seconds I could see a figure walking to the door. I was hoping it was not her father.

It was Rosa. I could barely see her behind the screen door. I could only see the white dress she wore.

"Can I come in?"

She looked behind her and opened the screen door and stepped out on the porch. She smiled and reached for my hand. I couldn't tell what she was wearing in the light from the half-moon. We held hands and walked to the steps and sat there together at the edge of the small porch. She placed her bare feet on the bottom step next to my dirty black shoes.

"Are you hungry, Doug?"

"No, I'm really not"

"Did you eat already?"

"Yes, at some rich people's house. I had to go for Dr. Randall. We had a fancy dinner, but I didn't like it."

"Did you have a date?"

"No, Rosa, no. ...I didn't have a date. It was a long boring dinner with an old lady that Dr. Randall and I have been treating. Afterward I had to listen to her play the piano. I snuck out before anybody noticed. Dr. Randall is out of town for the month, so I had to go for him. That's all."

I reached to hold her other hand too, and added, "I was thinking of you the whole time. In fact, I have been thinking of you the whole day."

"I was tired of waiting for you tonight. My mother said you wouldn't come and that she heard from one of the ladies at the market that all you students at the hospital had several girlfriends. "

"I'm not a student anymore. I graduated from all that, I want just one woman now and ...."

I wanted to kiss her. But she looked away. Her hair was loose and blowing in the gentle breeze. I touched her hair and her bare neck and pulled her close to me. She looked back at me with those deep dark eyes. The fronds from a wild palm growing at the edge of the porch cast a rocking shadow over her face in the breeze, like a paper fan. She closed her eyes slowly and I kissed her. I let go of her hands and held her in my arms. We kissed again.

She put her head on my chest and said, "Why did you do that?"

"I had to. You are so beautiful."

"Do you mean that, or should I believe my mother? She doesn't like you, you know."

"Really? But how about your father? I feel he likes me."

"No, he doesn't like you, either." She laughed.

"But do you, Rosa, do you like me, maybe a little?"

"Yes, I do, a little."

I kissed her again. We held each other. I smelled her hair, it was jasmine, made even more intense by the heat tonight. It was intoxicating.

"I like you too, a whole lot."

I reached into my coat pocket and pulled out a small burgundy colored cardboard box with a lid and gave it to her. She smiled and stared back at me. It was a little box that filled the palm of her small hand. She looked down at the box and opened it and gently lifted out a necklace. It was a brass necklace with a small brass rose pendant.

"It was my sister's necklace. I thought you might like it."

"When did she die?"

"She didn't die, she left it here when my family came to visit me in May."

She didn't look as excited now. But I added, "I had it engraved with your initial, 'R,' so it's yours now."

She turned the pendant over and tried to see the engraving in the moonlight, but it was too dark. It was an embellished upper case "R." She felt it with her finger.

"Which sister, what's her name."

"Winifred."

She was smiling again and said, "I love it, thank you so much." She kissed me again. I helped her put it on. "Rosa means rose in Spanish," she added.

"I know."

She held up the box and said, "And what a beautiful box, too." She was so special to even appreciate the box. I had lifted the box from a cupboard in the toilet before I left.

We sat for only a short time together that night. Most days I would hurry over after work. I usually arrived late, but she wouldn't mind just as long as I showed up. I was terrible at predicting how my workday would go. So, we spent most of our time together at her house. It was harder and harder to leave her house each time. She would make me leave before her father did. Walking home, time after time alone, was miserable. She always wore the necklace when we were together. Someday I would buy Rosa a gold necklace with a diamond.

My sister had written me about her necklace. She said that she left it on the table in my room after going to the beach and that she wanted me to send it back to her. She never liked her first name, so she went by her middle name, Rachel.

PART 3

"The medical man sees terrible sights, touches unpleasant things, and the misfortune of others bring a harvest of sorrows that are particularly his."

—Hippocrates

CHAPTER 9

The air was hot and sticky, but I suddenly felt cold and weak on the inside, standing alone on a ward full of patients and my arms full of charts. Several patients were talking to me at the same time while I stared out of the window northward, over the bay. A small homemade skiff was being tossed around in a stiff wind, with two boys hanging on for dear life. One boy fell off and the other reached out to save him. I put down the charts and reached for the window. The boy on board found a small rope and tried to throw it out to his friend. He was thrown off balance suddenly and fell backward into the water, too. The waves had their way with both, pushing them away from the boat and each other.

The empty boat was slowly rolling over now, its small mast now horizontal. I ran off the ward and down the central stairway and went out the back door. I ran the short distance to the water's edge and could see nothing but felt hot salt spray in my face from waves hitting the grassy water break. There was no sign of the boys or the boat, just waves with white caps sliding back and forth.

I had watched these boys in their little boat for the past few months. They were fearless, capable seamen crossing the bay in their homemade craft, not afraid of bigger boats crossing their path. I always felt happy watching those boys, even while the nurses would yell at me, or the faculty would brush me aside with their comments. How quickly they could launch their little boat, then raise its dark gray patchwork sail, and set out on a miniature adventure in the bay. They were about ten years old and never wore a shirt or shoes. I walked back and forth along the grass edge. They were lost.

I ran back inside the hospital and up the stairs to the ward and returned to the window looking out over the bay and again could see them no more. No sign of the boys, no sign of the boat. And no one had noticed? The ward was quiet. The windows had been shut to cut off the unusually stiff breeze blowing through the ward. Some patients were fanning themselves with whatever they could find. There was still no sign of them, just a bay too rough for a small boat. There were many large boats anchored in the bay, though, with their masts rocking back and forth in rhythm. Even the fat smoke-stacks of the large steamers were rocking a little. An old man tugged at my coat and asked me what I was looking at. I said "nothing," then he said he had some questions for me.

It was a Saturday morning in early September, and summer was still sweltering. Dr. Randall remained on vacation on the mainland, Houston, I think. He left by the train causeway across Galveston Bay several weeks ago. Many of the faculty were still vacationing in Europe, several left by steamer to New Orleans. And that meant that the patients in the hospital were left in the capable hands of the interns. The nurses anxiously awaited the return of the faculty.

I continued to work every day as I had done since my internship began in July. Weekends were less demanding. Call nights were added to long days several times a week, and I was on call again today, this time a Saturday. Sleep at work was not allowed, but we slept when we could in a storage closet off the nurse's room. There wasn't a bed, just canvas bags of dirty laundry stacked together. A nurse could be fired if found asleep, but we were found asleep all the time. We were reported to the faculty for sleeping, but Dr. Randall never brought it up with us.

This morning was unusually busy for a weekend. The ward was

becoming noisy with lots of coughing and wheezing, bedsprings squeaking as patients sat up and back down, and heavy shoes of the nurses walking back and forth carrying metal trays. Miss Aileen Duffy, a woman in her twenties who emigrated from Ireland a decade ago, had coughed since she arrived in Galveston, she said. She worked in a cramped sewing factory on the third floor in a building on the Strand with twenty other women. They were all coughing now, she said. She had lost a lot of weight over that time. With her thick Irish accent, she cussed the factory for the cough, and we all knew she had tuberculosis. There have been many from Ireland with TB. She told me today that she hated doctors, too.

Over the past year, she had lost a lot more weight. When she sat up in bed, I could see her collar bones protruding as she coughed. She couldn't breathe lying flat anymore. By her lung exam, she had a large amount of fluid in her left lung, probably a pleural effusion. And her lips and hands turned blue when she walked or got angry. Her coughing had been incessant. I wiped my face with my handkerchief after each conversation with her. The nurses kept their distance from her, and they continued to caution me about spending too much time with her. She worried me. A nursing student, Laura Pelley, was more help to her than the nurses. She didn't flinch with all the cursing and coughing she received. She gave the Irish woman a bed bath and combed and braided her long dark brown hair as it hung down over her white hospital gown. Her spine protruded in the opening where the gown was tied. She was too weak to braid her own hair.

Nurse Sanders was not on duty this weekend. I didn't miss her yelling and her heavy footsteps charging across the pine floor. The charge nurse was Nurse Willow, who was light-footed and more tolerant of the rest of us. She asked me to keep a close eye on a ten-year-old boy, Johnny Losico, at the end of the east ward. He now had a fever and a rash over his chest. He had a broken right radius after a fall off his bicycle a few days ago. I set the open fracture yesterday, and then casted his arm from his hand to above his bent elbow.

I went directly to see him, and now his arm above the cast was swollen and red and more painful. There was no fluctuance when I pushed hard. He was a tough kid, as he just winced and clenched his fists during my exam. His fingers at the end of the cast were not red or swollen. His armpit was tender. Usually there was less pain after the fracture was set and the arm casted, and they were usually back on their bicycles riding with one hand. But he was sleepy and shivering and in pain this morning. His father and mother ran a corner grocery store in town and were not with him here today. He couldn't go home as I had promised yesterday, as his arm was infected now.

"Can I go home?" he asked again.

"No, Johnny, I don't want you walking around, all right? Your broken arm has germs in it now, but we're going to get it better for you. How does that sound?"

"What are germs?"

"They are, well, bugs that you can't see causing your arm to hurt."

"I don't want my brother riding my bike."

"Just let him ride it awhile, okay?"

The bright red rash on his chest was the germ streptococcus from his open wound, no doubt. If the swelling got worse, the cast would have to come off.

There were several wealthy old people at the end of their lives on the wards. They had many visitors each day. The wealthy always wanted to die in the hospital rather than at home. A poor man would rarely have such an opportunity. Dr. Randall went out of his way to accommodate them. It was good for the hospital, he said. Some requested a morphine hypodermic for their pain. We knew it suppressed their respirations, but they seemed so peaceful after they took it. There was usually one family member present at their bedside, primarily to fan them. The heat and the mosquitoes were especially upsetting to the wealthy.

But most of the noise on the ward this morning was from just one woman, Nellie Connors, with postpartum hysteria. Her full-term baby was stillborn yesterday. She was in agony afterwards and had to be sedated with Lupulin through the night and again this morning. Her wailing was unsettling to the other patients and to me. She couldn't be calmed this morning even with cold water to the face from the nurses. Only Nurse Willow could calm her a little by gently stroking her hair while she sang softly in her ear. Tex was on call last night and had delivered her baby with some difficulty. Her husband and her mother rushed her here by carriage after twenty hours of labor at home. It was her first baby. Tex knew the baby was dead when he didn't hear the heartbeat with the long bell of the obstetric stethoscope. Maybe her family would come for her this morning.

Carl was forced into driving the ambulance this weekend because the driver, a temperamental old man, a Civil War veteran, refused to work anymore for so little pay. Carl wasn't happy about it, either. He had his own plans, but his mistake was frequenting the student nurse's home across the street from the hospital. He was easy to find.

The ambulance was a large box-like black carriage with tall walls and a hardtop roof, with the words "John Sealy Hospital" on each side. A matching old black horse with heavy hooves drew it; we nicknamed her Princess. When the ambulance was sent into the city to pick up a patient, the driver returned to the hospital and steered the ambulance through the archway under the raised steps of the front entrance and unloaded the patient stretcher through the first-floor door to orderlies or medical students who carried the patient upstairs to the wards.

This morning Carl had already delivered several patients to us, most with minor injuries. But this afternoon there had been an accident on Market Street downtown. An electric trolley hit several young men crossing the street and carrying a large wedding cake from a local bakery. Carl dressed their wounds and with the help of a few pedestrians nearby, loaded them into the ambulance. One had a head injury and was unconscious, the other was awake but couldn't move his legs. He screamed at the trolley conductor in another language as he lay on the ground, Carl said. Carl and the orderlies carried the two into the hospital up to the third floor.

"Hey, Dougie, I was hoping I wouldn't run into you today. The trolley on Market ran into these poor boys today. They were carrying this big white cake when they got hit. There's one with the fractured back. He had better calm down or he'll be paralyzed for good. I'm not sure what's going on with the other guy, his younger brother, but he should wake up soon. His pupils are equal, and he responds to pain in his arms and legs. I heard Tex had it pretty rough last night."

"He did and left me a lot of unfinished business."

"I guess I'm just the delivery boy this weekend. But I thought I could give a free tour of the island to some of the new nursing students, since I'm stuck in the ambulance. Then I'll have Princess take us to the beach, all done in style with the blessings of the Sealy family."

The stretchers were positioned next to each other on the floor, stretchers with four short legs supporting the white canvas that held the men. I looked back at Carl walking away and saw that his trousers were wet and covered in a coating of sand. He went to the beach? He should be reported to the faculty.

Sure enough, the other young man did wake up, enough to tell me his name and where he lived before he blacked out again. His name was Nichalous Stamoulis as was confirmed by his paralyzed older brother, Constantine. Their family ran a local bakery, and they spent Saturdays delivering cakes. They were in their early twenties, strong and tanned.

Nichalous opened his eyes and murmured a few broken words after I rubbed my knuckles over his sternum, but he didn't stay awake. His reflexes were all equal and his cranial nerves seemed to be intact. He did roll his head when I gagged him with a tongue blade. He had a large gash over his right temple that I would need to sew. I should do it while he was out.

Constantine was calm and not moving now. He was talking quietly to himself, or was he praying? When I came over to him, he quickly grabbed my hand and said, "Please help me."

"I'm Dr. Schuler, can you move your legs?"

"No, they won't move. What does this mean to me?"

"It means you probably have a broken back. Can you feel your legs?" I rubbed his legs below his knees.

"I don't know. Are my legs hurt too?"

"No, they look fine" I said as I lifted each one slowly. There were no leg fractures. "What happened to you both?"

He was tearful now and slowly said, "This good-for-nothing idiot smashed into my brother and me. I know the man; he knows the rush my brother and I are in on Saturdays. I don't hurt in any part of my body except my back, but I will find a way to make him pay."

"Why are you all wet?"

"The water from the bay is rising and covering the streets downtown. I lay in the street for a long time. Everybody wanted to move me, but I wouldn't let them. My father could have water in his bakery by now. Some will say that we fell in front of the trolley because the streets were wet. But he hit us first. We never dropped a cake before."

He had been hit hard; he didn't fracture his back from just slipping in the street. I would examine his back once we got him in bed.

What was Rosa doing? Was she thinking about me, too? I had been dropping by her house most evenings when I wasn't on call. I was on today, so I won't see her until tomorrow night.

By late afternoon, I went back to the north-facing windows of the east ward. There was a steamer struggling to enter the channel against the heavy chop on the bay. The waves were pushing hard against its tall side paddle wheels, making it twist and roll. Could those two boys somehow be alive? I put down a chart and left the ward and went down the main steps and out the back entrance. I stood in the grass at the bulkhead and saw nothing but hard breaking waves against it and me. I backed away from the edge as I was up to my ankles in seawater. I retreated to the hospital.

As the sun began to move to the west, the wards were still hectic, many patients were still unsettled, uncomfortable and complaining. The nurses were behind in their charting, and there was little time to pause and think. Days like this usually turned into nights like this. The nurses didn't help matters much, either. They were quick to tell you to be on your toes late in the day, that a night with a full moon meant you'd be delivering more babies, or that you'd better sharpen up because they just had a feeling that the night would be busy. Of course, if it was bad for us, it was bad for them. The faculty never worked through the night. The night was the time when we, the interns, ran the wards.

The student nurse, Laura, came to me to tell me that the patients were complaining that it was too hot on the ward, and we should open some windows. We were both sweating profusely, too. It didn't show on her like it did on me. I felt ridiculous standing there in my soaked pants legs and shoes. The student nurses were always dressed very well—clean, orderly, and well starched and pressed. We, the interns, on the other hand were the worst-looking bunch in the hospital, rarely ever clean, usually unkempt, and never starched and pressed. I don't know how they did it, they looked good day and night. But I knew they had, too. They were the standard for the hospital. If they weren't perfectly appointed in their uniforms, it would reflect badly on the whole institution. There was something comforting to the patients to see a well-uniformed nurse at their side.

We went to a few of the south-facing windows and as we opened each one, a very stiff wind blew the blinds inward, nearly slapping us in the face. We opened one next to an old drunk man sleeping and the noise immediately woke him up and he yelled at me, "What's wrong with you, shut the window!" We usually had several drunks brought here on weekend nights as the bars closed. They were passed out in front of someone's business and brought here by the police rather than jail. Typically, you couldn't awaken them during the night no matter what you did to them, like slapping their face or hitting the bottoms of their feet with a metal bedpan. But later in the day they would wake up on their own, so we just left them alone during the night. The nurses didn't tolerate them. They wanted the drunks off the ward as soon as possible.

Opening windows on both sides of the hospital seemed impossible without a stiff breeze running through the ward. That puzzled us all, so we didn't have a solution now for the stifling heat. Laura suggested that we pass out fans and glasses of water. What I wouldn't do for a glass of water with ice. Ever since Mrs. Landes had asked for it and since we had ice with our drinks at her party, I daydreamed about ice. The orderlies and students began bringing in large glass bottles of water from the hospital's cistern out back and placed them at the nursing stations in the east and west ward. According to Nurse Willow, we were not allowed to have any, it was for the patients only.

Some of the patients received visitors earlier in the morning but very few did by the afternoon. Mr. Stamoulis came late in the afternoon and was convinced that at least one of his two sons had died, so he brought along the Greek Orthodox priest with him. He was so relieved that they were both alive that he cried, kneeling between their beds. He told the priest that he could leave, but the priest was angry about being dragged down to this "God-forsaken place" on a busy Saturday. Mr. Stamoulis apologized profusely and kissed the back of his right hand, then slid paper money into it. The priest was gone after that. Maybe there were some other church members here, but he didn't bother to check.

As I saw all of this unfold from across the ward, the oldest son, Constantine, pointed toward me to show his father that I was his doctor. He walked over to me and began to cry again. What would I do now, I didn't have time for this? I put my arm half-way around him and told him that that his boys were doing just fine now.

He looked up at me and said: "You're not the main doctor in charge here, are you? You're too young! My boys need the best care from someone with experience."

This was the usual reaction that we got. He started pacing back and forth in front of me, shaking his head.

"I'm just one of the doctors taking care of your boys; my faculty doctor is Dr. Edward Randall," I said.

"Where is he, I want to speak to him, right away," he said, pointing his finger in my face.

"He's not here right now, but he knows about your boys and has planned everything about their care."

I knew that he knew I was lying. Laura was near enough to hear that as well, but didn't stop with her work for even a moment. I would never have said such a thing around Nurse Sanders. I would have been reported immediately.

Mr. Stamoulis took my right hand and said, "My boy, you are young like my boys, please tell Dr.Randall to take good care of my boys, their mother is dying from grief. Do you understand?"

"I will, Mr. Stamoulis, please don't worry. They will be okay. Please go talk to them, especially to Nicholaus. He is so sleepy after the accident."

He led me by the hand back to the bedsides of the two boys and began to speak to them in Greek. Constantine responded to his father's voice and pulled himself up resting on his elbows. Nicholaus was unresponsive but clearly breathing normally. His father could see the blood-soaked gauze wrapped around his head. He removed his hat and placed it on the bed next to him. He fell to his knees between the beds of his two injured boys and began to pray for Nicholaus to please wake up. He squeezed his hand tightly, but he didn't move. Constantine lay still but tried to calm his father with one hand. They were only speaking Greek. He hugged Constantine, crying on his shoulder. His father didn't realize that he was paralyzed.

"Why are you all wet?" I asked Mr. Stamoulis.

"My bakery and all of downtown is flooding. The electric streetcars have stopped running and the mule cars can barely move through the water. Their ears are flapping hard in the wind, and they refuse to pull. People are talking about another Saturday ruined by the wind and water. People are quitting work and walking to Broadway and the beach to see the high waves. Mama came down from the bakery to the street and stuck her finger in the water and yelled to me, 'Papa, it's salty!' She became more worried than ever."

To Constantine, he said, "I have to go back to the shop, you are better off here for now. Please wake up your brother."

Pointing a finger again at me, he said, "My boys are in your hands. God is watching you now."

He took his hat off the bed, kissed both boys on the cheek, and left. I knew it was going be a busy night for me. That's because the day never started out well. But I will see Rosa tomorrow afternoon even if I work all night and don't sleep. It won't matter, I will see her. As the sun was setting, we were all unsettled by the day's events. One patient after another was brought in by ambulance, by personal carriage, or wandering in on their own. One young boy had drowned in the surf, and after we got a call from the police, Carl went to the beachfront to retrieve his body, but only found his grieving mother.

When Carl returned, he looked windblown and wet and smelled of salt water, as he stood at the entry to the hospital basement under the main stairwell. He was standing in knee-deep water, as was the carriage, and the horse. I was in ankle-deep water standing in the doorway.

"I don't know what's going on, Doug, Princess and I have been sloshing through the sand, the water, it's everywhere. Even Broadway is under water. It's a storm, I think. I'm not going out anymore. I'm going home, my friend."

"Stay here, Carl, help me out. You can't go."

"Doug, the whole island is underwater!"

Rosa's house must be underwater, too. I told Carl to cover for me and then I ran out of the doorway in the direction of her house. She lived at least ten blocks from the hospital. I ran in the knee-deep water just in front of the hospital and as I reached the curb, fell forward off the curb and splashed hard to my knees into the street, deep with murky water. I stood up completely wet with the water forming small waves at my knees. I couldn't run so I just pulled myself across the street. I crossed two streets to get to the high curbs and the sidewalks where the water wasn't as deep. Branches were dipping down in my way from the strong wind.

People were scurrying about, retrieving their soaked young ones who were playing in the street, dragging them home out of the water. Horses were hobbling by, upset with the weather as well. Some carriage drivers had to jump off their seat and pull them down the street.

I kept walking along slowly, block-by-block, then past the alley where I lived. I glanced down the alleyway and saw high water and all sorts of things floating in the alley. My thighs were burning, and my feet were unsure with each step. I couldn't go down my alley now. As the sun was setting, the wind and water made waves in the streets. The water on the sidewalks was now above my knees and water began to enter the houses. This was especially true as I turned the corner onto Rosa's block where the houses were much lower and smaller and close together and close to the sidewalks. The sidewalks weren't elevated with bricks but were just sandy grooves in the grass. I was sinking in a sandy sidewalk as I saw Rosa's house. There was no one outside now on the street as I trudged through the thigh-high water toward her house. I stumbled up the two front porch steps that I couldn't see and pulled open the screen door and pounded on the closed door. There was water in the house.

I pounded again and again. I yelled out for Rosa. Then the door slowly opened. Her father pulled as hard as he could against the water in his home. He had an axe in his other hand.

"Please, *Señor* Lozano, I need to see Rosa, please," I pleaded.

"Get out of here, *muchacho*," he yelled back.

I pushed my way inside and stood with him in knee-high water in the front room. A chair was floating against the wall. He told me in Spanish that she was upstairs. I could hear her mother talking to the baby who was crying. Her father went over to the stairs and yelled, "Rosa, your gringo is here."

Rosa came quickly down the stairs with unbelieving eyes and her hair loose and wet. She stood at the last step above the water in her bare feet and I climbed over the railing. She wore a simple flower print dress with an open neck and hanging around it was the necklace. The dress was wet to her waist. She asked her father if I could come upstairs. He was staring out of the door with the axe in hand and nodded that I could.

She took my hand off the railing and grabbed mine and led me upstairs. Her mother was at the top of the stairs holding Rosa's little brother who was crying. The wind was beating hard against the house, and everyone seemed afraid, but the baby was the only one speaking out. Several candles were lit in the small hallway. The whole house was vibrating and weaving in the wind and every few moments it lifted. I heard muffled cracking sounds downstairs now. Rosa's father was breaking the floor with the axe, to let the water rise through the floor to keep the house from floating off its piers. The small divan from downstairs had been taken upstairs and was placed next to the small table with the candles.

We sat together and Rosa held my other hand, too, and with tears in her eyes said, "Doug, I'm scared, we're all afraid. Do you know what's happening?"

"I don't know, some kind of storm, I don't know how bad it's going to be. The water from the bay has risen all over town. The wind is so strong now it was hard to walk, but I had to come see you."

"You came all this way to see me," she said as she tried to smile. "What's going to happen now? My father says we should wait here for the storm to pass. But I don't know."

"Rosa, I've had to work all day, and I have to work all night, I'm so sorry. The hospital is full, and the patients are starting to panic. This will all pass. I think we'll all be okay."

She reached up and combed my hair with her hands. "Doug, I've never seen you look so bad."

"I've never been so glad to see anybody before, my love."

"Do you really love me?"

"Rosa, I couldn't be happier. I do love you. Do you love me?"

"Yes, Doug, I do."

I was cold and wet, but I felt warm now as I held her. I smiled back to her. The candles were dimming. We were alone in the hallway, so I leaned over to her and kissed her. Our faces were wet. The wind was blowing hard, and the house swayed with the harder gusts. Even the candles inside would flicker with the wind coming in.

"Doug, you have to go back to work?"

"Yes, I have to."

"My father and mother don't want you to stay long now. You should go now."

I felt warmth and love here in this little home. I stood up then pulled her close to me. I held her tight and kissed her again. She wasn't crying now. She took me by the hand and had a candle in the other and we walked down the steps into darkness. She went before me. She knew the number of steps and walked right down them all without hesitating into the water at the bottom. I went before her and led her outside with me. The flame of the candle was gone now. The wind was blowing so hard it was hard to stand together. I reached around her and held on to the door jamb with her in my arms. We swayed together in the heavy wind.

I yelled, "Please take care, Rosa, please. But this all will end soon, it has to. I will come over in the morning and help you clean up."

She yelled back, "You had better go now. We will be all be all right." I couldn't see her, so I felt her face with my free hand.

"I know you will. But please be careful, Rosa, for me."

"1 will, Doug."

As I went to the end of the small porch, I couldn't let go of her hand. She was holding onto the door jam and to me. And as I let go, she said loved me. I said I loved her too. I had never said those words before and really meant it. I stepped off the porch into the water above my waist now. Waves were blowing into me. She went back inside and slowly forced the door shut. I stood still in the water and couldn't move away from the house. The water was pulling hard on my legs now, pushing me away. I felt weak and wanted to crawl back to her house. As I walked away, I looked back, and there was no light coming from the house and it was moving up and down.

I felt whitecaps now breaking over me as I trudged around the last block before the hospital. I climbed into the basement entrance at the front of the hospital and dodged floating crates and baskets. There was no wind in my face now. I felt my way along the wall to the stairwell and finally climbed out of the water. I could see a flicker of candlelight above as I looked up the grand staircase. I hurried up the steps to the third floor. There were more flickers of candlelight as the staff scurried by.

“Where have you been, Doug?” Laura asked after tapping me on the shoulder from behind. She was sweating in the candlelight, but she was dry.

“1 had to check on someone near the hospital. It’s bad out there. What’s happening with the patients?”

“The electricity and the phone lines have gone down. Nurse Willow says that it could be a hurricane. She remembers one like this when she was a girl. But not to worry, these things pass quickly, she said. And this building wouldn’t lose a shingle, even in a hurricane. Douglas, you are soaked completely.”

“Water is up everywhere now, the island must be covered.”

“Come on, you’ve got some big problems with some of the patients.”

I followed her to the east ward but detoured to the linen closet to grab a towel and dry off. I straightened my wild hair and tucked my shirt back in. I felt for my tie, but it had washed away.

The ward was loud. The wind was raging, and the windows rattled hard. Patients were restless, pleading for assistance from the nurses and demanding to see the doctor in charge. It was loudest near the windows, especially the south-facing windows. I went to see the boy, Johnny Losico, with the broken arm. His skin was hot when I touched his forehead; no doubt he had a high fever. Nurse Willow came up behind me, pinched me hard on the back of the arm and forced his chart in my hand and said, “You had better look at his temps for today. That cast has got to come off. It should have come off hours ago, before you left.”

I felt his left arm above his cast, and it was exquisitely tender to the lightest touch. The cast covered most of the humerus with the elbow was at ninety degrees. The shoulder joint was red, tense, and tight. He was crying from the pain, so I held his other hand and told him we would have to take off his cast now.

"No," he cried, "It's not ready, my mom said it wasn't gonna come off 'til next month."

"Johnny, you have to trust me, your arm is broken but now it's infected and it's worse now. When we take off the cast, we'll put another back on later, a better one, you know."

He pleaded, "No, doctor, keep this one, please. You gotta wait for my mother and father."

"'Your mother and father won't be coming to the hospital now; you hear that storm outside? It's a real bad one."

"My father ain't afraid of a storm."

Nurse Willow brought over the cast saw and told the boy to please be quiet. His eyes grew wide in the candlelight.

"Hey now, I know this saw looks bad, but it only cuts off the cast and won't cut your arm."

"You do your arm first then," he said quickly.

"It won't work on me unless I have a cast."

I ran the blade across my palm, and it felt sharp, so I stopped. I glanced at it quickly to make sure it didn't draw blood, and then I showed him my palm. He inspected it very closely in the dim candlelight.

"Come on now, Johnny you see? I have got to do this now."

He shook his head no, but I stood over his bed and began to saw the cast longways starting at the wrist and moving upward. I stopped at the elbow. I then began to saw above the elbow and then he screamed. Was the saw cutting him? There was no blood. Just moving the arm even a fraction was excruciating, so I cut faster. He screamed and begged me to stop. Laura came over to assist me. She held him still and covered his eyes with her sleeve. After one last yell I had the cast cut in two and it came apart like a peanut shell. Johnny pushed her arm away and raised the arm to look at it.

After a few moments, he bravely said, "That feels better."

I looked closely at the arm and could see and then feel a tense, fluctuant area below the elbow. In the middle of it was the laceration that the fractured bone caused, and it was draining green. I told the nurse that I would have to open that up, too. She left to get the surgery tray.

Johnny understood what I said to her and pleaded with me not to. She brought a large bundle of long cotton gauze and as she unwrapped it, she discreetly handed me the long thin scalpel. Johnnie didn't see it.

"Now, Johnny, 1 got to cut that open so it can get better. It's going to hurt, too, but when it heals, you'll have the best-looking scar out of it. Now I need you to be even tougher than you were before. Can you do that?"

He nodded that he could. I rolled him on his side away from me and he grabbed the bed frame with his left hand. I examined the scalpel in the candlelight and it looked recently sharpened. I made a quick and deep incision along the top of the wound and pus came running out. He didn't make a sound, just exhaled hard afterward. She gave me the gauze to soak up the pus, then another in the wound and we wrapped the whole arm with the tail of the gauze. As I held pressure on the arm to soak up the blood, I stared at the window next to us. It vibrated against the wind.

One by one the windows on the south side of both wards began to break. We dove between the patient beds for cover with each shatter. Patients were frantic and those able to move also rolled off their beds. Some screamed with each fracture of window glass, but the screams were mostly inaudible in the face of the howling wind now inside the building. I crawled on the floor from patient to patient feeling their skin for fragments of glass with several pierced deep in their extremities. I removed the glass as quickly as I could and held gauze to the wounds. I grabbed their free hand to hold pressure while I went to the next patient. Laura, Nurse Willow, and I were removing large glass fragments from the beds with our hands and pulling glass out of ourselves, too. Many patients had crawled under the beds. I crawled back to the doorway. The nurses from both wards met in the storerooms and brought out thick blankets to cover the patients from the flying glass.

It wasn't much longer before the windows on the north side of the building began to break. The heavy iron beds were being blown slowly away from the south facing windows, leaving patients even more exposed. Each bed gave out a loud screech as it legs slid in small steps across the pine wood floor. The neat rows of beds were going away, and it was completely dark on the wards. A few beds over from me I saw Laura holding a blanket tightly around a patient and she was yelling for me. I stood up but was blown down, so I stayed down and crawled over to them, pulling bits of glass from my torn knees. It was an older lady who was no longer screaming. I felt no pulse at her carotid artery. I couldn't see if she was breathing.

"What should we do with her?" Laura asked.

I was just a few inches away from her ear and I yelled, "Let's pull her over to the hallway with the rest of them."

The nurse pushed as I pulled and as we both crawled from the ward to the central hallway. We slid her body against the near wall and her head was now sticking out of the blanket. I covered it back up. The patients that could walk had already fled to the central hallway and were huddled there and had shed the wool blankets. Several were holding one another. It was calm in the windowless hallway between the wards, with a few candles flickering. It was here that we felt the hospital moving in the wind.

The wind became stronger. It was so loud and so terrible and so hot. The mist it carried stung our faces and water ran off our clothes as they stuck to us. The wool blankets that protected us were now unbearable to shield us. I stood up in the hallway and went over to Laura and Nurse Willow who were passing water in small glass cups over to the patients huddled together there.

"We've got to everybody off the ward and into the hallway and stairwell, anywhere away from the wind. "

"But some of the patients can't be moved," Nurse Willow yelled.

They had tried to light some lanterns in the hallway, but they had all blown over except one. Laura and I crawled back into the ward and dragged some empty mattresses off the beds back into the hallway. Just then Johnny came running into the hallway barefooted and fell to his knees in pain. I picked him up and placed him on the mattress and felt his feet. I quickly pulled several pointed pieces of glass from each foot. He didn't make a sound. It was so dark. I could only see his face as the candlelight flickered. Could I get everybody out? How many were there, twenty, twenty-five?

I crawled back into the ward and found a pair of shoes under a bed. I took them to Johnny and told them to put them on and to give me a hand. I watched as he carefully slid the oversized shoes over his swollen feet and then carefully stood up. He said he was okay and that he wanted to help, with his entire right arm wrapped tight in gauze. We crawled together back into the ward, Johnny close behind me. I remembered the Stamoulis brothers and where they were on the ward, near the south facing windows, and headed that way. In the face of the wind, I couldn't lift a mattress to act as a windbreak. Most of the beds were completely blown over but the few beds that were standing were empty of their mattress and covered with broken glass. I crawled a little farther toward the window and found Constantine holding his unconscious brother at the outside wall under the windows. He had pulled himself off his bed and pulled Nicholaus to him.

"You've got to get out of here and into the hallway."

"We're not moving."

I reached around Constantine to feel his brother. Nicholaus' skin was warm, and his breath was palpable as I felt his nose and mouth.

"Let me help you, I can help your brother. Come into the hallway. Please, Constantine!"

What was left of the windows was just their tall, rectangular openings. The outside wall of the hospital that the brothers were lying against shook rhythmically, the bricks, the wood, the plaster. How long would it hold together?

I pulled Johnny close to me and told him to grab Nicholaus and help me pull him into the hallway. I felt his right arm and it was still wrapped, but completely wet. With both arms, he and I pulled Nicholaus by the shoulders and Constantine pushed his brother's legs while lying on his side. Constantine would be harder to move. He was heavier and insisted that his brother go first. We all moved along the floor, the four of us, unable to stand up because of the wind. Constantine pulled himself along behind us with just his hands.

There were more crashing sounds. In the windows every bit of glass was blown off. And all the blinds were gone. The floor was completely covered with debris, and it was in our way. Objects were blowing into the ward. They whisked by over my head. Again and again, I felt it. I pushed Johnny's head low. We stayed low and slowly slid Nicholaus into the hallway. I left them and went back to the entrance of the east ward to find Constantine. There I could see, but only faintly, flat dark objects stuck into the wet plaster of the north wall of the wards, like large imbedded oyster shells, but much larger. Constantine was not with us.

Carl came running up the stairwell in a panic and told me how he left the hospital earlier in the ambulance with the water as high as the wheels to go to his apartment but that once near the beach he was forced to turn the horse around because of the waves now breaking over the city. He was floating more than rolling back in the ambulance with Princess herself leading the way back to the hospital. He caught his breath, but then he remembered.

"Doug, the student nurses' house could collapse, we've got to get those girls out of there. It's leaning over bad and halfway off the foundation. Shingles are flying off the roofs."

"And flying in here, they could kill us."

"You have got to help me."

He began running back down the steps. I quickly lost sight of him as he left the barely lit hallway. I went over to Laura and Nurse Willow who were giving water to some of the patients in the hallway.

"We've got to get everybody out, take anyone that can help to make sure all the patients are off the wards. The student nurses' house is collapsing, I'm going there now with Carl."

Laura jumped up and got close to my ear, "Please Doug, that's where I live, my friends are in there."

"Stay here, take care of the patients. We'll get them out."

I left them both and felt my way down the stairs. I have been climbing and descending these steps for years but now they were wet and dark. I circled down from each landing to the very last one and then slammed into Princess standing quietly on the last landing, her wet fur against my face. I wiped my face and descended the steps from the last landing I entered the water. These were large stone steps. At the bottom of the steps, here in the basement, the water was chest high and rising and falling. Waves came in the open basement door and slapped my face.

"Carl...Carl where are you?"

I felt my way along the wall and at the open doorway reached outside when I felt Carl grab my other arm and pulled me back in.

"Doug, I found a rope. I tied it around my waist, Tie the other end to something that'll hold," Carl said as he handed me the rolled-up rope, then moved past me and began to swim out of the door.

I held the rolled-up rope in my arms and moved away from the door back to the steps felt the other end of the rope. I felt along one side of the wall and then the other and didn't feel anything, anything to tie the rope to. I never realized it before but there wasn't a hand railing on this narrow stairwell. I felt the waves pushing me over and sit me down hard on one of the steps. I stood up and leaned over to steady myself against the wall. I reached up with my free hand and felt an iron steam pipe running along the low ceiling of the basement. I should have remembered this pipe. I dodged it daily. I held on to it now.

I was good at handling the rope. I could quickly knot a rope on the horn of my saddle and jump off my horse and corral a loose calf with the other end. Pago, my horse, was the fastest and smartest horse in the stable. That's why the Mexican ranch foreman named him "lightning" in Spanish, Relampago. And as he sprinted, he would shine in the sun from his sweat. We would both sweat in the hot summer sun, working the herd in the open range. He was beautiful. He loved to swim in the cool waters of the Guadalupe River that flowed through our ranch.

I tied the knot quickly onto the iron pipe. I didn't need to see it; it was secure. I waited for a few moments at the foot of the stairs in the basement and pulled again on the rope. The waves crashed through the door and ran up my chest and neck and face, and over my head. I backed up a few more steps. What would I do now? I stared out the dark doorway. Should I go back upstairs? I felt the knot again, and it was fat and tight in my hand. The rope was still slack. I moved out of the basement, out of the water, and made my way to the landing. I felt Princess from her rear, then to her swayed back, and then pulled along her mane until I put my arm around her wet and drippy nose. I felt her warm breath on my neck. I started back upstairs finding each step with my soggy shoes, then running two at a time.

Nurse Willow was holding a lit candle to help me see the top of the steps. She was wet and wind-blown; her normally stiff white nurse's hat was wilting and her hair half down but still together. She was steady, even though the flame of the candle wasn't.

"Dr. Schuler, we can't find several of the patients, and we think they're dead," she yelled in my ear.

I thought of the very sick Irish girl. How could she breathe in a storm?

"Where is Aileen Duffy?"

"She's dead, her body's over there." Nurse Willow said pointing toward the storage room. Other alive patients were huddled in there too.

"Wrap her body up in one of the blankets and put her away from the rest of the patients. You know she had tuberculosis; she still could be contagious."

Nurse Willow looked a little taken back by that; she knew her body was lying with the rest of the patients. I began to go from patient to patient lying in the hallway. The hallway was lit by a few well-protected candles. It was loud and barely lit in the hallway, so it was difficult telling if a patient was alive. It was like a locomotive going by my head at full steam. For those not reaching back to me I yelled in their ear and felt their carotid pulse at the same time. Many were too weak to speak back or if they tried, I couldn't tell. I put the back of my wet hand next to their nose and mouth to feel breathing. I was barely able to feel each breath especially in some of the older patients, none as strong as the horse's.

Some were alive because they were clutching one another, or I could feel them sobbing. In the corner near the doorway was a body not moving. I made my way over to him. It was Nicholaus, still unconscious but I could feel his chest moving. He was warm under his wet clothes. I grabbed his shoulders and shook him. Come on, wake up, I need your help. He still didn't move on his own. And he was lying here alone. Constantine must still be inside the ward. All the patients on the ward were not accounted for. I found Laura sitting with and holding an older lady tightly. She was also trying to keep a candle going in her lap. I bent down toward her.

"Where is Constantine Stamoulis? His brother is still unconscious over there."

"Doug, I don't know where he is," she said, as loud as she could, her wet nursing hat long gone now, and her hair in strands dripping down her face.

I stood back and went back to the doorway to the west ward. All the patients had piled up against one another away from the entrance and out of the wind funneling into the hallway. I went down to my knees and began to crawl out onto the ward again. I crawled lower and felt glass gathering up into my shirt and cutting my chest. I began to spread some of the glass away from me with some parts of the broken blinds. I tried to remember where Constantine was last on the floor. I knew it was close to the windows. I reached that spot, and he wasn't there. I went down the wall under the windows farther and he wasn't there under any of them.

I moved back to the other far wall and that part of the ward was also empty. There were beds piled against one another and as I crawled through them, I felt a body. It was not responding to my hand. It was too loud to call out. I pulled myself close and reached up to the face to feel breath but there was none and no pulse either. I could feel the whiskers of a man, too, who was now dead. I reached down inside his shirt, and I felt a chain with a medal. I remembered the chain and medal around the neck of both Stamoulis brothers, a Greek Orthodox medallion. The medal was round in my hand. It was Constantine. His body lay tangled amidst the bed frames, blinds, glass, and so much debris. I was not able to pull him free. I pulled the chain from around his neck put it my pants pocket. I lay under the debris for a few moments.

Shingles were still flying in the window and embedding into the wet plaster wall. Perhaps one of these had struck Constantine? I crawled back into the hallway and stood up slowly, there were pieces of glass inside my wet clothes. I tried to shake some free as I untucked my shirt. It was like torn rags. I looked down the hallway at the small groups of huddled patients visible only by candlelight. Some were crying but all I heard was the wind.

"Doug, please...what about my friends at our house?" Laura pleaded, holding my forearm tight.

I saw her face, and it was dripping wet, but now from tears. I had to go find Carl, was he back? The student nurses' home was just across the street from the hospital, maybe a hundred feet. It was a simple, two-story building, wooden with a long front entry porch with several wicker chairs on the sides of the door. How many students were in there? As medical students we always walked by the house, hoping to talk with some of the students sitting outside on their time off, but I knew very few of them. The girls were discouraged from socializing with us. The housemother thought of us as irresponsible and growled at us when we dropped by for coffee. She complained to the school dean about our little visits. We worked with student nurses in the hospital. They were not allowed to call us by our first name. Even eye contact while standing facing each other on the other sides of the bed of a sick patient rarely happened.

I went back to the stairs and started back down. The whole hospital was vibrating. I felt it especially on the stairs. I had a lantern with me this time as I descended. Princess was still on the last landing; she seemed calm, her big eyes staring back at me in the candlelight. I stroked her wet mane as I looked down into the stairwell and the water over our feet. I hooked the lantern onto the steam pipe bending upward on the ceiling of the stairwell. The light was still intact somehow. I went down into the water from the top of the landing and with my hand on the pipe and felt my way down to feel the knot in the rope. I couldn't see, but it was still tied tight, and the rope was taut. I held my breath and swam to the doorway feeling the wall as I went. The water forced me back to the stairs and I climbed back to the landing on my knees. I pulled my hair back away from my face, then wiped my face to clear my eyes burning from the salt water. My clothes were clinging to me tightly and my soaked feet were swollen into my shoes. Was Carl alive and what about the nursing students? Were they alive?

I slowly stepped back into the water and took a deep breath and reached the rope and pulled myself out of the doorway of the hospital. I keep pulling and pulling until I couldn't hold my breath any longer. As a wave passed over my head, I took a quick breath and a quick look. I couldn't see anything. As I held tight to the rope the waves rolled over me. I pulled and pulled slowly along the rope. And the waves pushed against me. How far had I come? I pulled and each breath was mixed with salt water.

The waves didn't break my grip. I came to another knot. It was tied to the slick, wooden post on the porch of the nurses' home. I pulled myself up and my feet hit the front steps. I pulled my head up out of the water, but felt the next wave throw me off balance, off this porch. But I grabbed the rope again and pulled myself up over the rail to the porch and then swam across it to the doorway. The smaller waves from inside the house pushed against me but I swam through the doorway. I couldn't see anything as I took a breath. I knew the stairwell was to the right, a few feet away. I felt the bottom step with my shoe and with my hands on the banister pulled myself up the stairs.

Halfway up I was out of the water. I caught my breath. It was completely dark, and I could feel the wind and the rain against my face. I breathed deep without coughing. At the top of the stairs, I wiped my face and peered down the hallway. There were huddled bodies in flickering candlelight. I felt a hand in the darkness grab my arm.

"Doug, you made it. We're all right, we're alive!" Carl yelled in my ear.

"How many are here?"

"There's five of us, four nursing students. We don't have any water, but we have one candle. Do you have a dry match?"

"No, you fool."

I walked down the short hallway and collapsed next to the nursing students. As we huddled in the hallway, the house was moving, really moving, and leaning, leaning hard. There were flickers of candlelight on the ceiling and gaps in the roof. Rain blew and dripped onto us through the roof.

"Carl, we've got to get out of this house. It's going to fall."

"I told you we are all okay, we going to wait it out here."

"No, this house won't stand much longer, we're not safe here."

"Doug, I don't want to move and neither do the girls."

"Carl, can't you feel this house? It's moving hard and it's breaking apart. Look, half the roof is gone."

I was on my knees now and holding his arms. I was close to his face, yet I could barely see him.

My voice was going but I said, "As long as the house is standing, we can use the rope to get back to the hospital. The waves will push us that way. If the house falls, there's no more rope and then we're dead."

"All right...let's go."

"Tell the girls."

I walked back to the top of the stairs. The stairwell was black, the stairs invisible. Carl and the nursing students came over to me.

"Let me go first with one of the girls, then have the other two go together behind me and you bring up the rear with the last one.

Let's hurry," I said.

I could barely see Carl's face and only some of the faces of the students. None was smiling like my friend. I leaned over to the girl next to me.

"What's your name?"

"Victoria, and I can't swim!" she yelled back in my ear.

"Don't worry, just hold on to my neck and don't let go. We'll make it."

I grabbed her hand, and we started down the steps together. The water was half way up the stairwell. We rushed into the water into the darkness. I felt my way along the outside wall and on the last step, the water was chin high. Victoria stood two steps behind and let go of my hand. I reached for her and held her around the waist. She shifted her body to my back and squeezed my neck with both arms. As I stepped off, my face was barely above the water. I felt the wall and reached for the doorway and pulled us out onto the porch. I lunged for the knot on the post and held it tight.

Victoria had a good grip around my neck. I took a deep breath and pulled us over the porch rail with both hands on the rope. The waves were pushing northward, pushing us along. I took a breath when I could. Was Victoria able to take a breath between the waves? She was still holding tight to my neck with both arms. I pulled on the rope, hand over hand. It was about a hundred feet to the hospital. My hands slipped back on the rope, but I pulled. The waves lunged us forward.

Then my head hit the wall of the hospital. I felt it with one hand, and then I pulled my head out of the water and took a breath. Victoria reached up to the wall also and she was gasping and coughing. I shifted to face her. I took another deep breath and with one hand on the rope and the other around her waist, I pulled us both into the doorway of the hospital.

I still had her hand but let go of the rope and we crawled up the stairs together, coughing hard, clearing the salt water from our throats. We lay together quietly on the landing for a moment and then I sat up to see if Victoria was breathing. The lantern above us was still flickering and as she rolled onto her back. I could see that she was still breathing because she was coughing. With both arms, I reached beneath her and picked her and carried her up the stairs, past Princess and the other landings to the third floor.

She had stopped coughing and moving. I lay her down on the floor in the storage room off the hallway in front of Nurse Willow and Laura, under a dim light from a lantern. Laura sat next to her and called her name over and over, but Victoria didn't speak. I kneeled next to her and pushed her hair away from her face. Her mouth was open. I felt her mouth and nose. Her chest was lifting—she was breathing. I moved my hand down from her face and felt her carotid artery. Her pulse was rapid.

"Victoria...Victoria, we made it!" I yelled in her ear.

She opened her eyes and looked up directly into mine and nodded. She smiled a little, then closed her eyes again. I left her and ran back downstairs to the basement and at the last landing I saw two of the nursing students kneeling and holding each other. I asked if they could make up to the wards. The taller one said that they could. They stood up together and began to go up the stairs, arm in arm. They pressed their faces against the horse as they went by.

I did, too. I entered the water from the landing and reached for the rope tied at the steam pipe. I felt the knot and it was still solid. I worked my way back down the rope with my face close to the ceiling to breathe. I reached the doorway and felt the rope as it left the doorway. It was tight and moving from side to side in the doorway and then it felt lax. I pulled on the rope now with one hand and held on to the pipe with the other.

Then I felt a hand grasp the back of mine on the rope. I let go of the pipe to reach out with the other. Carl first and then the nursing student floated in through the doorway and then popped up on the stairs. He was talking and coughing but she wasn't. She was face down in the water. We both pull her along and up the steps to the landing. Carl laid her down on her back and shook her hard by the shoulders. He lightly slapped her face. He yelled her name. She was not breathing. Carl lifted her upper body and slid behind her. I held her by the knees. Several times he squeezed her chest hard against his and finally water shot out of her mouth onto her legs. He laid her back down on her back and placed his mouth on hers and gave her several breaths. He sat her up again and from behind her squeezed her even harder and forced more water out of her mouth. She coughed and moved all her limbs suddenly. Carl let go of her and she leaned forward to take deep breaths and cough more. She slowly sat back against him and started to breathe regularly without water gurgling in her chest. She faced me and looked back at Carl, then slumped forward and started to cry. Carl had his arm around her shoulders and with the other under her legs he lifted her gently.

"As we left the porch it collapsed and the waves moved us to the left, toward the steps. We were pinned there," Carl said.

"I think she's going to be all right now. What's her name?" I could only see their shapes in the dark as we climbed the stairs.

"Vivian," she said.

We reached the third floor and found the others. Nurse Willow and Laura were all attending to the patients in the central hallways and storage rooms. I went to find Victoria and the other students. Victoria was on her knees over the other two nursing students lying in the corner of the storage room under the lantern hanging on the wall. I kneeled next to her. I could see how small she was, the silhouette of her face with her long hair hanging down over the other students. They were all friends and Victoria hugged them both at once. One of them was sobbing.

Victoria told them, "We made it, we made it!"

I touched her back. She looked back at me and said, "I'm fine, I'm okay, really." I could barely hear her even though I was just a few inches away, so I got closer but that was all she said. I sat back on my heels and looked around at all the people in the hallway, everyone huddled closely together. Carl was kneeling over Vivian sitting in the corner. His arm supported her head.

Then I looked down at myself in the dim light. My clothes were shredded. My arms and legs protruded through my shirt and pants, with my elbows and knees bare. I sat back against the wall next to Victoria.

CHAPTER 10

I opened my eyes and looked straight up, straight into Victoria's eyes as she was looking down into mine. I lay on my back with my head in her lap. It was quiet. I could hear quiet conversations next to me. She was stroking my hair and smiling down at me. The sunlight was so bright! The storm had passed.

"Douglas...they told me your name was Douglas. You saved my life, you know."

I didn't know what to say as her long brown hair hung down onto my face. Her hair was a complete mess, but I could see her face well, her light blue eyes. It was hard to look away. But I did and then looked down at myself. I was awful with my torn clothes. Did she take my shoes and socks off? My feet were red, and the bottoms were hurting. She kept stroking my hair. She wiped the sweat from my face.

"Can you hear me?" she asked in a normal voice.

I nodded to her. I tried to sit up but was paralyzed from the pain in my arms and legs. But one by one I moved all my limbs and slowly sat up.

"How long have I been asleep?"

"You collapsed next to me a couple of hours ago. I couldn't wake you. I even slapped you face several times like they taught us to do, but you didn't move. You crawled into my lap, and I didn't have the strength to move you."

"I did?"

"Yes, but I didn't mind."

My head hurt, too. I felt the top of it and there was an open laceration covered with dried blood and my matted hair. Did I hit my head on the steam pipe?

"I cleaned up your scalp, but you will need some sutures, I think. I had to hold pressure to it for a long time."

I could see the dried blood across her skirt and down the front of what was left of my shirt.

"I think there is no tailoring your clothes," she added with a little smile. Her dress was intact and drying.

"I'm sorry my clothes are so torn." I didn't try to cover up as I stood.

After standing, I then felt the sharp pains in the bottoms of my feet. I examined them and there were many small lacerations all across them. I walked down the hallway past the patients most now sitting against the wall and to the east ward. In the ward was Nurse Willow with several orderlies cleaning debris from the floor—a tangled mixture of square slate roofing shingles, broken glass, boards, window blinds, mattresses, and bedsheets and pillows up against the north wall. Many of the metal beds were twisted or broken, many acting as a barrier over the windows. Everything was wet and there were puddles of dirty water on the floor. The orderlies were slowly separating it all, throwing most of the debris that had blown in back outside through the broken windows.

I wanted to find my shoes but only found a pair that looked like mine sitting by themselves in the storage room. I eased them on my feet; they were too small. Conditions on the west ward were similar. It was empty of anybody working and no patients present. I began to look at each patient in the hallway. Most were asleep but all appeared to be alive. Aileen Duffy was dead, though.

At one end of the hallway Carl was attending to Vivian. He was sitting next to her and holding her upper body across his lap. She was asleep but breathing rapidly and wheezing. I saw Victoria now attending to the boy, Johnny Losico. He was asleep, curled up in a ball in the corner.

"How's Johnny doing, Victoria?"

"He is in a lot of pain. He begged me to take off his shoes, his feet were cut up and terribly swollen. I didn't have anything to wrap his feet with. I didn't want to use the wrap on his arm. So, I just rewrapped his broken arm. He finally fell asleep now. Is there any morphine I can give him?" Victoria asked.

"I don't think so, all the medications are probably ruined."

"I'll find something to wrap his feet and to rewrap his arm."

"Everything is wet but use it anyway," I said as I turned to walk away.

"Douglas, are you leaving the floor? Maybe there are some supplies on the other floors?"

"I have to go; I will be back soon," I said. She looked away as I walked down the steps to the front door of the hospital off the second floor. The large wooden double doors had held during the storm. I wedged open one of them and stepped out on the landing.

What I saw I didn't recognize. All the buildings and the homes in front of the hospital were gone. There were large piles of debris, boards on top of boards piled high against the south wall of the hospital and on the lower front steps. The student nurses' home was completely gone. There were empty blocks covered with debris all the way toward the beach. Nearly everything was now leveled, everything that was familiar. Some homes off in the distance were partially intact lying sideways on the ground with their chimneys gone. All the fences that separated each home were gone. Between piles of debris stood large puddles of water. The streets and the land between them were all covered equally in a sea of debris. There were larger debris piles almost as a wall several blocks away. There were no people, no one walking about, no one looking through the wreckage. There were no sounds. Seagulls were moving overhead.

As I climbed over the debris lying over the lower steps, I found space on the ground to walk. Next to the hospital was the intact Medical Department building but with its spires blown off and all its windows broken. I kept walking westward and after several blocks could see large homes were standing and mostly intact, not too severely damaged, though all their windows were broken. Some were leaning a little off their piers. All the trees around them were uprooted and wedged against the iron fences except for several tall palm trees here and there. All of the sidewalks were covered with debris but seemed to be intact. As I walked closer to downtown most of the buildings were intact. There were a few dead horses still tied to their upside-down carriages.

Down the block toward Rosa's house the homes were less intact or gone. Some had just one wall left. After several more blocks, I couldn't tell—was this her street? On her block, almost all the houses were gone, nothing was left. I stepped over a layer of boards and poking out between them in the distance was the large palm. It was the one that stood next to her front porch. But her house was completely gone, as were all the other houses on the block and the blocks further south. There was only the bare ground where her house was. Even the small brick and mortar piers that supported her house were gone. As I got closer, there was nothing left, no windows, no furniture, no stove, no beds, nothing and no one.

It was Sunday morning and completely quiet, no wind, no people, no dogs barking. There were no babies crying, no little boys running in the street, and no church bells. Every Sunday morning each church in the neighborhoods across town took their turn ringing their bells. It would go on all morning for nearly every hour. At times, there was more than one ringing, as if competing for members, all within a few blocks of each other.

I turned back and headed westward again toward downtown, where there had to be people. But I wasn't walking in a straight line as the streets were laid out. Everywhere were large piles of debris to walk around. Much of the time I couldn't find a path around or through, so I climbed over it. There was one debris pile up against a large home. The home was leaning hard northward and off its piers but intact. The front porch was gone. The large cistern in the back of the house was on its side and partially collapsed. Under my feet were boards that had been torn off the sides of houses and piled in layers up the sides of homes. I could see exposed nails on the ends of each board. As several boards slid away from under my shoes, I saw an arm and hand of a small baby. I pulled several more boards away. She faced upward with her eyes closed in a small wet tan dress with lace along the edges. There was sand in her golden hair. There was a small gold ring on her finger. I moved some boards away and lifted her free, but she was cold and limp and not breathing.

What was her name? Where was her mother, her older brothers and sisters? What should I do with her? I looked around and didn't see anybody, no mother searching for her. The sun blazed against my head; there were no clouds. I gently put her back on the boards and moved some to cover her again to shade her from the sun. I crossed her arms across her body.

I slid down this debris pile and went around the corner and back to Market Street to head westward toward downtown. As I stayed in the middle of the street, near the larger homes on either side, it was passable. After several more blocks, I saw people slowly emerging from their homes. Some of the larger homes had debris in their yards piled up the sides of the houses and their wrought iron fences. And in between were large puddles of sandy water. The large buildings downtown had less debris against them, but all of their windows were gone. The streets were clear and people were walking up and down them and collecting on corners and on doorways of businesses.

Most seemed lost, lost and paralyzed into inaction, holding each other in disbelief. A man ran up and down one of the wide sidewalks wailing about the loss of his entire family. Perhaps he worked late yesterday evening and couldn't get home to help his family. He fell to his knees sobbing. A woman nearby wandered up the street next to me and was crying and holding her head in her hands. Another woman crossed in front of me to grab and hold that woman. Two young boys held hands and walked together in the street yelling for their father.

People were looking for each other and for water. The large water cisterns outside their homes were probably the first to go, smashing like a melon against a nearby home. They entered buildings in search of water to drink. Some businesses had potable water and brought barrels of it to the sidewalks under the canopy. People didn't use the water to wash the salt and sand off their faces, but they drank as much as they could. With their ripped clothes they had clung to floating debris in the churning sea that had covered the island, many with severe lacerations over their bodies. But they were alive, unlike the person that they couldn't hold on to any longer during the height of the storm, their child or their friend or their wife. A few had torn ropes tied around their waists.

As I rounded the corner at 22nd and Market I saw the Tremont Hotel with large crowds of people mingling together. Many men were tightly grouped together arguing loudly. It was chaos even among these important men. In a nearby building, a warehouse, someone had painted on a large board "Morgue #2." And a flatbed hand cart pushed by several men moved slowly toward it with a least six bodies, three on top of three. The men pushed hard across the sandy street and up the small ramp and through the door of the warehouse. I had not seen any horses alive that could have pulled the cart. I waited my turn to go inside and there was no wind, no breeze at all.

I went inside after the cart and saw that the large open floor that normally had hundreds of bales of cotton stacked high now was nearly completely covered with bodies, side by side in long rows. The men were unloading the cart and carrying each body down the rows looking for an available space one the floor. There were bodies of all ages lying together, most with shredded clothes and no shoes and with bloodied, swollen faces. And there were children and babies. The building had few windows near the ceiling that let in just a little light, and at midmorning it already felt like an oven.

Could Rosa be here? If I found her, then most likely the whole family had died. Her father would not have separated them during the storm. I didn't search. Some were slowly walking down the rows and then bending close toward a body, squinting through their sandy glasses in this dimly lit room. I didn't search. There were probably fifty bodies here, maybe sixty. I had to get out. How many other morgues were there, at least two? Hundreds must have died in the storm.

I stood in the middle of the street and two more carts loaded with as many as nine bodies each rolled passed me, heading toward the entrance, three more bodies on top now. Each cart was pushed by three Black men, all with clothes in tatters and none wearing shoes. One white man stood by in front of both carts, yelling at the men to hurry. He was wearing a broad straw hat and smoking a cigar. He had a pistol in a holster on his belt. His clothes were intact and clean, and he was wearing shoes. I crossed the street and noticed several other well-dressed men approaching him to confer with him. I left Market Street and walked between the buildings on 22nd Street toward Strand Street two blocks away.

The Strand was full of people, people crossing each other on the street and entering and leaving the crowded sidewalks with their high red brick curbs still covered with sturdy balconies. The Strand was one block from the bay. People also had to walk around the many small boats in the middle of the street and some were up against buildings blocking their entrance. Most were too big to be moved by a man. I looked toward the bay as I crossed 23rd Street and there were entire ships lying on their sides one next to the other on the wharves with their long masts extending outward in different directions and some piercing the backs of the buildings on the Strand. One large steamship on its side blocked 23rd Street, its deck fully visible to me. It didn't appear damaged, the supra structure was intact, and its large white smokestack pointed back toward me. I walked under it.

Most of the buildings downtown were intact except for their windows. Glass was everywhere on the street but not much other debris was blocking the way through. Roofs were damaged, as rays of light projected inside the buildings. The water line on all the brick buildings was over ten feet, at least. I walked up the Strand to the Hutchings-Sealy Bank building on the corner of 24th Street. Its beautiful carved stone façade was untouched by the storm. There were uniformed guards outside of both entrances. Each one stood next to its pink granite pillars with rifles drawn.

The Strand stopped at 25th Street where the large Union Passenger Station building stood and behind it was where all entering passengers would disembark. It was where I first arrived in Galveston and where I first marveled at this busy intersection, with the Strand and its magnificent buildings, and its electric trolleys heading up and down. There were no trolleys today, except the one that was lying on its side. Across from the bank building was a large warehouse building with a sign at the entrance, "Morgue #1." Several carts with bodies slowly plied their way toward it, down 25th Street. This street was where the mule trollies went up and back to the beach, taking recently disembarked train travelers to the see the Gulf, their first request upon arrival. But there were no mules or horses around. Manpower was the only power.

I stood to the side of the entrance while the carts entered the building by ramps. After the bodies of the first cart were unloaded, I squeezed around it and went inside. Like the other morgue, Morgue #1 was covered wall to wall in rows of bodies, but it was much larger. I walked quietly down one of the rows next to the bodies placed so tightly together, side by side. There were few windows in this building as well. I couldn't see the end of the rows, but my eyes adjusted as I went farther. All the bodies were placed on their backs, limp like dolls. They had all drowned at the same time just a few hours ago. They were all living a few hours before that. Just like the other morgue, most were without shoes and their clothes shredded. There were so many children. I walked down one long row slowly to the back of the building and back down another, female and male together, the old and the young, Black lying next to white lying next to a Mexican, next to whatever race next to whatever age, all united in the same death. All were represented but the rich. Money bought them protection in their well-built, elevated brick homes.

I didn't see Rosa or anybody else that I knew. I couldn't look anymore; my head was spinning. Other people entered the building to look for their loved ones. Some sobbed at the sad realization of finding the one they were looking for. But most did not find the one they had lost. There were simply too many bodies to look through. I left the building as quickly as I could. The air outside was as awful as it was inside.

There were many more bodies being carried toward the morgue, many on makeshift stretchers like a door that was found in the debris. How could I find her among so many dead? Perhaps just as many were washed out into the bay with the waves covering the island or drawn back into the sea as the water recoiled with the passing of the storm. I left the morgue and began walking down 25th Street toward the beach. After I crossed Broadway, the monument there was standing perfectly with wood debris piled up against its base. I climbed up the debris to the base and from here I could begin to see the complete devastation of the island. Walls of debris running east and west off in the distance, some as high as twenty-five feet, including parts of homes, their exterior and interior parts, forming a continuous barrier to the beach.

I slid back down to the street and walked as best I could east down Broadway between the mansions in the esplanade now without the large oak trees, and the wall of debris behind the south side facing homes. This wall was layered with so much debris of all kinds, but primarily boards from siding that had been torn apart and churned by the waves that had covered the island. There were doors off their doorjambs, tabletops without their legs, shutters without their windows. Nearly all these were from simple wood frame homes south of Broadway. All the debris separated from other debris during the storm and churned in the waves and then laid flat as it had floated into place, forming the high wall.

This long wall was nearly impossible to cross, but many people were trying, desperate to go back to where their home was. They tumbled back toward the debris-covered streets and yards as there was no gap in the wall, no path through it. People were pulling separated boards from the piles and peaking underneath, using ropes and poles and anything they could find that could begin to lift away the boards. They knew that there were many bodies under the debris.

I saw a gap in the top of the debris wall and climbed up slowly into it. The boards were loose and sliding under my feet. I pulled my shoes off the nails from the ends of the boards as I climbed. I saw beyond the debris wall to the south side of the island to the beach; it was completely without homes, just the debris lying flat and covering the south side of the island to the beach. It was a sea of wooden debris. Normal street patterns were gone. Occasional homes and parts of homes were punctuating the sea of wood. I slid back down to the street and saw that the mansions on Broadway were unharmed because they were made of brick and stone. The wooden debris was piled up against their wrought iron fences but little had gone over into the yards. It was as if the large wooden debris wall that was running parallel to the beach had acted like a storm barrier for these mansions and the buildings downtown.

I had to get back to the hospital. I was thirsty. I left Broadway at 23rd Street and walked down to Church Street to the Tremont House Hotel. It was only four blocks to the hotel, but it took me most of an hour to reach it, over and around large piles of debris. There were large puddles of seawater between the debris. Things were clearer in front of the hotel. There was a large crowd of people surrounding the hotel entrance. The high curbs around the hotel were clear and dry. As I walked through the blown-out entrance, it was obvious that water had entered the hotel lobby during the storm. The long white window drapes were still wet up to about ten feet.

Large groups of men congregated inside the hotel. These men were sitting on cane chairs in the lobby, as much of the wet furniture was moved to the side and stacked. The men were clean and dry with intact clothes, ties on pressed shirts, and straw hats in their hands. Their heads of hair were neatly combed.

I walked around them and got in line by the kitchen where employees handed out crackers and bread. There was always plenty of food at the hotel, much of it, the best of the best, imported foods and spices from all over the world, the finest cured meats, caviar, sardines, delicate snails sealed in tins, and bottles of champagne for the Mardi Gras balls. The wealthy people of Galveston were used to the best. I got crusty bread and a tall glass of water ladled from a wooden barrel. The men in the lobby began to leave and once outside gave instructions to the other men waiting near the entrance, the men with the pistols. Then they left the hotel entrance, stepping down off the high curb under the balconies into different directions.

I left, too, through the crowds on the sidewalk, to find a way back to the hospital. How was I going to find Rosa? I'm sure that she and her family made it out of the house during the storm and found refuge in another home, one made of brick. Maybe she and her father were looking for bread and water, too.

CHAPTER 11

The Strand was crowded now. People moved about with urgency. People were frantic, frantic to find their survivors, but they gradually faced the reality that their family members probably were not one of them. Others weren't moving, just frozen, lost, and didn't know what to do or where to look. They sat down on the street curbs with their bare feet in large puddles of seawater in the street and their heads in their hands. Everybody in Galveston had lost someone. There was no one to console the desperate because all were desperate.

I walked east to the hospital and passed a woman on her knees atop a pile of wood debris, searching, lifting one board at a time. She was alone, sobbing and her clothes were in shreds. I helped her for a while, but we didn't find her daughter. She had been holding her hand in the water after their house collapsed when the roof blew off and she had been pinned under some debris next to a brick smokestack at a nearby house after the water receded, she said. But her daughter was not here. I didn't have the heart to tell her that. I left her digging through the pile. She didn't notice when I walked away, she just kept talking.

At 12th Street and the wharf, a crowd gathered at a barge that was docked there. It was a long, flat metal barge with men walking on board and off again across a wide wooden ramp. I walked closer to the wharf and could see hand carts with bodies pushed up the ramps by groups of men. Other groups of men on the barges unloaded the carts and stacked the bodies in the bow of the barge. Several carts were in line in front of the ramp loaded with bodies and others were slowly arriving. And there was a large flat cart, fully loaded and pulled by a two-horse team. There must have been twenty bodies on it.

I felt myself pushed to the ground and as I turned to look back and up, there was a man standing over me pointing a pistol in my face.

"Get up," he said

"Why did you do that?" I said, as I stood up.

"Get behind that cart over there with that Negro and push it up onto the barge."

"Wait, I can't. I'm a doctor and I need to report back to the hospital. That's where I was going when you pushed me."

"Did you hear me? I don't care who you are, get behind that cart and push!" he said, as he pointed the pistol between my eyes.

I backed away and went to the cart and stood next to the black man, and we pushed the two wheeled cart slowly up the ramp onto the barge. I couldn't see where we were pushing it due to the bodies stacked in front of me. There must have been six bodies on this cart. We pushed it near to the men who were unloading the bodies at the front of the barge. They grabbed a body by the feet and shoulders and swung it on the pile. The bodies were stacked on top of one another, eight to ten deep and they were going to be dumped at sea.

After the cart was unloaded, we turned the cart around and headed back to the ramp. After going down we were met by another man with a pistol who told us to follow him. He held the pistol by his side and walked next to me.

"I can't do this, sir. I have got to be back at the hospital. I'm a doctor there, they're expecting me. Please sir!"

"Shut up and push or I'll shoot you dead." He said as he moved behind me.

I could feel the pistol now at the back of my head. I stopped the cart and stood straight and turned and looked directly at him. Before I could speak, he struck me across the forehead with the pistol butt and I fell to the ground. He stood over me and grabbed me by what was left of my ripped shirt and pulled me up with both hands. He was wearing a metal badge on his shirt that was stamped "Sheriff."

"What's your name ... doctor?"

"My name is Douglas, Douglas Schuler. I'm at the John Sealy Hospital."

I stood as straight as I could. I was a little taller than he was. He looked back at me with light blue eyes that didn't move.

"Well, doc, I told you to push the cart!" he said as he shoved me back next to the black man at the cart.

I fell headfirst against the cart, and landed on my knees before it, with my face in my hands with my hands full of blood. I felt the laceration on the top of my head, it had reopened. The skull bone in the laceration felt smooth, though. I ripped off what was left of my left sleeve and put pressure against it, as I pushed with the other hand. The scalp took forever to stop bleeding.

After about 10 minutes of pushing, the sheriff reached down and ripped off the sleeve of the black man and told him, "Tie the clothe around his head."

He did and I thanked him. Then the sheriff told us to shut up and push. Without the bodies on the cart I could see where we were going. There was a path in a gap between the debris as we were headed back to the Strand. Other carts laden with bodies came slowly toward that gap. All the carts were accompanied by a man with a pistol, the ones I had seen at the hotel. They all had their pistols in their hands and yelled frequently at the men pushing the carts. They would lead the carts around the debris and through large puddles of seawater by waving their pistols in the air. Where we were going? We pushed the cart for blocks back to the large wall of debris on Broadway, then waited in line behind other empty carts. There were crews of men sifting through the debris and pulling out the bodies from the wall.

It didn't matter who they found, young or old, large or small, male or female they were all handled the same, lifted to the cart by two men and stacked with their feet towards the back of the cart. Babies were tucked in between adults. Several men inspected each body on the cart before another was stacked on top of it. They were looking for jewelry of any kind that they then removed and placed in a large wooden box on the ground. They struggled to get the rings off fingers, as all hands of the dead were swollen. They had knives to cut the fingers off the bodies to get to the rings. The bodies were stiff now from rigor mortis and easier to move, and their cut off fingers didn't bleed because the blood in their bodies had coagulated. There was no blood on their knives.

"Why are they taking off the jewelry," I asked the black man next to me.

"I don't know. I heard it's so the bodies can be identified. Or anything left could be given to the families."

"Why aren't they taking the bodies to the morgues first? There might be families there looking for the bodies?"

"There are just too many bodies, ... thousands I bet."

I felt my head and the bleeding had stopped. I didn't want to remove the bandage to disturb the clot. My head pounded and I saw double again. But I wasn't vomiting, so no bleeding within the skull hopefully. They loaded more bodies onto our cart. One of the bodies, a small young woman, rolled off the cart. I walked around to the side to pick up the body.

"If I see you stoop down over that body I am going to shoot you!" the sheriff said.

I stood back up, "I was going to pick her up and put her back on the cart."

"You want to steal that necklace she has, don't you?"

I looked back and saw a bright silver necklace around her neck. Her long hair was completely covering her face and part of the necklace. He yelled for one of the men to come and get the necklace. A man came over and ripped the necklace from around her neck and threw it into the box.

He looked back at me, "Get back to the back of the cart."

As I walked back I saw other empty carts waiting down that long wall of debris behind us. Maybe thousands have died? The black man was leaning against the metal rail that we were pushing and was quiet and looking down to the ground.

"Did your family make it?" I asked.

"I don't know. I was working late at the jute factory downtown and couldn't get back home to my family in time. The water was way up in our building. It came so fast. My house was a small house on the other side of that wall. I know the house is gone. It wasn't much of a house. I hope my family didn't stay in it. But from what I can see there is not a house on the other side of that wall that made it."

"How many children do you have?"

"Three children. Two boys and a girl. My girl is only a year old. I think they are all gone and I am stuck here pushing this cart," He said with tears running down his face.

"Don't give up on them. Maybe we can get off this cart somehow. What's your name?"

"Elijah."

"My name is Doug." He reached out and shook my hand. Ours hands were hurting. His hands were thick and callused. Mine were soft and blistered. He had done most of the pushing. Our cart was now loaded so we walked the cart sideways together to begin the journey back. I was so exhausted. We were given some water out of a barrel before we left. I looked back as we pushed and could see the sheriff talking to other sheriffs. I couldn't clearly hear what they were saying but I heard "martial law" several times and that the last morgue, the fourth, was filling up.

As we pushed the cart through the streets downtown, people didn't stare at the bodies on the cart. We were not stopped by anybody who was searching. I could hear the sheriff behind me screaming at us to go left or right as we slowly rolled across town, block after block. Nearer to the barge there was more debris and it was harder going. We stopped when we heard a gunshot. I saw a sheriff standing over a dead man near the large window of a business. The man was caught looting.

It took us a long time to get back to the wharf. As we got near the barge, we waited behind other fully loaded carts with their pushers and we rested a bit. The barge was filling with bodies, more than half full now.

I said to the sheriff, "Are they weighing down those bodies?"

He ignored me, but then walked over to several other men with guns, interrupting their conversation and pointed at the workers on the barge.

I turned to Elijah, "Dead bodies are going to float. They don't know that. A drowned body even with lungs full of seawater would still float."

"There is no number of morgues that can hold all these bodies. Maybe there are more dead than alive looking for them. They're gonna have to start burning them, not putting them in warehouses or carrying them around town on carts," Elijah said, as we kneeled on one knee and leaned against the rail of the cart.

The sheriff came walking past me and I told him, "The bodies are going to have to be burned and soon. Disease will be here if you leave the bodies decomposing in the morgues."

"Get your cart moving up the ramp now, ... doc." He said as he turned and stared at me, then spit on my shoes.

My shoes were ripped and wet and sandy and I couldn't feel my feet, they didn't hurt anymore. We pushed the cart slowly up the ramp to the workers unloading the bodies. Some of the men were tying burlap bags of sand around the feet of some of the dead. We slowly slid each body off our cart and swung him or her to form a pile. I couldn't look at their swollen faces. Over the bay, the masts of hundreds of capsized boats stood above the water, pointed in different directions. A small tugboat slowly steamed along between them towing another barge toward us.

"That's not gonna do it," Elijah said looking at the sand bags.

"I've got to get out of here."

"Don't try it man. They won't think twice about shooting you. And nobody is going to ask any questions about why an innocent man was shot today."

We reversed our cart back down the ramp and the sheriff left the others and stood behind us again. The large horse drawn cart returned laden with even more bodies. The sheriff pushed us as we pushed our cart back across town to Broadway to the large wall of bodies and debris. We loaded again and headed back to the wharf to begin loading the second barge. We pushed hard the rest of the day making several more trips to the wall and back. If we saw a body along the way we didn't stop to pick it up. Elijah said that if the sheriff saw you stooping over a body he may shoot you for looting the body. So we didn't stop for anyone alive or dead. People were still everywhere, searching frantically but seemingly not finding who they were looking for. The storm had killed them and washed them away from where they lived, even off the island.

It was getting dark now, and we were allowed to rest at the wharf after unloading. A third barge was loaded and ready to be towed, the other two already taken out to sea. The second tug and barge I saw far off in the harbor, slowly steaming eastward. The tug puffed a dark black cloud, the only cloud in the sky. This last barge was full, maybe with 300 bodies. There were now a dozen or so of us "porters" sitting at the water's edge. We were given some food and water. The food was dried fish out of barrel from a ship that was looted, Elijah said. It smelled awful but we ate it. I used some of the water to wash my scalp a little, after removing the crusty sleeve.

We were commanded to all stand and form a line and march back downtown. All the carts were left at the wharf. The sheriff wasn't around now, but several of his deputies were in charge of us. I pleaded my case again, to be able to leave but they didn't listen. We walked slowly as the sun set over the bay, sending pink and purple strands of light over us. Seagulls were everywhere overhead, loud hungry survivors of the storm. We felt a little sea breeze as we walked.

In the last twenty-four hours my life had drastically changed, and Elijah's too. My hands were blistered and my feet were throbbing. With the sun setting what would happen tonight in the city? It was going to be really dark and really quiet.

We were all led to a large square brick building on the water side of the Strand, and then around to the back where there were several boats up against the back of the building. We were told to all move one of them that had landed on a concrete ramp leading to a large metal door. With all of us pulling, we slid the boat away and down the ramp. It spilled seawater as it rolled over. A deputy opened the door and with his pistol he pointed the way and we all walked in. Several others with pistols had gathered as we moved the boat and had unlit lanterns and entered after us. We all saw large bales of cotton stacked high before us. The lanterns were lit and we were led around to an open area with benches. We were surrounded by the large bales, stacked high to the ceiling. One of the men told us all not to try to leave, that we were still on duty and would resume our work in the morning. Several of us pleaded with the men, but we were told that we would be shot if we tried to leave.

The men put back their pistols and left us with a small barrel of water and a single lantern for the night. I heard the heavy metal door shut slowly close and then locked. We all sat on or around the benches.

Elijah stood and walked around with the lantern held up and said, "All these bales have been ruined by the seawater, they're soaked through. There's going to be some angry men losing a lot of money over this ruined cotton."

"Do you think it will burn?" I asked.

"No, it won't burn. Do you see the jute wrap on each bale, that's what we make in the factory. That jute comes in on a ship from India and we weave it and shape it for each bale. When it dries it will burn."

"I wish I had a match."

"Shut up and get some sleep. We'll be back at it tomorrow."

Expanding wet cotton caused many of the jute wraps to pull away from the bales and the cotton spilled out. It looked like snow at our feet. Many of the other men were quiet, not saying much to each other. Then as the evening passed, they spoke out angrily, then tearfully, then quiet again. None of us wanted to share stories about a loved one who was missing. We were numb and tired and now mute. What we had seen today was too much to speak about to anymore.

But it was dark now and we were here, captive and it was quiet outside. The city had stopped searching for the night, but my mind still searched. The babies were the easiest to load and carry. I carried one in my arms today. Before I put her on the pile with the others, I looked at her face. Her eyes were closed. She was at peace, but I wasn't.

CHAPTER 12

"Elijah, I've got to get out of here."

"No, Doug," Elijah said without moving, asleep on his back on a bench.

"I was thinking about what you said about the jute on the bales. Let's get some off the bales and tie them together."

"If you try to burn the jute, we will all die."

"No, not burn it but use it to make a rope to climb out of here. There is a moon tonight and I can see the windows at the top of the walls, right above us, we could climb out. We can't climb on the bales, I tried already."

He moved his head toward me and then slowly sat up and looked up. About twenty feet high was the ceiling and there was a small, closed window at the top of the wall. Above the window were iron girders in the ceiling that ran the width of the building.

"I'm not gonna do it, but I'll help you," he said.

We pulled hard on the jute bale covers around us and slipped them off the bales. We tied the ends together forming a long rope. Looking around, we found a metal bale hook that we tied to one end.

I held the bale hook in one hand and the rope in the other. Elijah stood back near the others who were still asleep. I threw it toward the ceiling girder, but it didn't catch. It landed without a sound in the piles of wet cotton. After several times, the hook hit the ceiling and moved across the girder and swung down next to the rope. I pulled on the rope so that the hook would catch the girder.

Elijah came up next to me and was smiling. "Man, you are a cowboy! I didn't believe you. I thought that hook was going to kill you or me."

"I didn't miss too many times."

Elijah walked back to the benches where all the other men were still asleep.

"Go ahead, don't worry about the jute, it will hold you. What are you going to do outside?"

"I've got to get back to the hospital. I've got to try to find my girl, too."

"I don't how you will ever find her. Don't look at the morgues anymore, look down by where her house was. Maybe she could find you at the hospital if she is still alive." Maybe she could find me?

"Doug, once you get to top, pull the rope through the window and let yourself down the outside wall. Look out, there may be a guard posted at the door."

I tested the rope and it felt strong. I pulled myself up the rope, walking with my feet up over the cotton and then to the exposed wall.

"Be careful, they will shoot you on sight."

I still couldn't feel my feet. I grabbed the hook at the girder with one hand and let go of the rope and pushed open the small window. It was heavy glass reinforced with wire and had not broken in the storm. With my legs holding my place on the rope, I was lying on the open windowsill and looked outside. In the moonlight I could see down the wall and toward the door. There was no one there. I put all my weight on the window and fed the rope through the window. After it was completely out, I leaned out of the window grabbed it with both hands and swung the rest of me through the window and onto the rope. Elijah was right about the strength of the jute. I held my place with my feet and legs and looked around again. There was nobody around in either direction. I slowly let my myself down the rope to the wood debris piled up against the building. I climbed down and then slid down the debris to a patch of grass. I ducked under the keel of a sailing boat that lay on its side in the grass. There was no guard.

There was a small way through the debris from the back of the building to the street. What street I was walking down? The buildings along the street were visible in the moonlight. I found the high curbs of the Strand. I walked east down the Strand slowly, the other direction from the morgue, and didn't see a soul. Each building was dark and open and quiet. The downtown was usually loud with music and people from the taverns downtown, and the horse's hooves, the carriage wheels, and the street vendors calling out. Even a few electric trolleys ran late. But tonight it was quiet, not a sound.

Every window in the entire city had lost its glass. The tall gas lanterns were dark, the ones still standing, that is. Some were lying in the middle of the street and each one had lost the glass in its light chamber. As I made my way back to the hospital, the darkness was broken in a few buildings where a lantern was lit toward the back, and I could make out a few people huddled around it. They were guarding against looters. I didn't want to be taken for one of them, so I walked quietly in the middle of the street, broken glass cracking under what was left of the soles of my shoes. There was no one behind me.

I left the downtown and continued east toward the hospital. Even in the moonlight I couldn't tell what street I was crossing. The moonlight cast unfamiliar shadows over the debris. There was less glass in the streets, but the debris piles were higher in the blocks without homes. I turned back south to find Rosa's neighborhood but after several blocks I couldn't tell if I was in it or had crossed it. It was a cloudless night, and the stars covered the dark sky. I quietly wandered between mounds of boards lying across one another and between puddles of water. The streets were made of red bricks, but most were covered with sand now. I wandered alone. There was an occasionally lantern rocking off in the distance as if someone was carrying it as they walked. But it would disappear quickly as we both moved around more debris piled high. I found what I thought was her block as it was empty of homes, homes destroyed and then washed away.

Where I stood seemed to be that block. I walked over the curb and kept walking within it until I found the lone palm tree, the one we sat under, next to her front porch. It appeared to be completely unharmed. There was a slight sea breeze now and its fronds were moving slightly, casting a shadow on the empty ground that was her house. I walked over to the sand that was the house. It wasn't even the same sand. I sat down in the new sand and took my shoes off. I felt for any pieces of glass left in my feet. They felt better as I shuffled them in the cool, wet sand.

I walked back to the palm and sat in the small patch of exposed grass with my back against its large round trunk. I reached up and felt its rough skin on my sore hands. I looked straight up and could see that it was not broken, not even bent, even a little. It was standing completely straight pointing toward the stars like the mast of a ship that would not be broken. What seemed to be weaker than the many oak trees before the storm was still standing when they were not. I put my shoes next to my leg. I crossed my hands across my lap and felt my stiff, salt-soaked clothes in tatters. I rested my head against the palm and closed my eyes and felt the warm breeze drying the sweat on my face.

Rosa walks with me through the sand, our feet bare. She laughs with me in the bright sunlight, her long dark hair blowing across her face in the warm breeze. As she kicks sand on me, she falls backward laughing. I sit down next to her and brush the sand off her foot. She runs her fingers through my hair.

I woke and looked around, adjusting my vision to the bright sunlight. I could see and hear many people walking about me, some working together in lines to orderly move debris to clear a path. And some dug in the debris alone, haphazardly. I bent my stiff legs and reached for my shoes, but they were gone. I stood up and got a better look at all the people and then at myself, my clothes. My ripped white shirt had lost most of the buttons and was dirty and gray. I tucked it into my pants. My ripped black pants had ripped through to the end of the pant legs from the knee and they were gray, too. My knees and elbows were scraped and exposed, and my feet were swollen and cut. I rubbed the bottoms of my feet, one at a time, and didn't feel any glass.

I left the palm tree and walked back toward the hospital the usual way from Rosa's house. I was walking over the boards covering the streets and through the water puddles with sand oozing between my toes. After several blocks of nothing but debris, there were more homes intact and less debris. Many were not destroyed but were fixable and only a little sideways. They had shifted on their foundations. As I passed the entrances to the alleys, many of the homes there had collapsed or were gone. Most alleys were blocked by their remnants. Though I couldn't clearly see them, I found an elevated sidewalk in the neighborhood. Some debris was against the larger homes but had not pierced them and all windows of these homes were broken. People were entering and leaving their homes. I could smell wood fires burning in stoves inside. I didn't hear any chickens clucking or dogs barking. At one home, I saw a horse standing in the front yard tied to the iron fence. The horse must have been on the front porch during the storm or even in the house with the family. The storm-water line on every house was the same, higher than the front porches.

I kept walking east but wasn't sure where I was again. My bare feet throbbed with each step. Many trees were down and across the sidewalks too, and it was difficult to find a way around or under branches. Some large oak trees were unbroken and leaning all the way down to the curb and were stripped of their leaves. After walking around a tree in the middle of the street, I could see the large, bright red brick home on the corner. It was the Landes home, standing straight and proud except for a few broken windows on the first floor, and with its large black wrought iron porches with all their paint. Some well-clothed persons were standing on the front porch and others were walking into and out of the home. Several of the servants were sweeping the glass off the porch after bringing water in large flowered, ceramic pitchers to the people on the porch sitting in white wicker chairs.

I entered through the open iron gates and walked up the sidewalk, which had been cleared to the front porch. I walked up the tile-covered steps and stood on the top step. and the tiles felt warm and smooth under my feet. The whole porch was inlaid with mosaic tile. People were going in and out of the house. I followed an older woman in through the front door and made my way to the kitchen where many people were standing quietly in a line. The servants had emptied the ice box and large sections of beef were being sliced and then cooked on the wood stove. I grabbed a decorated china plate from a tall stack of plates and a silver fork and served myself a steak and then made my way back out to the front porch and found an empty chair. I drank several glasses of water before eating. The cistern must have survived the storm. But they had indoor plumbing, too. The water was clear in the sunlight and just a little salty.

Mrs. Landes was walking through the house and onto the front porch, asking if everyone had had something to eat. She was dressed impeccably in a long flowery dress and shiny black laced shoes. She saw me as I was finishing my steak and asked if I would like another. I said "yes" and stood up to go back inside. Before I could, she looked at me and my clothes and then told me to sit back down, that more food would be brought to me. She glanced down at my bare feet too and took my plate and fork and went back inside. Did she recognize me?

Mr. Landes came out to the porch a few minutes later and found me sitting in the chair and said, "My dear, Douglas, is that you?"

"Yes, hello, Mr. Landes, it is me," I said as I stood and looked down at my clothes and straightened my hair with my fingers.

"My wife said that she thought it was you," he said. "And that you looked terrible. Look at you! Come into the house and rest in the parlor with me, will you?"

"Are you sure, sir? I could just stay out here."

"Absolutely not."

"Yes, thank you, sir."

I followed him into the house and into the parlor where several other well-dressed men and women were sitting and drinking water from tall clear glasses. And each glass had a little ice!

"I'm sorry, Mr. Landes, for the way I look but I was at the hospital during the storm and the debris blowing into the hospital shredded my clothes and..."

"Have you been back to your home yet, Douglas?"

"No, I haven't had a chance yet. I'm overdue at the hospital, though."

"How did the hospital fare during the storm?"

When he asked that question the busy conversation in the room came to a halt and all eyes were on me. I was sitting in a small wooden chair in the corner near the end one of the two long sofas and was visible to all.

"The hospital did fare well except that all the windows are gone. The spires on the Medical Department are gone but the structure is intact, as well."

"Did you lose anybody during the storm?"

"Several of our patients died during the storm. The home for the student nurses was completely destroyed."

One lady on the sofa near me spoke up, "Those poor girls, so young, so eager to serve their fellow man now lost in this dreadful storm along with so many others."

"No, ma'am, a friend of mine and I were able to get them out just before the house collapsed."

"How many were you able to save?"

"Four were in the home. Some were on duty at the hospital already."

"That is magnificent, young man. An orderly like you should be proud of being able to save a life rather than carrying bodies away in death to your morgue."

Mr. Landes spoke up, "This is Dr. Douglas Schuler, a recently graduated physician working as a house intern under the supervision of Dr. Edward Randall at the John Sealy Hospital. He is no orderly. No doubt, by his appearance he has been through a terrible ordeal as we all have."

They didn't look too bad.

She asked me, "Shoes are not mandatory for physicians on duty?"

Before I could answer, Mr. Landes said, "Will you all excuse us, please?"

He walked over to me and helped me up by my arm and told me to walk with him. I followed him past the main stairway to the long hallway to the back of the house. There was a small stairwell, and he began to go up. I went with him to the top floor and then down the hallway past several rooms to what appeared to be a large bedroom. Mrs. Landes was sitting in a chair next to a dressing table.

"You didn't bring him up the main stairs, did you?" she asked.

"Of course not. But I couldn't stand the way they were looking at him."

"Take him to your room, please."

He took me to the adjacent room through a connecting door from her room and past his bed and near his dressing armoire. He opened its large heavy doors and inside were a row of dark suits. He reached in and picked out a black suit and held it near to my chest to size me. We were about the same size, though he was a taller man, well over six feet.

"I'll get you a shirt."

He pulled out a white shirt with a tall, starched collar out of his bureau and handed it and the suit to me.

"You will need a pair of underwear as well, no doubt," he said.

Mrs. Landes stuck her head through the door and said, "You just can't have him put those things on, he's filthy, he smells like death."

Mr. Landes took me to the water closet down the hall and there was a basin of water and a bar of soap and a towel.

"Douglas, there isn't enough water for a bath."

"Thank you, sir, thank you very much. This will do fine."

"Please forgive Mrs. Landes. She is exhausted from feeding the whole neighborhood. I think as many as two hundred people sought shelter in our home during the storm. They keep coming back to eat and we are running out of food. But she has had little time to worry about her arthritis."

I went to the water closet and bathed from head to toe with soap and water. It was terribly hot inside the water closet now at midday and I began to sweat as I put on Mr. Landes' clothes. I put mine in the corner, to be burned. Overall, the clothes felt good, just a little long on the pants. These were expensive clothes, probably made here in Galveston of imported silk. I had never seen such suits as the men wore here. There were many tailors on the island I was told, some from New Orleans. I walked back into his bedroom, and he returned to see me from the adjoining door.

"It looks good on you, Douglas. Here are also a pair of shoes with socks."

I squeezed into these black shoes with matching black socks with little problem and stood before a long mirror on a wooden stand. I had never seen my whole body in a mirror before. I stood sideways and straightened my posture a little. My waist was too short for the rest of my body. And I was flat footed.

"You need to shave, but my man to do that is not here, hopefully he's at home, alive. Comb your hair, will you? It has gotten so long again. You had better put some oil on it."

I put a little oil in my hair, then combed it over to the right, out of my face with a large black comb with mother of pearl on the handle. I looked at myself, all of me, in the mirror again. I stood in a rich man's bedroom wearing his suit, combed my hair with his fancy comb and smelled pretty. Who would believe me? My feet were too big for my body and my arms looked too long, protruding too far through the coat sleeves.

"Thank you, sir, I will return the suit to you when I get to my home and can change."

"No, keep it, keep it all, you might not have a home to go to or anything left to wear. And Douglas....Mrs. Landes will need more Aspirin soon. Her arthritis will be worse with the storm."

"Yes, of course, I will let Dr. Randall know. He should be returning soon."

"Yes, I heard that many of your professors spend the summer months away. How convenient that they were not here to experience this tragedy as we have."

"I'm sure that they will all rush back."

"You and your house interns were the ones in charge of the hospital, unsupervised?"

"Well, yes, but we feel we are well trained to handle most any patient problem."

"I bet you do. Your professors are not from here. They don't realize that we get storms in the summer in Galveston? Shouldn't several have remained behind?"

I could see that he was exhausted. He took a few steps toward me and readjusted my coat by the lapels. He tugged at my sleeves to cover my wrists.

"Will they help us rebuild Galveston?" he added.

"I am sure that we all will."

"First, rebuild your hospital, we are going to need it. The crisis we are going to face here is just beginning, you know. I'm sure many will say that we should abandon the island. But I will never let that happen. I have built my home here, out of brick. I knew no storm could destroy it. Glass I can replace. You know, Douglas, I have raised my family here and we're not leaving."

I thanked Mrs. Landes also as we walked back to the hallway. She looked up at me and smiled briefly and said, "Now take him down the main stairs and see what our friends have to say about that."

"Yes, my dear," he said, and then to me, "Most of our friends are skeptical about your hospital and what good it will do for the people of Galveston. But now everything is different. The storm, I think, has killed hundreds, maybe thousands. We will need outside help, help from the people of the state, maybe the entire country. The train bridge to the mainland I am sure is destroyed. There is no telephone line. Maybe no one knows what has happened here. As an island we are isolated, and we are trapped here now."

"Many of the survivors will become ill after the storm as well, I'm afraid."

"I've heard today that the makeshift morgues downtown are full, all four of them. And there are still many more bodies. We've got to start burning them, right along with the debris. There is no time to identify them all."

"Barges left the island yesterday loaded with bodies, to dump them at sea."

"Yes, I heard. I was not in favor of that. Dead bodies will float, right Douglas?"

"Yes sir, they will unless they're weighted down."

"I hope they thought to do so. Nobody is thinking logically now. People are looting everywhere. People will become very desperate, very soon. Galveston will become a very dangerous place."

"Yes, sir. I've got to get back to the hospital." My shoes felt so good as we walked to the main stairwell.

"Where are you from, Douglas, were you born on the island?"

"No, sir, I am from Santa Clara, a small ranching community near Seguin."

"You can't leave now. You have to stay to do your part to rebuild our city."

"No sir, I am here to stay to do whatever I can to help."

"I'm afraid it will be a while until you can get a message to your family, that you survived. Do have family living?"

"Yes, I do. My parents, my younger brother and sisters."

"When they read about the storm, they will probably think that you drowned."

"Yes, sir, I know."

"Let's go now. Don't be ashamed. They may not recognize you now."

"I hope they don't."

We stood at the top of the stairs, the main staircase with its paneled wood walls and its carved banister and its little bronze statue on the pedestal at the end. Mr. Landes went first. As I walked down behind him, very little of the home had been damaged or even rearranged by the storm. All the paintings on the wall were straight. The thin white drapes were lightly blowing in the breeze but were dry and unstained. It was unthinkable to Mr. and Mrs. Landes for a storm to destroy this home. They wouldn't tolerate it. These shoes didn't hurt my flat feet as a new pair of shoes normally would, and they were so shiny!

CHAPTER 13

As I made my way back toward the hospital, I was the best dressed man in the neighborhood. Every other man wore torn and dirty clothes while working to clear their property and the street in front of it. I avoided the Strand and the waterside street behind it where the barges were docked. I looked too important to be recruited again to push the cart. I saw the Medical Department building and the hospital off in the distance and walked around the debris in the streets, off and on sidewalks, to the main steps of the hospital. I loosened my tie a little before I entered.

It was very quiet inside as I climbed the steps to the wards. I could only hear my new shoes with each step. I opened the doors on the third floor and looked to the left and to the right at each of the wards and it was still very quiet. I went to the east ward, and it was empty with much of the debris cleaned up. The beds were back in their spots, spaced across the floor one opposite the other. I went to the west ward, and it had been cleaned also and was full of patients, each bed occupied and each bed where it belonged. There was no glass in all the windows, no glass on the floor. There was a light breeze blowing through.

I saw Carl at the far end of the ward sitting on the bed with a patient. He was sitting next to Vivian who was sitting forward in her bed, grasping her knees. He had his stethoscope placed on her back and was listening to her lungs. With each breath he moved it to the other side of her back to listen again. I walked to the foot of her bed, and she was wheezing loudly with each inspiration and expiration and her lips were blue. She lay back down and began coughing. Carl stood up and watched her cough and then wheeze between coughs. He looked at me at the foot of the bed and then back at her. Finally, she stopped coughing and rolled on her side away from him and began to cry.

I knew Carl didn't know how to help her. The normally talkative Carl didn't know what to say to her, either. She had nearly drowned from inhaling all that salt water and her lungs were full of fluid, edema, fluid that filled her lungs after all the salt water had been absorbed into her body. And there was no coughing it up. Laura came over to sit with her. She fanned her with a small decorative fan and held her hand. Then she lifted her light brown hair off her face and then wiped her tears dripping down her face to the pillow.

Carl walked toward me. "Where were you, Doug?"

"I was in town searching for survivors."

"Tex hasn't shown up either. I heard his apartment building was completely destroyed."

"Why don't you go look for him? I can stay with Vivian. Have you been back to your apartment?"

"No, but I'm sure it's not there. I went to the top floor of the Medical Department yesterday and saw that the whole neighborhood is gone, just wood everywhere and a few brick chimneys standing alone," he said. Then he looked closer at me and added, "Where did you get those clothes?"

Carl looked terrible in his salt water soaked, shredded clothes, and he looked exhausted. We walked back to the nurses table together.

Carl stared back at Vivian and said, "I don't know if she is going to make it. She survived yesterday but she's getting weaker and weaker. She's exhausted. I've given her injections of Epinephrine that have helped her wheezing but only for a few minutes."

"Where's Johnny, the boy with the broken arm?" I asked.

"I don't know, I think he left, walked out of here with Victoria."

"Victoria's gone?"

"She was here all day yesterday, but Nurse Willow sent her to take the boy home. He was better and had tried to run out of here several times."

"She'll never make it. The city is in ruins and the streets are nearly impassable, except downtown. There's a mountain of debris on the south side of Broadway. Go now, I'll take over. There's some food and water at the hotels downtown."

"Okay, I'll go look for Tex. I'll take the horse. I'm sure Tex is alive. Those apartments at the beach are made with brick."

"Don't let anyone steal the horse. There's looting and stealing everywhere."

"Doug, just so you know, several people were looking for you yesterday, Dr. Smith, later Dr. West. I told them you were lost or hurt or something, I don't remember now. Where did you get the suit?"

"It's not mine, it was loaned to me," I said.

Carl left the ward, and I went back to see Vivian. She was wheezing loudly but asleep. Laura stood up; she had been crying.

"Go home, Laura, you've got to get some sleep. I'll keep an eye on Vivian and the other patients today."

"I don't know where to go. I guess I could go to my church."

"I don't know how many churches are still standing. Go to the home of Mr. and Mrs. Landes at 16th and Postoffice. They have food and fresh water there."

"Is that where you were?" she asked as she stood.

"Yes, just briefly earlier today. Mrs. Landes will help you. You can't do much more for Vivian now."

"I know," she said as she turned to leave left ward. Then she turned back toward me and said, "Oh, the head nurse was looking for you yesterday, Nurse Sanders."

"Oh, okay, is she coming today?"

"No, Nurse Willow is back on today," she said.

So, Nurse Sanders was looking for me too. That was all I needed.

I began to look at the other patients on the ward. Most were quiet and stable, with several wanting to leave, all were thirsty. We had potable water to give them. All the patients were here during the storm. Many had questions for me about the condition of the city and certain neighborhoods. No new ones were admitted since the storm, and there were no visiting families on the ward today, except the husband of Nellie Connors. I overheard him describing the conditions on the island, the number of the dead, the loss of their home. He sat next to her on the bed and held her hand as he cried. She was consoling him by running her fingers through his hair as he spoke without shedding a tear. She had been so calm the morning after the storm assisting the nurses, providing water to the other patients. She had badly cut her feet on the broken glass. I rewrapped the gauze on her feet now before they left. They left together, childless.

I came to the bed of Nicholaus Stamoulis and saw that he was sitting on the side of the bed, holding his head. I asked if he remembered me, and he said, "No," and that he didn't know how he had gotten here. His headache was severe, and he vomited frequently. I explained what happened to him and his brother two days ago now. I checked his eyes and his pupils were equal. He could look in all directions, so I knew his extra ocular muscles were intact. He had a large contusion on the left side of his head but besides the symptoms of vomiting he most likely did not have a brain hemorrhage. He was able to stand and walked without too much dizziness, too. I explained that he was hit on the head very hard, and he was unconscious for about forty-eight hours. He remembered the time just before the accident, that he was with his brother, but didn't remember the storm. He wanted to know where his brother was.

I told him what happened to his brother, that he suffered a broken back but was never unconscious, that Constantine took care of him during the storm, even protected him from all the flying debris. But that he died from it. Nicholaus sat back down and began to cry, holding his head. He seemed so young. I never knew his age, maybe twenty-one?

"So, you're saying that my brother protected me during the storm?"

"Yes, we all moved you to a safe area in the hallway, but we couldn't get back to him to save him. He helped us move you, and he was shielding you from the debris. He was paralyzed. I am so sorry to tell you this. He was so brave."

"He always felt like he had to take care of me. My father always told him to," he said as he sobbed. I sat down next to him. He was moving his arms and legs without difficulty.

"You can leave now, there's not much more we can do for you," I said as I stood. "But give me a minute first."

I left and went downstairs to the basement, to the morgue. It had been flooded but it was in use again. With a candle lamp I walked through the basement and found Constantine's body on a stretcher and took off his shoes. I carried them back upstairs and gave them to Nicholaus.

"These are your brother's; you will need them. The island is covered with debris. His body will be here in the morgue if you want to come later for it."

The bodies in the morgue would begin to smell in the heat. I added, "Please come soon."

He put on the shoes and stood again and walked without difficulty, though a little wobbly. He drank more water before he left. He hugged and thanked me. I told him that he may later regain some memory of what happened. He left the ward and after a few minutes I went to the south windows and watched him walk away;

he was fine. As I looked out over the city, I felt the laceration on my scalp, which was, dry and some of my hair was stilled matted with old blood. The sea breeze felt humid and cool, and my head throbbed less when I closed my eyes. So everybody thought I was AWOL, that I left my position here, my duty. How could Rosa have survived the storm?

Later that evening, the ward was quiet. It was hot but the sea breeze picked up and there weren't too many mosquitoes. There were some dry goods in storage that we opened and gave to the patients to eat. A small group of medical students who had stayed in the city for the summer came by the ward. They were lost. Later, Dr. Henry Cooke, the Dean of the College, who had not left for the summer and who went through the storm in his home, appeared on the ward and spent time with the students. He was our Chief of Pediatric Studies and an authority on yellow fever and an excellent anesthetist. I heard him tell the students that his home was not severely damaged during the storm and if they needed to live with him for a while, he would allow it. The students left with him as it was getting dark and we were lighting the lanterns for the night at the nurse's table. Several hours later after many of the patients were asleep, Dr. Smith appeared on the ward. I was charting on the patients at the nurses table when he tapped me on the shoulder.

"Hello, Douglas, it is nice to see you today. How long have you been here?"

I stood up, "Hello Dr. Smith, I have been here since this morning."

"I understand that you were here during the storm Saturday and that you left yesterday morning, I was wondering why?"

"I left Carl in charge, and I went to search for my friend. I have no family here in Galveston."

"Was this friend so important that you felt comfortable leaving your post?"

"Well, yes, I was afraid she and her family could have been lost in the storm. I went to her home, and it was entirely gone. I spent the morning looking for her but didn't find her. Right afterward, I was forced at gunpoint to push a cart the rest of the day. A cart to carry the dead to the barges to bury them at sea. I pleaded with the sheriff to let me return to the hospital, but he wouldn't. I was locked up with others for the night in a warehouse but escaped by climbing out of a window in the middle of the night. I reported this morning directly."

"By your appearance, you look better than most of us."

"My clothes were shredded during the storm. I was loaned this suit before coming here."

"I believe you, Douglas. I and my wife and son suffered through the storm at our home just a few blocks from here. Our house was lifted off its piers and we survived upstairs in the only room that wasn't severely damaged. We lost many valuable things and just to be alive is a blessing. Our emotions are strained as I'm sure yours are and the rest of the staff. Have you been to your apartment?"

"No, sir, I am not sure if I could reach it. It might not be standing. I had no valuable things to think about. Being here at the hospital during the storm, I am fortunate to be alive as well."

"Well, we have much work to do now and for the months ahead. I have been to the Medical Department building and all the microscopes and my entire lab in the basement has been destroyed. I don't believe your story about being taken captive but it's not me who you have to worry about, it's Dr. West. Your fellow intern, Dr. Hornsby, did not report yesterday, either. Have you seen him since the storm?"

"No, but I'm sure he's okay."

"All of the other faculty members are expected back soon. I'm sure they will soon hear of the storm and rush back. I hope the whole world will hear about it. The loss of life is, no doubt, in the hundreds."

"Beg your pardon sir, but I think it will be in the thousands. We were loading barges as many as seven hundred bodies at a time. There are mountains of debris everywhere, especially on the beach side of Broadway. The morgues downtown are full."

"If you have no place to stay you can stay in the hospital in one of the empty storage rooms or on the empty ward. Other students, medical and nursing, will no doubt need temporary housing as well. The student nurses' home was completely destroyed."

"Sir, we have one of the students from that home here who was a near drowning. She is struggling a great deal to breathe. If you could examine her, it would be much appreciated," I said, handing him my stethoscope.

"Yes, I will. I am sorry to hear about your friend, I hope that she and her family survived. Many of my own neighbors were washed away, I'm afraid. Was she affiliated with the hospital, or was she a nurse at St. Mary's Infirmary?"

"No, she wasn't," I said as we walked together to examine Vivian. She was not breathing loudly anymore, just hardly at all. Dr. Smith helped her sit up as she was barely conscious.

After examining her with the stethoscope, he said, "Her lungs are full of water. She probably won't survive." He gently laid her back down.

"All the water in her lungs is not allowing her to breathe in any air, any oxygen," I said.

"That's right." He kept staring at her, thinking. "We've got to get oxygen in her body, somehow," he added.

He handed the stethoscope back to me and began walking away, then said, "Douglas, come with me."

I left the ward with him, and we hurried down the stairs and left the hospital down the long front stairs. We went next door to the Medical Department building and made out way through the debris piled up against the south wall to enter the basement door under the grand staircase. This was his lab that we all knew well. But as we peered inside by candlelight, we could see that it was completely unrecognizable. It had been completely underwater. Now all the shelves of books and the table of microscopes and benches of glass tubing had all been completely turned upside down. It was all still there but piled on top of one another.

"Don't just stand there, start looking" he said.

"What are we looking for?"

"I was running experiments on my rabbits of the benefit of oxygen therapy. I simulated lung damage in them by having them inhale chlorine gas and later they seemed to improve with continuous oxygen gas therapy. I just received a new tank of oxygen. If we can find it, we could use it on your sick young lady."

We were overturning table and chairs and other furniture looking for the tank. It was dark but I saw that the cage for his rabbits had broken open. Towards the back of the lab, after overturning several bookshelves and stepping and breaking several glass tubes and syringes, he found the large flat rectangular metal tank that had the word "Oxygen Gas" stamped into its side. He lifted it from under some fallen chairs and handed it to me.

"How can we use this?" I asked, as I felt the metal valve at one end of the tank.

He continued to search. "We need some rubber tubing and a large glass jar with stoppers." He quickly found these, and we made our way back to the door. I carried the heavy flat metal tank, and he had armfuls of rubber tubing and a large wide glass jar with a long narrow neck. We hurried back to the hospital and up the stairs and onto the ward. We found a small table and carried all these to Vivian's bedside. We lay the tank on the floor next to her bed and on the table, we placed the glass jar. We connected the rubber tubing to the tank and the other end to the glass jar through a hole in a stopper in the top. And then through another hole in the stopper connected another rubber tubing, this one shorter. The other end of the rubber tubing he gave to Vivian. I opened the valve on the tank.

"My dear, please put this in your mouth and breathe as deeply as you can," Dr. Smith said.

She was too weak to object. We sat her up and slowly she began to breathe the oxygen that had been collecting in the glass jar. There was another hole in the large stopper that acted as a vent for air to be drawn into the jar as she inhaled. Slowly she was able to inhale, deeper and then deeper. After a few minutes she opened her eyes and looked at us. Dr. Smith pulled the tube away from her and asked how she felt. She didn't speak but just nodded. He gave her back the tubing and she continued to breath from it, faster now.

It was amazing, I had never seen such a treatment! He said that it was experimental, that there were case reports in the Boston Medical Journal about the benefits of breathing oxygen in cases of terminal pneumonia. And his rabbits seemed to like it! I had heard of the wealthy and their oxygen water that they like to drink, that it would help with facial wrinkles and bad breath. Vivian was getting better!

One of the other nursing students who we helped out of the house put down the bed pan and came to Vivian's bedside to watch. I explained what we were doing. She sat next to Vivian on the bed and pulled away her hair from her face and wiped it with a cool cloth. Vivian withdrew the tube from her mouth and smiled at her friend and said, "Thank you."

I had my stethoscope and listened to her lungs while she breathed the oxygen. I still heard all the fluid in her lungs, but I heard air gurgling through, in all five lobes. Dr. Smith and I left the bedside and left her breathing on the tube. We walked back to the nurse's table.

"Let her breathe on it all night, the tank should last her several days if she needs it. She should not breathe it directly. Do you know why?"

"Yes, I do. It may be toxic to her lungs in the long run."

"You see, Douglas, we faculty can be of use to you interns who think you know it all," he said with a smile, then looked back at Vivian. We had left a lantern on the table at her bedside. It was the only light on the ward. We could see that she was sitting up and talking to her friend.

"By the way, remember that oxygen is flammable," he added as he left.

I walked back to her bedside and took the lamp away from the table. I could see that she was better. I told her not to talk too much but to keep breathing on the tube for now. In the candlelight, I could see her nod in agreement and smile a little back at me. I walked back to the nurse's table and spoke with Nurse Willow about Vivian. She went to her bedside to see for herself.

I sat down and gathered my charts beneath the light of the lantern. Where was Tex? We called him Tex because he tucked his pants legs inside his boots. This completely baffled the faculty, as most of them are from the East Coast. He was from West Texas, some little town near Abilene that no one ever heard of. He was a fish out of water, living here in Galveston, or a Texan out of Texas, living here on the island. He wasn't sophisticated like the rich society people here in Galveston with their imported French perfume and silk suits. His accent was thicker than mine and many people had trouble understanding him. But he was a good doctor and a good friend.

CHAPTER 14

"Wake up ... wake up, Dr. Schuler. You can't sleep here. Wake up immediately!"

I woke up to see Nurse Sanders standing over me. I don't remember when or how but I was asleep in a chair at the nurse's table on the ward. I straightened up in the chair and looked back at her and tried to smile a little.

"I'm sorry, I didn't mean to sleep here," I said as I stood.

"Well, you know you can't. It's against the rules. You are still on duty."

She didn't look as well arranged as she normally did, with her perfectly pressed long white apron and her hair perfectly tucked up under her nurse's hat. I had never seen her in wrinkled clothing or with a lock of hair fallen down.

"I guess the storm didn't hit you too hard," I said.

"You don't know anything about me. But I know all about you, you look awful as usual. I guess you have an excuse now, the storm."

"How do you like my new suit?" I looked away and over at Vivian. She was sitting up with her legs hanging over the end of the bed and still breathing the oxygen.

Before she could answer, I said, "And don't touch that set up we have for Vivian. It's keeping her alive." I began to walk to her bedside with Nurse Sanders following me.

"I have never seen such a ridiculous arrangement for a patient. Take that out of your mouth, Miss Callaway," Nurse Sanders ordered.

I raised my voice now. "I said don't touch that device. Doctor's orders per Dr. Smith, as of last night. This is oxygen gas to manage her hypoxia."

Nurse Sanders stood motionless and gave me a cold stare. I stared back. "Doctor's orders."

She turned and loudly walked back to the nurses table to look for a written order for the oxygen and there was none, but I didn't care.

"Vivian Callaway is your full name?"

She took the tube out of her mouth, "Yes, it is. I don't know your name, though."

"Dr. Schuler, Doug Schuler. I'm one of the interns. Do you remember anything that happened to you?"

"No, not really, I remember leaving the house in the storm with Carl and waking up here the next morning, but not much after that," she said as she replaced the tubing in her mouth.

"You were severely hypoxic from all the water you swallowed, you needed oxygen, so Dr. Smith and I got this set up together for you last night."

"It is helping me. I'm not coughing as much, either."

"Keep using it but try breathing without it for short spells. I think you will need it for at least another day more. By the way, how old are you?"

"I'm twenty-one."

"Where are you from? Do you have any family here?"

"I'm from Houston, my older brother and his wife live here. He works at the Waterworks building downtown." She put back the tubing in her mouth.

I walked around behind her to listen to her lungs. She was still wearing the same blouse and dress from before the storm. I lifted her blouse in the back and listened with my stethoscope. I could still hear some fluid in her lungs, but air was moving through it well. I felt her forehead and face—no fever.

After a few deep breaths of oxygen, she continued, "I don't know what to do. I would like to get in touch with him."

"All the phone lines are down, there is no electricity to the island anymore. Don't worry too much about that. I saw some of your friends on the other ward. I think they will be staying there for a while. Maybe they could find some clothes for you. I will have them come see you."

"Thank you so much, Dr. Schuler, for everything." She held my hand.

"Sure, and don't worry about Nurse Sanders. She hates that she has to take orders from me, a house intern."

"She's awful," she said, smiling with her bright white teeth showing between her pink lips shining in the sunlight.

I smiled back. "I know."

Rather than go back to the nurse's table, I had to check on the other patients. It looked like no one had died during the night. I sat on the bed of an elderly man who was asleep. In his file I saw that he was admitted yesterday after the storm with head trauma and a skull fracture. Carl forgot to tell me about this one.

I felt the back of his head under his bandage and could feel the small concave indentation. He woke briefly from the pain but fell back asleep after following a few commands from me, like "squeeze my hand" and "touch your nose." I looked up and could see that one of the student nurses was bringing water to the patients. She spotted Vivian and walked immediately to her. They hugged briefly and Vivian explained what her contraption was.

I was exhausted and hungry. I needed to leave to look for Rosa. Maybe she will come here looking for me? Or maybe she won't leave her family wherever they were? Where could they be staying, perhaps with friends? I never asked if she had any family in Galveston, but she was born here. I didn't know many more details of her life, though. I told her everything I could think of about me and she told me I talked about myself a lot.

I stood to go on the next patient and looked up and saw Dr. Randall entering the ward. He was talking with Nurse Sanders, and she pointed across the ward to me. He signaled me to come to him. What did he have to say to me?

"Welcome back, Dr. Randall."

He looked me up and down. "I got here as quickly as I could, Douglas. I was on a train to St. Louis when I heard the news. I got back on the next train to Houston. I had to take a barge from the mainland to get here. The railway bridge is out, as are all the electric lines. I passed other barges going the other way, leaving Galveston with women and children."

"Have you been to your home yet, sir?"

"No, I haven't but I'm confident my home is still standing. Douglas, come with me and tell me about the storm."

We left the ward and went downstairs to his office. His office door was difficult to open due to the debris inside against it. We pushed it open together. Everything was out of place and on the floor. The electric chandelier above his desk was broken but still hanging. Debris was knee-deep on the floor. He pulled a slate shingle from the wall. His office had a view facing southward, with the windows broken, without any hanging glass fragments. We lifted his desk off its side and made room on the floor for where it was. I found his heavy wooden desk chair and a chair for myself. We sat facing each other to the side of the desk. He was speechless for a moment.

"Well, Douglas, the storm has devastated the island. I think we came out better than most here at the hospital."

"Yes, sir. It was horrible. Where is your home, sir?

"It is on Broadway and 20th Street, but that doesn't matter now. We've got a tremendous amount of work to do here at the hospital."

"I've been down Broadway and the homes aren't damaged too

badly. But everything south of that is virtually destroyed. There is a massive wall of wooden debris that extends the length of the island, parallel to the beach on the south side of Broadway. It is full of destroyed homes and their belongings: furniture, stoves, chairs, clothes, everything. And I think that wall protected the homes where you live and most everything north of that. And in all that debris are bodies, hundreds, maybe thousands of bodies." I wasn't speechless anymore.

"I know, it is truly a crisis of humanity on a scale, I don't know, maybe never beforehand. But we have to pull together and focus on preserving life now. It will be a great test for us, for our hospital. If we don't act fast, disease will begin to sweep across the island. There is a tremendous stench already."

"I don't smell anything, sir."

He smiled a little, "I bet you don't, Douglas."

I sat back in the chair and realized he was right. I smiled back a little, but I wanted to cry. I leaned forward again and put my head in my hands. There was a little blood on my hands from the forehead, it was still bleeding a little.

He stood beside me and patted me on the shoulder, "I know you have been through the worst of it, but I'm afraid death is not going away so fast. Gather yourself for the challenge we face. And what happened to your head? That should have been closed with sutures, you know."

"I know," I said as I wiped one hand on my pants leg. "Dr. Randall, I haven't seen Tex, I mean Homer, one the other interns, since the day of the storm. His apartment is on the beach. Carl went yesterday to find him."

He had his back to me now, he was searching through a large wooden chest, standing on wet volumes of books scattered covering the entire floor. He found his doctor bag.

He turned back to me. "I was wondering how many of our students might have died. Most of the medical students haven't returned for the fall session yet. The hospital and the Medical Department building didn't suffer too badly. But for those students who weren't here on duty? We have to take an accounting of them, and, of course, of Homer."

"I didn't see any medical students. But on the ward, we have a nursing student who was a near drowning that Dr. Smith and I cared for. He brought oxygen gas for her to breathe, and I think it saved her life. I'm trying to wean her off before the gas tank empties. All the other patients on the ward are more or less stable. Many of them left to go look for their relatives. Many count themselves fortunate having been here, ill during the storm, but are convinced their families in their homes didn't make it. Most of them are probably poor."

As he stood over me, he reached inside his black bag and lifted out a spool of thread and a curved suture needle.

"I'm going to close that laceration on the top of your head," he said as he started to sew my scalp together. He spoke as he sewed. "I want to hear more of the details later, Douglas. We've got to prepare for the worst: dysentery, malaria, yellow fever, tetanus, that will begin to affect the survivors, also pneumonia, tuberculosis, even insanity and hysteria. The doors of the hospital have to remain open for the citizens of the city. Leave and go find Carl, go to your apartment, but return later today. I will examine the student and see what more we can do for her." It didn't take him long. He cut the loose end after the last knot. He put back the needle and thread spool and then reached into the chest and pulled out several rolls of what looked like fish netting.

We both left the office and stood in the hallway. He added, "I got to get a telegram somehow to the mainland. The whole island will need a lot of help from the outside. We are captive on the island. We've got to protect our patients with this netting to go over their beds to protect them from mosquitoes. We will be swarming in them in no time."

He had spoken to us about this netting for mosquitoes before, but we were skeptical. I would do whatever he told me. Just then Carl entered the front entrance and met us on the stairs.

"Dr. Randall, you're back."

He walked toward us and shook his hand. He added, "It is horrible, the destruction, the debris, so many dead bodies. Doug, I went to find Tex and it took me forever to make my way there, even with Princess. There is very little left of Lucas Terrace, nearly completely gone. I don't know how anyone could have survived. Has Tex come by?"

"No, he hasn't," I said.

Carl said, "I went downtown to the morgues and didn't find his body. They were crowded with people desperately looking through all the bodies. But I couldn't stand the stench and there are just so many bodies. There is a wall of debris probably thirty feet high on the beach side of the island. But the worst was the bodies, the dead bodies that were dumped from the barges are floating back onto the beaches. Large crowds of people with carts are down there gathering up the bodies."

Dr. Randall asked, "They took bodies out to sea, to dispose of them?"

"Yes, they did, the day after the storm," I said.

"Why would they do that? Did they identify the bodies, notify the families, gain consent from the families? This is a travesty!"

"No, Dr. Randall. I think, there were just too many dead. They were removing jewelry, rings whatever they found on the bodies that could be used to identify them later. Many of the bodies had missing fingers as they were loaded on the barges."

"You witnessed this happening, Douglas?"

"Yes, I tried to convince them to at least to weight down the bodies."

"You took part in this?"

"I had no choice. I was forced to at gunpoint."

"You are suffering from hysteria as well, Douglas?" he asked with disgust, and looked away.

I walked around to stand in front of him. "Please believe me, I was forced to collect bodies on a cart, and push the cart across the city to the barges. Me and another man pushed the cart for hours the day after the storm. They were looking for men to do that. Most of the horses had drowned. I told them that I was a doctor and had to return to the hospital, but they didn't believe me. I think they were sheriffs or city officials; I don't know. Some of the men pushing the carts were shot, accused of stealing jewelry off the dead. They locked us up in a warehouse for the night, but I escaped. I was out looking for my girlfriend when I was taken prisoner. I couldn't report back to the hospital until the next morning. I haven't left here since."

They both stood silent and stared at each other.

Carl said, "I didn't know you had a girlfriend."

"Taken prisoner at gunpoint?" Dr. Randall asked. He wasn't smiling.

I was desperate for Dr. Randall to believe me. "Please, Dr. Randall, you've got to believe me. You weren't here to see what transpired after the storm. The sheer panic, the desperation in the faces of the living. The shock people felt. I think everyone lost someone."

"We'll talk more about this later, Douglas. Now please leave, go collect your thoughts, clear your mind. Carl, please change your suit, you're a disgrace by the way you look," Dr Randall said with a stare of disappointment at us both.

To Carl, I said, "Vivian is alive, breathing oxygen gas from Dr. Smith. Help her wean off the tank before it runs out." They walked up the stairs together and left me standing alone. Dr. Randall told me to leave but I'm sure he meant for me to come back as soon as I could.

I made my way back to my apartment. As I turned the last corner, I could see that most of the homes were not severely damaged. The Hendersons' home was missing a few shutters on the front and the trees in the front yard were down. I kept walking down the sidewalk and around the corner to the alley entrance where there was debris piled high. Wood siding and beams and flooring were all stripped apart from the board it was nailed to and piled up together with table legs, and doors, and other broken things. The debris blocked my way, but I walked to my apartment over it gently. I had to lift boards and beams out of my way and trust the wood stacked beneath me to hold my weight. The alley was completely covered in debris, from back fence to back fence. There were exposed nails everywhere, sticking in the bottom of my new shoes.

But I kept going. I made it to my apartment and removed the debris covering the bottom half of the staircase. The small window in the door was broken but the cloth shade sill hung over it. The small windows in the apartment were all broken. The furniture in the apartment was blown to the back wall. I put back the cot and realized that there were puddles of water on the floor, and everything was soaked, including my cot. All the clothes in my closet were damp. I looked up and saw a large hole in the ceiling and roof.

I grabbed a drinking glass from the floor and left the apartment. I went down the stairs and jumped the rail to the Hendersons' yard and landed on the lawn. I noticed less debris, only a few boards scattered about. I went to the cistern that was still in place and got some water to drink. It looked clear and tasted only a little saltier than usual. I drank several glasses. The small outhouse was blown over. I walked up to the back porch and knocked on the door and no one came. I looked inside the window on the porch; it wasn't broken, and I could see no one there, but the house looked intact, no furniture out of place. My little back house over the stables seemed to block a lot of the wind and debris that would have hit the house. I went back to my apartment. On the stairs, I could see the Grandma Sam's little alley house was gone. Where it stood was now replaced by wood planks shuffled together like cards. Where was she and was she still alive?

The Petteways' little alley home was there, intact, but it had shifted off its short brick piers. It probably had six feet of water inside during the storm. It was heavily damaged. Debris was piled up in front of it. But the door was cleared as if Moses had been there to clear it, to go inside. Was his family alive? Maybe they made it to another house, a bigger one? Maybe Moses went across the alley to take Grandma Sam and the others in the alley to a safe house on the main street, or maybe to the front house where Angelina cleaned? But that was unlikely; they were probably not welcome in the bigger houses on the main street. Maybe Moses took his family and Grandma Sam to the waterfront to weather the storm in the large brick building where he worked?

The storm caught everybody by surprise. The poor had a tougher time finding shelter, no doubt. And afterward, if they survived, where would they go? The rich probably thought that the storm was a minor inconvenience. The Hendersons were alive, I'm sure of it. The house was empty because they probably decided to stay in a hotel downtown where there was food and clean water. Stubborn Grandma Sam probably refused to leave and drowned. Maybe her body was under the debris where her home stood. Down the alley, other small homes were gone or heavily damaged.

I went back inside and got my clothes from the closet, a few suits and a few shirts, and left. I couldn't stay here. I found a shoebox with some letters from home. They were damp also. I took them out of the box and put them in my pants pocket. I went back to the window by the door and saw that the curtains that my mother had made for me were still hanging down over the window, intact and wet. I could feel thin shards of glass embedded in them. There was a stench in my apartment and it wasn't just death or rot or me. My apartment had started to mildew. Those curtains probably would turn black in a few days. Where could I go? I needed to get a message to my family but that was impossible now.

I climbed out of the alley and back toward where Rosa's house was. It was so hot and I was so hungry and so tired. I weaved my way around much of the debris blocking the sidewalks. It was easier just to walk down the middle of the street. I turned the last corner to her street to see the empty lot where her house was. There were few people around and it was quiet. I think most were out looking now for food and water instead of their lost relatives. I crossed to the empty lot and sat down under the palm tree that was the only living thing in her little corner of the world. I wanted so much to talk to Rosa about what had happened to me, that no one believed me, even when I was telling the truth. I should have taken her and her family out of their house and to the hospital. Everybody lost someone.

The sky was so clear and all the trees that had provided shade were gone except this palm. The sun was bearing down on me. It was so bright. It was more powerful than the electric surgical lamps that the hospital had just purchased. This palm that seemed insignificant amongst the proud oaks in the neighborhood before the storm was the lone survivor. I sat down underneath it again in the small sandy circle of shade that it provided. I could feel the breeze coming off the water now. Maybe this could be my new home. I lay my clothes across my lap. I was dehydrated. My lips were cracked. But my eyes were not dry, they made tears that landed onto my black coat in my lap.

CHAPTER 15

I pulled my head forward from the palm trunk and looked up at the sun. What time of day was it? I didn't know what day it was, but I knew it was four days after the storm—then it must be Wednesday. I stood and gathered all my things and began to walk back to the hospital. I was dizzy, dizzy from the sun. Near the curb I saw a smashed hat, a black derby under some boards piled up at the curb. I pulled out the hat and slapped it against my knee to get out the sand, then straightened it out and put it on. It was mostly dry, and it fit good enough.

I kept walking until I got to the hospital and went up to the fourth floor and found a place to lay my clothes. I went back down the stairs looking for water. I went down to the morgue then out of the back of the building where the potable water was held in large cisterns. They had not been damaged but hopefully weren't flooded. They were elevated on tall wooden legs. I found a wooden bucket and was able to get some water out without wasting too much. It was fresh tasting. I drank as much as I could. I rinsed my face and hair with what I couldn't drink. I washed some of the dried blood off my scalp. The sutures felt intact and in place.

I went back through the morgue in the basement and went out the side door. Grazing on a small patch of exposed grass was the ambulance horse, Princess. I went back inside to find the wooden bucket and filled it again and took it to the horse. She drank it down. I poured the water left in the bucket over her and wiped her down with a rag to get the salt and sand off. Her coat glistened black in the sun. She was calmer than most horses and smarter, too. She found a way to get out of the rising water on her own. I talked to her a little about my plight and she listened with sympathetic eyes. She wouldn't be needed for the ambulance. No wagon could pass through the streets of the city, especially in the far east end of the island where we were. She still had her bridle from when Carl rode her yesterday.

I gently rubbed her mane, then jumped on her back, talking to her the whole time. She shifted around a little but didn't seem to mind and I didn't mind riding bareback. I just missed being on a horse. I sat up tall and grabbed the reins and gently encouraged her to go forward. She did and we began walking toward the front of the hospital. From my vantage point and looking westward toward the city, I could see the endless sea of debris on the land in front of us. I pulled her around and began walking eastward instead. There was an opening in the debris along the waterfront and we walked through it. Here the debris wasn't piled as high but was flat and spilled to the bay at the water's edge. We were able to follow a path between debris piles east until the amount of debris was less and I could see the water where the bay and the beach met. After a few blocks, we reached the grass that led up to where the dunes were. Small clear waves were gently spreading out on the sand as we walked through the wet sand. The water was clear and green in the bright sunlight. It was quiet and we were alone.

We stopped and I eased off the horse and took off my outer clothes and stockings and shoes and threw them on the dry sand and walked into the water. I went out far enough, past the second sandbar to completely submerge myself. It was a relief, a complete relief. I looked back at Princess; she wasn't tasting some of the salt grass. I had to get back to her before she wandered away, but she hadn't moved too far away from my pile of clothes. I floated back to the water's edge and walked to her and grabbed the reins. She stayed beside me while I put my clothes on. I jumped back on the horse barefooted and placed my shoes with the stockings in them in my lap. There was still no one else here with us.

We wandered slowly down the beach following it toward the city. My horse back home would wander with me like this as we crossed the land, working with the cattle. The land was rocky in places. Outcroppings of red rock surrounded tangles of brush. From their edge, I could see lots of wild grass scattered with prickly pear cactus, not a lot of trees except by the creeks and the river. The creek had the tall bald cypress trees closely following it. And it was always nice and quiet by the creek. The calves were always noisy, looking for their mothers. No noisy people in crowded spaces like Galveston. We walked back toward town, and I closed my eyes to feel the breeze, to hear the waves and the hungry calves, and Princess was following the edge of the water nicely.

As I looked down the beach, toward town, I could make out small pillars of black smoke from separate fires off in the distance. The closer we got, the more I could see that they were large fires, maybe fifteen in number, that were burning hot with wood stacked high inside them. Crowds of people were standing around these fires. There were a few horse-drawn wagons nearby the fires. I stopped the horse. There were bodies on the carts. I could see men lifting them into the fires. And at the water's edge I could see lines of bodies, tangled with one another being detangled one by one and loaded onto the carts. The dead that had been buried at sea had washed back up on the beaches.

We were several hundred yards away and I didn't want to get any closer. Was what I did wrong, taking part in the illegal disposal of unidentified bodies, as Dr. Randall said? But I was forced to do it. Now the dead were returning home, searching for a proper burial. Was there still a chance that they could be identified and the next of kin notified and then properly buried? Where would you bury so many and how? Galveston is an island of shifting sand. It would be impossible to identify them and floating at sea would completely alter who they were. No, the bodies had to be burned. I put my socks and shoes back on.

I turned the horse away from the beach into open areas of land that were once neighborhoods. There were signs everywhere that homes were once here—an occasional broken brick chimney, scattered brick piers no more than a few feet tall and still in their place, defiant, even after their homes had floated away. There was the occasional heavy iron stove sitting on the ground after the ground floor and the rest of the home had collapsed. And there was a porcelain bathtub lying completely face down. Off in the distance, farther west, I could see the occasional brick building or home that seemed to survive with debris piled high against it.

I made my way back toward the city through the maze to find higher and higher debris piles. The smell of fresh sea air was replaced with what reeked from the large mounds of burning wood and flesh. I could see the large wall of wood in the distance. Within it were many bodies, the dead that would never be identified. The sheer weight of all that wood would take days, maybe weeks to remove. And this wall of debris seemed to stretch for several miles, running parallel to the beach. I rode next to the wall for a couple of blocks and came to where people were crossing through the wall. I rode a little farther and saw it was a diagonal gap about six feet wide. I crossed through it as others were passing the other way for about fifty feet. They were not bothered or making way for the horse. Few people had been on the side where I was. But as I crossed to the other side of the wall, the street I entered was bustling with people, with the mansions on Broadway intact. I slid off the horse and led it by the reins, being careful to avoid people busily crossing the streets. Many were looking for others in the crowd, weakly calling out their names. And nobody answered.

I walked past Broadway toward the downtown buildings, toward businesses, toward normalcy? Many people were cleaning up their storefronts, having placed wet or ruined items outside to dry. People were passing into grocery stores and buying canned goods. Many people in Galveston had plenty of money and now they just needed a place to buy what they needed, food and water. I saw many walk out with bent cans of food in their arms, cans without labels that appeared bright silver in the sunlight. Their labels had gotten wet and fallen off or were blown off. People didn't seem to mind because they were hungry. Some children had gathered in front of the store, perhaps because they had misplaced their parents? They were not allowed in the store, and a few were pacing and crying outside. I saw one small boy in a military uniform sitting still by himself on the tall red brick curb, looking down at his bare feet. It was Frankie Madera, Archie's friend at the orphanage.

I walked up to him, leading the horse. "Hello soldier, would you mind watching my horse for me?"

He stood up and just stared back at me without speaking.

"Frankie, it's me, Dr. Schuler. Archie and I rode out to see you a few weeks ago."

He sat back down on the curb and then looked down at his feet and said, "I remember you."

"What are you doing here, so far from your home?"

"I don't have a home anymore," he said.

I sat down next to him, "Where's Archie? Is he with you?"

"No, I think he's dead, along with everybody else, and the sisters that took care of us, too. There's nobody left, just me...when the storm hit, the house started shaking bad. Water was coming in through the ceiling. The wind was so loud. The sisters gathered us all together in the room where we eat. Each sister got a rope and tied it around us and her. They told us to hang on to them. They started singing and told us to sing too but I couldn't. Big waves were coming into the room and knocking us over and pushed me away. I grabbed a pole in the middle of the room and tried to hang on. Archie was hanging on to me by my belt. I mean, I think it was him, but it was so dark. I was trying to hang on to his hand, but I couldn't hold him. The water pushed me off the pole against the wall. I looked up and the roof was gone. I tried to climb the pole, and it was slippery. I couldn't hang on anymore. I wasn't afraid but I didn't know how to swim."

He started to cry and hung his head again. He removed the little military cap and squeezed it in his palms.

"Dr. Schuler, I never had been so afraid in my whole life."

"Did you hang on to that pole?"

"No, it started to fall over, and I jumped on the altar from the corner of the room that was floating by. I kept sliding off. I don't know how I stayed on it. I was looking for Archie to pull him out of the water, but it was so dark. I couldn't see him or anybody else. I yelled for him, but I didn't hear him. I just hung on. I tried to pray but I was too scared. The whole building fell apart, and a wave threw me and the altar out of it, all the way. The altar floated away, then got wedged in the tree behind the building and I jumped onto a branch. I stayed in the tree during rest of the storm. The waves almost threw me out of the tree, but I wasn't gonna let go."

He wasn't crying now. And he continued, "I fell asleep in the tree and woke up when I saw the sun coming up over the water. I could see that there was nothing left of our home. Everybody was gone, all gone, and no dead bodies on the sand. There was just me by myself in the tree and there were no more leaves on the tree."

He stood again and got close to me. I put my arm around him and hugged him but not for very long. He pushed away from me and went to stand closer to the horse and he reached up and touched her neck. I put him on her back. He lay forward and hugged her neck.

"I walked down the beach. I knew which way it was to town. I walked and walked all morning. I did see a few dead animals along the way, but I didn't touch them. I walked all the way down to Fort Crockett. I saw that their buildings were still standing, and the soldiers were cleaning up. One of the men saw me and told me to come inside. I looked down at myself and I only had my pants on, and they were almost ripped off. I was almost naked!"

"On no, what did you do?"

"Well, I was walking almost completely naked and several of the soldiers sat me down next to them on a bench and handed me a cup of water, then a piece of dried meat. I told them the story about my home just like I'm telling you. They left me alone and told me not to move. They came back with a captain or someone important and his wife. She told me that they would get me some more clothes. I fell asleep on the bench, and they brought me this uniform that she fixed for me. It was a man's army uniform, but they cut it down to fit me."

"That is some uniform. Do you like it, Frankie?"

"I sure do. It's the only thing I have to wear, but they didn't have shoes for me. They told me I would have to leave, but they showed me how to salute. I got to salute a bunch of the soldiers. They gave me some more dried meat to eat. I told them I didn't have anywhere to go, that I am an orphan. They said that I should walk toward town to find somewhere to live. That there is another orphanage, that maybe I could maybe live there."

He paused and looked off in the distance, then said, "Dr. Schuler, I sure am hungry. I saw a bunch of kids outside this store, so I thought I might be able to get some food here. The other kids were laughing at me, making fun of my uniform."

"Don't move Frankie, I'll be right back, okay? Stay on the horse and yell out loud if anybody comes near it."

"Okay, I will."

I went inside the grocery store and could see there wasn't much left on the shelves. I rushed over to the farthest wall and grabbed a can off the shelf with no label. I felt that I had a fifty-cent piece in my pocket. I went to the owner behind the counter and paid for the can. I asked what he thought might be in it. He said, without looking at me, that he had no idea and that he wasn't giving me any change back. There was nothing in that can that could cost fifty cents. I turned around and went back to the wall and took another can and walked out.

I went outside and saw Frankie talking to two men while sitting on the horse. They were too close to him, so I walked off the curb and stood between them and Frankie. They backed away without saying anything more.

"What did they say to you?" I asked.

"They wanted your horse, but I told them 'no.' That you and I were in the army and were soldiers."

"Good work, soldier. Let's open up a can and see what we can eat!"

I left him on the horse, and we walked away holding the reins, back toward the middle of town, toward Broadway. I found an empty curb and slid Frankie off the horse to sit next to me.

"What do you think of my knife? My brother gave it to me."

"Wow, I like the handle."

I put a can between my feet and punctured the tin can with the knife and worked it back around the lid. I pried up what was left of the attached lid. I smiled at Frankie.

"What's in it?" he asked, leaning over to see.

"Okra," I said with an even bigger smile. "Reach in and grab some".

"I hate okra, it is so slimy. They made us eat it at the orphanage."

"Frankie, you've got to eat it. So do I."

Frankie reached in the can with his dirty fingers and pulled out several pieces. I watched him eat them before I took some. We finished the can and I gave him the water in the bottom of the can to drink. I told him how my grandfather used to grow okra on his farm back home. And we used to put them in cans for the winter.

"Frankie, do you have any family here?"

"No, I don't think so. I may have an older brother I heard, but he doesn't live here." He hung his head and shuffled his bare feet on the bricks of the sandy street.

I put my arm around him. "Don't worry, I don't have any family here, either. Where have you been staying?"

"Nowhere, really. I found a doghouse last night in an alley. The dog wasn't there."

"Let's go find some better place for you to stay."

I climbed onto the horse and reached down and lifted him up to sit behind me. He knew to hold on tight. There was another orphanage in town, on 21st Street, but on the beach side of town, beyond the wall. I headed south from downtown toward Broadway. I asked several people on the street where the orphanage was located and was it destroyed. Most knew where it was but had no idea about the condition of the home. I found the gap again in the wall and crossed at about 19th Street. I headed west to 21st where there were intact buildings and down several blocks to Avenue M. There I saw the orphanage, a large light yellow brick building three stories high surrounded by a tall iron fence. It had sustained significant damage—a collapsed roof in the middle of the building with loss of part of the third floor and, of course, broken windows all around. Most of the homes around it were destroyed. I rode up to the building and into the open gate. We heard loud children running inside.

As we got close to the entrance, Frankie jumped off the back of the horse and ran through the open front door. There was broken glass everywhere. I tied up the horse to some nearby debris in the yard, a jumble of furniture and siding next to a patch of grass. I tucked the other can under a broken table leg. I went inside and found that much of the first floor had sustained damage but had been cleaned. And it smelled clean, like ammonia, the way the hospital smelled most mornings before the storm.

I walked past the hallway stairwell to the back of the building. Groups of children were sitting together in a large room, perhaps as many as fifty children. Most were sitting in chairs, but there weren't enough small chairs for all of them. Some were eating dried fruit out of a dark brown cardboard box. I looked for Frankie but didn't see him. I kept walking to the north end of the building and found him sitting at a small desk in a small classroom that looked completely intact. An elderly woman was walking around looking over the children's shoulders.

"Is this your little soldier?" she asked.

"Yes, I know him. He's been wandering around downtown looking for food. He seems to be the only survivor from the St. Mary's Orphan Asylum. He walked back to town, not before the soldiers at Fort Crockett made him something to wear." I looked at her until she looked up at me, "He's got nobody, no family, nobody."

"He is welcome to stay with us. We are, of course, over capacity after the storm. I am proud to say that none of our children were lost in the storm. But if we receive any more children we will have to send some to Houston or Dallas. Our food supple is getting scarce."

There were many more orphans roaming the streets downtown. They were made orphans by the storm.

"We have sustained severe damage to the third floor, where they all slept," she continued. "So, we moved them all downstairs. The whole floor collapsed. The second floor is being cleaned now. There has been a lot of water damage there. Much of our staff is upstairs cleaning. I am the director of the orphanage, Mrs. Finch."

"My name is Douglas Schuler, I am a doctor, a house intern, at the John Sealy Hospital. I could help if any of the children were injured."

"We have a few with minor injuries, mainly from flying glass, small lacerations only, I think. We have them lying down on cots in the other room, trying to keep them calm."

She took me to the south side of the building where makeshift cots were placed. The whole area had been covered with broken glass. All the children were wearing clean clothes and shoes. Some were sleeping, others were trying to escape. I asked all the children to take off their shoes. Most didn't want to because it hurt. Many of the children had small lacerations to the bottoms of their feet. The lighting was good, and it was easy to see small pieces of glass in many of the children's feet. I could feel the pieces, too.

"Mrs. Finch, would there be anyone to assist me, perhaps with some tweezers or sewing needles?"

She left the room after nodding to me that she had someone in mind. Some of the children had glass in their arms and legs, too. Some were large enough to remove with my fingers. Most didn't complain about the pain. One small girl with thick, long blonde hair was convinced that she had glass in her hair and her scalp but that she couldn't find it. I stood and examined her hair and moved it all around so as to see her scalp. I found there were several small pieces of glass deep enough in her matted hair to grasp it.

"Maybe this would help you, Douglas?" It was Victoria holding a pair of long tweezers. She smiled at me, then stepped in front of me to sift through all that hair.

"What are you doing here, Victoria?" I said, smiling more than a little to see her.

She made the little girl scream when she pulled a small shard of glass the size of a long tree thorn. The girl stood up and put out her hand and said to Victoria, "Give it to me. I want to show Mrs. Finch that she was wrong. I knew all along that I had glass in my hair."

Victoria answered, "Why don't you sit back down and keep your mouth shut for a moment so I can get more glass out of this mop of yours."

The little girl plopped back down on the cot. Victoria went back to work. I started on the feet of the boy next to the little girl.

"I left the ward Sunday with Johnny. Nurse Willow insisted that I go with him. We walked across town to find his home. It took us hours to find it. His family owns a small corner grocery store not far from here, 21st and P 1/2. The entire family lived upstairs. I tried to support his arm as we walked. I made a makeshift sling for him, but he wouldn't keep it on. When we finally reached where his home was, he collapsed in tears. I wasn't sure if we were in the right spot, but he was sure. He refused to leave. We found an abandoned, nearly destroyed home to sleep in that night. Yesterday, we came here and we stayed the night."

"Why are you here?" she asked.

"I found a little boy I know downtown. He was an orphan at the St. Mary's Orphanage down the island, the only survivor, I think. He was close with a boy that I took care of in the hospital. I wasn't sure where to take him."

It took a lot of looking by Victoria to convince the little girl that was no more glass in her hair. I finished pulling out glass out of the foot of the last boy. I told them all to stay put and keep their shoes off for now. Victoria and I walked out of the room together to find Mrs. Finch.

"Douglas, I have to get back to the hospital. For two days now I have been gone. I've been helping Mrs. Finch clean here for the day. I don't know where else to go. She said I could stay tonight but if I don't get back, I could be expelled."

I looked around the room and could see the sun setting in the west side empty windows. "Don't worry, Victoria. I'll take you back. Where's Johnny?"

She took me back to the large room where the children were,

and I saw him sitting with others playing marbles. He was throwing them with his left hand. He looked up at me and let me examine his arm and put the splint back in place. I took off his shoes and felt his feet and didn't feel any glass. He was an orphan now, like so many. Victoria hugged him and we left to find Frankie. He returned to the big room with all the other children. I told him that this is where he would be living now. He smiled and seemed happy about it. Victoria told Mrs. Finch that she was going back to the hospital. They shook hands and she thanked Victoria for all her help. We walked back into the hallway and out the front door. Outside, I showed her Princess tied to a table leg.

"This is my way home? I don't know how to ride a horse," she said.

"You don't have to know how to ride, you only have to know how hang on...to me."

I went to untie the horse, and reached for the can of food and wedged it into my pants pocket. I then climbed on the horse and extended my hand to Victoria, but she didn't take it. She looked small from my perspective on the horse. She was still wearing her uniform, the blue dress under the dirty white apron. Of course, she didn't have her mandatory nurse's cap on. Her wavy long dark brown hair was down and blowing in the breeze.

"I'll pull you up."

She hesitated a moment, then she grabbed my right hand with hers and I dragged her up the side of the horse. She let go of my hand and lay on the horse on her stomach behind me with nothing to hold on to. The horse became a little restless. I held her in place by the back of her legs. She reached up from behind me to my shoulder and straightened herself, placing both legs behind mine, straddling the horse as I was. She probably didn't realize that most women ride side saddle.

She said in my ear, "I hope you know how to ride this thing."

"Trust me, I'm really a cowboy."

"I don't believe it, because you're a doctor, and you can't be both."

"Well, then you'll have to take your chances."

She pulled off the apron and dropped it in the debris, then put both arms around my waist, and then we, the three of us, walked out through the gate of the orphanage.

CHAPTER 16

Standing outside the gate, I wasn't sure which way to turn. The horse wanted to go back toward downtown, to return to the hospital. Princess knew the way back, having led the ambulance all over town. She knew the city like the back of her hoof, but I turned her south toward the beach. Victoria and I didn't speak as the horse walked down 21st to the beach. There were a few homes and business still standing but not standing straight; nearly everything was crooked now. The electric poles that followed the street were all leaning northward. Walking in the middle of the street, there was no one else.

I recognized Avenue O and turned westward. As Princess sidestepped debris scattered across each city block, I noticed off in the distance a large building with debris piled high against its southern side. As we got closer, I saw that it was the German Club dance pavilion. The octagonal building was completely intact except for the tall spire from its rooftop. All the tall, beautiful windows were intact except for missing their glass. As we got closer, we could see a tremendous amount of debris inside the building. One brass chandelier was left hanging. The clubhouse was gone. All the grounds, the tennis courts, lawn bowling lanes, and croquet fields were completely covered in wooden debris, some piled over ten feet high. I slid off the horse and was able to lead her around the building to the north side where several men were pulling planks of wood away from entrance and digging out the sand under them. I recognized

August Schlueter among them.

He straightened up and leaned on his shovel, "Hello, Douglas Schuler, I see that you survived."

"Yes, we did, as did the hospital. This is Victoria, a nursing student at the hospital. We just left the orphanage on 21st Street. Did your home survive?"

"Yes, it did. I live on 14th Street, north of Broadway and most of the homes there did have damage but not too severe. Many club members weathered the storm in our home. As you can see, the clubhouse has been flattened. But as long as our dance hall is intact, our jewel, we can rebuild everything else. She was hand built by the club, of strong Louisiana cypress. I knew she would make it."

"Mr. Schlueter, do you have any water?"

"Yes, the cistern here at the back of building didn't break."

The cistern, also made of cypress, was perfectly intact except for a layer of sand. Mr. Schlueter filled several glasses for us and a wooden bucket for Princess.

"Douglas, we are not rationing water, so your horse can have some too. Have you been able to contact your parents."

"No, I mean, I don't know. I sent a telegram."

"I will send one to them also, to let them know you are alive. You must come over to my house to eat, you look terrible, you know. But we all look terrible on this island."

"I don't have much free time from the hospital, but I would like to. Thank you for the invitation and for the water."

"We are going to rebuild the club, and I expect to see you soon."

I waived goodbye to him as I led Princess back into the street. I climbed back on the horse, and we began walking eastward. After a whole bucket of water, Princess was walking faster. We went back down to 21st Street, then turned south to the beach.

After several blocks, Victoria asked me to stop. It was where the Losico family store and home stood. Johnny had told her all the details of the home. That it was a small corner grocery store like so many here in town. He said the building was like a big square, it was two story, all made of wood. The entrance opened right at the corner. Now, there were only small brick piers that punctuated the sand where it once stood. There were no scattered belongings on the lot to search through, like a lone chair or clothes dresser, not even the heavy cash register. The lot where the house and store had been was wiped clean of anything and everything that had looked familiar to him.

It was getting dark now as the street ran out at the beach. There had been businesses, fishing piers, bathing houses here, but they were all gone. So were the bathing house pagodas that extended over the water. We turned eastward down the beach. She was sitting upright and holding my shoulders now and said that she was fine, just exhausted. I could see in the distance that the fires were still burning. As we walked eastward toward them, the salty smelling sea breeze gave way to the stench of burning flesh. The fires were so large now, some three stories high and so bright in the dusk. She lifted one hand off my shoulder to cover her face.

"All those fires, what are they burning?"

"Many of the bodies that were dumped at sea have washed back onto the beaches. And now they're burning them."

We were familiar with the smell of burning flesh. There was a large furnace with a tall smokestack behind the hospital where everything was burned—surgical and pathologic specimens, cadaver parts, and unclaimed bodies. As we rode slowly by, we could see bodies stacked three and four deep next to each fire, each one waiting their turn. The fire tenders had left for the night, left the fire to burn itself out. There were so many fires and so many bodies. Victoria began to cry at the sight of it.

"Don't look. Just hang on," I said.

I felt her bury her face in between my shoulder blades and her arms grasp tight my chest as I put the horse into a gallop and I was able to dodge the rows of bodies and the fires. We ran for probably a mile before we were clear of them all. We slowed down and she lifted her head to look around and then behind her.

"How awful this all is," she said.

"They will be back tomorrow to finish the job."

We both shook our heads a little to clear our minds. The breeze was off the beach, and it smelled only salty again. She eased her arms from my chest. It was very dark now as we slowly followed the water's edge.

"Look," she said as she pointed at the moon coming up over the water. It was just above the horizon and bright yellow and orange and completely full.

"The moon seems like the only thing that wasn't damaged in the storm," I said.

"Doug, I have seen so much death in the last few days. I've seen bodies in the streets under piles of wood, dead animals everywhere. After the storm, Johnny and I were walking past a large pile of debris, and I saw something reflecting the light between all the wood. I was holding Johnny's arm in one piece. But I let go and reached out toward it. It was a little gold ring reflecting the sunlight on the hand of a baby. All I could see was the hand sticking out of the debris. I knew the baby was dead, but I felt I couldn't leave her. But Johnny was pulling me along."

"I try not to think about it, but I have seen these things, too. I'm not sure if I will ever forget what I've seen."

There were horrible scenes playing over and over in our minds. This was not what we bargained for when we came to Galveston. We had been trained to put off death, to keep diseases from consuming the healthy. But death was everywhere since the storm.

She put her head back against my back, then looked to the side toward the moon. She didn't say anything else. It didn't help to talk about what we had seen since the storm. Princess wasn't breathing hard now. I only heard the waves gently breaking on the beach and the horse's hooves shuffling in the sand, and Victoria sobbing.

After a mile or so further, she tapped me on the shoulder, "Doug, can we stop. I feel terrible. I am so sore all over."

I stopped the horse and swung my leg over the mane. She reached out her arms, grabbed mine, and slid down to the sand. Her feet sunk in the sand, and she fell to her knees. I helped her up and held her hands in mine. I saw a clear spot where we could sit, a few yards from where the water was wetting the sand. I tied the horse to a small bush at the edge of the grass and we walked holding hands.

"Let's rest a little while. Are you hungry?" I asked.

"Yes, I'm starving."

I pulled the can of food out of my pocket. It reflected in the moonlight as I showed it to her.

She smiled. "A can with no label? I hope it's food?"

"I bought it from a grocery store this afternoon with Frankie. We will have to take our chances."

She smiled at me. "I don't mind. I'll eat anything, or almost anything...but maybe not okra."

I was hoping it was something different even though it was from the same shelf. I pulled my knife out of the other pocket and punctured the lid. I felt the juice come forward to my fingers and tasted it.

"It's peaches!" I pried open the rest of the tin lid and around the sharp edges I could feel peach slices. I lifted out several for her.

She pulled back her hair and said, "Put them in my mouth. One less dirty hand." I put two slices together in her mouth. She closed her mouth and just tasted the peaches awhile before she chewed them, and then she smiled at me. In the moonlight, I could see her bright smile and her sooty face with her tangled hair. She was so pretty.

I licked my fingers and reached in to grab a slice for me. I took one and ate it slowly. I reached in and grabbed more peaches for her, two at a time. I was careful not to touch the sand with my sticky hand.

"You take some, I can't eat them all," she said.

"I already had some food with Frankie, this afternoon. The other can was okra."

She laughed a little and tossed her hair back in the breeze. "Poor Frankie, he would have liked this better."

She took the can after I handed her the last slice. She drank the juice. I tried to warn her to be careful with the sharp edges, but it was too late.

"I didn't eat earlier. I didn't want to take some of the food from the children," she said with her eyes focused on the moon. I focused my eyes, too.

She continued after a few minutes. "Doug, who knows if there will be enough food for everybody. Some people might starve here after the storm. Maybe the rest of the world doesn't know what has happened here."

"The rest of the world with have to know about the storm. Dr. Randall came into the island by boat this morning. He said he heard about it the day after it happened and hurried back."

"I am so worried about my family. They probably think I'm dead."

"Mine, too. Where are you from? Wait, what is your last name?"

"I know your name, but you doctors can never remember our names."

"Had we met before?"

"No, we haven't. I'm just kidding you. My last name is Cleary and I'm from Fort Worth."

"Are you Irish?"

"Yes, I am, but I was born here in Texas. My parents got married in their hometown in Ireland and then ran away to America. They landed here in Galveston, then found their way to Fort Worth. I have an uncle who sponsored them, who took them in. What about you, where are you from? I see that you are German."

"I was born in Santa Clara. My family has a ranch there, outside of Seguin. Why did you come here for school?"

"My father is a blacksmith and my mother a seamstress. My mother wanted me to be a seamstress, too, but I wanted to be a nurse. One summer, when I was about twelve years old, my younger brother got sick. The doctors didn't know what he had but he didn't last the summer. I took care of him while my parents worked. He was only five years old. After he died, his doctor told me that he probably had leukemia. That he should not have lasted six weeks but since I took good care of him, he lasted three months. After that I told them I wanted to become a nurse. They knew some Irish families here in Galveston, who recommended that I come here to the school. The school is the only one in Texas. It was new and would provide housing for me. And I could get a diploma."

She added, "If you grew up on a ranch, why did you want to be a doctor?"

"I don't know. I guess, I knew our family doctor well. I am the oldest and I was around when he delivered my brother and sisters at home. He was always available if we needed him. My father would give him beef or a live calf for his services. I didn't really want to live on the ranch anymore. I went to college in San Antonio but left early to come here. My professor recommended me. He told me it would be an honor to serve others, more dignified than raising cattle. And I could be trained right here in Texas, I wouldn't have to leave the state for training. And I wanted to see the ocean."

"Me, too," she said.

She was quiet for a little while. She looked back at me, "You know that laceration on your forehead doesn't look good. It's still bleeding a little, I think. What happened?"

"I fell against a cart a couple of days ago in town," I said, as I reached up to feel a little fresh blood. My hair was matted again from it. The sutures felt dry, though.

It was cooling off and the moon was climbing higher in the sky. I didn't want to leave. Victoria looked at her dress, her uniform. She unlaced her shoes and pushed her feet into the sand. I took off my shoes and socks and rolled up my pants legs a little. The sand was deep and dry.

"I have been wearing this same uniform for more than three days, I think. I know I look horrible. I think it's ruined."

"That's okay, don't worry."

"Please don't think me as terrible, but I must go for a swim, to rinse off all this soot, and the sand too."

"Of course, I understand. I will be over by the horse."

I stood up and brushed off the sand from my pants and grabbed my shoes and walked over to the horse nearby. I combed her mane with my fingers and rubbed her face with my back to the water. After a few moments I could hear her splashing and laughing in the water. I didn't look for a few minutes, but finally I turned to see that she was waist high in the water wearing her long white underdress. The white dress was bright in the moonlight reflecting off the water. She was splashing around, then seemed to slip a little and go completely under. I moved a little closer to the water, then she came up moving her hair away from her face. She began to walk back out of the water. I turned back around to the horse and put my socks and shoes back on.

I could hear her walking toward me. I turned around and she was holding her blue dress in front of her.

"I feel so much better now," she said.

"I'm glad you do. I went in earlier this afternoon. The water was clear then."

"I think I like the water better at night. The moonlight cast over the water is so beautiful."

"I think we should be heading back now, don't you?" I said. I could see the moonlight in her clear eyes.

"Yes, but I don't want to put my uniform back on just yet. It is glorious here, feeling the cool breeze when I'm wet. I feel so much better." She smiled a little, then said, "Will you get down on your knees?"

I did. She reached into a waist pocket and pulled out a handkerchief and touched it to my forehead and wiped a little of the blood away. She was using the moonlight to treat me. I closed my eyes. It was wet and cool. The pain it caused didn't matter. Next, she got down on her knees in front of me and wiped my face. I closed my eyes.

She pulled back the handkerchief and smiled, "Now that is a little better, I think. We are so dirty, you know."

"Thank you. I can't imagine how I look, probably awful." I wanted to touch her face, too, and gently lift her wet hair from around her face.

"No, you don't look too bad," she said with a broad smile. "Just quit hitting your head," she said as she replaced the blood-stained handkerchief into her dress pocket.

I stood and pulled the horse around and jumped up on its back. She handed me her dress and I held it in one arm. I extended my free hand to her. This time she got up on the horse a little easier. She slid in behind me. I felt her legs against mine. She had her shoes in one hand. Her other arm was on my shoulder.

We pulled off the salt grass back to the sand then walked slowly by the water's edge. She put her free hand around my chest and held on tight. I could see that her hand was so small. Her hand looked clean now. As the horse walked, I held the reins with one hand and her blue dress across my lap. I could feel her cool, wet underdress against me, the wetness seeping through my shirt. She was quiet for a while with her head between my shoulders.

"Douglas, really, I have nowhere to go."

"Let's go back to the hospital. Dr. Randall told me that the faculty were arranging for the student nurses to stay in the hospital for a few weeks until something better is found."

"I don't mind. I want to telegram my parents that I'm still alive, but they will insist that I come home. I don't want to yet. I want to finish the program now. In May I will get my diploma. I have been thinking about Vivian, she looked so poorly when I left. Did you see her?"

"Yes, I think she will be fine. Dr. Smith was able to give her oxygen gas to breathe, which helped her. When I left this morning, she was much better."

"Oh, thank goodness, she is my dear friend."

"She's not going to die, I promise."

She was quiet again for a while. I thought she fell asleep, resting her cheek on my back. Her grip at my chest relaxed. I looked down to see her small feet above mine on both sides of the horse. We wound around toward the north, leaving the beach before it ended and headed directly back to the hospital. In the moonlight, I could see my way around and between the piles of debris, slowly making our way back. I looked toward the hospital and further downtown. It was all completely dark. The lights of downtown before the storm never dimmed. When we reached the hospital, it was dark and quiet, too. I steered Princess to the side where she was tied up. Victoria was asleep.

"Victoria? Victoria, we're here."

She slowly lifted her head off my back. I swung a leg over the neck of the horse and jumped off. I reached up for her and she leaned toward me. I caught her under her arms and could feel her wet underdress. She landed on the ground in front of me and rested her head on my chest.

"I'm okay," she said, as she pulled away.

I took her dress off the horse and gave it to her. I turned around and tied up the horse. I could hear her putting on her dress.

"I don't want to put my shoes back on now. I can't see anything, can you?"

"I think so," I said as I walked back toward her. I reached down behind her back and her legs and picked her up in my arms. She put her arm around my neck. We walked toward the rear door of the hospital. I carried her through the door and slowly made my way through the morgue.

"Can you really see where you're going?" she asked.

I had been in the morgue many times over the past four years. I could see my way by the moonlight coming through the small windows. I carried her through the door leaving the morgue and down the hall to the main stairwell. I climbed to the first floor. I could see clearer now. The moonlight was shining through the large front windows of the hospital. The fragments of glass left in the windows edges were like broken teeth all around. As I walked, I didn't hear glass under my feet.

"Doug, you can put me down." She held her shoes in her hands, and we quietly climbed the steps together to the next landing.

"Victoria, keep going to the next floor and go to the east ward. There are no patients there and I think that's where you and the other students are staying."

"Are you coming up?"

"No, I want to bring some water to the horse, and I will find somewhere to sleep, maybe in the morgue or on the top floor."

She was looking up at me as we stood together on the same step. Then she stepped up on the next step and turned around to look at me directly in my eyes, standing on her tiptoes. She dropped her shoes and then put her arms around my neck and kissed me on the cheek. She leaned away from me and smiled.

"Well, Doug, so you've rescued me again. That's twice in one week."

"I guess it is. There's still time for a third."

"I wouldn't mind it. You handled that horse really well, for a doctor."

"I told you I could," I said.

The moonlight was directly on her face, framed by her wavy dark hair. Her eyes were so clear, so bright, like the moon and I stared into them. I pulled her closer and kissed her, on the lips. After a moment, she lowered her head in front of my face.

"Victoria, your hair is such a mess." We both laughed a little but not too loud. It was quiet in the hospital.

She raised her head and looked at me, "So is yours, Douglas. And your clothes are so filthy."

She gently pushed some of my hair away from my scalp wound and then straightened my shirt collar before she let go of my neck and rocked back on her bare heels. She bent over to pick up her shoes and then turned and headed up the stairs. I watched her until she got to the next landing. She stopped on the landing and then turned back to me and smiled again. Her bright smile parted her long, curly hair hanging across her face. The front of my shirt felt wet and clung to me. She went inside the ward. The nurses never smiled at us; it was against their rules.

I went back the way I came as quietly as I could. I found the water bucket outside behind the hospital and filled it with water at the cistern and then took it to the horse standing in the patch of grass. From this side of the hospital, I could see the bright moon high in the sky and the light reflecting off her mane and her back. I patted her down and told her what I was thinking about Victoria. Where could I go now? Would I be trespassing; was I welcome to stay here? I was probably in some trouble. Why did she kiss me?

Princess was a good listener. She let out a snort and moved her head up and down—in approval? I looked up the wall of the hospital, at the broken windows, one in line above the other. There was no light shining outward from any of them. I knelt on the grass, moved away some wood planks away from the wall, and sat down next to the stone wall of the hospital. What time was it? I think it was Tuesday night? It didn't matter. I leaned my head back and then touched the cheek where she kissed me. The sea breeze blew my hair away from my face and drops of sweat ran down it.

CHAPTER 17

The morning sun was directly in my eyes as I sat forward from the wall of the hospital. I swatted a mosquito biting my face. I stood and looked around, then down at myself. I was so dirty; my untucked white shirt was a grimy gray, and my black trousers were sandy. I tried to dust off most of the sand, but my new suit was filthy and where was the coat?

I went to the back of the hospital and entered the morgue. It was lit by a little sunlight coming in through the low outside windows. I easily walked around all the fallen tables that I had navigated in the dark last night. I went to the front stairs and then to the main entrance here on the first floor, which was brightly lit by the morning sun.

As I climbed the stairs, I heard could hear voices on the wards. I opened the doors to the wards and looked toward the east ward where Victoria had disappeared to last night. I didn't see her and it was quiet there. I walked toward the west ward and saw Dr. Randall talking with Nurse Willow in the middle of the ward. He glanced over toward me but turned back again and continued giving orders to the nurse. There were just a few patients, most of the beds were empty and I didn't see Carl. I walked back to the storage room where we used to get our morning coffee but there was none.The storage room was stacked with supplies, wooden crates with tools, rope, glassware, and there was a long table in the middle next to a sewing machine. It had Dr. Randall's netting folded high in the center.

Dr. Randall came over to me as I went back into the ward. Before he spoke, he looked at me, noticed carefully my terrible appearance. He paused a little longer and took a deep breath.

"Come here, Douglas, and sit down."

He motioned to a chair at the nurse's table. He stood over me and looked at the lacerations in my scalp. Nurse Willow came over to see it too.

"Dr. Randall, they look pretty clean," she said as she moved the hair away from the laceration and he probed the sutures with his index finger.

"I had it cleaned with salt water last night," I said.

He grabbed a towel to wipe his hands and said, "I don't think the skull is broken, Douglas."

"It doesn't hurt like it did."

Dr. Randall walked away. Nurse Willow returned with some Permanganate of Potassium in a glass jar and turned it upside down over some gauze and then thoroughly cleaned my scalp. She was rough with it, not soft like a handkerchief. I closed my eyes.

"You've got to be more careful, quit hitting your head," she said quietly, while shaking her head.

I stood up and thanked her. It was still stinging but I knew it would for a few hours. We used to use that on our horses with their leg wounds, and they would dance around afterwards. I walked over to Dr. Randall, who was assembling a large, rectangular piece of his netting over a bed of an older man who was sleeping. I wasn't sure what he was trying to do; neither was the man in the bed after he felt the netting on his body and woke up, but he didn't say anything.

"I have read in *The Lancet* how Punjabi fisherman used to sleep under them and had very low rates of malaria. Dr. Ronald Ross, a Scotsman living in India, reported his observations about malaria and the mosquito. I had ordered these rolls of it before the storm. I'm as convinced as he was that it's the bite of the Anopheles mosquito that transmits the parasite, the kind we have here, too," Dr. Randall said as he was busy fitting the netting to the bed. He reached and held the center of the netting off the patient.

He added, "We need to find a way to suspend the netting away from his body. He could still be bitten if the netting is on his skin."

We looked up at the light fixtures hanging from the ceiling. We were thinking the same thing.

"Douglas, have you been to your apartment?"

"I have and it is heavily damaged. Part of the roof is gone."

"Do you think the Hendersons will take you in?"

"I don't think so. I think he wouldn't think it proper."

"Mr. Henderson owes me favors after caring for his mother. All those house calls after his nervous phone calls to me in the middle of the night. He made it worse for her with all his worrying."

"I'm would rather not ask him, sir. He always seems to look at me with....I don't know, disdain."

"I think you're overreacting, Douglas. He's just averse to what we do as physicians."

"If I could stay here in the hospital? I could be available to work day and night."

"You can't stay here. Dr. Cooke, the Dean, is making arrangements for the students to stay here at the hospital or the Medical Department building, or the Breckenridge Hall until they can find other suitable housing."

"But I haven't seen any medical students here yet. There's just been the nursing students with us for the summer."

"I know how you interns have concerned yourselves with the whereabouts of the nursing students this summer," he said. "But the Dean does not want to start the school year late. He stayed during the storm and has been busy with telegrams to our Senator and, I believe, the Governor as well. They are determined to start the fall session on time."

"But, Dr. Randall, the medical students don't have any idea about what has happened here. I don't think they will fulfill their commitment to return."

"You don't know that. I am in full support of the Dean and I 'm counting on you and the other interns to support the mission of the school."

"Yes sir, of course, we will." He turned to Nurse Willow who had brought another sewn net. We all stepped to the next bed that was empty and she helped him spread the net out over it.

He continued, "But as I said, you cannot stay here or at the other buildings at the university. We are allowing the student nurses to stay here because their home across the street was completely destroyed. Did you know that?"

"Yes, sir, I did."

What did he mean? He had always been honest with me, but he didn't care about me or Carl and Tex, just like the other faculty doctors. We had come to disregard the negative opinions or personal insults by the other faculty, but Dr. Randall's opinion meant a lot to us.

Dr. Randall sighed and with his hands on his hips said, "But you do need a place to stay, and probably Carl and Homer, too. Though, I think Carl is more resourceful than the two of you."

I knew what he meant by that. That Carl knew how to communicate better with people better than we did, better with patients, better with women. I don't care now about his opinion.

I sighed again and said, "You all can stay with me. My wife and our children are still visiting with family in St Louis. I told them to stay put until it's safe on the island. I have a small house in the back of my home where you all can stay....temporarily."

"Thank you, sir, for your kindness. And, Dr. Randall, I haven't seen Tex since the storm. I'm worried about him. Have you heard from him?"

"No, Douglas, I haven't. I'm afraid he didn't survive the storm.

Carl said that his apartment building was destroyed."

I slowly backed away before he changed his mind. Could Tex have somehow survived the storm? Did he float away to the mainland and is just waiting to come back?

I went to the storage room and found a small spool of rope and brought it back to the bedside of the first patient. He was awake and not moving a muscle under the net and he looked like a corpse under a funeral veil. He had listened to the whole conversation; patients will do that when you think they're not.

I grabbed the center of the net over him and bunched it in my hand. I had the spool of rope in the other and wrapped the bunch of netting at the bottom of my fist to make a knot. With the other hand I tossed the spool over the light fixture directly overhead and caught it as it fell back to me. I cut the end of the rope with my pocketknife and tied the loose end of the rope to the foot board, suspending the net above the patient a few feet. The patient nodded his head in agreement with what I did.

Dr. Randall turned to Nurse Willow and said, "Our Dr. Schuler is from the ranch. At least, he knows how to use a rope."

"And he didn't break the glass chimneys, because they were all broken by the storm," Nurse Willow said looking at the fixture as it was rocking slightly and now tilted.

"That will work for now; do the same for the other beds. But don't break anything."

"Yes sir."

We did. I saw Nurse Willow instructing one of the student nurses to finish the sewing of the nets according to the dimensions that Dr. Randall specified. It wasn't Victoria. Where was she?

We had enough netting to cover half the beds in the west ward, about fifteen. We mainly covered the beds on the north side of the ward where there might be the most mosquitos, the bay side of the hospital. With the rope, I was able to elevate all the nets. I ran out of rope and went to the storage room to get more. I glanced to the east ward but didn't see anyone at the entrance. Some of the ropes were looped on more than one light fixture as there were fewer fixtures than beds. The whole set-up looked a little awkward but I was working well to hold the nets in place.

I assumed it was my night to work. Carl, Tex, and I rotated every third night since we began in July. I know Carl worked last night and I did the night before. During the day, I was hoping to see Tex walk through the door of the ward, but he never did. It had been five nights since the storm and no one had heard from him or seen him. I knew Carl had left as early as he could.

It was a relief to work with Nurse Willow for the day. She looked exhausted and I wanted to tell her to go home but I knew she couldn't leave until her shift was over. And it wasn't my place to recommend that to her or to have a personal conversation with the nurses or nursing students. Maybe she had to work the night, too, or did Nurse Sanders have night duty?

Dr. Randall returned to the ward before the end of the day to inspect each net over each bed and then approved our work. He confirmed that I had duty tonight and that still he had not seen Tex. He mentioned that we should have fresh water later today. The waterworks building was not damaged severely and the primary water main to the island was still intact. We heard that many sought shelter there in this brick-and-stone building and that the tall smoke stack was swaying during the storm but didn't fall. He had the orderlies drain the hospital's cisterns so they could be refilled with fresh water. He spoke with Nurse Willow before he left, and she was shaking her head in disagreement. Maybe he had recommended some rest for her, maybe her home was destroyed? Was she married? Did she have children? I wasn't supposed to know or be curious about it.

Before dark, I got some clean water from the cisterns out back.

They filled very slowly from the main water source as the hospital was at the far east end of the island, far from the waterworks downtown. The sun set over the bay while the water trickled into the buckets. I carried several full ones back to the west ward for the patients, but also left a full bucket at the east ward door. Several women were talking behind the closed door. Was Vivian still was breathing easier? Was Victoria there? It would not be right to knock.

The night was quiet and breezy. There were just a few patients remaining. No one was near death and all were sleeping. The ward was especially dark without the electric lights. But Nurse Willow lit a small lantern at the nurses table and sat down in the small wooden chair with her patient charts. There were no fevers or rapid pulses to document. Our normally boisterous ward was quiet because putting patients to sleep was not easy. But we did have our supply of opiates to quiet the few who were in constant pain.

Dr. Smith came by to inspect our netting over the beds and he approved also. He had heard rumors about it. I told him what Dr. Randall mentioned about the Punjabi fisherman and the Anopheles mosquito. He recounted how he showed us the flagellum of that mosquito in his microscope lab as a student and how he has been trying to develop a mosquito repellant from a combination of Alum, Chloroform, and the Essence of Pennyroyal. Now, he was working night and day to restore the microscope stations in the Medical Department building before the new class of medical students began. He commended my knots on the foot boards of the beds as he tested each one.

When it was very late, I walked through the ward to check on the patients and all were still asleep. And I checked on the nets that we had rigged and made sure that all the knots were not slipping. I looked back at the nurse's table and could see Nurse Willow asleep over her charts next to the only lantern on the ward. I crawled under the mosquito netting on the empty bed at the far end of the ward, took off my shoes, and closed my eyes, only for a moment.

When I opened my eyes again, it was daylight. I sat up as fast as I could manage and looked around the ward, through the netting. I didn't see Nurse Willow at the nurse's table or any other nurse at that moment. Two of the orderlies was standing at the bedside of the old man. They had a stretcher waiting. I swung my legs over the side of the bed facing the wall and lifted the netting and looked out the window. A small piece of paper had fallen from my chest to the floor. It was a small cream-colored card folded in the middle. I opened it.

> Dear Douglas,
>
> I found you tonight under this net. For a moment I thought you were dead, but I then could hear you breathing. I wanted to let you know that I am fine. Vivian is getting better. Please don't lose track of me. There's still time for a third!
>
> Yours,
Victoria

I looked out the window; maybe I would rescue her a third time. I had a few days left. I put my shoes on and stood and looked back across the ward. I put the card in my back pocket and walked to the entrance of the ward. I saw the bed where the old man was with the orderlies waiting. One of them said that I needed to pronounce him so they could take him to the morgue. He had just died, or the head nurse waited to let me sleep a little.

I lifted the netting and could see that he had died. He wasn't breathing, no chest elevations. I felt for a carotid pulse and there was none. His skin was cool, so he died several hours ago. I told the orderlies that they could take him now. I went to the nurse's table and sat in the chair and grabbed his chart. He had terminal cancer of some sort, most likely liver or stomach cancer, as his liver was very large and rock hard on palpation. His family said he was a drinker, and we weren't sure why they brought him to the hospital yesterday. He survived the storm only to die a few days afterward here.

I looked up again and didn't see Nurse Willow; hopefully, she was relieved of duty. I began to look at the few remaining patients. They had not wanted to stay under the netting and moved to the other side of the ward to the beds without the netting.

I could hear Nurse Sanders walking on to the ward with her heavy footsteps and booming voice. She was with Dr. Randall. They walked toward me, and I stood in front of the table. She paused to stare at me with disgust, as she usually did. She could tell that I just woke up. She complained about the netting and the irregularities of this sort of arrangement on a hospital ward, and for not following the prescribed protocols. He insisted not to take down the netting, not to even touch the netting, and that the chandeliers were fine. She concluded the conversation by saying that she wanted to consult Dr. Thompson or Dr. Clopton when they returned. Dr. Randall left the ward.

I moved next to her and added, "Don't touch the netting" as I stared back at her. I hurried to catch up with Dr. Randall. He stopped and looked back at me, up and down, and shook his head. He was upset with Nurse Sanders; I could see it. How did he look so professional?

He sighed, "Douglas, your appearance is horrible. You've got to go clean up; launder your clothes, for goodness' sake."

He was still inspecting me when he reached up and pulled a white handkerchief out of my shirt pocket. It was lacy and delicate and had the letter "V" embroidered with pink thread in the corner.

I hadn't noticed it. It was perfectly white, without a blood stain. He stared back at me with more disgust.

"This doesn't belong to you, does it? I won't ask you how you came to acquire it. I don't want to know."

I gently lifted it out of his hand and put it back in my shirt pocket. "It was a gift."

"Your shirt should be as white as that handkerchief. Clean yourself up."

"I will. Can I go to your house now? And I will clean up."

"Yes, do you know the house?" I nodded that I did.

"Enter the back house through the alley, don't go into the main house. You'll find soap to launder your clothes. Is this all you have?"

"No, I have some other clothes that I placed downstairs. Thank you again, sir for letting us stay with you."

"Yes, just stay in the back house."

How did she get the blood out of the handkerchief? I didn't see Carl as I left the hospital to give him a report, but I just kept going.

I began walking down the Strand toward downtown after I got some fresh water to drink at the hospital cistern. I splashed my face and hair also. I smelled the handkerchief, and it smelled like soap. I put it in my back pocket with the card. As I walked block after block, people were beginning to clean up much of the debris and pile it higher on the sidewalks to clear the streets. One man on the bay side of the Strand was trying to pull a boat lying on its side away from his house with a mule and a chain. Much of the Strand was passable now as the downtown district sustained the least amount of damage. Everywhere people were cleaning, sweeping, removing what was broken and piling it high.

I made my way several blocks over to Market Street. I wanted to go to the morgue there, Morgue #1. I jumped on the elevated sidewalk and walked down to the entrance. The doors to the morgue were locked. The handmade sign that said "Morgue #1" was lying sideways against the wall. I asked several persons walking by about the morgue, that I was looking for someone, and no one knew where to go. I saw a store owner sweeping his storefront and he told me that the morgue was emptied yesterday, and the bodies were taken to be burned near the beachfront and that all of the morgues were closed now. Could Rosa and Tex still be alive? Maybe they floated to the mainland and were waiting to come back? Or are we waiting to find their bodies? Would it do any good to search for them any longer?

I headed down 22nd Street toward Broadway and there were women with their wooden buckets of water washing away the storm from front porches. Grocers were selling more things besides unlabeled cans. I smelled bread baking over open fires. A furniture store had some of its pieces on the sidewalks to dry and to sell at a marked down price. As I continued to walk, I saw a boy with a large white linen bag over his shoulder. He was yelling what was printed in black ink on the bag "Galveston Daily News." People were gathering around to buy a copy for a nickel. I made it to Broadway and could see the mountains of wooden debris in the distance, running parallel southward to the wide street. And there were many fires in the tallest piles of debris at their peaks. I crossed over Broadway and several blocks more to get close to one of the fires. This fire was blazing high, but I could see that the dead had not been removed from it, but were being burned where they were. There was the smell of burning flesh and salt, and wet wood as these piles were now funeral pyres.

As I walked eastward down Broadway, people were moving up and down the street. The tall wrought iron fences were still intact to keep the crowds out of the expensive properties. Many people were working their way south through the mountain of debris as there were many paths through it now, and over it, too. If you looked closer you could see parts of bodies within the wood, and other things from houses: lacy curtains, a flattened bowler hat, children's toys, a piano, an armoire, table legs, and many mattresses now ruptured of their cotton. The paint of these boards had been blasted off by the wind. Many homes were painted bright colors, but the wood looked like new, ready to be used and painted again.

I stopped when I saw a tiny hand protruding from the bare boards. There was a little gold ring on the first finger reflecting the sunlight. She will be cremated with all her fingers. I think if a body was seen in the pile, it might be nearly impossible to extract. The sheer weight of the wood on top of the body kept it trapped. People were helplessly looking and looking, afraid to stop, and afraid of what they might find as the fires would slowly make their way down to them. How do you stop searching? I should search for Rosa and her family, but where would I start? Or was she just washed away, like their house? How could she have survived when thousands had died? She hadn't found me. Tex hadn't shown up. We were living, but why?

Things had to be repaired, put back together. But what if there was nothing left to repair? How can you fix your home when it is just gone? That was the situation for so many, especially the poor. Their smaller homes on the southside of town were built by someone who labored six days a week and saved up just enough to build a small wood frame house for his family. These simple wood frame homes were no match for the storm. Nearly all were completely gone, sacrificed during the storm to make up the wall of debris that seemed to protect the rest of the island, the rich side, the business side.

At 20th Street I found Dr. Randall's house in the middle of the block. It was one of the smaller houses on the north side of Broadway, tucked between the mansions. It looked completely intact except for a few broken windows on the first floor and a few missing window shutters. There was some debris in the yard behind the tall iron fence, mainly from fallen branches. I went around back to the alley and found his back house and entered the property through a wooden gate. The cistern was intact and in place next to the back of the house. Closer inspection revealed that it had ruptured and was sitting slightly tilted on its base, and empty of water. The outside privy had been blown over. I went up the stairs to the back porch of the main house and looked inside the window beside the kitchen door. Everything seemed in its place inside.

I went back into the yard and then climbed the stairs of the back house and went inside. It was a single room over the garage. The windows facing the main house were broken but the floor was dry on the inside and the ceiling intact was dry. Carl was asleep on a small daybed. He had cleaned up the broken glass on the floor. There was a small wood stove in the corner, and a small table and chair against the wall. It all smelled of mold and the plastered walls were spotted with it. I left the room and went back down the stairs to the garage to find tools to fix the cistern. Could there be a list of the dead in the newspaper?

PART 4

"The youngest of us who today hold his newly won diploma will have in his first unsuccessful case no deeper sense of misery than he who has had the experience of half a century."

Jacob M. Da Costa, M.D. , Jefferson Medical College,
Philadelphia, 1891

CHAPTER 18

In the week that we had been at Dr. Randall's back house it was hot and dry. Most of the mildew spots were disappearing and the house smelled better. Carl and I fixed the cistern and removed all the debris from the yard. We, of course, lifted the privy back to its original location in the corner of the rear yard. We picked up the window shutters and after we found a ladder in the garage, we nailed them back to where they were before. One day when I wasn't on duty, I used the ladder to climb on the roof of the main house where several slate shingles were missing. I found spare shingles in the alley and completed the repair of the roof, and the roof on the back house. From that vantage point, I could see the debris piles burning even bigger than before; the strong stench of burning bodies hung in the air day and night. And the southern breeze off the Gulf blew it our way.

What was worse than the stench, though, were the mosquitoes. They swarmed everywhere. The smoke from the burning debris piles helped reduce them, but not by much. They bit us at dusk and during the night and buzzed in our ears as we tried to sleep. Throughout the city there were large puddles of seawater after the storm, slowly evaporating but not before the mosquitoes could reproduce and then feast on the islanders. Everywhere I went they would swarm me, especially close to the hospital that was next to the bay. Mosquitoes were a way of life in Texas, but I had never felt them so thick and so hungry.

I bought the newspaper daily and searched through the list of those confirmed dead. There were hundreds on the list, and it kept growing with each publication. I didn't see Rosa or Tex on the list. There were many more missing than confirmed dead. There was no list for the missing.

The mule cars began plowing their usual course through the city again. Some new mules were brought in over the repaired wagon bridge from the mainland, as most of the animals had drowned. The mule cars had been toppled but with makeshift repairs they were back on the tracks, slowly squeaking across town. That bridge also carried the electricity and telegraph and telephone lines into the city. A few of the businesses downtown had electricity as they stood alone illuminating a dark city. The Cotton Exchange building on the Strand with its enormous imported electric chandeliers was shining brightly. Wealthy businessmen sat beneath them late into the evening in the large oak-paneled main room smoking dry cigars and planning how to move all that wet cotton.

I managed to get a telegraph to my family a few days ago. The Western Union office had reopened, and I waited in a long line to send the telegram. I made it a one-line message, just to let them know that I was alive. I didn't want to worry them about the minor details of my life, not yet. The banks downtown had reopened, too. I had an account in the bank where my former landlord, Mr. Henderson, was on the board of bankers. He vouched for me to get it. My account was running low, and I think Mr. Henderson took out the entire September rent from it. It was early October now and I had not been paid. I had withdrawn money to buy food, to send the telegram, and to pay rent to Dr. Randall. He refused my payment. He didn't want us living there too long.

The mail had not been delivered since the storm. I had told my family that if they wanted to write, to send letters to the hospital and that I wasn't sure where I would be living in the near future.

I had heard that the railroad bridge that ran alongside the wagon bridge had been repaired also. Many railroad cars behind the 25th Street terminal had been tossed on their sides and stacked on top of one another during the storm like toys. Since living in Galveston, I could tell the difference between the train whistles and the horns from the steam tugboats navigating the harbor. Most of the time, it was a noisy place. But there were no train whistles since the storm.

People were returning to the island now by boat and by carriage. They would travel down to Broadway to see all the destruction that they had read about: well-dressed men in their dark suits and ties and their clean bowler hats. No doubt, they were dignitaries from Houston or Austin who wanted to see it all for themselves. It seemed that only a few women made the trip. But they were all well-dressed women in their bright white, lacy dresses holding their white parasols in their white-gloved hands. They covered their mouth and noses with lacy white handkerchiefs to block to stench of burning flesh. It was easy to tell that they were not from here. Galvestonians who survived the storm did not have clothes that were black and white anymore; theirs were dirty browns and sandy grays. We didn't realize how bad we looked until we saw the visitors.

I heard that many of the homeowners on Broadway had spent the summer abroad or in New York City. No doubt, they read about the extensive destruction and the thousands who had died, but they returned to a sturdy brick home with minimal damage and to their lives not terribly inconvenienced. There wasn't much food on the island in the first week after the storm. Some desperate men had scaled those tall wrought iron fences and broke into a few of these homes looking for food, and some were shot on the spot. These owners had arranged for lawmen to patrol their premises in their absence. And there was a great deal of looting just after the storm. Of the residents who did, most were desperate, looking for food, and when they were caught they were not jailed but were shot.

There was much less looting now, though the island remained under martial law.

And these wealthy Galvestonians who had left for the storm for some advantageous reason were also returning. They were the most astonished of all, the most upset at seeing their beloved city in such devastation. Of course, many less-well-to-do didn't find their homes at all. They had been washed away. No heirloom pieces or photos albums lying around the property to gather up, or to hold close to their chest while they cried.

Now two weeks after the storm, the newspaper notified us that several sites across town were set up for food and water distribution by the City Committee on the storm recovery. There was one near the hospital at the home of Dr. West on 13th Street and Postoffice. This was food brought by steamers from New Orleans and Mobile, and I ate as much as I could get my hands on. I had never known such hunger in the first week after the storm. At one point, I hadn't eaten for nearly three days. I was trying now to put back on the weight I had lost. I would take some of the dried food with me and walk the several blocks to where Rosa's house was and sit under the palm tree to eat. I wrote a letter to her and pinned it to the tree with a loose nail. Just a dry, stained piece of paper I had found nearby and written with the pencil I carried around. It wasn't much of a note. I wanted her to know that I was looking for her and for her to come to me. Every time I walked by the palm tree after picking up food at the Dr. West home, I saw the letter still pinned to the palm and spinning in the breeze.

The public water fountains were working again for man and for beast to equally partake. The water looked clear but tasted a little salty. I didn't mind drinking directly from it even if I was in line after a horse. Carl and I took turns bringing bucketfuls of water back with us from the nearest downtown fountain to the back house after working the night. I made a round wooden cover for each bucket. I bathed outside at night with the water that I didn't drink.

The hospital was nearly empty in the first week after the storm but now the wards were full. The nursing students that were housed on the west ward had been moved to another home and to Breckenridge Hall. I would have to find out where they were. But some left Galveston and the nursing program to return to their hometowns. Nurse Willow, who had worked so hard during the storm, had resigned. All the faculty were back as the new medical students were scheduled to begin the first of October. This was the time the faculty usually returned from their extended vacations. The faculty were all over the wards, talking loudly, running us ragged. They were at first shocked after seeing the condition of the hospital, then angry that much of the debris had not been moved away from the front of the hospital and that the windows had not been repaired.

But there was very little building material on the island. Most everyone who could repair their homes were waiting on ships or barges or anything that could bring it in. Most of the faculty had offices in the Medical Department building and all the windows there were broken, too, so what was in their offices was destroyed, missing, or ruined. Dr. Thompson wanted to know why his office had not been cleaned and why his surgical volumes were not sanitized. I heard that they were all over the floor and black with mold. His precious volumes were ruined, as were all the other faculty's, except Dr. Randall's. Dr. Randall, who hurried back right after the storm, was able to dry his medical books and save them. Dr. Smith, though, who stayed for the storm, never wanting to leave his experiments unattended, lost his books in his basement office. They just floated away.

I was present on the ward when Dr. Randall informed the rest of the faculty present that one of the house interns was missing, probably drowned. They all looked at me. They seemed disappointed that it wasn't me. He mentioned that it was Homer Hornsby. Several were a little confused about who that was. Dr. Clopton spoke up and asked if it was "that tall Texan boy"? Dr. Randall and I nodded that it was. He explained how his apartment building was completely destroyed, but that the other two interns survived because they were on duty here the night of the storm.

Dr. Clopton asked why Tex didn't take shelter here in the hospital? And why the other interns didn't go get him when the water started rising? Dr. Randall calmly responded that there was no warning about the storm, no one knew that it was imminent on that Saturday, now several weeks ago. Dr. Clopton then told the faculty that he knows Tex's father and that he had recommended an internship here for his son above other hospitals on the East Coast. I knew that Tex's father was an important man. They all suggested to Dr. Clopton that he get a telegraph to the father as soon as possible.

Mosquitoes were swarming throughout the wards, biting us all as we tried to work and the patients who tried to get better. Several of the faculty, especially Dr. Clopton, demanded loudly to Dr. Randall that the mosquito nets be removed at once. We removed a few of them but the patients under them were truly protected from the swarms of mosquitoes that happened every evening and they pleaded with us to leave them. I saw several of the other faculty lingering under them after they examined a patient. But not Dr. Clopton, whose face was the most mosquito bitten body part that I had ever seen, as he refused to reach up to swat a mosquito like the rest of us were doing constantly. He spoke to everyone who would listen about the ridiculousness of the nets—that they would do nothing to prevent a yellow fever epidemic, like the ones that he had lived through here in 1867. He said that the miasmata of disease and filth present on every corner of the island after the storm is the cause of the yellow fever. And that he knew personally the father of Texas medicine, Dr. Ashbel Smith who described in beautiful detail the yellow fever plague of 1839 when the Republic of Texas and marshy, unsanitary Galveston were in their infancy.

Our own Dr. Smith had spoken to me of the disease and the observations of Dr. Ashbel Smith on it when he did the autopsy on the last confirmed case of it when I was a student two years ago. He said that Dr. Ashbel Smith was correct in saying that it was not contagious. He tried to prove it by even tasting the black vomit, the fatal last symptom. But our Dr. Smith had told me that we were scientifically past those days of self-injections or of tasting vomit, which didn't prove anything. Our Dr. Smith agreed with Dr. Randall that mosquitoes were the vector for many diseases—malaria, and dengue fever—but he couldn't find the parasites by microscopy of the blood.

His first day back, Dr. Clopton had a small audience of students and nurses on the west ward, and he related his experiences this summer traveling "back East." How he had the privilege of meeting the great Dr. William Osler in Baltimore, even dining with him one evening at a feast with many other prestigious physicians. That Dr. Osler spoke of his many accomplishments in patient care, the unsolvable cases that he had solved, of his unique diagnostic methods, and how Dr. Clopton was inspired to donate his brain to the American Anthropometric Society as Dr. Osler had planned. And that Dr. Osler even spoke to him directly during the dinner. Dr. Randall asked Dr. Clopton what he said to him and Dr. Clopton said, "'My dear man, could you please pass the potatoes.'"

Dr. Smith was not listening to Dr. Clopton expound on the finer points of Oslerian medicine but was busy spraying his homemade mosquito repellent throughout the wards. He did this every few hours during the day. The scent of camphor made our eyes and noses burn. Of course, he wasn't around during the evening hours to spray when the mosquitoes feasted on us, as rarely were the faculty were ever around in the evening. During the night we took some of the discarded nets from the supply rooms to cover ourselves, sitting between two chairs with the net draped over them in the storage room. I learned two things—that mosquito nets do work and how to sleep sitting up.

Electricity had not been restored to the hospital or the Medical Building. On my nights at the hospital, we would light the wards with lanterns until we ran out of kerosene. Then we would light candles. There weren't enough candles to illuminate the wards well and it was very dark on this part of the island. The only light I could see was from the harbor where a few boats were anchored with their dim cabin lights shining and bobbing. The harbor lighthouse at the southern jetty was damaged and not working. I used to watch its rotating light over the harbor on quiet work nights.

Many boats in the bay had sunk. I could see parts of them protruding out of the water during the day, the pointed masts or the chubby smokestacks pointing skyward, but at an angle. It looked like a graveyard of ships with their exposed superstructures as tombstones. How many sailors were entombed in these boats?

CHAPTER 19

Nearly every patient had high fever this morning, Carl said as he gave me a report and then left for the morning. High fever with chills followed by heavy sweats as the fevers broke. High fever was nearly always a part of a severe illness, most with an uncertain diagnosis. We were supporting them the best we could with fresh water and a little food. Most didn't feel like eating or drinking. They were all dehydrated. Not having a clear diagnosis just added to the misery of most of our patients. Carl was particularly worried about several young children with fever, vomiting, and diarrhea. They were all at the far end of the west ward.

But we had some medicine on hand to give them. Dr. Randall told me that a relief ship, the Winona, had arrived the second week after the storm. It had come all the way from Washington, D.C., and maneuvered past all the sunken ships in the harbor to dock downtown. It was loaded with fresh food, medical supplies, medicines, clothing, volunteer nurses, and overseeing it all was Clara Barton, head of the American Red Cross. She was working with the Galveston City Committee and setting up medical tents downtown. He said, proudly, that they even brought some bed nets similar to the ones he had fashioned.

I went to see the children first. Laura Pelley was sitting with a young girl who was five years old. She was placing a cool cloth on her forehead and stroking her hair. The little girl was curled up on her side in pain with one hand over her stomach and the other holding Laura's. Laura pulled her hair away from her face and tucked her necklace into her adult-size starched white hospital gown. The other three children were quiet as well. Sick children who were quiet was a worrisome sign.

"The Belladonna is helping her diarrhea, but her stomach pain seems worse," Laura said.

"What's her name?" I asked.

"Zadie...Zadie Rosen."

"Hello, Zadie, I'm Dr. Schuler. How are you feeling?" I asked.

"My stomach hurts so bad." She was crying a little, but she was too dehydrated to make tears or to speak clearly; her tongue was sticking to her palate.

"Can you roll on your back?"

Laura helped her roll over slowly and I went to the other side of the bed and sat next to her. I observed that her stomach was protuberant under her white cotton hospital gown. As I palpated it gently, her face winced but she let me continue. She was squeezing Laura's hand as hard. I heard bowel sounds with my stethoscope. When she opened her mouth, her tongue and mouth were extremely dry. I lowered her eyelids one at a time and could see that her conjunctiva was dry, as well.

"Is she taking in fluids?" I asked.

"No, not really," Laura said.

"Zadie, are you thirsty?" I asked. She nodded that she was.

"Would you like some water?" She shook her head no.

"She hasn't had much to drink, and she vomits right after she drinks," Laura added.

"Give her a few drops of Turpentine oil to see it that will calm her stomach," I said as I stood. "We've got to get more fluids in all these children. Where are Zadie's parents?"

"I don't think she has any. She was dropped off by an aunt, I believe. Probably, her parents died in the storm."

Zadie and the other children were sleepy from the Belladonna and were having less diarrhea this morning. Laura and Vivian were busy with these children, holding them while they vomited and frequently changing their soiled gowns. They had to be given fluids a little at a time, sometimes with a little scolding to make them drink. They cried as they drank. A small sip was a victory.

Most likely they had enteritis with diarrhea, but could this be cholera, as Dr. Randall feared? Could this be the beginning? Of all the diseases that we had read about, of all the outbreaks we had heard about, cholera was what we feared the most. We didn't even want to utter the word to the nursing staff as it would terrify them. I had never seen a case and I don't think there had been one here in Galveston, or at the hospital in the last ten years. But after the storm we all knew the conditions were right for such a lethal disease to appear. People had been forced to drink contaminated water and to eat rotten food, and the corpses in the city, human and animal, were not buried or burned, and all the standing water was full of mosquito larvae. But with all the death in our midst, the rats survived. I saw them everywhere after the storm, crawling in and around debris. Live rats transmitted disease through their bites and through their excrement.

A few adults came to us with severe abdominal cramping and diarrhea but none that persisted for more than a day or so. Of course, the symptoms of one of the men ceased when he did. He died of dehydration or the effects of it on an already diseased heart or liver. These young children had been sick for three or four days. As I sat at the nurse's table, Dr. Randall entered the ward.

"Douglas, I need your help."

We left the ward and went down the steps to the bottom floor and in the ambulance were several orderlies unloading large glass bottles of distilled water. We each grabbed one and carried it up the stairs to the wards. I went back down and grabbed another. We placed them all in the storage room of the west ward, and several more in the hallway between the wards, maybe twenty all together.

"Sir, if I can ask, what are these for?" I asked as we ascended the steps the last time. He was carrying a large heavy cardboard box with a bound journal volume under his arm.

"I got these from the relief ship that just arrived from New Orleans," he said as he lowered the box in front of him. "I also have vials of Sodium Chloride, Potassium Chloride, Calcium Chloride, and Sodium Bicarbonate."

I opened a flap of the box and saw a dozen liter-size glass bottles full of white powder and their wide mouths stoppered with a cork.

He continued, "We are going to make a solution for rehydration that we will give to our patients intravenously, like the one made by Dr. Sydney Ringer from Australia, who published its formula in *The Lancet.* He created it to perfuse frog heart muscles in his experiments. But in some parts of the world, it has been adopted as a means to rehydrate a person while replacing essential minerals. Douglas, look at me, we have to do this. We've got to be ready for the worst." He meant cholera.

We moved a large table to the center of the storage room and unloaded all the glass vials from the box. He opened his large bound volume of *The Lancet* to a page that he had dog-eared and lay it open next to the vials. He placed a large glass jar of distilled water on the table. After studying the solution in the article and converting grams to ounces in his head, we began spooning small amounts of each of the four mineral salts into the large glass vial of water. And then together we picked it up and turned it upside down over and over. Once it all seemed dissolved, we found a few empty quart glass jars with long necks and poured the solution into several of them. He did say intravenously?

I had heard of an intravenous injection of water dissolved with table salt. I had given an intravenous injection of boiled starch water to one of the children that wouldn't drink it. It had tincture of opium stabilized with acetate of lead to control the diarrhea.

Dr. Randall found a long spool of rubber tubing that he now cut into several pieces each about six feet long. He placed a rubber stopper in the mouth of the quart bottle. It had a piece of straight glass tubing through it.

"Now we have to take a needle from a syringe, preferably a larger one, maybe 18 French, and attach it to the tubing."

"And we are going to infuse this solution into the vein of a patient?" I asked. He looked back briefly with a disappointed expression but didn't say anything, I had just stated the obvious.

I found a syringe and removed the needle and forced its dull end into the other end of the tubing. It was a tight fit. Just before, he had placed a metal tube clamp over the tubing end and tightened it. He attached the other end of the tubing to a rubber stopper that had glass tubing through it. He gave it to me to hold and I held it high. He opened the clamp, and the water passed all the way out through to the needle and onto the table. He retightened the clamp and gathered it all up in his arms and we left together.

"I have the perfect patient in mind for this," Dr. Randall said as we walked to the east ward and to the very end of the row of beds where a young man in his twenties was sleeping quietly.

"Douglas, this young man is a machinist downtown and has had diarrhea and vomiting for a week and has taken very little by mouth. He's stopped urinating. We've got to get some fluids in him somehow."

The man lay on his back in a white cotton gown. His face was withdrawn, and pale and his eyes were sunken.

"What vein are you going to use?" I asked.

"I'm not sure. All his veins have collapsed due to the dehydrated state," he said.

Dr. Randall sat next to the patient and began to examine his arms and legs, looking and palpating for a vein. His skin was dry and inelastic. I began to look, too. We didn't find any. The patient had awakened but was too ill to protest.

"I think we have to use the external jugular," Dr. Randall said as he had turned the man's head away from him and palpated the side of his neck. I could see the vein, too, though it collapsed easily after he palpated it.

"Mr. Singer, we are going to put this needle in your neck. Hold still," Dr. Randall said. The man was alert now but didn't move as I held his neck to the side away from Dr. Randall. The patient gripped the sides of the mattress. Dr. Randall handed me the bottle and he took the needle and placed it downward into the vein in his neck. He quickly looked back at me, and I immediately raised the bottle above my head. With his free hand he unclamped the clamp. We waited a few seconds and then Dr. Randall felt the tubing with his free hand.

"Douglas, feel the tubing for flow, what do you think?"

"Sir, I think it's flowing."

The tubing felt stiffer and full. I looked up at the upside water bottle and saw a few bubbles floating up. I wasn't sure what we were going to do now. We had held the bottle for about ten minutes and the patient seemed to tolerate the infusion. He reached up toward his neck with his right hand, but Dr. Randall pushed his hand back down and told him to "hold still." The water level in the bottle had definitely gone down. I heard the heavy footsteps of Nurse Sanders.

"Dr. Randall, what are you doing to this patient?"

"We are rehydrating this man, Nurse Sanders. Now would you take the bottle from Dr. Schuler so he can go find some tape?"

"No, I will not!" she said and turned back around and walked away. Dr. Randall didn't look back at her.

"Douglas, lower the bottle beneath him," he said. I did and

watched the tubing and could see blood coming back into the tubing past the needle.

"That's fine, hold it up again. We are still in the vein." He stood and said, "Give me the bottle and go find some surgical tape."

I handed him the bottle in his free hand and hurried back to the supply room. I found a roll of white surgical tape, four inches wide. As I walked, I began to tear away thin pieces of the fabric tape and stuck them in a row hanging from my sleeve. I reached Dr. Randall and took the bottle from him and raised it above my head. He saw the strips of tape and took them one at a time and taped the needle in place to the side of the patient's neck. He again told the patient not to move and Mr. Singer didn't.

"Douglas, what do you think?"

"I think you have infused half the bottle."

"No, Douglas, it's we. You know you are part of this, too," he said with a smile.

I smiled back. "You know, Dr. Randall, I have learned more medicine since the storm than during my four years of medical school."

"Then we need to do a better job of teaching," he said excitedly.

"Keep holding the bottle up. Pull out the needle when it's empty," he said as he hit me on my shoulders and walked away. The patient was looking up a me but just with his eyes, sideways. I walked around the foot of the bed and to the other side so he could see me straight away. I was still holding up the bottle.

"How do you feel, Mr. Singer?"

"A little better, I think."

"We are giving you water directly into your body through a vein in your neck. Don't move."

One little movement of his head could displace the needle. He was cooperating but was getting a little restless. The bottle was emptying slowly and so was the strength in my arms. I was trying to think of a way to hold up this bottle while the patient stared up at me, careful not to move.

"Doc, you know, I could make a round metal bracket to fit on the end of that bottle and a hook on the bracket to hang it by," Mr. Singer said, as he was now feeling better. Could I use this on the children? It was amazing to think that a patient could be rehydrated without having to drink.

"Then you could hang the bottle from a hat rack, or a metal pole." He was smiling now.

As the last of the fluid was leaving the bottle I walked back to the other side of the bed and stood right over the needle. I put the bottle down onto the bed and closed the clamp in the tubing and lifted the tape away enough to pull out the needle. I held pressure on the venipuncture site with my fingers for several minutes.

"Don't move, Mr. Singer."

After a few minutes I had him sit up and made sure there was no bleeding. I replaced the tape over the site.

"Are you dizzy?"

He shook his head no. I held his wrist and felt his pulse. It was strong and I knew his blood pressure was better, too. I took the bottle and the tubing and the needle back to the nurse's table. I also took the volume of *The Lancet* with me. I went to the west ward and sat at the nurse's desk and opened the volume to the article by Dr. Ringer. How did Dr. Randall think to apply this frog heart bath solution to the rehydration of humans?

I closed the volume after reading most of the article and went downstairs to Dr. Randall's office. His door was open, and he was sitting at his desk. He looked up after I knocked.

"Douglas, have a seat. How is that young man, Singer?"

"I think it's amazing what you have done. He is sitting up and talking."

"No, remember it's what we've done, you're just as guilty as me," he said again.

"I wanted to return the volume. I've memorized the recipe for the intravenous solution."

"Good. I think some of our other patients may benefit from it. In fact, there is a man named Atchison, a tailor downtown, with persistent high fever and lethargy who I think may have dengue. There are several others that may have it too, but he is the sickest. Would you look at him for me?"

"I will. But I was thinking about the sick children on the west ward. They all seem to have enteritis with diarrhea. They are all severely dehydrated. Can I use the rest of the solution on them? I can start with one, the sickest, a young girl who hasn't drunk any water for two days."

He sat back in his chair before speaking. "How would you find a vein on a small child? It isn't easy to see their veins when they're well."

"I would like to consult with Dr. Cooke about that." Dr. Cooke was Professor of Pediatrics and the Dean of the medical school.

"I think that would be prudent. He may want to alter the solution somewhat for a child, though I can't see why. He is an expert on the yellow fever."

"Thank you, I will," I said and got up to leave.

"Douglas, I have been meaning to ask you, did you ever find your girlfriend?"

"No sir, I haven't. She's still missing."

"Well, you have to realize that by now, three weeks after the storm, she is probably dead. I'm sorry to put it to you so strongly but I want you to be realistic.""

"I don't know, sir."

"I want you and Carl to dine with my family one evening."

"Yes sir, I would like that." I was touched that he said that.

I didn't know how both Carl and I could dine with them as we worked every other night and most days during the week together.

When Tex was alive and sharing night duty, Carl and I were off. The faculty had no clue about our schedule or our lives, nor did they care to know, except for Dr. Randall whom we reported to. The faculty didn't care what goes on at night at the hospital, either. It was always rare to see a faculty member on the ward after dark. They were more likely to stay late to care for their experiments in their labs than to assist us with patient care.

I left Dr. Randall and the hospital and went to see Dr. Henry Cooke next door at the Medical Department building. His large office was on the first floor at the top of the large outside stairway and through the grand oak doors. I knocked on his heavy closed office door and waited. He came to the door and invited me in. He returned to his large desk. I had heard that he was from a long line of physicians in Virginia. He had thick white hair and a large mustache, mutton chops facial hair, and wore gold wire spectacles. He was known for his poor eyesight as he was the only faculty to wear them.

"Pardon me, Dr. Cooke for the interruption, but I would like to consult with you about the sick children on the west ward."

He nodded and waved me to the chair in front of his desk. He was a man of few words, so I explained the situation with the children succinctly. I wrote down the recipe for the solution that I had memorized and passed it to him. I explained the benefit this morning to the dehydrated man. He sat back in his chair and held the recipe close to his spectacles.

"I was part of the yellow fever epidemic in 1896 when I lived in New Orleans. But the children do not sound like they have it. I suggest that you limit your efforts to the treating of enteritis. But I am fascinated by the Ringer solution. By all means proceed, give it a try. I think of the children we could save if we could just hydrate them. Reduce the amount of Potassium Chloride for the children." He reached for his pen and altered the recipe and handed it back to me.

"But Dr. Cooke I do have a question, what vein should I choose?"

"Well," he sat back in his chair again, "I am not sure."

He put down his pen again. "I think the brachial would be too small. Try for the femoral vein. Remember it is lateral to the femoral artery. Please make me aware of the results, Dr. Schuler."

"Dr. Cooke, you know that my fellow intern, Tex, I mean, Homer Hornsby is missing after the storm?"

"Yes, I know. Dr. Randall and Dr. Clopton have informed me." I waited for him to continue but he didn't. I thanked him and returned to the hospital.

I returned to the west ward and saw that Laura and Vivian were walking back toward the nursing table. When I first saw Vivian earlier this morning, I thought it was Victoria. She was short, too. She still had a cough.

"Laura, if you are not too busy, I would like to show you something that might help the children."

"Of course, Dr. Schuler."

We walked together to the storage room where we had mixed the Ringer solution. I explained what it was, how we mixed it, and how we gave it to an adult patient, rehydrating them. She had an apprehensive look on her face.

"Dr. Randall wants you to give it to the children?" she asked.

"Yes, of course, he has approved it, as has Dr. Cooke. I want to start it on Zadie as a trial. Is she still not taking water?"

"No, she's still not. I'm worried about them all, but I think she is the sickest." I poured some of the solution into another quart bottle and took another piece of tubing and another rubber stopper.

"You can't use that big needle on a child. I don't think Nurse Sanders would approve of this," Laura said.

"I know I need a smaller one, maybe a 22 French. We need some surgical tape. Could you tear some strips so we can secure the needle? I am ordering this for Zadie, and Nurse Sanders has to follow my orders, but don't tell her."

"Yes, doctor, I won't tell her."

I found the smaller needle and put it on the end of the tubing. The glass jar was full, and I primed the tubing with the solution. I remembered to mix less Potassium Chloride. I carried it all to the far end of the west ward and put everything on a small table next to Zadie's bed. She was quiet but some of the other children were crying a little as they rolled from one side to another. A sick boy sat up to watch. I sat next to Zadie on her bed and felt her forehead. She rolled to her left side and held tight the small pendant on her necklace in her left hand. She had fever again. She opened her eyes a little when I said her name, and she looked when Laura said her name. Laura explained to her what I was going to do.

I stood to better see the side of her neck. I couldn't see or feel the external jugular vein. I extended her right arm to me. I opened her hand. The brachial vein was the largest in the arm but I couldn't clearly see it or feel it. I didn't want to try for the femoral vein. I gently rolled her on to back. Her eyes were closed, and she held the pendant tightly. Her breathing was rapid but regular. I took the needle and inserted it in the middle of the bend of the arm and saw some blood return in the tubing. I nodded to Laura to raise the bottle as high as she could. Zadie hardly moved. I could feel by the hardness of the tubing that the solution was flowing through it. I took the tape pieces and secured the needle. I took the bottle from Laura and raised it over my head. Laura sat down next to Zadie and stroked her hair while she held her arm still. She took her left hand from her pendant and tucked her necklace inside her hospital gown. She stroked her left arm and hand.

"Zadie, try to relax. This is going to make you feel better," Nurse Pelley said.

Zadie hardly moved during the infusion and at the end of the infusion, which took longer than Mr. Singer's, I removed the needle from her arm. Her radial pulse felt stronger now. I looked at Zadie and she looked back at me. I held her hand.

"I think you are a good doctor," Zadie said.

"Zadie, I'm going to get you better, I promise. But you have to drink more water, too. Just try small sips first."

"Okay I will. I promise too, doctor."

Zadie sat up on her own and looked at us and the other children. She didn't seem lightheaded. I hoped that she wasn't afraid. The infusion was amazing! I walked backward away from the children and Laura stayed with Zadie.

I had to check on the tailor, Mr. Atchison, for Dr Randall. I went to the east ward and found him lying quietly on his back under the mosquito netting. He was somnolent and difficult to arouse, and his skin was hot and dry. I laid back his gown from his shoulders to his waist and could see that his skin was a little yellow in the evening sunlight. He didn't have the unusual veins over his chest and abdomen that many of the alcoholics did with cirrhosis of the liver. I reached up to pull down his lower eyelids and saw his eyes were bright yellow; he was jaundiced. He withdrew his hand when I squeezed his fingernail bed with my thumbnail but didn't awaken. His pulse was weak. He could have dengue, or the yellow fever or malaria or something else. According to his chart, he had been vomiting for two days, but hadn't had diarrhea, so cholera was unlikely.

But he was "very sick," as Dr. Randall liked to say. He was the last patient I gave the IV infusion for the day. I ordered some Quinine for his fever and Bismuth salts for his vomiting, and we had to somehow wake him enough to drink them. I left his bedside but paused when I remembered that there was no mention of the examination of his blood smear in the chart. I went to find one of the needles I used for the infusions and cleaned it with a cloth and took a syringe and test tube and returned to the bedside. It was still sharp. I drew a syringe full of blood from his right arm, then transferred the blood to the test tube and put the tube in my pocket. I left Mr. Atchison asleep and saw a few more patients on the ward before I went back to the west ward to see the children, and Zadie.

"I would not have believed it if I hadn't seen it," Laura said, smiling and standing near her bed. By now it was near the end of the day and Zadie had sat up and asked for something to eat and had eaten a few crackers and had not vomited.

"I know it is amazing. It's just water and minerals," Laura said as she covered all the children with their bedsheets, and we walked back to the nurse's table. I had gathered the infusion bottle and the tubing and the needle.

"Have you spoken with Victoria?" she asked.

"No, I haven't seen her. Where is she?"

"She went home to Fort Worth. Her family received her telegram and then sent one back demanding that she return home."

"Is she coming back?"

"She told me that was. She wanted me to tell you that."

"Thank you for letting me know."

I walked away from the ward toward the storage room where I put back the bottle and tubing. I took the needle out of my pocket and wiped the blood off with the cloth, then wiped the blood off my hands.

The rest of the day and night we infused the Ringer's solution to other patients, only the adults, and they all seemed to get better. Some refused the treatment despite our insistence. The needles I saved were getting dull and more difficult to pierce the skin. It was dark, and there was no longer enough light by the dim electric lights on the ward to see the veins clearly.

Very late that evening, Dr. Thompson brought me to the fourth-floor surgical suite to assist with an emergency surgery. I kept the patient sedated with ether while he prepared to explore the abdomen. He made a large midline incision in the older woman, who had a rigid, painful abdomen. He was right when he told me that he suspected a ruptured gallbladder. He removed it skillfully in less than two hours. I helped him close the large incision with the cat gut sutures. He was too tired to criticize my technique, but I wasn't too tired to admire his. He was so fast when closing the skin of a surgical incision, and I couldn't keep up. I had mentioned during the surgery about our intravenous infusions to rehydrate our patients and that she might benefit from it, as she had lost a lot of blood. He said absolutely not, he wouldn't allow it.

I accompanied the orderlies holding her stretcher down the elevator to the ward. The orderlies carried her back to her bed. Dr. Thompson left for the evening. When back in her bed on the east ward, she woke up briefly, but I made sure that she had enough morphine solution to drink to keep her quiet for the night. An hour or so after the surgery, I gently pushed on her abdomen, and it didn't wake her.

During the night I went to check on the children on the west ward. They were all sleeping and seemed to be stable. I had heard that they had not vomited anymore. They were all the same, lethargic with weak pulses and dry skin. I woke up Zadie, and she said that she felt better and that she was a little hungry. She let me push on her stomach, and she didn't wince. I held her hand a little as she fell asleep. One of the children had a mother that came to visit for a few hours, I heard. Had Zadie's aunt come to visit her?

Midway through the night, most of the patients were asleep as I made my final rounds, and a few adults had died, but not Mr. Atchison. I sat back at the nurse's table on the west ward. I took a few of the needles that I had used during the day and started to sharpen them with a file. The very tip of the beveled needle had to be sharp to penetrate the skin cleanly. They, of course, were hollow which made them harder to sharpen and easier to bend. I bent several of them at the tips, so I put down the file. We could never use a needle that had been bent. I felt alone and it was quiet. Victoria didn't need me anymore?

CHAPTER 20

Vivian shook me awake while I was asleep on a cot in one of the storage rooms. Daylight came through the small window. She told me that Mr. Atchison was vomiting again, that she was worried about him. I jumped up from the cot and went to his bedside on the west ward. I usually slept at the hospital with my shoes on. Another nursing student was there at Mr. Atchison's bedside and holding a shiny metal emesis basis to his chin. He had propped himself on one elbow and pulled up the emesis basis closer to his mouth.

"Mr. Atchison, I am Dr. Schuler. I work under Dr. Randall. He asked that I take care of you. Do you remember me?"

He didn't look up at me and was breathing rapidly. He shook his head "no." I stood by his head and felt his forehead. His skin was cool and sweaty. His fever had broken this morning, and he was shivering all over.

"Mr. Atchison, I want you to take some medicine now. It will help your vomiting."

He said shaking his head, "I can't, I will throw it up, too."

He began to shake all over. I had him lie back down flat. He did so very slowly and moved his hand and the basin away from his mouth, pushing it toward me. His stomach felt tense, and he winced with pain at the slightest touch. The whites of his eyes were bright yellow, glowing. As I pulled down his gown, I could see that his skin was also yellow, especially over his chest. He suddenly sat up quickly and pulled the basin to his mouth again and vomited. He vomited so hard that it bypassed most of the basin and landed on his chest and on my hand and sleeve. It was black, black as tar. It was coagulated blood. He collapsed back down in the bed and dropped the basin by his side next to me, spilling more on my pants. The nursing student grabbed the towel at the foot of his bed and began to wipe down the patient.

He said, "I'm so sorry doctor, but I can't stop vomiting."

I grabbed the clean end of the towel and wiped my hands. Even on the white towel it was black, completely black. Then I wiped my shirt sleeve.

To the nurse, I said, "Please get some more towels and his dose of Bismuth. No wait, change it to Belladonna, it's stronger."

I examined his stomach again and it was less tense since he vomited. I felt on his right side of his abdomen and his liver was enlarged, swollen and tender. And on the left side his spleen was palpable.

"Mr. Atchison, do you drink?"

"No, no, I don't, not at all," he said while breathing rapidly. What was his diagnosis? He had been bitten by mosquitoes as we had all been and it didn't seem like dengue, or malaria, but maybe the yellow fever as he was very yellow? But what caused black emesis? I had studied several diseases that had that symptom as their trademark, the "black vomit." Absolutely, you knew it when you saw it. I stood up by his bed to think. I could see at the far corner of the ward, the four young children with enteritis sitting in their cotton gowns with their bare legs and feet handing down over their beds and talking together. I kept wiping my shirt and pants with a new towel.

He added, "I haven't passed any urine in two days, doc".

"Okay, Mr. Atchison, let's give the medicine time to work."

I went to the storage room and rinsed my shirt sleeve, removing most of the blood. I straightened my tie and put on my suit coat and left the ward. I went to the Medical Department building next door to the basement to find Dr. Smith. It was early and I knew he would be in his microscopy room. I entered the room and found him looking at a collection of photos that he had developed there in a small side room he had converted to a dark room. He didn't notice me until I was standing close to him. I stared at the photos.

"Good morning, Douglas," he said, then stopped what he was doing to look at me. "You know, you look absolutely terrible today," he said with a smile.

He was looking well put together, as usual—clean dark suit, clean shaven, combed hair, but red stained hands and nails. I combed my hair with my fingers and stood straight.

"I have been taking some photos and developing them this morning. I have adapted one of my smaller cameras to replace the eyepiece lens in order to photograph tissue specimens."

I examined the grainy photograph of the normal cells of the liver.

"That is genius, Dr. Smith. It could replace the drawings in the textbooks one day."

"Well, we still have a long way to go for that."

"I have a patient that I would like to ask you about, a patient of Dr. Randall's. He is a tailor in town who has jaundice and fever and vomiting. He has no alcohol history. This morning his vomitus was black, really black like tar."

Dr. Smith took off his glasses and looked directly at me and said, "the black vomit." He was listening now.

I continued, "I know we have been suffering with the mosquitoes since the storm and the timing is about right for the yellow fever. But his liver and spleen are very enlarged and tender. He most likely has nephritis as well. He vomited blood this morning for the first time. I'm not sure what he has." I paused again. "I took a blood sample from him last night after I realized that his blood smear had not been examined." I pulled out the test tube in my pocket and held it in front of him.

He reached for it but with a small towel, then wrapped it up and placed it on the table. I pulled up my coat sleeve and showed him the blood stain on my shirt sleeve.

"Yes, that's black, all right. Let's have a look," he said.

After he removed the rubber stopper, he took a dropper and removed a few drops of blood and placed them over several glass slides and smeared the blood with another slide directly on top. He dipped it in an open beaker of methanol and let it dry for a few minutes. Then he took a dropper of a purple stain and placed one drop at the edge of the slide. He placed it under the microscope. He replaced the rubber stopper on the blood tube and held the tube up to the light.

"The blood is not coagulating as it usually is. So, this may give us a clearer look," he said.

He placed a slide under the microscope and examined it carefully, adjusting the mirror on the microscope to allow as much sunlight as possible to reflect off the mirror at the bottom of the microscope. Microscopy was best with the morning light, he always said.

"His cells, red cells, white cells, platelets all appear normal. But there is a strange spirochete floating around that I haven't seen before." He sat back, grabbed his glasses off the table, then stood up for me to have a look. I sat down and leaned in to see exactly what he was talking about. It was a long corkscrew appearing bacteria moving across the field—several, in fact.

"I am not sure, Douglas, but I think your tailor has Leptospira in his blood, the bacteria that causes Weil's disease. It's a disease named after the famous Dr. Adolf Weil in Germany. It is also described in the Orient, and called, I believe, 'rice cutters jaundice.' I have never seen that bacterium before except in drawings and there has never been a case of it here, I'm sure. I believe it is transmitted not by mosquitoes, but by rats. Your patient must have been bitten by an infected rat."

"There have been rats everywhere since the storm. I don't why they didn't drown like all the other animals."

"Douglas, I want you to know that his blood and his bloody vomitus is extremely contagious. You should wash your hands and arms thoroughly and wash that shirt in boiling water, maybe that entire suit," he said as he walked around me, carefully looking at my suit.

He added, "It is a shame to ruin such a nice suit."

"I will convey these findings to Dr. Randall. Thank you again, Dr. Smith."

I left the Medical Building and walked back to the hospital. The tailor could have Leptospira or Weil's disease? I had never heard of it. In the sunlight, I looked again at my suit and could see the large blood stain on the pant leg. This was Mr. Landes' shirt and suit, and they were now ruined. I had had blood on my clothes before, we all had. We would remove our suit jackets and roll up our sleeves to keep the blood off them, but only at the end of the day, after the faculty had left. It was usually impossible to get blood out, even with lye. Grandma Sam cussed me if there was blood on my clothes. She could get out almost any stain, but blood was "near impossible."

I looked up the large entry staircase of the hospital and several men in suits entered before me. They carried briefcases. I watched them climb the stairs to the top where the wards were and then stand at the top landing and look around. I came up behind them and asked if they needed help. They said they were looking for Dr. Cooke or Dr. Randall or Dr. Clopton. I entered the east ward ahead of them and waiting for them were the three doctors that they had mentioned. I went to the nurse's table.

"Good morning, doctors." The taller man spoke and extended his right hand to them all. He held his large black cowboy hat in his left. "My name is Roy Hornsby, and I believe my son Homer is working here as an intern under you gentleman. This is my congressman, the Honorable Jonathan McCallum, who insisted on joining me on my trip here to find my son."

Mr. Hornsby was taller than the doctors and now had a deep frown beneath his bushy grey handlebar mustache. The three doctors introduced themselves as members of the University of Texas faculty.

Dr. Clopton spoke up first. "It is my delight to meet you, Mr. Hornsby, and we are honored to have you both at our hospital. As you know we are still in the process of repairing the windows due to that awful storm several weeks ago. But we and our hospital are standing strong, her foundation is strong. It would be my pleasure to give you both a tour of the hospital and our beautiful Medical Department building next door."

Dr. Randall interrupted him, "Mr. Hornsby, did you get our telegram about your son?"

Tex's father said, "I did, and it couldn't have been more vague. I have one question for you all and I will not leave until I have the answer. Is my son alive?"

Dr Randall answered, "We don't know. His apartment building was completely destroyed in the storm, and we haven't seen him since." He turned around and pointed to me and said, "Dr. Douglas Schuler, a fellow intern, has been to the building to search for him, and didn't find him."

The congressman spoke up, "Did any of you gentlemen, faculty doctors, also go in search of Homer? I believe you all called him 'Tex'?"

Dr. Cooke spoke up next. "I was here during the storm but most of the other faculty were not here, they were on assignment abroad. The medical students had not yet arrived for the year. I personally did not search for Homer. All those who took shelter here in the hospital survived."

The congressman said, "So there was no loss of life of any of the faculty? All of the other faculty are accounted for because they weren't here? Well, who may I ask ran the hospital during the storm, the nurses?"

"The three hospital intern physicians for that period of the summer did. Dr. Heath and Dr. Schuler were assigned here the night of the storm. Mr. Hornsby, your son was off duty that night," Dr Randall said.

Mr. Hornsby said, "So if I am correct, my son was not encouraged to take shelter in the hospital with his fellow intern physicians?"

Dr. Clopton spoke up, "Well, sir, we had no warning that day of an impending storm. No one was aware of the danger."

"Is that what you were told later after the storm, since you were on a holiday during the storm, Dr. Clopton?" the congressman asked.

Mr. Hornsby added, "So you are saying that you think my son is missing?"

Dr. Clopton, "Yes, we feel he is missing, as I stated in the telegram. Thousands have perished in this horrible storm. And thousands are still missing."

"Of which group do you all think my son is in? To me he is dead either way." Mr. Hornsby was bending the rim of his hat in his broad fist as he spoke.

Dr. Randall spoke up, "Yes, we think he has died. His body is missing as are most of the victims of the storm. They have drowned. I am so sorry to tell you that, Mr. Hornsby."

The congressman responded, "It was our strong suspicion that Homer could have died in the storm. I have prepared Mr. Hornsby for that possibility. We are all aware of the thousands who have died here. It is known all over the state. What I don't clearly see is that you do not even have his body, nor did you search for him! So, he will be denied an honorable burial in his family cemetery back home."

Dr. Cooke answered, "I am afraid that we do not have his body. We have nothing left of his. I am deeply sorry."

The congressman continued, "I encouraged Mr. Hornsby to send his son to Galveston for his training at this new hospital that the Texas state legislature proudly built. That it would be an excellent training experience, not the cause of his death!" The congressman now shouted, "And you cannot even produce his son's body because you all were either not here, nor had the desire to search for it. That is disgraceful, gentleman!"

It was completely quiet on the ward except for a metal bedpan that was dropped and clanged loudly throughout the ward.

The congressman continued in a calmer tone after a long pause, "And you do not have any of his belongings?"

I stood from the table. "We have his stethoscope. I am sure it is here. He kept it hidden in a closet between the wards."

All the men were quiet as I walked past them to look for the stethoscope. I knew it was initialed like mine. I found it on the top shelf in a closet and brought it to the father. It had his initials on the silver band holding the black tubes together, "HTH." The "T" stood for Timothy, Tex told me.

The father accepted the stethoscope and stared at the silver band, ran his thumb across the band and said to me, "Thank you for thinking of my son."

And after looking directly at the faculty, and then back at me said, "And thank you for searching for him."

"My fellow intern, Dr. Carl Heath, also searched for him the day after the storm. He reported to us that his apartment building by the beach was destroyed. And he didn't find him. I searched again the following day."

Mr. Hornsby said, "Thank you, son." And to the congressman, "I want to leave now. I have nothing else to say to these gentlemen."

As they were turning to leave, Dr. Randall said, "Please, sirs, could you wait just another minute. I remembered that I do have something of his."

Dr. Randall left the ward, and Dr. Clopton asked if they would like to sit while they waited, and he offered them tea. They refused both. Dr. Randall returned in less than a minute and presented a rolled-up canvas to Mr. Hornsby. It was tied with a black ribbon.

"Tex drew this for all of us here, for the school."

The father unrolled the large canvas and stared blankly at it. It was an anatomical drawing of the human body, highlighting the entire vascular system, the arteries in red, the veins in blue. It was beautiful. He drew it as a first-year student and Dr. Randall had kept it and would show it to the new medical students each year. The father continued to stare at it. After a minute or so, his eyes migrated down to the right lower corner of the canvas where he spotted what Tex had written in the same ink as the arteries, "Tex Hornsby '96." Tex had underlined his name with a swirling blue line with the ink for the veins, like a lasso. His father's face softened.

"Homer was an excellent artist and had a great grasp of human anatomy, even as a student. All of his drawings have been studied by the other doctors and students here. He was very talented," Dr Randall said.

Mr. Hornsby rolled up the canvas in his hand. A few tears had welled up in his eyes. He just nodded his head to Dr. Randall and then slowly left the floor followed by the congressman. He held a tight grip on the canvas and his hat, one in each large fist. The black stethoscope tubing was dangling out of his side suite pocket. Before the congressman left, he told the faculty that the matter was not closed, that further inquiries would be made, and that he expected the full cooperation of all the faculty. Dr. Cooke reassured him that they would have it.

After the two men had left the building, the three faculty discussed what had just happened. Dr. Clopton was speaking the loudest and then punctuated his sentence with his fist slamming on the nurse's table. Dr. Cooke was trying to pacify him. I had moved away from them to attend to a patient nearby. Dr. Randall said something quietly to him, as well, then left the group and walked over to me.

"Douglas, thank you for searching for Tex and for remembering his stethoscope. But the faculty would like to meet with you and Carl this afternoon in the main salon of the Medical Department building at one o'clock. Let Carl know, please." And then he left the floor.

I found Carl later in the morning on the west ward and told him about the meeting we had. He suggested that we get some coffee and talk about it. We sat together in the supply room and drank hot, bitter coffee as there was still no sugar after the storm. I told him that I was not told what the meeting was about. Carl pulled out his pocket watch to wind it. It was a few hours away. He told me, laughing, that not to worry, that they wouldn't fire us. We were their slaves, that they couldn't manage without us, that it would mean more work for them, especially with the new class of medical students coming any day now.

I told him about the meeting with Tex's father and his congressman and the dressing down they gave to the three faculty. I felt tense as he rambled on, but the coffee relaxed me, but only a little. I told him there was some food in a crate on the floor below, rations from the steamship. We walked together to find some. The faculty would be in no mood to go easy on us, to listen to my side of the story.

We arrived a few minutes early to the main salon on the first floor of the Medical Department building, the building where all the faculty had their offices, except Dr. Randall. We wore our suit coats with our sleeves rolled down and cuffed. I pulled my coat sleeve down low to cover the blood stain. Carl looked cleaner than me as he didn't work last night. I borrowed his pocket comb to comb my hair. It was too long, below my collar now. Dr. Randall opened the double doors and invited us in. All the faculty were present, all nine of them. Eight of them were sitting around the three sides of a large, square oak table. They were all sitting in large oak chairs. There were three empty chairs on the side nearest us. Dr. Randall sat down in one and we sat in the other chairs next to him. Carl gave all the faculty a nod and a broad smile. They weren't smiling.

"Dr. Schuler, Dr. Heath we wanted to meet with you concerning the events of the storm and your behavior," Dr. Randall began. "Since the return of the faculty, we have heard many rumors, stories about your behavior, that cannot be ignored. I must inform you that discipline by the faculty may be in order, or possibly your dismissal."

The broad smile on Carl's face collapsed. I wasn't smiling when I entered, but now I felt a sharp pain in my neck and throat as I tried to swallow.

Dr. Thompson stood. "Dr. Schuler, I was appalled when I heard the most serious of all the rumors that you were absent without leave for your shift the day after the storm. That you were gone for almost twenty-four hours, leaving Dr. Heath in the lurch by himself to care for the sick? Head Nurse Sanders confirms your absence!"

"Dr. Thompson, sir, I was taken captive the morning after the storm by a law officer at gunpoint, to man a cart to load the dead. I explained to him that I was a doctor and was needed back at the hospital immediately. He wouldn't let me go. I worked all day pushing that cart to the barges on the docks waiting to be disposed of at sea. I was held captive and even locked up in a warehouse for the night, but I escaped in the middle of the night."

"Who told you could leave the hospital?"

"No one, but our census was low, and the patients were stable. I only wanted to search for a friend."

"Is this true, Dr. Heath, that Dr. Schuler left the morning after the storm?"

"Yes, he did, but...." Carl said.

"Was it acceptable to you to allow him to abandon his duty at that critical time? I see, Dr. Heath, that you were burdened with the care of all the patients present then. This was not your decision to make."

"Well, yes, but Doug was correct, there were only a few patients in the hospital during the storm," Carl added.

Dr. Clopton stood also. "Do you expect us to believe such a ridiculous story, Dr. Schuler? That you were taken prisoner, that you pushed a cart full of bodies? I doubt, very seriously, that that ever happened. In fact, in our enlightened city, that would never have happened, to handle the dead in such an unlawful way. It is a disgrace that you even mention this before us." He sat back down hard.

"It was what truly happened, sir. You were not here to witness it," I said.

Dr. Clopton continued, "And you both did not ensure the safety of your fellow intern, Dr. Hornsby, who no doubt perished in the storm, in part, thanks to you. Boys...you will have that on your conscience until your dying day."

Looking around the room, Dr. Thompson asked, "Have you all ever heard of such a thing happening after the storm?"

All the faculty shook their head "no," except Dr. Smith.

After a few moments, he spoke. "I was here during the storm and afterwards it was utter chaos. I heard rumors of carts of dead bodies pushed by survivors. There were no horses to pull a cart. The bodies taken out to sea on barges but then floated back up on the beaches the next day. There was local law enforcement in charge of maintaining the peace. Many survivors were shot on the spot if they looted."

Dr. Cooke spoke next. "I was here, as you all know, during the storm and I had heard of the carts of dead bodies that Dr. Smith mentioned. I witnessed the chaos on the island, but I can't confirm that it happened. It is hard for me to imagine that the citizens would tolerate such barbarism. It is hard for me to imagine that a physician would participate."

I didn't know the name of the man who held me at gunpoint or anyone else during that day, except Elijah. I didn't know where to find him but they would not believe the testimony of a Black man.

Dr. Thompson spoke again. "Whether the rumors be true or not, we have a decision to make concerning the behavior of our house intern, the reproach that such an allegation could bring to our institution is enormous."

All of the other faculty that hadn't spoken did, except for Dr. Randall; Dr. Keillor, the professor of anatomy; Dr. Paine, the professor of obstetrics and gynecology; Dr. Morris, the professor of toxicology; and Dr. Cline, the professor of pharmacy. They all had their say and took their turn against me and my alibi. Dr. Clopton suggested that the authorities should be notified, too, to prosecute me for defamation of the dead. Other accusations were raised against us both, that Carl was a womanizer. They knew this because of the complaint of the nurse's dormitory mother and Nurse Sanders. Carl had no defense and for once, he was speechless. But they came back to the accusation against me, the abandonment of my duty.

For over an hour the verbal beating continued, and Dr. Randall did not speak up in our behalf. I looked over at him, but he only looked straight ahead. He was not here during the storm. I did tell him what happened when he arrived, and he seemed to believe me then. We were asked to leave while the faculty deliberated. We walked out together and back to the hospital without speaking.

"I believe your story, Doug."

"I know you do."

"If they fire just one of us, I think it will be you," he said, smiling. I smiled too and couldn't help nodding in agreement.

"That was rough. Why don't you go home now, I can handle everyone from here."

"The four kids with enteritis, I think their families are coming for them later today."

"Got it, my friend." Carl said putting his arm around my shoulder.

I needed that. Without Tex, he was my only friend. I walked slowly down the street in front of the hospital and every other street on my way to my new "home," Dr. Randall's back house. If I am fired, I will have to leave, leave the back house, leave the island. I would head back home to the ranch. Maybe I should send a telegram for my family to expect me soon.

But I was too tired to send a telegram or do anything else but sleep. I had to wash the suit, to find a way to get rid of the blood out of the pants. Near the back house I could smell the fires of people cooking outside or maybe washing clothes. Everyone was burning debris of all kinds now. The smell of burning flesh and every other rotten thing was still strong in most neighborhoods.

I reached the back house and entered the property through the alley entrance. I climbed the narrow stairs and went inside after I took off my shoes and left them on the small landing. I took off my clothes and put my shirt and suit and my socks in a bucket of cold water. I rinsed off my face with water in a basin on the kitchen table. I was only wearing my underclothes when I went over to the cot to sleep. I was more tired than worried about my internship, the internship the faculty convinced me to take.

I awoke with a knock at the door. It was Dr. Randall, and he asked if he could come in. It was dark now. I opened the door all the way. By his expression, he didn't look pleased to see me. We sat together in the two chairs at the small kitchen table. I lit a small candle and put it between us.

"I apologize, Dr. Randall, I can get dressed if you like."

"No, Douglas, this won't take long," he said, then added, "You and Carl were not fired today."

"I don't believe it!" I was awake now. "Why not?"

He pulled out a letter from his coat pocket and said, "I read this letter to them that I received a few days ago about you and Carl."

He handed the letter to me. I looked at the bottom, the writer of the letter. It was from Nurse Willow. She spoke of the heroism that we showed during the storm, how we rescued the student nurses during the height of the storm, risking our own lives. How I moved all the patients into the hallway away from the flying debris. How I helped all the patients stay calm and safe with little regard for my own anxieties and health during the storm. I handed the letter back to him.

"I read it to the faculty, but they all wanted to see the letter for themselves. After they had all read it, Dr. Smith made a motion to keep you both on, not to fire you. And it was unanimous, they all agreed."

He saw how stunned I looked. "Did you tell Carl?

"Yes, before I came home. He was worried about you and suggested I tell you as soon as I could."

"I don't know what to say, Dr. Randall. Thank you so much. You have helped me so much. What can I do?"

"First of all, don't keep insisting on that story about why you were not at the hospital the day after the storm. All right? Nobody believes it."

"Okay, I will, but do you believe me?"

"Yes, I do," he said smiling in the dim candlelight, "but I'll deny that I ever said I did."

CHAPTER 21

The smell of coffee roasting was in the air as I left Dr. Randall's back house this morning, and a cool breeze washed over my face. After I took a sponge bath, I put on a clean shirt and my other suit. The suit that I had been wearing, Mr. Landes' suit, was hanging out to dry this morning after a good scrubbing with soap. And I shined my shoes.

I followed 20th Street down to Market Street and stepped up over the high curb to the sidewalk and walked past a few open businesses. The door to my favorite bakery was open. I peeked inside and smelled fresh bread. I saw the family working in the back by the oven, pulling out large metal trays of hot bread and placing the loaves in large wicker baskets. Large white burlap bags were stacked high against a wall and stamped with the words "King Arthur Flour." The storefront window used to say, "M. Antonelli Bakery."

I grabbed a few small loaves out of a basket and placed a quarter on the counter and began to eat as I walked down Market Street to 18th Street. I found the door of the barbershop I used to frequent open and the barber inside. He saw me and waved me inside. He had two large swivel chairs facing a large mirror on the wall in a long and narrow room. The mirror was gone as was the barber pole outside. He wasn't wearing his usual black barber's smock. He gave me a shave and a haircut for twenty-five cents. I had removed the sutures from my scalp the day before with small scissors and a hand mirror.

Much to the dislike of the faculty, Carl and I preferred to cut off our beards. A clean-shaven face was the modern style we preferred, but to the faculty, to not have a beard or at least a mustache was seen as rebellious. I especially disliked Dr. Clopton's large lamb chop sideburns. I remember his lectures on hygiene and how he said that the beard of a man was not just a marker of masculinity but a protection for the skin. We didn't believe it.

I finally looked good again but there wasn't a mirror anywhere to confirm it. Most of the businesses downtown would have a mirror on the wall in their entryways, many with advertising painted on them. I walked over to the Strand and then east to the hospital. Several steamships slowly worked their way toward the piers along the waterfront. On the 16th Street pier, a large crew of men was busy unloading a large bright white steamship that was held snug against the pier, balancing wooden square crates with hand carts down a steep ramp and then stacking those crates high on the pier. The name on the bow was Winona.

As I walked past the Medical Department building, I could see several repairmen perched on the point of the steep red tile roof on the west wing of the building where the tower was. Many new students were coming and going in and out of the building, up and down its long grand staircase just as we did and, no doubt, spending the day there, listening to endless lectures, dissecting a cadaver on the top floor, microscopy in the basement, and hours upon hours of reading in the library. It was a good life, but being an intern was more gratifying because of the live bodies that we got to touch, and they spoke back. I was disappointed, though, about how few people got better by the time they made it to the hospital and we treated them.

The hospital was just as busy with workmen on all floors repairing the windows. I felt good as I climbed the front stairs and entered the building and then up the stairs to my "real" home on the wards.

I found Carl on the east ward.

"Well, come shake my hand. It looks like they still like us after all," Carl said.

"I know, isn't it hard to believe?" We laughed a little together.

"I think we fooled them again. Listen Doug, I had a long night and I'm ready to get out of here," he said as he looked me up and down. "Okay, you look really good. I wasn't sure it was you."

"Sure, go ahead and go, I got it from here. What happened during the night?" I always looked better than Carl.

"Dr. Randall's patient, Atchison, is still alive but barely. He's not vomiting now but his breathing is labored. I admitted an old lady last night named Stevens with high fever and pneumonia. Not sure if she is going to make it through the day, either. We have an alcoholic seaman here from New Orleans in delirium tremens. His tremors were severe, so we had to restrain him. I gave him opium injections every four hours, which calmed him down, but only after the third dose.

"What about the four kids with enteritis, are they gone?"

"Yes, they all left. I mean three left. The littlest one, Zadie, she died in the middle of the night after the other three left earlier in the day. Her aunt is here to claim her body."

I grabbed him by his dirty white shirt. "Carl, what happened? You let her die! I can't believe you let her die! Were you asleep? I told you to pay attention to her."

"Wait, wait, Doug, I did pay attention to her. You remember how sick those kids were when they came? The chance of all four of them surviving was slim. You knew that," Carl said. He pushed my hands away and walked away.

I followed him down the hall, "You miserable ass! I worked hard to get her better and you go and neglect her!"

"Now come on. What's wrong with you? Take it easy. You know, like we say, some live and some die. We gave it our best."

"You didn't."

He stopped and turned back to me, "Hey calm down now. We still have our jobs. You can't turn on me now."

I hung my head and paced in a circle. "How did she die?"

"The nurse called me to her bedside in the middle of the night. She had a lantern at the bedside. Zadie was lethargic and cold to touch with weak respirations. We tried to wake her. We tried to get her to drink some water. She wouldn't respond and didn't last much longer. She wasn't in pain when she died."

I pointed a finger at him and said again, "You let her die!"

I walked away still pointing at him and went down the main steps to the bottom floor to the morgue. I never should have trusted him to take care of her. She was getting better under my care. The other children had parents who came to visit, even siblings. But not Zadie, poor Zadie. Her aunt never came to see her, not once did I see her visit.

As I entered through the heavy iron door of the morgue, I saw a woman standing at the other end of the room talking with an orderly in front of the wall with a set of small square wooden doors one above the other, three sets high and five across. Only one door was opened and it was lined with lead. She stood next to a flat wooden tabletop that had pulled out of the wall of doors. As I walked toward her, Zadie lay on it, her small body taking up less than half the length of the table. The sheet covering her had been pulled back enough to show her face and upper chest. She was still in the same, large hospital gown. I leaned over her to see her face clearly. Her locks of hair falling back to the table. I looked back up at the aunt. What would I say to her?

"Hello, my name is Dr. Schuler and I cared for Zadie. You are her aunt?"

She was a tall woman dressed in a long black dress with white gloves, and said, "Yes, I am Mrs. Sutton, her aunt. I want to thank you for all your efforts to save Zadie. Poor little thing, she was always such a tiny girl, and she suffered so much after the storm."

"Did her parents die in the storm?"

"Yes. they did. Zadie happened to be staying with me and my husband while my sister, Zadie's mother, was in labor just before the storm. She had a baby boy the day before, but I'm afraid they all died, including Zadie's father. Their home was completely washed away. Our home sustained some damage, we lost our roof, and the first floor was underwater, but we all survived."

"Did she have other siblings?"

"No."

"Did you get to see her while she was here? Did you come to see her, did you come even once?"

"No, I didn't, I couldn't. Dr. Schuler, I have my own children to care for," she continued, "I didn't expect her to make it. She was so upset after the storm that she hardly ate or drank anything. Even when we found some food, she barely touched it. But she has always been a frail little girl."

She looked away from me as we both looked again at Zadie, who was gray. I leaned closer to see the details of her face again. I reached for the edge of the turned back sheet.

"Dr. Schuler, before you cover her, could you take the necklace from her neck so I can have it?" She stood some distance from her now.

"Yes."

I leaned over and slowly reached behind her cold neck to undo the clasp of the necklace that was entangled in her hair. It was a thin necklace with the pendant tucked under the hospital gown. I released the clasp and gently lifted it from her. I saw the pendant clearly now. The light from the window was shining directly on her face. I held the necklace higher in the light and the pendant in my palm. The pendant was a small brass rose. I turned it over and engraved on the back was the letter "R".

"Mrs. Sutton, where did you get this?"

"After the storm, we were at the city morgue looking for my sister's body. We didn't find her, so the sheriff suggested I look through a box of jewelry that had been collected from the victims, to see if there was anything of hers. I saw this necklace and the engraving that it had and thought Zadie would like it, that it might cheer her up. Rosen means rose in German, you know."

"I know it does."

She continued, "The engraving on the back, I thought, would make it more personal. I told Zadie that it was a gift from our family."

I stared at the necklace in my open hand, then closed my hand. Zadie grasped the pendant when we gave her the intravenous infusion. And it had been Rosa's, it had been my sister's.

"Could I please have it, Dr. Schuler?" Mrs Sutton extended her hand to me.

I held it tight in my hand. I looked up into the sunlight and saw Rosa, sitting next me on her front porch, wearing the necklace, and holding the pendant in her hand too. And her bright face I could see in the moonlight, with the necklace hanging around her neck. But she was now gone. I was not going to find her.

"Can I have it, please? I want to send it to her grandparents, to remember her by. I will be sending her body to them in San Antonio to bury. There are no burials on the island anymore."

I opened my hand to see the necklace again and then handed it to her. I took another look at Zadie. Her eyes were closed. I covered her completely with the sheet. I glanced back at her aunt and then left the morgue. I went outside of the hospital through the small side door in the back and walked a little on the grass levee. I knew Rosen means "rose" in German. She didn't love Zadie like I did. Rosa was gone.

But Rosa was found, her body, and she was wearing the necklace. I didn't want the necklace. I could see Rosa holding her little brother sitting next to me in her front room of her house, so calmly, so peacefully, rocking back and forth in the chair to keep him quiet. And he was gone, too. The smallest stood no chance against the storm. And Zadie lost her newborn brother whom she never saw. The aunt said that Zadie had always been a frail little girl. She must have been terrified that night of the storm. But to die now after surviving it, to die from drinking contaminated water. Poor Zadie. Poor little Zadie.

CHAPTER 22

I went back inside and upstairs but stopped by Dr. Randall's office before going back to the wards. He wasn't in the office, but I went inside. On his desk there was a large bound volume of some journals held open by a clear bottle of white pills. I walked past the desk and looked out one of the windows. They had all been repaired now. I saw several eager students laughing and talking below. Who could I talk to about Zadie or about Rosa? I was ready to quit, to resign. I couldn't take it anymore. I wasn't cut out to be a doctor.

I wasn't welcome to just loiter in his office like this. So, after a few more moments I left his office and went back upstairs. I would finish out the workday here, at least.

I saw Mrs. Stevens, the old lady with fever and pneumonia. By late afternoon, her fever had broken, and she was alert but still short of breath and wheezing. She begged me to stop the cold compresses to her chest. I ordered some mercury sulfate tablets to ease her wheezing. She spoke to me about her family in short, measured sentences between wheezes. She didn't know how she survived the storm when her husband didn't. She thought her dog had drowned but he showed up the next day and had been by her side ever since. That the dog had given her some reason to live and that she wasn't going to give up now.

The drunk man with DTs was calm now by the afternoon and, in fact, was snoring loudly, still in four-point restraints to the bed frame. Several of the other patients wanted me to wake him as his snoring was disturbing them. I was not going to; he could relapse back into DTs. When he finally woke, he asked for more rum, that it would ease his symptoms. He told me a crude joke and laughed out loud at the punch line. This poor drunk had more to live for than me.

By mid-afternoon Mr. Atchison was dying. His breathing was erratic and labored. He wasn't responding to pain or any other stimulation. I sent word through one of the medical students tagging along with me to find Dr. Randall. He showed up soon afterward and I told him what I was observing about Mr. Atchison. He went to his bedside and watched him for a minute or so. He took his hand and pressed his thumbnail into the patient's thumbnail as hard as he could, but the patient didn't withdraw his hand or grimace. He listened to his heart with his stethoscope for just a few seconds, then stood back up and stared down at him. Then he walked over to me.

"Yes, Douglas, you're right, he's dying. I'm not sure what else we can do for him now."

"I'm sorry I couldn't do more, sir."

"Don't apologize, you're not going to save everybody. I'm looking forward to the pathologic findings at autopsy so that we can understand more about this disease and maybe we can help the next person with it."

"I will get a message right away to his family. And Dr. Randall, I need to speak to you about something very important." My resignation was only proper.

"No, I will do that. Will you do me a favor, though?" he asked as he reached in his side coat pocket and pulled out the clear glass bottle of white pills.

"I need you to run this bottle of aspirin pills to Mrs. Landes this afternoon. She was expecting them this morning, but I haven't had the time. She is having an afternoon tea and recital and wanted them before it started. We can talk later, maybe tomorrow."

"I'm sorry, Dr. Randall, I can't leave the hospital on my call day."

"Please, Douglas, I will cover for you until you get back," he said as he handed the bottle to me. He patted me on the back and walked away. He didn't want to go to her house, either. What is an afternoon tea?

I left the hospital by the front steps and made my way to the Landes home. Several couples dressed in formal wear entered before me. I went in behind them and looked around the foyer for Mr. Landes. I peeked into the parlor and saw rows of empty white wooden folding chairs aligned before the piano. In the dining room was a large crowd of people, and Mr. and Mrs. Landes were standing at the head of the table. They were all ready to sit when Mr. Landes spotted me and waved me over to the side of the room as he moved through the guests to meet me. He shook my hand and escorted me into another room.

"Douglas, you have Mrs. Landes' medication?"

"Yes, I have it," I said, as I reached into my side coat pocket and gave him the bottle.

"Good, we were expecting Dr. Randall, but he sent you instead," he said while inspecting the clear glass bottle with its glued brown paper label with the word "ASPIRIN" written in the center. Dr. Randall had the powder made into pills.

"He was tied up with sick patients and couldn't leave. He hated to miss this, he told me. He had been looking forward to it all week."

"Well, this event is going to bore you and me to death, but it means a great deal to Mrs. Landes and her friends. She had the idea that we needed an event to lift the spirits of our city. She has invited many of our old friends, and many new ones too, ones that passed the storm with us here. Please stay, Douglas."

"Yes sir, I was hoping you would say that."

I ran out of excuses. I would rather be back in the hospital talking to that alcoholic, and I needed to talk to Dr. Randall, but Mr.

Landes had been so generous to me.

He returned to the head of the table next to his wife and announced that all should now take a seat to begin the tea. I didn't take a seat but stood back a little in the doorway of the adjacent room. At the large table, about twenty-five people took their seats, and all were dressed beautifully. At the far end of the table, near Mr. and Mrs. Landes were "ordinary" dressed people, as well. There were a few of their small children running around the room. All were served tea by their servants with small cookies and cakes placed perfectly on silver plates. Mrs. Landes said that this was how they did it in England. Everyone seemed to be enjoying themselves.

I didn't know how I could escape. Mr. Landes discreetly gave his wife a few pills in a laced napkin. One of the servants brought me a small chocolate cake. I had never had chocolate cake before. How could I get another? But the servant never came back my way.

After the tea, Mrs. Landes announced that all should move into the piano parlor. Slowly everyone did and took seats in the folding chairs that all faced the piano. The ordinary looking people with their small children sat in the back. Mrs. Landes walked to the front of the room next to the piano and faced her audience.

"It is a great pleasure to see all our friends taking time out of their busy day to join Mr. Landes and myself for tea. Some of you are old friends and some of you are new friends, and we love you all. I applaud the courage and the compassion that you have all shown in these weeks since the storm."

All of the audience loudly applauded her, and she bowed to them with one arthritic hand on the piano.

She continued, "I have written a song for all of us, entitled 'The Great Galveston Storm.' I hope it will be a song of healing and a song of hope for all. I want you to sing along with me. I will sing the first verse and then please join me in singing the second and the third."

The audience applauded again as she walked around the piano

to sit at the bench facing the audience. Mr. Landes had passed out small sheets of paper that had the lyrics printed on them and then stood proudly with me in the back of room. He put his arm around my shoulders. I put the sheet in my coat pocket. She began to play the piano and sing. It was a slow tune with loud chords in a minor key that described the winds and the water in the darkness and the terror that we all felt. By the time she finished the first verse, I could hear small sobs in the crowd and during the second, there was more sobbing than singing. Mr. Landes let go of my shoulder.

Few people were able to continue, and Mrs. Landes' voice began to falter, but she kept playing. By the time the lyrics of the third verse began, that spoke of the bravery of the people of Galveston, nearly all were sobbing, even the men. Mrs. Landes could continue no more and stopped playing. She stood and walked to the far edge of the piano and leaned her body across it covering her face with her right hand. She was loudly sobbing with everyone else in the audience. Mr. Landes rushed to her side and put his arm around her and gently raised her off the piano and she buried her face in his chest. Sobbing husbands were consoling their wives while they cried. The children stood still and then cried when they saw their parents in tears.

I pulled back a few steps and found a large leather chair to sit in and found a handkerchief to wipe my face. A little boy who was crying in the arms of his mother saw me and waved at me and tried to smile. I half smiled and waved back. Many in the parlor were going up to Mr. and Mrs. Landes to hold them and cry with them. I had to get out of there. I stood up and moved to the back of the house and walked through the empty kitchen and left through the back screen door. I knew the way.

Before I went back to the hospital, I walked in the other direction toward where Rosa's house was. I had not been there in several weeks. I saw the palm tree in the yard where the house was.

Much of the debris of the entire block was now gone. Many small red brick piers that used to hold houses still were scattered around the empty block. I went up to the palm and the note was gone. It had blown off the nail. I looked around the base of the palm and didn't see it. Everything about her was gone. It just wasn't fair.

The epidemic after the storm that had consumed the island now was not the yellow fever, or malaria or cholera but sadness, melancholia. All persons on the island were not only affected by the storm, but also were altered, even destroyed by it, and felt guilty to be alive as survivors. Thousands had died during the storm, and many were still dying, like Zadie, and the grief was unending. I had to leave this city. Why did I survive, and Rosa didn't? Why did Carl survive and not Tex?

As I left the palm tree and walked back to the hospital, I read the words of Mrs. Landes' song that were in my coat pocket. It was a song of hope, of rebuilding, of looking to the future, of personal strength. Was I defeated too, by the storm? Yes, or I don't know, but I was not going to quit my job. I had to continue, to fight back against what the storm did to me, too. Thank you, Mrs. Landes.

PART 5

"He will be the physician that should be the patient."

—William Shakespeare

CHAPTER 23

The fires across the city were burning out. The constant sky of gray and the smell of burning flesh had given way to a clear sky with the smell of sea. Ash was now blowing around the city and coating the buildings downtown. A good rain would help, but it hadn't rained much since the storm. The ash blew on my suit and in my face as I walked north through downtown on my way to work.

It has been about two weeks since Zadie died, and I still thought constantly about what I could have done differently. But it was no use, it didn't change the outcome. Was Carl right? That we did all that we could? That just wasn't acceptable. I didn't plan on getting close to her. I don't know why I did. But I did and now I wish I hadn't. Is that the way I should feel?

Carl moved out of the back house. I saw him almost every morning, but he wasn't speaking to me. He and I were invited to dinner at Dr. Randall's home last week and we didn't say much to each other then. Mrs. Randall made roasted beef with potatoes and carrots. The dark mahogany dining table was covered with a lace tablecloth. It was six of us at the small table, including their young daughter and son. Mrs. Randall, fortunately, carried the conversation and didn't ask too many questions of us or of our friendship. She mostly asked about what we did the night of the storm. Carl and I had worked closely together that night, but neither one of us went into much detail about it. I wanted to eat, not talk. I hadn't had a home-cooked meal in a long time. Mrs. Randall even brought out a bottle of red wine. We drank the red wine in tall carved wine glasses. Dr. Randall could sense the coldness between Carl and me, but he didn't say much that night, either. Carl left soon after eating the meal. We both thanked Mrs. Randall for the delicious meal. She probably was glad to see the evening end early, but she said that we would be invited back soon. But Dr. Randall wasn't too happy with either of us.

As I walked past the Medical Department building, it looked as if all the repairs were now complete. The towers on either end of the building were replaced with sky lights. Each wing of the building was rounded, containing many small windows closely in series on each floor. They illuminated the surgical amphitheaters inside. They had all been restored.

The hospital was restored as well. Nearly all the windows had been replaced, including the grand ached window in the entrance that illuminated the central stairwell. On the east ward was the sweet smell of fresh paint. The holes in the walls had been plastered over and painted. Everything was white again. The bedsheets had been cleaned and pressed. The metal bed frames were given a coat of white paint to cover their chipped legs. It all matched the nurses' aprons and their tiny hats that held their hair high on their heads. A few nursing students had worn their hair down after the storm but that was would no longer tolerated. And I had to have a necktie on at all times. The mosquitoes had had their run of the place since the storm but even they knew that it was over. It was a new day.

The new class of first-year medical students were here, but their number was less than expected. Many cancelled their enrollment after the storm and the faculty were in a bad mood about it. I heard them talking about it on the ward a few days ago, that nearly a third of them didn't show up because of the fear of an epidemic on the island. I had received a letter from my mother asking me to leave because she had heard of epidemics affecting the island after the storm. She said the whole state was talking about it and in Austin, the state officials were having many meetings about it. My parents had travelled to San Antonio to listen to a public forum discussing the impending disaster in Galveston given by their local congressman. They were warned to not travel here.

But there had not been an epidemic on the island after the storm. I let her know that in a telegram. I let her know that I was still alive and healthy. I never let her know about the weight I lost after the storm since I had gained most of it back.

The faculty had been pushing the workers hard to finish by today. I had heard that a special visitor was expected this afternoon. Carl and I weren't told about it; we were rarely included in important conversations that the faculty had. But by early afternoon several of the new nursing and medical students were milling around the wards, in expectation of that visitor. I was attending to all the patients on the east ward when a large group led by an elderly woman entered the ward. She was of average height and wearing a long black dress with an ornate white lace collar with an enameled round pin of a red cross on a white background pinned at the top of it. Her bright grey hair was pinned up high without a hat. It was Clara Barton. Dr. Thompson and Dr. Clopton were speaking to her enthusiastically as she stood and looked around the ward rather than at them. Dr. Cooke was present as well and Nurse Sanders was not far behind. The students were leaning in to hear her speak. I was at the far end of the ward and stood up as she slowly walked toward me, but not looking at me. Nurse Sanders and I had made eye contact from behind Mrs. Barton, and she glared at me and put her index finger to her lips. I looked away and sat back down on the foot of the bed. Dr. Randall walked onto the ward to join the group. The doctors were explaining to Ms. Barton the damage done by the storm and what had been done to repair the hospital. The ward was full of patients, and they were all quietly listening as well or too sick to notice.

I could hear Dr. Clopton. "Nurse Sanders and myself have personally overseen the repair of the hospital. We have eliminated any chance of an epidemic with the speedy repairs that you see before you."

Mrs. Barton didn't say anything but kept looking around, scanning all corners of the ward. The smell of the fresh paint seemed to overwhelm her a little, so she took out a handkerchief to lightly cover her face. Her dark piercing eyes met mine briefly and I stood up again and nodded. But she kept walking slowly past me, carefully scanning every corner of the ward.

At the end of the row of beds, she finally spoke, "Well, Dr. Clopton, your repairs have been expedient and fortunately for you and the people of Galveston, an epidemic didn't ravage the city. I have never witnessed such death and destruction as I have seen since I have arrived, and I have travelled the world. It looks like you have made good use of the medicines and supplies that we brought. But I have heard rumors of the intravenous infusions you have created here. I believe you call it a Ringer's solution?"

Dr. Clopton spoke up. "Well, Mrs. Barton, some of the physicians have created such a solution due to the dire nature of dehydration that many of our patients were in. But I would never condone the continued use of such a radical treatment."

Nurse Sanders stepped forward and said, "Yes, Mrs. Barton, it was done while some of our patients, and to state it honestly, some of our physicians were in a hysterical state of mind after the storm."

"And there were rumors of netting hanging from the light fixtures? You allowed that, Nurse Sanders?" Mrs. Barton added.

Dr. Randall said, "Yes, Ms. Barton we did those things and I believe we saved lives with our Ringer's solution and even prevented an epidemic with the netting. Galveston has had its outbreaks of the yellow fever and malaria over the years. I had read of both as lifesaving measures, and I was determined to implement them here immediately after the disaster. It was from a relief ship that I acquired the ingredients to prepare the intravenous solution."

"What was the storm like for the patients under your care?" Mrs. Barton asked.

Dr. Cooke said, "I was at home during the storm, caring for my family."

"We were not here for the storm, but our house intern, Dr. Schuler was. He can tell you all about it," Dr. Randall said pointing at me.

She looked toward me then back at them, "Well, where were you all? I am hoping to include in my report to the Washington office a few stories of your heroism during the storm. But it doesn't look like I will have much to tell."

Nurse Sanders said, "Please know that we returned as soon as we could, and I did everything in my power to dismantle those nets and block the infusions. I want to report that I was overruled by Dr. Randall on many an occasion, though most of the faculty supported my written protest."

"Nurse Sanders, I will put it in my report that you were not here during the storm and that you blocked efforts to alleviate suffering from critical dehydration. And that you put patients at risk for malaria by taking down the netting. That is extremely unethical in my opinion!"

Nurse Sanders took a step back and hung her head.

She continued, "I am grateful for the initiative Dr. Randall took, with the help of this intern here, to save lives. To put their own fears and their pride aside for the betterment of the courageous people of this island. Thankfully, they didn't allow you to interfere."

I stood straighter now and stared at Nurse Sanders.

She continued, "In my report I will note the expediency of the minor repairs to the hospital. I credit the builder and the architect for building such a well-made hospital. It truly did withstand the storm as it claimed it would. But for the faculty to desert the hospital and its patients in its hour of need during the season when the storms frequent the island is unthinkable. I am compelled to include that in my report."

She left the other three and walked over to me, "Dr. Schuler, I would like to hear what the storm was like and what you did to preserve the lives of others. I heard you acted quite selflessly. Will you visit me at the Disaster Committee Office downtown?"

"I would be happy to, Mrs. Barton."

Dr. Randall walked over to me and added, "Douglas spent many long hours assisting me after the storm. He knows the Ringer's solution and how to administer it better than I do."

"I know it was a difficult time for all. Young man, you look as if you have had little time to recuperate." And to Dr. Randall said, "Maybe he needs to see a doctor himself."

As she turned away, Dr. Randall looked at me directly in the eyes and then took a step back with shock on his face.

Dr. Randall stepped forward and took me by the arm and led me off the ward. He didn't say anything as we walked downstairs to his office. In his office, he led me to the window to stand with him in the sunlight. He faced me and pulled down the lower lids of my eyes.

"Take off your shirt."

I did as he asked. He looked closely at my face and then my chest and abdomen and then turned me around to see my back in the sunlight. He then stood back against the window.

"You're jaundiced, Douglas, very jaundiced."

I looked down at my arms. He asked if I had fever or chills or headaches or any other symptoms. I told him that I didn't. I confirmed that I had been fatigued and had a few nights of sweats and chills, but I had had many nights like that; it was just how we all felt since the storm. And that I don't drink much alcohol. He kept staring at my bright yellow eyes. As I looked back at his, he was thinking about the diseases that we had just talked about with Mrs. Barton. I could only think of Mr. Atchison.

Mr. Atchison died a few days after I carried his blood around in my pocket and on my clothes. Dr. Randall never warned me that whatever he had could be contagious. Dr. Smith did but it was too late.

Dr. Randall walked over to his desk and pulled out a small square mirror from his desk drawer and gave it to me, a mirror that he used to comb his mustache. I could see that the whites of my eyes were yellow and my face and neck, too. I kept blinking but the yellow didn't go away. He told me to sit down. I put my shirt back on. He took a small glass thermometer out of another drawer and shook down the mercury level and then placed it under my tongue. We waited a few minutes together without talking.

He took the thermometer out of my mouth and read it. "Your temp is 102." He leaned back against the desk in front of me and sighed and shook his head. We were taught to never shake our head in front of a sick patient.

"Doug, you have a rash on your back."

"Dr. Randall, I really don't feel too bad."

"Does your back itch?"

"No."

"Think back now, how long have you been feeling bad?"

"I really don't know, maybe just a few days."

"I want you to come in the hospital. You're practically here all the time anyway," he said, smiling.

I still didn't know what to say. I wasn't smiling but I was glad that Dr. Randall was. Could I really be sick? I did have a pretty bad headache the other evening with some hard chills, and I vomited once. But I thought I had drunk some bad water; the cistern at Dr. Randalls house was still tasting salty. If I'm not able to work that would mean Carl would have to work every night? I would have to pay him back for that. He would make sure of it.

I wanted to go home and sleep a little, but Dr. Randall insisted that I not, that I could be risking my health if I did. He left to go to the ward to arrange for a bed at the end of the ward. It was late afternoon, and I had fallen asleep in the chair when he returned to his office to get me.

"Douglas, I have a bed for you in the corner of the west ward. I put up a screen around the bed to give you some privacy. Are you ready?"

I stood up stiffly, "Yes I'm ready." My muscles were very sore now.

We walked up the stairs slowly and went to the west ward. He left me at the bed in the corner as he said. There was a white cloth screen on a large shiny metal frame positioned next to it. On the other side of the bed was the west wall with windows. Directly across from me on the other side was an empty bed. Next to my bed next to the window was a small wooden table with a pitcher of water and a glass. A cotton gown was folded up on the pillow. I took off my clothes behind the screen and put on the gown and laid down on stiff white sheets. I had not slept on bedsheets for a long time. I folded my clothes and put them under the bed.

Later that night I woke with hard chills. The sweats followed a few hours later. I vomited once in the emesis basin; there was no blood. It happened again before morning. My mouth and eyes felt dry. In the morning, Dr. Randall came to see me.

"How are you feeling, Douglas?"

"Well, I had some fever and sweats through the night, I think."

"I can't order anything for your fever until we know what's causing it. Can you lie on your back?" I had been lying most of the night on my side because my abdomen and the muscles in my legs hurt less that way. He examined me, from head to toe. I watched the expression on his face as he did. I knew what he was feeling for when he palpated my upper abdomen from side to side. It hurt when he did, and then he pushed down hard with both hands in the center of my abdomen, then let go quickly. But I didn't recoil from the pain, so no peritonitis.

"Your liver and spleen are enlarged. But you don't have peritonitis."

He stared at my eyes again but didn't say anything. I stared back and tried not to blink.

"Am I still jaundiced?"

"Yes, I'm afraid so. Your bilirubin is very elevated."

"Dr. Randall, I am worried that I have what your patient had, Mr. Atchison, the Leptospira described by Dr. Weil."

"Why do you think that?"

"Well, I drew some blood from him and carried it to Dr. Smith to examine it. He noticed blood on my hands. Plus, he vomited on me, you know, the 'black vomit.' I didn't wipe it all off. I couldn't. I'm worried that I might have it."

"Let's sure hope not. Dr. Smith told me how you assisted in making the diagnosis. I was initially skeptical about it. But the autopsy confirmed it. His liver was necrotic, and he definitely didn't have malaria. But I still think you could have malaria or the yellow fever, though, there hasn't been a case of it here in Galveston in four years."

"And it is no longer the summer."

"Yes, I thought of that, too. Dr. Smith is going to come and draw your blood to examine it. To check your white corpuscles, as well. To rule out malaria in your red corpuscles."

He listened to my heart in the center of my chest and lungs on the sides with his stethoscope. It was painful to take a deep breath.

"Good, no heart murmur." he said as he stood up straight. "I'm going to order you opium as a suppository in case you vomit. It will help your muscle pain, too. Just ask the nurse for it," he said.

"I will, thank you, Dr. Randall."

After he left, I rolled back on my side toward the wall. I could see a few seagulls flying by.

The nurse on duty that afternoon asked if I wanted the suppository. I was not going to take a suppository. A nursing student who I didn't know came by and refilled my water and emptied my emesis basin. She didn't make eye contact with me. I sat up for a while to look out the window. I could see the Medical Department building next door. The pigeons were stationed on its window ledges again. Where had they gone during the storm? The bright sunny morning had given way to a cloudy, dreary afternoon. I could see a few sailing boats drifting by in the bay. I had to lie back down because my eyes felt heavy.

I don't remember Dr. Smith coming by to see me. But I saw the venipuncture site on my right arm where he must have drawn the blood. He had covered it with gauze and tape. I looked outside and it was dusk. The nurses must have brought me a blanket, but I couldn't take it, I was sweating again. My skin was burning now.

I opened my eyes; it was morning again. I was so thirsty. I sat up and poured myself a glass of water. I could see that the day was bright. I looked at my arms and legs in the sunlight and they still were yellow. I had a terrible headache, and the sun was too bright. I couldn't look outside. The screen had been folded back to the wall. I could see the whole ward, but it was too bright to see what was going on. I closed my eyes and rolled back away.

I jerked upward suddenly and vomited, vomited on the floor before I could reach for the emesis basin. It was dark on the ward and dark outside and my head was still hurting, now pounding at my temples. I lay as still as I could; just moving made it hurt worse. I dreamed of riding my horse back home directly into the sun, galloping through the tall grass.

It was daylight, and I was too weak to sit up. There was a bottle of clear fluid hanging above the bed from a dark metal stand. It was draining into a rubber tube that was going into a needle in my left arm and was taped down tightly to a board under my arm so I couldn't bend my arm. Dr. Randall came to my bedside.

"How are you feeling this morning, Douglas?"

"I don't know." My mouth and tongue were sticking together. Did he understand me?

"You're on your fourth bottle of Ringer's now. You stopped drinking several days ago. Our former patient, Singer, came by with a metal tower he made to hold the infusion bottles. And a metal bracket for the base of the bottle. He said that you and he talked about it. It's rough looking but I think it works pretty well."

"Am I still, still yellow, still"—what was the medical word?— "still jaundiced?"

He stared into my eyes and then lowered my gown to my waist, "Yes, you are. Have you vomited?"

"Yes."

"I'm giving you injections of atropine to control your vomiting."

"Dr. Randall...could you please apologize to Mrs. Randall for my behavior the other night?"

"Don't worry, I already did. I will check on you later," he said staring down at me with a serious face.

He looked away and then walked away without saying anything more, nothing to make me feel better about whatever it was that I had. I looked down at my gown and didn't see any blood or any black stains on it. The cotton felt thick and smooth like my grandmother's quilt that was on my bed back home. My feet were sticking out from under my long gown. I still had all my toes. It hurt my head to count them. My toenails didn't look right, too long, like the claws on a hawk. From my horse, I could see a flying hawk holding a small rabbit in its talons. I curled my toes to hold the rabbit.

I opened my heavy eyes and saw both Carl and Dr. Randall standing over me with serious faces, but I couldn't focus on their bodies.

The light was too bright. They spoke but I didn't hear any words. I closed my eyes, but they pulled my eyelids open. I still couldn't hear them as they talked between themselves. Why were they yelling? Was I deaf?

Rosa was riding a bicycle in the street in front of her house. The bicycle bounced on the red brick street. And she laughed at me as she made circles around me. I had never ridden one before and she laughed as she told me that I was too afraid to try. It was harder to ride a horse than a bicycle, I told her back. It was my turn. I sat on the bicycle, but it had only one wheel. I could see my heart through my open chest, and it was pounding out red and blue blood and there were wires coming out it.

I opened my eyes and I saw Carl again, and it was dark. Why was he shaking me by the shoulders? I felt his hand on my forehead. Did he apologize to Mrs. Randall? I tasted the roast again.

Zadie was running at the beach, wearing a white lace dress. Her long curly hair blew backward, and she was laughing. I ran toward her as she splashed in the ankle-deep water. We were barefooted. She saw me and stopped. I held out the necklace to her.

CHAPTER 24

I opened my eyes and stared at the ceiling. My eyes wouldn't move away. I could smell something, something sweet. I moved my hands and feet now, just a little. My legs felt warm, very warm. I lifted my head and could see Victoria rubbing my legs with oil. I put my head back down. I took a deep breath, as deep as I could. I lifted my left arm and there was no needle in it; there was no metal tower above me holding an infusion bottle.

"You're awake," she said as she stopped rubbing my legs and stood up straight over me, placing her hands on her hips. She smiled brightly.

"What are you doing here? Did you come back or am I dreaming?"

"I didn't know if you were going to make it."

"I got sick, very sick....When did you come back?"

I looked down at my toes. My toenails were too long, but they were just toenails.

"Laura sent me a telegram about how sick you were, and everybody wasn't sure if you were going to make it. But I wanted to finish my nursing certification, so I decided to come back."

"Did the nursing program take you back?"

"Yes, they did. There are not as many nursing students now since the storm. So I guess they needed me a little," she said, still smiling. She rearranged her hair a little on the top of her head with the back of her hands, careful not to touch it with her oily fingers.

I was looking up at her. She was wearing her uniform, a long clean blue dress with a long white lace apron over it, and with her hair pulled up and pinned up under the small white hat.

"I liked your hair better hanging down. Will you unpin it? I don't know how much longer I have." I tried to smile back. The screen had been back in place, so no one saw us talking.

"Douglas, Dr. Randall said you are getting better. You know I could be fired if I let my hair down." I remembered how she looked that night in the stairwell when she kissed me.

"Am I still yellow?"

"I can't tell, it's getting dark outside now."

My head wasn't hurting anymore. I looked at my hands and they didn't look yellow anymore. I slowly leaned to the side and reached for my clothes under my bed and lay my pants across my lap. I took out the mirror from my pocket. I blinked and blinked, and my eyes were not as jaundiced. I had a beard. I felt it to make sure it was real. How long have I been sick?

"Can you sit with me?" I asked.

"No," she said, as she backed away a little.

"What were you rubbing on my legs?"

"Oil of cloves in a liniment. Dr. Randall said it was okay. You were in such pain, and you kept refusing the suppositories." She closed the bottle of the liniment and put it back in her apron pocket.

"I like the way it smells. It feels really good. Thank you." I propped myself on my elbows and then slowly pulled my legs over the side of the bed. I pressed my feet to the warm wooden floor.

"I want to stand," I said as I reached out for her with both hands. She hesitated a little but then grabbed them and slowly helped me stand. It felt strange to stand again. I was a little dizzy but okay as long as I didn't let go of her. I looked at her small hands in mine and then at her. She looked up at me.

I said, "So, you came back. Did you come back to see me?"

"Of course not, I came back to finish the nursing program. And you should sit back down now, Douglas."

"I feel just fine standing." I didn't want to let go of her hands. My hands looked a little yellow compared to hers.

"When did you come back?"

"Last week."

"I don't know how long I have been sick. Maybe a couple of weeks."

"I think so. I have been checking on you every day. You had everybody worried. Dr. Randall and your friend Carl have been keeping a close eye on you. Even Nurse Sanders gave you a bed bath, I think. Now sit back down, I don't want you to fall." She helped me sit back down, but didn't sit next to me. She quickly let go of my hands.

I looked back up at her. "I'm glad that you were checking on me." I lay back down. "Nurse Sanders gave me a bath?"

She poured a glass of water and put it on the stand. "You will need time to recover. Drink the water, too, all of it please," she said without looking at me.

"I will, I promise."

Maybe I said too much to her. Would she keep checking on me now that I'm getting better? She pulled the screen away to the wall before she left.

"Wait, Victoria, don't leave."

I reached again into my pants pocket and pulled out the lace handkerchief that she had given me. "I've been carrying this since you gave it to me." She walked back to my bedside, and I handed it to her. It was stained with blood again.

"Keep it," she said as she ran her finger across the raised letter "V" before she handed it back.

"I know how to get blood out of things now."

"That's good. Now get some rest, don't talk anymore," she said as she left my side.

I watched her walk away again. She didn't look back at me. I felt weak now after we talked. I pulled myself back up only to drink the water. I drank it all without feeling any nausea, and I was a little hungry now. I balled up the handkerchief in my hand. My muscles felt better with the liniment. Maybe I was getting better?

I slept without chills or a headache to wake me, and no fever and ate a little breakfast. I sat all the way up to see the rest of the ward. Would Dr. Randall see me this morning? What has been wrong with me? It was late morning when he came to the ward. I watched him talk at length to Nurse Sanders at the nurse's table before he walked to the end of the ward. I sat up and swung my legs over the side of the bed.

"Well, Douglas, I heard you were feeling better."

"Yes sir, I am feeling stronger now. I had a little breakfast, and it stayed down."

He sat down next to me and looked closely at my eyes, then reached for my hands and put them in his and turned them over several times.

"Lie back now," he said as he stood.

I did and he bent over me and felt my abdomen. It wasn't tender anymore. He felt under my right ribs for my liver and then my spleen under the left. He palpated my neck for lymph nodes and then gently elevated my head with his palm under the back of my neck. I remember how it hurt to do that, but not now. I knew not to talk while he was examining me.

"Well, I think you are getting better. It looks like you still have some jaundice, but not like it was. Your liver and spleen are not as enlarged. Nurse Sanders told me that you haven't had fever for twenty-four hours now."

"Dr. Randall, do you know what is wrong with me?"

"You have the Leptospira in your blood, Weil's disease, like you thought. Dr. Smith confirmed it when he examined your blood.

I think, you got it when you handled the blood from my patient, Atchison." And when he vomited on me.

"Did I have the black vomit?"

"Yes, you did. That was when I was worried the most. You don't remember that?"

"No, I don't remember too much of the past week."

"Are you urinating now?"

"Yes." I pointed to the metal urinal on the bedside table that was half full from this morning.

"Good. I have stopped the quinine because your blood smears have not shown malaria. And I stopped the carbolic acid injections because I don't think you have the yellow fever. You're young so you're only allowed to have one near-fatal disease at a time." Dr. Randall said with a smile. I needed a little humor, too.

After a moment, just staring at me, he continued, "I may stop all other treatments, too, so you can get your appetite back?"

"Yes, sir, but please don't discontinue the liniment with the cloves. It helps me quite a bit. My muscles hurt less with it."

"Okay, I won't. Doug, you are going to be weak for a while, I don't know for how long. You are going to need some days to recover, maybe weeks. I want you to stay here for at least a few more days, until you get stronger. You have lost a lot of weight. But I can say confidently that you will recover."

He reached into his coat pocket and handed me several letters.

"I notified your family about your condition. I'm afraid I didn't paint too pretty a picture. I got two letters back. You should let them know that you are getting better as soon as you're released."

"Yes sir, I will. Thank you for notifying them."

There were two letters, one from my mother and one from Anna. I opened the one from Anna first:

My dearest Douglas,

I have received word from you mother that you have been very ill. She suggested that I write you. I didn't want to write because it has been so long since you have written me. I have not forgotten about you, but I fear that you have forgotten about me. I promised that I would wait for you when you left for Galveston, but it has been more than four years now, when you said that it would be only three.

Douglas, I don't feel that I can wait any longer for you. You are living in a rich city now and probably not ready to live a quiet life in the country with me again. I must confess that I have met someone else now. A fine young man from a respectable German family in New Berlin. I have promised to marry him. I am sorry to break my promise but I feel that you have already broken your promise to me. I hope that you don't die before you can read this letter.

With kind regards,
Anna Warnicke

I read the letter from my mother afterwards. It was a better letter, and longer, too. She still loved me even though Anna didn't. My mother wanted me to come home right away, that she couldn't take it anymore, first the storm, now my illness. That she had been against this whole risky medical career and that ranching was a safer occupation. Wasn't she the one who had encouraged me to be a doctor? She had Dr. Wallace talk to me about it. I put both letters in my pants pocket.

I read Anna's letter again later. Was I relieved, a little? I remember when we sat together on the back porch of her house looking out over Cibolo Creek down the hill. It was a hot summer evening but the breeze off the creek was cool. Our families were close; I've known her since we were young. Everybody approved of the two of us except her father, but he eventually did after I told him that I had asked her to wait for me. It would be the last time that I would see her. My mother was convinced that I really didn't love her. Anna was probably different now and so was I. It was good that I lived to read her letter.

As the hours slowly went, I was itching to get out of the hospital. I didn't like being a patient—being on the other end of things, so to speak. It was awkward, even strange, lying in bed next to the other patients and wearing a hospital gown that opened in the back. I looked at each patient on the ward and I was definitely the youngest. There were no sick children on the ward. I couldn't help noticing the old man next to me. His breathing was erratic, at best.

A few of the other faculty members came by to see me, after they made their morning rounds. I coughed loudly a few times when Dr. Thompson was seeing a patient just a few feet away and he nodded to me but didn't speak. Maybe he didn't recognize me as a patient? I saw the medical students rounding with Dr. Cooke, bed after bed, but they didn't come down as far as my bed. He sent the students away then came over to check on me. He checked the whites of my eyes to see that the jaundice was improving. He encouraged me to get out of bed more. That it was important to regain my strength. And that he would bring a liver tonic for me to drink daily. A small group of nursing students were following Nurse Sanders around and taking orders from her, emptying bed pans, applying gauze dressings to wounds, taking temperatures. All the while Nurse Sanders closely watched their technique. I pulled the sheet over my face when they were close to me.

Later, I sat up to see how long I could, this time with my back to the ward, and stared outside the window at the sunset. I didn't have the strength to open the window. I could hear the low and slow horn of a pilot boat cruising in the harbor. At the end of the day, it was getting quiet on the ward. I sat up for several hours before feeling dizzy again, but the pounding didn't return.

I fell asleep and when I woke it was dark and quiet on the ward. The screen had been moved back next to my bed. I sat up again and saw that the water glass on the bedside table was full. And I smelled cloves. I leaned back across the bed and moved the screen a little to see the whole ward. The lights had been turned off except for the lamp at the nurse's table. There was a student nurse sitting with her back to me, but it wasn't Victoria. I drank the water and lay back down and stared at the ceiling. Why did she really come back to Galveston?

The next day I walked a little on the ward after breakfast and I could feel how sore my buttocks were from all the injections. I walked with the help of one of the other nursing students who didn't say much when I tried to have a conversation. She was taller and stronger than Victoria and held me by the arm; she held me up, in reality. I kept the screen in place because I didn't want to see who wasn't going to come see me today. I asked her to help me to the nurse's table. Nurse Sanders was back on duty this morning. I walked slowly but steadily past the rows of beds.

"Hello, Nurse Sanders," I said, as she put down the clipboard and looked up at me. "I want to tell you that I appreciate very much that you gave me a bath and that you helped take care of me. And I appreciate what a good nurse you are and how much I have learned from you as an intern. I feel awful that I have spoken harshly to you in the past."

She picked up the clipboard again and looked down at it and said, "Thank you, Dr. Schuler. But I didn't give you a bath. You must have dreamt that."

I stood by the table for a few moments more, silent and just looking at Nurse Sanders, but she never looked up at me. My legs shook now, so I turned back toward my bed. The nursing student held me tighter while we walked away from the table.

Dr. Randall came by in the afternoon and said that I couldn't leave yet. He didn't want me walking around Galveston even a little jaundiced; that it made the hospital look bad. But my appetite was coming back, and I ate all the food that was brought to me. And my head felt clearer, and my skin wasn't as itchy, so my jaundice had to be better. I looked in my little mirror, angling it to get as much light as possible, to see if the whites of my eyes were white again. It was getting dark and quiet on the ward when Victoria peeked her head around the screen. She looked back toward the nurse's table before she came around. I sat up on the side of the bed.

"How are you feeling today, Doug?"

"Better now," I said with a big smile. "Though my muscles are aching again," I added with a frown and elevated my feet to be even with the mattress.

"Hmmm, I bet they are," she said, as she reached for the bottle of liniment from her apron pocket and handed it to me. She added, "I think you're ready to start putting it on yourself."

I let my feet fall back to the floor. "Will you sit with me, Victoria?"

"No," she said standing several feet from me.

"Could I ask you a question?"

"Yes."

"I was wondering, where are you living now?"

"My family insisted that I live with someone they knew, so I am living with my mother's cousin. She has been living here for several years after she immigrated from Ireland. They asked her by telegram if I could live with her in her apartment at the Rosenberg Women's Home on 25th Street. There wasn't much damage to the home during the storm and the home accepts charity cases."

"Is she a nurse?"

"No, she works as a seamstress downtown. My family invited her to move to Fort Worth to live with us after she landed in Galveston, but she decided to stay here. There was more work here. There are a lot of other women from Ireland living there, too."

"Victoria," I carefully stood up so I could face her. "I was hoping that I could get to know you better. Could I call on you where you live, to see you outside of the hospital?"

She hesitated a moment and took a step back, and said, "Yes, you can."

"I would like to get to know you better, away from the chaos that we went through with the storm, and now my illness."

"Yes, I would like that too."

She reached out for my hand and held it tightly now and looked up at me with her bright eyes. The eyes I remember in the moonlight.

"I hope to be feeling stronger soon. I have been living in Dr. Randall's back house since the storm. My apartment near the hospital was ruined and I hope to find a new place to live soon."

"Doug, I want to ask you a question?"

"Yes."

"Do you have a girlfriend?"

"No, I don't, not anymore."

I would have to tell her about Rosa someday, and about Anna. She stared into my eyes now and suggested that I quit talking and lie back and get some rest. But I didn't want her to leave so I shook my head "no." It was dusk, and the sky was still bright and clear this fall evening and there were brilliant streaks of pink in the sky reaching out toward us from the sun cradled in purple over the bay. There had been so many beautiful sunsets since the storm; maybe it was the weather or maybe just that I noticed them more. I stared at her and she stared back at me. The sunlight in her green eyes made them glow.

We didn't say anything as we held hands and looked out the window together. We were fortunate to be alive. Was she thinking the same? That she and I were surrounded by death everywhere on the island, and as we rode down the beach, we ran from it. We had been surrounded by sadness, but that night on the beach together, in the moonlight, I saw her bright clear eyes and that she was able to smile. Despite all the death around us, she was able to smile. I could still feel her holding me tightly around my waist as we rode down the beach.

I looked at her now, but she kept looking at the sunset. She let go of my hand and with both hands she pulled the long pins from her hair. Her wavy auburn hair fell all the way down her back and the nurse's hat hit the floor. The sunlight shone brightly on her face as her eyes captured mine. She rescued me.

ABOUT THE AUTHOR

Paul Remmers is a physician with more than forty years' experience in internal medicine. He was born and raised in Galveston, Texas, where he attended the University of Texas Medical Branch and later returned as a faculty member. He also has served on the faculty at Baylor College of Medicine in Houston. He is married and has four grown children.

www.ingramcontent.com/pod-product-compliance
Lightning Source LLC
LaVergne TN
LVHW091316270325
R18631400001B/R186314PG805034LVX00001B/1
9781965766125